PRETTY VENGEFUL QUEEN

RUTHLESS HEARTS #3

CALLIE ROSE

D1369025

For updates on my upcoming releases and promotions, sign up for my reader newsletter! I promise not to bite (or spam you).

CALLIE ROSE NEWSLETTER

MADDOC

THERE ARE TOO many guns pointed at us. I fucking *know* that, but it doesn't stop my mind from racing through a hundred different scenarios where I rip Austin McKenna's face off and get Riley back.

He laughs as he snatches her gun away—the one she just had pointed at me—and I almost lunge for him and do it.

My whole body hums with the need to attack, retaliate, destroy...

It's only the pleading look in Riley's eyes that stops me.

It also fucking guts me.

Watching McKenna shove her into the back of the car that cornered us in this alley feels like getting my heart ripped out... but watching him actually drive away with her is even worse.

I tear after them as the two West Point vehicles peel away, spraying gravel that hits my body like shrapnel.

I don't even feel it. Pure emotion takes over, raw instinct driving me. There's no strategic thinking, no room for the calm, clear-headed approach I've trained myself to use as leader of the Reapers. All I feel is the thud of my feet pounding on the pavement and the burning rage that pulses through my veins as West Point speeds out of sight.

They take a corner and disappear, and I let out a primal roar of fury.

It does fucking *nothing* to fix the situation, and I keep chasing after them for a few more steps anyway, but when I get to the cross street they took... they're gone.

I finally stop running and force myself to bottle up all the savage anger inside me until I can do something useful with it.

And for that, I'll need my brothers.

I turn back, not surprised at all that Logan and Dante are already headed toward me, Chloe in tow. Logan's face is completely blank, which I know damn well means it's taking everything he has to hold in his own murderous wrath at what just went down. Dante is another story. His green eyes flash with fire.

"Plan, Madd?" he bites out, his face set and grim.

"The fucking plan is we get her back," I rasp, my lungs burning as my heart rate starts to slow from the flat-out run I was in. "Get the car. We need to catch up to McKenna. Follow his trail and figure out where the fuck they're taking her."

Neither of them point out how impossible that will be. It's pavement and a car. There is no trail.

Still, Logan spins on his heel and heads back to collect the Escalade, and Dante gives me a sharp nod.

"We'll find her."

"Damn right, we will," I growl.

A small sound of pure pain escapes Chloe, but she doesn't say anything. Dante's got an arm around her shoulders, and she looks shell shocked. Her face is streaked with tears and her eyes are glassy as she stares off in the direction West Point disappeared with her sister.

I press my lips together. I'm not used to caring, but the girl's been through hell, and just when it was set to get better, she's on her own again.

No, she's got us.

She's Riley's little sister. We'll do right by her.

Right now though, I'm glad Dante's the one making sure Chloe stays close and stays safe. With my blood still bubbling over with rage, I can't spare anything extra to help Chloe deal with the fact that Riley just fucking sacrificed herself for us.

Not that there's any way in hell that I'm going to let that stand. We *will* get her back.

Logan pulls the Escalade up and Dante helps Chloe into the back while I take the passenger seat. It's pocked with bullet holes and the entire driver's side got banged up in that fucking alley. It's gonna need some serious body work, but the only thing that matters right now is that it's still drivable.

"Go," I say as Logan floors it, taking the turn where I lost McKenna's car fast enough to put us up on two wheels.

None of us are surprised to see empty road in front of us.

"Head toward Cliffton," I tell Logan, naming a part of the city in West Point's territory.

Dante shakes his head. "They're not that stupid. McKenna has to know we'll try to get her back."

"We're not going to *try*," I snap, fisting my hands so hard that my blunt nails draw blood from my palms.

"Dante's right," Logan says, even though he's heading in the direction I told him to. "McKenna won't take her into their territory or stash her in any of his usual haunts. He'll need her somewhere completely off our radar until he can figure out how to get his hands on her inheritance."

We all go silent for a moment. He's right, but it leaves us with fucking nothing right now.

I can't accept that.

The only safe house I knew West Point to use was the one I saved Chloe from, and obviously that one is blown now.

During the entire time we were searching for Chloe—Logan tapping into every electronic surveillance method available in Halston, and Reapers scouring every street—we didn't come up with any off-the-grid leads, but we're just going to have to dig deeper.

"Is she really going to marry Austin McKenna?" Chloe asks quietly, her breath hitching.

I clench my teeth so hard it feels like my molars are about to crack, but it's Logan who answers her.

"Now that she's claimed the Sutherland inheritance, it's the only way he'll have a chance of getting his hands on it."

"But she only said that so he'd stop his men from shooting at us," Chloe says, sounding young and scared. "Right?"

None of us answer her. Of course that's why Riley fucking said it. That doesn't change the fact that McKenna is a sadistic bastard who will do whatever he needs to, to put West Point on top.

Chloe lets out a shuddering sigh and turns her face toward the window, silent tears trickling down her cheeks. I half expect her to start losing her shit, but she's got the same strength her sister has.

And right now, she's gonna need it.

Logan starts driving a grid pattern, all of us keeping our eye out for any sign of that silver Charger McKenna stuffed Riley into. Or, hell, *any* sign of West Point activity outside their borders.

There's nothing.

As we crisscross the streets of Halston, I send out instructions to our people to keep their eyes peeled too, and Dante reaches out to our allies with the same request.

All we get back is a fuck-ton of even more nothing.

"McKenna got too much of a head start," Logan finally says, making me want to fucking punch something.

"Madd," Dante adds after a minute, "We need to do this another way."

I can feel a muscle ticking in my jaw. I want to get my hands on McKenna and make him bleed. I want Riley safe and back where she belongs, with us. I want to fucking *find* her already. Turning back feels like admitting defeat.

But my brothers are right. Getting Riley back is our only priority right now, and the only way that's going to happen is if we focus on doing shit that might actually help. And clearly, driving the streets of Halston isn't doing that.

I unclench my jaw and force words out that I hate. "Head back to the house."

The Escalade is shrouded in thick silence as Logan drives us there, and once we get back and start to head inside, Chloe follows us out of the vehicle, then hesitates.

"Should I come in, too?"

I nod. "You'll stay with us until we get your sister back."

I move behind her as I'm speaking, ready to grab her if she bolts. Keeping her here is for her own safety, and because I know for fucking sure it's what Riley would want.

What I don't know is any of the details about what went down when West Point was holding Chloe—either the first time, or the second—or how much Riley had a chance to tell her about our... relationship. I can imagine, though. And after everything Chloe's been through, it wouldn't surprise me at all if she has trouble trusting me on this.

She doesn't resist, though. She almost looks relieved as she looks up at me, nibbling her lip in a move that sends a sharp pang through me.

I've seen Riley do the same thing.

Finally, Chloe gives me a shaky smile. "Okay. Thanks."

I nod sharply, ready to be done with the uncomfortable emotional shit. I still put my hand on her back to get her moving into the house, though. And dammit, I can't resist trying to reassure her a little bit too, for Riley's sake.

"You'll be safe here. You know your sister would never fucking forgive us if we let something happen to you while she's—"

I snap my mouth closed, refusing to say "McKenna's captive," or let myself imagine any of the things he might be doing to Riley right now.

I'm pretty sure Chloe's imagining the same exact shit though, because as we follow Logan and Dante into the kitchen, she looks down, her expression turning bleak.

"Hey," I say gruffly, tipping her chin up so she has to look at me. Her eyes widen. "I'm not gonna let anything happen to you, and we *will* get Riley back."

Chloe holds my stare for a moment. I can see she wants to believe me, but she also knows the kind of sick bastard Austin McKenna is firsthand. "Do you think he'll hurt her?" she finally asks, her voice cracking a little in the middle. "Or... or worse?"

"No."

I bite the single word out, then rage steals my voice... because it's a fucking lie. But I *can't* think that shit, or else I'll do the kind of damage that this city—and the Reapers—won't recover from.

I close my eyes and draw a slow breath through my nose, reaching for the clear mind I need right now.

Thankfully, Dante jumps in.

"All McKenna wants is the Sutherland money."

I meet Logan's eyes behind Chloe's back. We both know that's not true. He's getting a sadistic pleasure out of taking my woman again too. But Chloe doesn't need to hear that.

"That fucker *needs* Riley," Dante goes on, reassuring her. "Wherever she is, just remember that McKenna knows it. He'll take care of her. He needs her alive to get access to her inheritance."

Dante has never been one to sugarcoat things, but he's damn good at making people believe what he wants them to, and in this case, it works. Chloe's shoulders relax, and she gives him a tentative nod and a small smile of appreciation.

Must be nice. I've managed to lock a mask of calm in place,

but underneath, my skin itches with agitation as my mind races through dozens of scenarios that I'll take my whole fucking gang to war over if it comes down to it.

I'm not worried about McKenna taking Riley out... yet. Keeping her alive is only gonna be guaranteed until he gets what he needs from her, but that's not what fuels the burning sense of urgency inside me. There are too many shitty things short of death that a fucking sadist like him could be subjecting our girl to right now to count, and no matter how tough Riley's core of steel is, she's not going to be able to stand against the entire West Point gang.

"Logan," I snap, "go tap into city surveillance and track down McKenna's fucking car. We need to know where he took her."

Logan nods, his blond hair messier than usual. He's already been tapping away on his phone, no doubt getting a start on doing exactly that, but at my order, he turns and heads out of the room to pull up the more powerful system he has on his computer.

"Dante." I jerk my head toward my office. We need a fucking plan.

Dante hesitates, though.

"What about...?" he starts, indicating Chloe.

I dial back my impatience, because he's right. We need to keep her out of the way, but we also need her to stay fucking calm. Knowing how headstrong both Sutton sisters are, I figure Chloe is likely to either make herself a distraction or put herself in danger if we don't take the time to make sure she feels confident that we're gonna handle this the way it needs to be handled.

"Grab their bags, then get her settled up in Riley's room," I tell Dante, pulling out my phone as he follows my orders.

I tune him out as he talks softly to Chloe, then heads out to grab the girls' things out of the Escalade. A tiny spark of satisfaction flares to life before dying again when I see him bring Riley's things back inside, then head upstairs with Chloe to unpack them.

Planning on sending Riley away was... necessary.

Having her shit back in the house feels better, though.

I start making calls. We already alerted some of our people on the drive over, but we need more manpower on this.

It's not just a matter of getting Riley back. That's a given, because there's no way in hell that I'll stop until she's free of his clutches. But even more importantly, it's a matter of getting her back right the fuck *now*.

Before McKenna does something to her that will force me to rip this fucking city apart.

2

RILEY

I TRY to blink my eyes open and can't, and I feel like I should be panicking about that, but I can't seem to do that, either. Everything feels muffled and distant, but it's not until someone lifts me—*out of a car?*—and starts carrying me somewhere that I realize I've been drugged.

There are muffled voices around me, and I don't recognize any of them. I push through the fog and try to remember where the fuck I am, and finally manage to blink my eyes open only to wish I hadn't.

Austin McKenna. Leader of the West Point gang. The man who took my sister in payment for our father's debts. The enemy who's at war with the three men I love. And the monster whom I promised to marry today.

My skin feels like a thousand ants are crawling over it, and my eyelids each weigh a thousand pounds. I give in and let them drift closed again, and for a moment, I'm almost grateful for the way whatever that motherfucker drugged me with is muffling the world around me.

It was hard as hell to leave the Reaper's house with Chloe this morning, knowing I'd be leaving them behind forever. Signing all those papers to claim my inheritance from the

Sutherland estate was surreal. But West Point lying in wait for us afterward is something I *wish* I could forget.

When they pinned us down in that alley, I saw the truth in my men's faces. Neither Maddoc, Dante, nor Logan had any intention of backing down.

And that would have gotten them killed.

"Where do you want her, boss?" the goon carrying me asks, the question breaking through the drugged fog I'm stuck in.

I shove against his chest, struggling to get loose even though I'm not sure my legs are ready to hold me yet.

It doesn't matter. I'm the one who voluntarily offered myself up to Austin, and I'd do it again in a heartbeat to save my sister and my men.

But that just means that it's up to me to get myself out of this now.

"Shit, she's awake," the goon holding me grunts, his fingers digging into my flesh as he hauls me into a tighter hold.

Someone laughs. "The feisty ones are fun."

"Fuck you," I rasp, ramming an elbow into my captor's ribs and twisting away as much as I can.

The men around me just laugh, and one of them loops something around my ankles, binding them together, while the goon holding me lowers my feet to the ground, groping me along the way.

Then they tie my hands too.

I'm still too weak from the drugs to stand, and I hate being right about that almost as much as I hate the feeling of helplessness as they let me slide to the floor at their feet.

I blink up at them. Four men. All blurry. Then one leans down, his face looming into focus above mine.

It's Austin.

He's smiling, and it turns my stomach.

"Riley Sutherland," he says, his smug, possessive gaze

making my skin crawl in a way that has nothing to do with the drugs.

"Sutton," I correct him in a hoarse whisper. "I'm Riley *Sutton*."

Not that I'm proud to carry Frank's name, but if this fucker is going to gloat, he needs to get it right.

Something ugly flares in his eyes, but his smile only gets wider. "Good to know. It's the details that matter, isn't it? Otherwise, our marriage wouldn't be real."

I glare up at him, wrapping my anger around me like a shield to hold off the panic those words bring. "It will *never* be real."

He reaches down and strokes my cheek in a disgusting parody of affection.

I jerk my head away, and he laughs.

"I think what you meant to say was until death do us part," the smug bastard says. "After all, you're the one who proposed to me. And as much as I would have enjoyed spilling a little more Reaper blood in that alley, I do appreciate how easy you made it on us. I'll even forgive you for all the time we wasted chasing after your little sister before we figured out that *you* were the one getting all the Sutherland money."

He moves closer. Close enough that if I wasn't so fucking weak I could headbutt him in the balls.

I flex my arms, pulling against whatever it is they tied me with as I imagine doing it, but even that makes my muscles feel shaky. I glare at him instead of crying, and he leans down until I can feel his breath on my face.

"Maddoc Gray is a fucking idiot."

His men laugh on cue, and I bite my tongue to keep from spitting out how much better of a man Maddoc is than him.

I can't. Not while I'm weak and at West Point's mercy like this.

But I can tell Austin reads it on my face anyway by the way

his smug smile suddenly drops, a flash of rage breaking through as he reaches for my face again.

This time, he digs his fingers into my chin so I can't jerk away.

"He had you living with him for what, weeks? Months? And all that time he thought you were fucking worthless... or else only worth fucking."

I refuse to give him the reaction he's looking for, and he drops his hand and straightens up, throwing his arms out like he's putting on a show for his minions. "*We* figured it out, though. It's why we were there to snatch you as soon as you signed that shit that made you actually worth something. You don't think that makes Gray an idiot? He had his chance to get his hands on all that Sutherland money you just inherited, but now *I'm* gonna be the one to benefit."

One of his goons grumbles something under his breath, and Austin's eyes flash with that sadistic rage that lives inside him again before he quickly masks it and grins magnanimously at his men. "I mean, West Point will benefit. West Point... and all of Halston."

They all laugh, and I fucking hate the smug way he gloats. But that's not important. Nothing he says is important. The only thing that matters is that I got them to drive away without hurting Chloe or the Reapers.

West Point had too much firepower, and we had no way out of that alley. All the people who matter to me would likely have died if I hadn't voluntarily come with Austin... and I'd do it again in a heartbeat, no matter what hateful things he tries to taunt me with now.

I think of the calm facade Maddoc always projects to his crew, the blank mask Logan wears like a shield, the way Dante disguises his killer instincts behind warmth and charm. I remember having each one of them inside me, and I use that to pull my own armor on, drawing on everything they mean to me.

Austin narrows his eyes at me, but this time, I don't give him anything.

"Pick her up," he snaps to his goons, turning away and stalking across the room.

The guy who carried me in here yanks me roughly to my feet, holding me steady as my legs try to crumple again. I hate that I appreciate it, but I do. There's no fucking way I want to let myself look weak right now, even if those damn drugs they gave me mean it's still true.

I blink a few times in an effort to get the room to come into clearer focus as I try to remember how long it took Chloe to shake off the effects of the drugs they used on her after we got her back from that West Point safe house.

Actually, that doesn't matter. And not just because I don't know how long I was unconscious, but because Austin heads my way again, but this time, I can see clearly enough to make out the guy he brings with him.

More importantly, I can see the distinctive collar around his neck.

He's a fucking priest.

"Ready to say some vows, baby?" Austin asks, rubbing his hands together like some kind of cartoon villain.

I press my lips together tightly, knowing I can't say no even though my stomach flips at the thought of pledging *anything* to this man. But I knew this was the end game. It shouldn't feel like such a shock even if I didn't realize it would happen this fast, because of course Austin isn't going to waste any time. All he wants is my inheritance, and marrying me is how he'll gain access to it.

The priest doesn't even look at me, and he sure as shit doesn't pull out a bible. "This is your fiancée, Mr. McKenna?"

"This is her," Austin says with a sadistic grin, tunneling his fingers through the back of my hair and digging them into my scalp as he yanks me forward. "Let's get on with it."

The priest glances down at the paper he's holding. A marriage certificate. "Do you take Riley Suth—"

"Sutton," Austin cuts in, snatching the certificate from his hands and glaring at one of his minions. "Pen?"

The guy fumbles one out of a pocket and hands it over. Austin scribbles a quick correction on the form, then thrusts it back at the priest. "Yeah, Father. I *take* Riley Sutton to be my wife." He smirks, then winks at me. "Your turn now, baby."

My stomach clenches tight and I glare at him, my heart trying to pound its way through my chest.

"And you, Ms. Sutton?" the priest asks me in a flat voice, not making any effort at all to pretend this "ceremony" has anything to do with love or what I actually want. "Do you take Austin McKenna as your lawfully married husband?"

He stares at me, waiting for my response, and I know what I have to do, but my tongue locks up.

The West Point goon holding me upright yanks on my arms, making my shoulders scream with pain. "Boss is waiting, bitch," he growls in my ear.

"How romantic," I snark before I can stop myself, my nerves getting the best of me.

I half expect one of them to hurt me for it, but Austin just grins and steps in closer, gripping my chin again. Something hard digs into my stomach. He holds my gaze with that sadistic smile that I don't want to admit terrifies me, and ice water seeps into my veins.

If it was his cock, I'd be disgusted, but it's not—it's a gun.

A reminder that no matter how hard it is to make myself say the words he wants to hear, I have no choice.

"Say it," Austin demands, his bruising grip making my jaw ache. "Tell the good Father that you want to be my wife. That you accept me as your lawful husband. That you fucking begged me for this back in that alley."

He pushes the barrel of the gun deeper into my navel, and I force the words out.

"I do."

The words scrape my throat raw.

Austin's eyes flare with a sick heat. The fucker is getting off on this.

"You do what?" that fucking sadist asks, taunting me.

"I... accept you as my husband."

He doesn't take his eyes off me as he snaps another order at the priest. "That's what you needed, isn't it, Father? We're married now?"

The man nods. "Yes, Mr. McKenna. I now pronounce you husband and wife. I just need your witnesses to sign the certificate and then it will be official."

Austin waves the priest off with his gun hand, then shoves the weapon into his waistband as two of his men follow the priest across the room to seal my fate.

Austin fists my hair, yanking it hard enough to make my eyes water as he forces my head back. Since the dickhead still holding my arms doesn't let go, I'm sandwiched between the two of them when Austin tightens his grip on my jaw and slams his mouth over mine, kissing me hard enough that his teeth cut into my lips and I taste blood.

My skin crawls, and I gag. I can't help it.

Austin abruptly releases me, licking my blood off his lips with a predatory smile. "You heard him, *wifey*. We're married now. What's yours is now mine."

I want to tell him to fuck off, but my legs wobble when he steps away, and I blink back the hot sting of tears instead. Austin's goon tightens his grip on my arms, holding me up, and I want to fight him, but it's impossible. I can barely stand on my own.

Austin gives me a slow once over, then sneers and turns away. "Lock her up. I've got shit to do."

He turns and strides away without a backward glance, and his minions drag me through the sparsely furnished house and toss me into a windowless room the size of a shoebox that has three thick, steel locks installed on the door. It also has a narrow bed with a thin mattress, and nothing else.

"Are you going to take these off?" I ask the asshole who gropes my tits as he shoves me down on the bed, holding up my bound wrists.

"Boss didn't tell me to," he says with a lascivious leer, "but if you wanna be extra nice to me, I can ask."

I glare up at him. "You mean, you'll ask my *husband?*"

The word almost makes me vomit in my mouth, but it does the job. He grumbles something and backs off without molesting me any further, stomping out of the room and throwing all three of the locks.

Without untying me.

3

LOGAN

"Where, where, where," I mutter, my fingers flying over the keyboard as my eyes jump from screen to screen, scanning the security footage I've got pulled up.

The multi-monitor computer setup I've got here in my room is extensive for a reason. If something happens in Halston, I want access to it, and by now there isn't a single public camera in the city that I haven't tapped into. And not just the public ones.

Unfortunately, the area that West Point took Riley in has shitty security coverage.

It took me longer than it should have to find an image of McKenna's car speeding away from that fucking alley, and so far, I've only been able to trace it up to a point before the sightings start falling off. And the last image I've been able to confirm makes it look like McKenna was running parallel to the border of his territory.

"Were you stupid enough to veer north, you piece of shit?" I ask, widening the radius of my search.

I don't think he did. North would have taken him into Cliffton, and as I said to my brothers earlier, my guess is that McKenna won't try to stash Riley in West Point's territory.

So... fucking *where*, then?

My hands go still on the keyboard as I close my eyes, reviewing a mental map of the area around that final sighting of McKenna's car that I picked up. It was a shot of the silver Dodge Charger's rear license plate, captured by an ATM machine's camera about three miles from the alley.

I've already done a street-by-street surveillance search in a twelve block radius around the location and come up with nothing. The longer it takes for me to pick up the trail, the colder it grows. It's like that bastard drove her into a fucking vacuum, leaving me with nothing but a black hole of information.

"Unacceptable," I bite out, keeping a tight rein on the emotions that threaten to distract me so I can focus—*again*—on sorting through every sighting of McKenna's car, cross-referencing maps of the city as I build up a picture of the route he took as it correlates with all the known connections West Point has in the city.

It gives me a probable direction... *if* McKenna was acting logically.

I start searching block by block through all surveillance systems along my predicted route. Again.

And come up with nothing.

Again.

I press my lips together tightly, breathing in through my nose to the count of six, then breathing out for the count of eight. I repeat it over and over to activate my parasympathetic nervous system, desperately needing to eliminate the unsettled feeling that keeps intruding on my concentration.

I fail.

I feel... out of control.

When a thing happens, there is a record of it. When a car travels through Halston, it leaves a trail. This is simply another puzzle to solve, and not being able to do that makes me feel off balance and out of control, a feeling I hate.

But it's more than that. It's not having Riley here. That's making me feel off balance and out of control too. It's... wrong.

I know it was the plan all along.

She was going to leave even before West Point took her.

It made sense and was safest for her and her sister, but that was wrong too. I can see it clearly now. She should never have gone anywhere. She belongs here with us.

Once we get her back, I'll need to tell Maddoc that.

And... I should have told Riley.

I want her here. I want more of what we had before she left. Not just the sex. She's important. She's *necessary*. For as much as I hated how disruptive her presence was when she first burst into our lives, now the house—my *life*—feels wrong without her in it.

If McKenna hurts her...

I grit my teeth and forcefully shove the thought aside, then get back to searching. If he does, it's a given that he'll die. But letting myself imagine it now isn't going to bring Riley home, and right now, that's my only priority.

I pull up a satellite view of the city and zoom in on the location of the ATM machine where I last caught sight of McKenna's car. I'm about to input new search parameters into my surveillance mapping program when a soft noise from behind me freezes my hands on the keyboard.

I spin my chair around to face my bedroom door, the door I *always* keep closed whether I'm in here or not.

It's open.

I left it open.

That should bother me. It's another sign of how much today's events have thrown me off-kilter. But Chloe is standing there, no doubt responsible for the noise that caught my attention, and a soft, unfamiliar feeling comes over me, muting the reaction I would normally have to someone intruding on my space uninvited this way.

But Chloe isn't just "someone," she's Riley's family. Her little sister. And if Riley belongs here, then Chloe does too.

But there's a lost, defeated look in Chloe's eyes that I don't like. It awakens memories of my own little sister, along with the feelings of fierce protectiveness I had when faced with the monster I failed to save Emma from.

Riley didn't fail, though. Riley was able to save *her* little sister.

And until we get Riley back, someone else needs to look after Chloe.

"Sorry," she says, the nervous hesitation in her voice making me suspect that she finds my silent regard unnerving. "I didn't mean to disturb you, I just..." She trails off, her shoulders slumping. "I'll leave."

Maddoc and Dante are undoubtedly as focused as I am on getting Riley back, so Chloe has most likely been left to her own devices ever since we got back to the house. If she's anything like her sister—which it's clear from the way she survived out on the streets that she is—she'll want to help get Riley back too.

She starts to turn away, and I blink, realizing I haven't done that since discovering her in my doorway.

"No."

She turns back to face me, her eyes widening. "No?"

"Come in."

The words come out stilted, but surprisingly, I mean them. It feels weird to allow another person in my room—no, to *invite* someone in—but in a completely illogical way, Chloe's presence also soothes some of that feeling of wrongness inside me from not having Riley here.

"Um, Maddoc said you had a way to track Austin McKenna's car?" she says, approaching my desk hesitantly. "Is that what you're working on?"

I pull out the second chair that I brought into my room when Riley was here helping me search the city for Chloe. The synchronicity gives me an uncomfortable pang in my chest.

"Sit," I tell Chloe.

She does it, and I surprise myself again by how much it helps me quiet and focus my mind—exactly what I was reaching for earlier and failed to accomplish on my own—when I start to explain what I'm doing.

"You can see through the traffic cameras?" she asks, leaning forward with a look of fascination on her face.

"I can access them," I say, because "seeing through them" is both imprecise and incorrect. "Depending on the model, some only take still photographs when their sensors are activated, while others live stream but don't record." I switch views and bring up an image of the intersection at Broad and Leavenworth, using my cursor to circle the camera prominently mounted next to the traffic lights. "Other locations use dummy cameras to deter drivers."

"You mean, that one does nothing?"

I grimace, annoyed because yes, it does nothing. "Correct. But as you can see, I'm still able to monitor that particular location by accessing another camera. In this case, it's part of the security system for the pawn shop on the corner of Broad."

Chloe's breath hitches, her eyes turning glassy as she covers her mouth over a little sob.

I frown. "What is it?"

She smiles at me, dashing the wetness from her eyes. "So you *will* be able to find her. When Austin drove off with her I thought... I thought..."

"We will find her," I confirm quickly before she can become even more emotional. It makes me uncomfortable, but at the same time, I'm also overcome with a strange feeling of satisfaction over having changed her previous look of despair to this more hopeful one.

I turn back to the monitors and walk her through the details of the various surveillance systems I've tapped into around the city, explaining the logic I've applied in searching for traces of McKenna's route. Talking through it gives me a clearer perspective, and Chloe murmurs quiet, insightful questions as I redefine the most probable search area and explain some of the rivalry between the Reapers and West Point and the resources we'll use to get Riley back.

"We'll also tap our allies for help—" I cut myself off abruptly when Chloe makes a small, pained sound. "What?" I ask sharply, wondering if she has information that I don't about the other gangs we've forged relationships with. It's possible she overheard something while West Point held her captive, but it's equally likely that she saw or heard something while she was hiding out on the streets. I narrow my eyes as dozens of unsavory possibilities for betrayal flip rapidly through my head. "Tell me."

"Sorry," Chloe says, shaking her head. "It's just... I can't believe Riley gave herself up like that."

I blink, recalibrating my thought process. Chloe wasn't having a reaction to the information I provided. She was having an... an *emotional* reaction.

Before I can determine if it requires me to comfort her, she huffs out a watery laugh.

"What am I saying? Of *course* I can believe it," she says. "Riley would do anything to protect the people she loves."

I stiffen. *People.* The word sends a visceral reaction through me, not unlike the painful awakening of blood rushing back into a limb that's fallen asleep.

But this isn't a limb. This is a deeper part of me.

Riley loves Chloe the way I loved my sister Emma, and yes, Riley *would* do anything for her. She already has. But Chloe said "people." Chloe thinks that Riley sacrificed herself to protect... people.

People whom Riley loves.

Chloe puts her hand on my arm, cocking her head to the side. "Logan?" she says, searching my face in a way that should feel intrusive, but doesn't. "I don't know exactly what's happening between my sister and you, all three of you, but it's something, isn't it? Something real?"

I hesitate, then give her a stiff nod, still reeling from the casual way she used that word.

I am not... lovable.

Other than my brothers, who would die for me, people do not *love* me.

Chloe gives me a tentative smile, squeezing my arm one more time—a touch that should repel me, but that, strangely, I find comforts me instead—and then pulls her hand back. "I wasn't sure about you guys at first. I mean, come on, the Reapers? Your gang has a reputation and the three of you are pretty intimidating, but Riley was different after you guys got me back from West Point the last time. Different around you and Maddoc and Dante, I mean. Different in a *good* way."

"We... are different too," I admit.

She nods, then sniffles before scrubbing at her cheeks with a self-deprecating laugh. "Good. That's... that's good. I never thought I'd see the day she actually fell for someone after all the losers she's dated. But I'm glad, you know? She deserves a guy— um, *guys* who will kick some ass for her."

There it is again. She's talking about Riley falling for me and my brothers. Caring for us.

Loving us.

Chloe smiles. "It really means a lot to see how hard you're all working to get her back. Thank you."

I go still, her gratitude and everything she's just implied sending me into a tailspin, completely out of my element.

I want to rub at my chest, thick and tight with emotions that feel too big to fit inside it. But I don't. Hiding that sort of weakness, learning not to display feelings that I don't understand and have no strategy for dealing with, is a self-preservation strategy I internalized at a very young age. Instead, I give Chloe a stiff nod.

Then, belatedly remembering certain social niceties, I force my tongue to unlock from the roof of my mouth. "You're... welcome."

Chloe grins. Then, thankfully, she stops emoting and turns back to my monitors.

"Let's find her," she says with a renewed determination in her voice that bolsters mine. "Where else can we look? There are a ton of places near the plaza here, the one with the fountain, that have security systems, right? Can you hack all their cameras, too?"

"I already have access," I confirm, refocusing on the search and grateful for the chance to let the bewildering swirl of emotions inside me settle into the background again as Chloe and I pour ourselves into the only thing that matters right now.

If she's right, if Riley... loves me, there's nothing to be done about it until we get her back.

So we will. We have to.

I won't accept anything else.

doing is necessary," I answer her honestly, "even when it hurts you. They'll justify that it's for the best, but what they really mean is that it's best for them."

Sienna's face hardens. She thinks I'm trying to hurt her, but I'm just telling her the truth. I have no idea why she decided to betray Maddoc, or if she actually has the feelings for Austin that she claims to. I just know that the way Austin's treating her isn't love... and even if she believes it actually is, is that really what she *wants*? A man who'd marry a woman he doesn't give a shit about just for money, rather than do what's right for the woman he's supposed to love?

"You just don't understand him," Sienna sneers, reminding me that I actually don't give a shit what she feels or why she feels it. "This isn't your world, and you're either stupid or naive if you think you know anything about what men like Austin and Maddoc actually care about. Once all your money is in Austin's hands, things will be different. He'll finally be able to do whatever he wants. He'll be able to *have* whoever he wants, and trust me, it won't be you." She smirks again, backing toward the door without taking her eyes off me. "He won't have any use for *you* at all. At that point, you'll just be a liability."

My gut twists. She obviously just came in here to try to make herself feel better by tearing me down, but I've got plenty of practice letting shit like that roll off my back. The only people whose opinions matter to me aren't in this room, so she shouldn't have been able to get under my skin.

But as she stomps out and leaves me on my own again, I can't deny that she did.

Not with her jealousy... but with the reminder that Austin only has one use for me.

"Shit," I whisper, my heart pounding and my hands getting sweaty.

I wipe them on my pants, but my knees betray me, giving out and depositing my ass on the edge of the narrow bed.

I'd give up a lot to keep the people who matter to me safe. Hell, I already did. But... I don't want to die. And the way Sienna was talking, it sounds a hell of a lot like once Austin doesn't need me anymore, he plans on getting rid of me.

Permanently.

5

RILEY

I FEEL BLESSEDLY numb inside as I pick at the overcooked piece of meat these assholes gave me for dinner, trying not to let myself compare it to the memory of all the delicious meals Logan has cooked for me.

Or, hell, maybe this mystery meat is supposed to be breakfast?

I've got no fucking way to tell since they haven't let me out of this windowless room other than to pee a couple of times every day, and even though I've been trying to track time here based on when they feed me, it's not like I trust that they're doing it on any kind of regular schedule.

Still, I think I've probably been West Point's prisoner for a week or two by now, and every day—or at least, every time I wake up from my longest sleep—I try not to get my hopes up that the Reapers will come rescue me.

"Oh god," I whisper, the shield of all that numbness cracking for a moment and letting my actual emotions through. I cover my mouth to hold in the pained noise that tries to escape, because even though I'm alone, I refuse to be weak here.

All I need to remember is that the men not coming for me is a *good* thing. I shouldn't even want them to since I did this to protect the three of them and my sister. If they suddenly burst in here just to try to save me, here where they'd be even more overpowered than we were in that alley, then what I've done for them would be worthless.

But, more importantly, it doesn't even matter.

No one comes. I'm left alone with nothing but my thoughts and the occasional plate of food that always tastes like cardboard soaked in ass. And time keeps ticking downward toward a feeling of doom.

"But I'm still here. I'm still alive," I whisper to myself, needing to hold onto that.

I make myself take another bite of the food they've given me. I still have no plan other than survival, but I know that if I get an opportunity to do something more than that, I'm going to need my strength. And that's all this food is. It's not pleasure, it's barely sustenance. But it's the only fuel I've got for the dwindling spark of hope inside me that somehow, some way, I'll find a way to make this motherfucker pay for what he's putting me through.

And for what he's stealing from me.

I haven't seen Sienna again after that first day, and other than the neckless wonder who escorts me to and from the bathroom down the hall from this windowless hell, Austin is the only person I've seen since they brought me here.

He brings me paperwork to sign periodically, pressing a cocked gun to my temple while he stares at me with an even cockier grin, and it's not just the fact that I've been signing over the fortune I inherited to my new "husband" that's fed my hatred of the man. It's the sick pleasure I can see he takes in how much power he has over me.

I've got no choice, though. Not if I still want to live... which I do. Bit by bit, Austin is forcing me to give him access to all of it. All I can do with my overflowing anger and the choking sense of helplessness that comes over me every time the door opens to reveal his gloating face is store it up inside and promise myself that I'll use it later.

I won't make it easy for him to "get rid" of me the way Sienna said. Not without a fight.

I look up as I hear the locks disengage. I'm not surprised to see it's Neckless. Now that they've fed me, they usually give me a bathroom break.

I force myself to shove the last bite of the meat I've been toying with into my mouth before standing up, briefly letting myself fantasize about smashing the plate over his head. But then what? On my brief walks to and from the bathroom, I've seen far too many gang members hanging around—and heard the voices of even more—to think I'd have any chance of getting very far even if a dumb move like that actually did anything more than piss my guard off and give him an excuse to hurt me.

"Coming?" he asks gruffly. "'Cause if you'd rather piss in the corner and stink this place up, that's on you, bitch."

I don't bother replying, and as soon as I get within arm's reach of him, he grabs my arm and digs his fingers in, keeping me close as he turns and marches me down the hallway.

Out here, there are at least some windows I get to walk past. I can tell by the light outside that it's probably sometime in the afternoon, closing in on evening. I've also been able to piece together the little glimpses I get of the world outside this fucking house, enough to realize that it's not in any part of Halston that I'm familiar with.

It's got to be another safe house he keeps hidden, like the one Maddoc saved Chloe from. Somewhere he plans on keeping me squirreled away while he works through all the legal bullshit to get my money transferred into his name.

It's a straight shot from the room they're keeping me in to the bathroom, but since we pass a few other rooms along the way, along with an open entry to what looks like the front of the house and a stairway just past the bathroom, I've done my best to make a mental map of the layout of the place. It may not be totally accurate, but at least I won't be running completely blind if I ever get a chance to make a break for it.

We reach the bathroom, and Neckless follows me into the small room. It's another windowless one, and they've taken out every single amenity other than the roll of toilet paper and a single, thin hand towel. There's no way my guard is under orders to watch me like this. I'm not going to escape if I'm out of his sight for a few minutes while I pee.

No, the sick bastard does it—every single time—purely because he gets off on having power over me.

I've known plenty of bastards just like him and used most of them to pay our bills back when I was stripping at Club M. My skin should be thick enough that his lascivious stare doesn't bother me, but the truth is, I hate it.

Being stuck here is wearing me down. I don't want that to be true, but I can feel it.

What I can't do—*won't* do—is show it.

I ignore him and do my business, quickly peeing and then washing my hands at the sink. I don't flush. It's a small rebellion, but it's one tiny fuck-you that I have control over, so I take it.

As soon as my hands are dry, Neckless puts his clammy hands on me, meaty fingers splayed across my lower back as he starts to usher me back to my room. I don't give him the satisfaction of reacting, but his touch makes my skin crawl, and when two more gang members exit one of the rooms near mine, turning toward us in the narrow hall, my heart starts to race with an anxiety I fight not to show.

For a split second, they look surprised to see me out of my room. Then their expressions quickly morph into leering sneers, and they saunter closer, blocking the hallway.

"I thought she wasn't supposed to be out of her room," one of the new guys says to Neckless, licking his lips as his eyes rake over me. "The boss know you're having a little fun while he's out, Tony?"

"Yeah, real fun," my guard—Tony, apparently—says sarcastically. "All I'm allowed to do is take her to the bathroom and back."

"Sounds risky," says the lip licker, staring down at me. "You never know what she might cook up in there. You sure she hasn't snuck anything past you?"

"I watch her," Tony grunts, fisting his hand in the back of my shirt and yanking me back against his 'roided up chest like he's trying to prove that he can keep me from making a break for it.

"That's good," purrs Lip Licker, taking another step toward me, standing so close that I have to tip my head back to glare up at him. "But do you *check* her?"

His hand lashes out with no warning and he grabs my pussy, grinning when I flinch.

"Fuck you," I spit out, hating myself a little for showing any weakness.

"Maybe I'll do that when the boss is finally done with you," Lip Licker says like a sick promise, groping me with rough, demanding fingers as his breath speeds up with excitement. "I can fill this hot little pussy up for you *real* good."

Not if his dick is broken.

Old instincts kick in fast, and I slam my knee up, aiming for his balls.

I only graze them, earning a vicious curse from the guy, because Tony is faster. The fucker yanks me backward before I can connect and do the damage I want, his moist breath on the back of my neck sending a disgusted shudder through me as he leans down to whisper in my ear.

"None of that, bitch. Jackson's right. Once Austin gets what he needs from you, he ain't gonna have any more use for you. And you know what he does with bitches he has no use for?"

His cock starts to swell against my back, and I struggle to get away from him, answering his question with a string of curses that gets me nothing but dark laughter from all three of them.

Tony yanks my elbows behind me, sending a shooting pain through my shoulders. "We've been stuck here watching over you, bored out of our fucking minds. Pretty sure he'll let us pass you around since we deserve something for that."

"You deserve to rot in fucking hell," I grit out, panting as I struggle against him.

"Nah, like Jackson said, what we deserve is a little fun," he says, wrapping a meaty hand around my neck and squeezing until I'm forced to go still. The shithead he called Jackson seems to take that as an open invitation, closing in on me again and grabbing my tits hard while Tony holds me in place.

His eyes are mean now that I've gone for his balls.

"What do you think, *Mrs. McKenna?*" he asks nastily as he gropes me. "Are you having fun yet?"

The front door bangs open before I can tell him to go fuck himself, startling all three guards. The guy against the wall straightens up and looks toward the front of the house, and Jackson backs off too.

It's Austin, looking so fucking smug as he approaches that the brief surge of relief I felt at the interruption goes up in smoke. If he's this pleased about something, there's no way it can be anything good, and the way he's looking at me sends my heart into my throat.

"All good, boss?" Jackson asks, backing off even more to give Austin room to pass.

"Very, very good," Austin answers, his eyes locked onto mine as he walks right up to me. Tony quickly drops his hand from my throat without letting go of my arms, shifting back a few inches.

At least I don't have to feel his cock pressing against me anymore.

Tony clears his throat. "I was just taking her to the bath—"

"*Shh*," Austin says sharply, holding up a hand. I hear Tony's mouth snap closed behind me, and Austin smiles. "It's official, wifey," he practically purrs, leaning in. "What's yours is all mine. The accounts have all been officially transferred into my name. And do you know what that means?"

I don't answer him, and I don't give him the satisfaction of flinching away when he reaches out and strokes my cheek with one finger, either.

"It means I don't need you anymore," he says, slowly dragging his finger down to my throat before jerking it sideways in a vicious slicing motion.

I swallow hard, both adrenaline and fear stabbing through me, and Austin grins, a dark hunger flaring to life in his eyes. For a split second as he holds my gaze, I think he's going to do it right now. But then he rocks back on his heels, tucking his hands behind his back.

"I was going to kill you, but Sienna gave me a better idea."

He pauses, dragging it out, but I'm not going to feed his sadistic pleasure by begging to know my fate.

"You do still have *some* value," he finally goes on, watching me with an avaricious gleam in his eye. "No monetary value, not anymore, but since there are three men who still seem to want you anyway, you're still going to be useful to me."

For a single, horrifying moment, I think the three guards were right. Austin is going to give me to his men. He'll let them pass me around and use me as their cum dump until I *wish* I was dead. But then the gloating expression on his face gives way to ugly rage, and he spits out a word that makes my heart sing.

"*Reapers.*"

My breath hitches, and as quickly as Austin's mask slipped, he has it back in place, grinning at me with smug satisfaction.

"That's right. Maddoc Gray and his seconds still have their

people sniffing around for you, and Sienna pointed out that that gives me an advantage against them."

My heart lurches. Are they really still out there looking for me?

Something both painful and warm spills into my chest, because I don't even have to ask. Of course they are. I can't deny that the three men I was living with... care about me. They've shown it, proven it, over and over. Just like they've proven that it's not about the money.

Austin's right. They *will* still want me, even though it's gone.

But I care about them too. I don't want them to pay for their feelings for me like this. I don't want Austin to use me as leverage.

He will, though. He'll make them pay. He'll use me to hurt Maddoc, Dante, and Logan.

West Point is going to blackmail the Reapers.

6

DANTE

"I WANT to hear about it even if you're not sure whether they're working for West Point or not," I say, lifting my take-out cup to my mouth even though the coffee tastes like ass.

"Yeah, yeah, whatever you need, Big D."

Scales, a runner for the 17th Street Gang who owes me for saving his ass when he got into a tight spot with Halston's finest a few years ago, bobs his head in a quick, jittery nod that tells me he's using again.

Fucking stupid of him, but not my problem. What is my problem is that just like every other contact I've checked in with out on the streets, he hasn't seen anyone from West Point doing anything that would point us toward where they might be keeping Riley.

I drain the last of the truly shitty coffee I picked up at the convenience store behind us, the one Scales somehow holds down a part-time job at when he's not moving product for his organization, and toss the cup into the dumpster we're standing next to.

"I'm serious," I tell him. "It's not just McKenna's people I want to hear about. If you see anyone you don't recognize and they so much as fucking sneeze in a suspicious way, I want you to call me."

We don't know who West Point is allied with at this point, but it's almost guaranteed that McKenna has our girl locked down somewhere outside his own borders. The problem is, Halston ain't big, but it's not exactly small, either. No matter how far our reach is, we can't cover all of it.

Scales nods again, his fingers flicking urgently against his thigh as he promises me that he'll keep an eye out.

I let him go, then give in to my frustration and punch the side of the dumpster with a vicious curse, welcoming the hot burst of pain across my knuckles.

I've got no fucking clue if Scales will actually remember the promise he just made me after he gets his next fix, but *someone* has to have caught wind of McKenna's movements lately. I just have to fucking find that someone... and after two weeks of looking and coming up with fuck all for the effort, I want to do a hell of a lot more damage than just leaving a few smears of my blood across a back alley dumpster.

I've already tapped out all my informants and contacts today though, so I scrub a hand over my face and head back to the car, absently noting the rasp of stubble on my jaw as it catches on the calluses on my fingers.

Fine, it's more than a fucking rasp. I'm probably getting close to full-on beard territory. I honestly can't remember the last time I shaved, but I care even less.

"Fucking McKenna," I mutter as I slide behind the wheel of the piece of shit SUV I've been driving ever since the Escalade got shot up.

I head for home, the agitation I feel over another fucking day with no leads to follow making me drive a little more recklessly than I probably should... maybe not entirely by accident.

The way Riley's extended absence is getting to me, I'd

seething anger I expected to see is definitely there, there's nothing but murderous determination in his eyes as the three of us share a look.

"We're getting her back," Logan finally says, his voice flat and irrefutable.

"Damn fucking right we are," Maddoc growls.

"We've got a shit-ton of planning to do and not a lot of fucking time to do it in," I add. "How do you want us to get ready for this drop, Madd?"

"Come on," he says, not waiting for either of us as he turns and heads toward his office. "Let's go figure that out."

Logan follows on his heels, and I'm right behind the both of them when Chloe stops me with a hand on my arm.

I look down at her, half expecting big, teary eyes and trembling lips. Understandable, but not gonna lie, we don't have time for that shit right now. But once again, what I get instead is a reminder to stop assuming stupid shit about people who care about Riley.

Of course Chloe is torn up about McKenna having her sister, but they've both got the same inner core of steel, and she doesn't waste my time whining about how bad this could go or drowning in fear over shit that's out of our hands at the moment. She just lifts her chin and locks her gaze onto mine. "Are you really going to get her back?"

She doesn't need me to sugarcoat it. She needs the unvarnished truth.

"Yeah, we are," I say, giving it to her. "Riley's coming home tomorrow."

It's more than the truth. It's a promise. A motherfucking vow.

No matter who we have to take out to make it happen.

7

RILEY

I ARCH MY BACK, reaching for the ceiling, then let out a long, slow breath as I reverse it and bend forward, folding at the waist until I've got my arms wrapped around my calves and my chest pressed against my thighs. Then I let out a stream of viciously muttered fucks and flop backward onto the piece of shit bed West Point has so generously provided for me, staring up at the pattern of textured bumps that I can probably draw in my sleep by now.

If I *could* sleep.

"Fuck," I whisper again, squeezing my eyes closed.

It doesn't help.

I've been on edge and feeling anxious ever since Austin dragged me out of this windowless cell of a room and forced me to listen in on that call he made to Maddoc yesterday. But even with my eyes closed, I can still see the look on Austin's face as he taunted Maddoc over the phone, trying to hurt him. Threatening to hurt *me* if I so much as made a sound or attempted to let the Reapers know I was there.

West Point's leader truly is a sadistic fuck. It's the only reason he had me listen in like that, and the smirk he wore the whole time just confirmed it.

Austin made sure to hold the phone away from his ear as the two of them spoke so I could hear the muted sound of Maddoc's voice, and my heart clenches all over again as I remember the leashed fury behind Maddoc's words as he demanded to know where I was.

He didn't even hesitate before agreeing to trade his life for mine.

I never expected that.

"You asshole, Maddoc," I whisper into the stale air, my throat tight with a wave of emotion that threatens to overwhelm me.

I came here to protect *him*. All of them. But even when Austin told me he was going to use me against the Reapers, I didn't anticipate the fucked-up terms he offered them, or I would have fought it like hell.

And I couldn't have prepared myself for how it felt when Maddoc said yes to those terms.

I can't be the reason Austin hurts him.

That thought sends my emotion bubbling over, and they burst out of me in a short, sharp laugh that sounds almost hysterical. It's got nothing to do with humor and feels all too close to tears, and I quickly slap a hand over my mouth to stifle it because, even all alone in here, I can't stand to hear it.

And I won't be alone in here for long. Even though I can't properly tell time with absolutely nothing in here to tell me how quickly it's passing, I know the hand-off will be soon... and I'm torn.

I don't want my men in danger.

I can't stand the idea of Maddoc giving himself up for me.

But I want to see them again. I want it so badly it almost scares me.

I think I've been falling for them from the start. The feelings between all of us grew slowly, and sometimes they felt a lot more like hate and terror along the way, but even when I couldn't see it and didn't want to admit it, the connection I feel with each of them has become the one thing, besides Chloe, that matters most to me. The one thing that's sustained me in this West Point hell over the last couple of weeks.

I was willing to give up everything for my men, and the idea that Maddoc is about to do the same for me is overwhelming. It shows me the true breadth of these feelings—mine for them, and theirs for me—and suddenly I'm not fighting off tears. I'm pissed the fuck off at Austin for daring to threaten it.

And pissed off is better, because caring this much makes it really fucking hard to stay strong. If I let myself think too much about how hard Maddoc, Dante, and Logan are willing to fight for me, it's going to knock me right over and make me even more terrified about what's going to happen when we all show up to make that trade.

I don't trust Austin. Not even a little bit.

But I'm powerless against him right now, and the only hope I have to cling to is knowing that the Reapers trust him even less than I do. Whatever happens, even if it all goes to shit, they won't let him win.

The door to my room opens so suddenly that it sends my heart into my throat, and I leap to my feet, my pulse pounding. Austin stands in the doorway, and I can see a couple of his henchmen and Sienna waiting in the hallway behind him.

"It's time," he says, his eyes roving over me like I'm a piece of meat. "Move your ass, bitch."

I bite my tongue and do it, but of course Austin has to keep playing his little power games even when I obey him. When I get to the doorway, he doesn't move aside, forcing me to squeeze past him instead.

The feel of his body against mine as he takes the opportunity to grope me makes my stomach turn. It also pisses off his girlfriend, even though she quickly masks it.

After that one flash of fury across Sienna's face, she keeps her gaze utterly impassive. She's not, though. I'd bet anything she's regretting talking Austin out of killing me right now.

We lock eyes for a moment, then I decide to ignore her.

So does Austin.

"You really are the gift that keeps on giving," he says to me, moving up behind me and pulling my back against his chest. His hands slide down my sides and settle on my hips, forcing my ass back against his groin. "I never thought I'd see the day Maddoc Gray was stupid enough to trade himself for something so worthless. Can you explain that to me? Why the fuck does he want you so bad?"

I keep my mouth shut. I'm not playing this sick game of his.

Not that that stops him.

Austin pushes my purple and blue hair off my shoulder, baring my neck. Then the fucker licks it.

I shudder with revulsion, my stomach twisting.

"If you're not going to answer me, I'm gonna have to figure it out for myself," Austin says, still holding me tightly against him. "Maddoc knows the money is gone, so I figure he thinks your pussy is made of fucking gold too. Is that it?"

This time, I manage not to react. At least, not until Austin slips his hand between my legs and gropes me while dragging his nose up the line he just licked on my throat, sniffing me like he's a goddamn dog.

"We never did bother to consummate our marriage," he murmurs when he finally reaches my ear. "But don't worry, *wifey*, there's still time to fix that before we have to leave. Unlike those fucking Reapers of yours, I'd never be stupid enough to leave gold on the table without taking some for myself."

Sienna's mask cracks for a moment, and if I wasn't so fucking disgusted, I'd almost feel sorry for her. I don't actually give a shit about whether she's hurt or not, though. She made her bed and she can rot in it.

But despite my best efforts at keeping my real feelings from showing, I tense up, giving away how much Austin's sick game affects me.

It's a mistake. It turns him on. His cock starts to swell against my back, and he spins me around, fisting my hair with one hand while the other gropes my ass. He grinds us together and takes my mouth hard, his teeth cutting into my lips and his tongue thrusting deep enough to make me gag.

So I bite it.

"Fuck!" he bellows, rearing back and shoving me away from him. "You goddamn bitch!"

I stumble, and he backhands me, sending me crashing into the wall.

Then he's on me, his face twisted in fury as his fists rain down pain. He punches me in the ribs, and the pain is so sharp and sudden that I cry out before I can stop myself. I bring up my arms to block him, but that just leaves my stomach exposed, and the uppercut he drills into me almost has me retching.

I double over and get two hard blows to my kidneys and a brutal knee to my thigh that almost sends me to the floor, then Austin fists my hair and uses it to yank me upright again.

"You want something to fucking remember me by?" he shouts, bloody spittle flying in my face. "I'll give you fucking something."

He lands another blow to my ribs, then abruptly stops, a terrifying glint in his eyes.

"If this is how you want to play, maybe I'll just keep you," he says in a frighteningly gentle tone, his eyes caressing my face in a fucked up parody of a lover's gaze. "I'll keep you right here, where I can teach you the kind of respect a real wife would owe me. I'll deny the Reapers any of that golden pussy and show you what it means to belong to a *real* man."

I go cold all over, the threat terrifying me in a way that a simple beating never will.

Austin's hand is still fisted in my hair, pulling hard enough to sting my scalp, and he forces my head back even farther, his eyes dropping to my mouth.

"Fuck you," I bite out before he can try to kiss me again.

His gaze turns hard in an instant, going so ugly and dark that I know it's not my pussy he's thinking of now. If he didn't have to deliver me to the drop to exchange me for Maddoc, he'd kill me for that.

For a second, I think he just might.

Then he backhands me again, keeping me in place with that grip on my hair, and spits a wet gob of bloody saliva on my face before shoving me at his men.

"Lock this bitch's wrists behind her back," he snaps at them as the disgusting fluid drips down my cheek, pooling in the corner of my mouth.

I press my lips tightly together and duck my head toward my shoulder, trying to wipe it off.

Austin's fingers dig into my chin hard enough to bruise, forcing my head back up before I can. "Leave it or I'll slice up that precious pussy of yours before we get to the drop."

I obey him because I have to, and someone yanks my arms back and snaps a cold pair of handcuffs onto my wrists. I blank my mind and stuff down my emotions as they lead me out of the house and load me into a car.

Pain doesn't matter.

Nothing Austin does to me matters.

And I can't let myself think of what he'll do to Maddoc after the exchange, or I'll break.

The drop point is in the warehouse district, and the West Point driver pulls up behind an abandoned-looking building not far from the one we burned to the fucking ground when we got Chloe back the first time.

The whole area is deserted, which makes it easy to see when an unfamiliar SUV finally approaches.

For a second, my heart plummets. It's not the Reapers'

Escalade, and my first thought is that Austin has reinforcements coming to ambush my men. But then Maddoc, Logan, and Dante all pile out of the SUV, and the tight rein I'm keeping my emotions under loosens enough for my heart to give a single, painful thump.

"Ready to earn your keep, wifey?" Austin asks with a cruel smile, dragging me out of the West Point car. "Let's go cut off the head of the Reapers."

My fear rises up so hard and fast that I gasp, stumbling in Austin's brutal grip. He doesn't stop walking, and I manage to get my feet under me before he has to drag me.

Then I look up and meet Maddoc's eyes across the deserted parking lot.

His jaw clenches tight, and even at a distance, there's so much packed into his gaze that it threatens to overwhelm me. When I lock eyes with Logan, then Dante, and find the same intensity with both, it almost brings me to my knees.

They came for me, and I can't lose them. Not any of them.

I don't want Maddoc killed. I can't be a part of that. And whether it's here and now or after Austin drives away with him, that *will* be Austin's end goal.

The Reapers have arrayed themselves in front of their SUV, but McKenna leads his people a little closer like the cocky fuck he is.

"Stop," he barks out at his men, leaving about thirty feet of empty space between the two groups. Too far, but also too close when I know what my men are risking.

"Send her over," Maddoc demands in a gravelly voice. From here, I can see the way that familiar muscle tic flares in his jaw, a telltale sign that his outward calm is only a facade over much deeper emotions.

He's got his eyes locked onto Austin now, but both Logan and Dante stare at me with unwavering gazes, one filled with icy determination and the other with vibrant green fire.

Austin smirks at all three of them and yanks me closer, dragging his finger through the disgusting traces of himself he left on my face. "You never did tell me why you wanted my little wifey here so badly."

"You proposed this trade, McKenna," Maddoc says grimly. "Are you going to honor it, or not?"

I think he is. I think he is, and it makes me want to cry. But he's not going to hand me over until he manages to wring every ounce of sadistic satisfaction over having the Reapers jump to do his bidding, I can tell.

They trade a few more verbal barbs before Austin finally agrees to start the exchange. Then, just to fuck with Maddoc a little more and prove that he's the one winning here, he yanks me back as soon as Maddoc starts to walk forward.

Maddoc freezes, and Austin sends him a smug smile. "Oh, I almost forgot..."

He holds his hand out, and one of his men gives him something. Austin holds it up.

The key to my handcuffs.

Of course he doesn't unlock them, though. All he wants is another chance to show off his power, and he does it by groping me in front of my men, making a show out of feeling up my breasts before pushing them together to form cleavage.

I keep my eyes on Maddoc's while Austin shoves the key into my bra, scraping the rough teeth against my skin and digging it into the bruising that's already starting to form there. Then, finally, he shoves me forward.

"Enjoy her," he calls out as Maddoc resumes walking too. "Up to you whether you want to take those cuffs off her or not. If it were me, I'd probably choose... not."

None of my men react, and my heart is pounding so loudly that it's easy to ignore Austin's parting taunt. I can't believe this is actually happening. Pain pulses through my veins, filling every part of me. Not from the beating, but for Maddoc.

He meets my eyes as we approach each other, and for a moment, nothing else exists. With anyone else, I'd try to hide my fear and anguish behind anger, but I've got no armor with this man. I don't want it. I let him see everything I'm feeling. If it's the last chance I get, I want him to know how much I fucking hate this.

I want him to know how much he matters to me.

Maddoc's face is set in stone, but there's something intense churning behind his eyes. When they flicker to one side, the tiny, almost imperceptible motion catches my attention. He does it again, and my pulse jumps, hope slamming into me so hard that I can't breathe for a moment.

He's giving me a signal.

That must mean they have some sort of plan.

Oh god, please let them have a plan.

I tense as we cross past each other, half expecting Maddoc to reach for me. But he doesn't.

Instead, he shifts his body directly behind me, shielding me from West Point as a deafening crack breaks the tense silence.

too many emotions I had to keep bottled up when it wasn't safe to show them, and they need an outlet.

But instead of reaching for his belt, when he breaks, it's to crush me against him.

"Fuck, Riley," he mutters in a ragged whisper as he buries his face in my hair and tightens his arms around me. "I was fucking terrified. Two straight weeks of not knowing if we'd lost you or not. *Jesus*. Just... just don't. Don't do it again, butterfly. Please."

I nod, and he pulls me even closer, breathing out. Then breathing in again. Then out, tension flowing from his body as my breath syncs with his, his chest rising and falling against my aching ribs.

"Good," he says quietly, pressing a long kiss to my temple. "That's good."

I can feel Logan's eyes on me, watching with the quiet intensity he brings to everything. I can't *not* be aware of him, the connection between us thrumming in my blood and beating in my heart. Just like it does for each of them.

Dante is on my other side, his hand still resting low on my back, and when Logan's hand comes to rest on my hip, all three of my men touching me now as they surround me, something deep inside my soul starts to truly relax for the first time since...

Well, since the night I had sex with all three of them.

They were all worried about me.

They *all* have some kind of feelings for me.

This is real for all four of us now.

It's a lot to process, and I'm not in the headspace to really do that... but I also know none of them expect me to. Not right now. Right now, we all need the same thing, and it's as simple as this moment.

They're my home.

And I want to stay.

I stop trying to hold any part of myself back and cling to

Maddoc, giving in to how badly I need to touch him. He wasn't the only one terrified that he'd lose someone who mattered today.

We stay like that, all of us, for I don't know how long. But then the sound of light, rapid footsteps racing toward us causes Maddoc to finally loosen his hold on me, and I'm already half turning to face the door when my sister bursts through it.

"*Riley.*"

She throws herself into my arms, and just like that, my heart is complete again.

9

RILEY

Maddoc releases me, shoving his dark hair out of his face as I hug Chloe tight, murmuring low words of comfort to her. All three of the guys step back to give us a moment together, but the sense of being surrounded and protected by them doesn't change.

"Oh god," Chloe says, her arms still locked around me. "I was so scared for you."

She starts to tremble, and I hush her, running my hand over her hair just like when she was little. "I'm back now. It's fine. We're okay. It's okay, Chloe."

"Dante, Logan," I hear Maddoc say quietly before issuing instructions to his brothers that I suspect they don't need. Something about clearing the weapons out of the vehicles, post-mission coordination, and clean up. He's not just coordinating shit with his seconds though. He's also giving Chloe and me some space, and it hits me in a rush that I didn't worry about her while I was kept prisoner.

The whole time Austin had me locked in that fucking room, for the first time since our Mom died when Chloe was small, I didn't worry about her once.

I knew these men would take care of her.

I knew she wasn't alone.

She finally loosens her grip on me, stepping away with a sheepish smile. "Sorry—"

"No," I cut her off. "Never."

She bites her lip, then blurts, "I'm just so glad you're back."

"I know the feeling," I say, arching an eyebrow as she wipes the moisture from her cheeks.

The dark humor makes us both giggle a little, a sound of pure relief, and after Dante passes through on his way from the garage to somewhere deeper in the house and grins at us, Chloe tugs me close again.

"They were totally wrecked, you know," she whispers. "They're all really into you. Like, *really.*"

"It goes both ways."

She snickers. "You mean... all four ways?"

"Yeah, that." I shove her shoulder playfully, things almost feeling normal for a second as she razzes me about a guy—guys —just like she's done dozens of times before.

Except... these guys are different.

"I really care about them, Chloe."

She nods, a serious expression on her face. "Good. You wouldn't believe how hard they worked to find you. And once that asshole offered up the exchange—"

"Austin?"

She makes a face. "Yeah. *Prick.* But they put in, like, a *ton* of effort to make sure they'd be able to get you out of there okay after they knew where it was going down. They called in a bunch of other Reapers and planned out the whole thing."

"I know," I say, and it's true. But hearing her talk about it as she starts to tell me all about Logan letting her help out with the digital search, and some of the other lengths my men went to, affects me more than I'm prepared for.

Or maybe that has something to do with how comfortable Chloe is with them.

I can tell by the easy, familiar way she talks about Maddoc, Dante, and Logan as she describes the time she spent with them that she feels secure here, just like I do. I can tell she not only likes the three of them; she trusts them too. And normally, Chloe doesn't trust any easier than I do.

It means something to me that she's obviously found a place for herself here.

I like it.

She hugs me again, and when we separate, Maddoc is standing in the doorway, watching us. "We need to talk."

Something in his tone has me tensing up, and Chloe picks up on it.

"What? What are you talking about?" she asks, worry filling her eyes all over again. "We got her back. Everything's good now, right?"

Maddoc sighs and scrubs a hand over his face. "Can you two come into the living room?"

Dante and Logan are already in there, and no matter what Maddoc is about to spring on us now, having everyone I care about all together is always gonna be a good thing.

"It's good to have you home, wildcat," Logan says with a small, enigmatic smile that earns him a sharp glance from Maddoc but warms something in the center of my chest.

I squeeze Chloe's hand, pulling her along with me to the couch where Logan's sitting. We settle next to him as Dante lounges near the wall, hands in his pockets. His stance is relaxed, but I can read the signs of tension in his body that belie the outward appearance of ease.

"What is it?" I ask Maddoc, cutting to the chase.

He doesn't sugarcoat anything, either. "We need to get you two out of here."

"She just got here!" Chloe bursts out.

"I said both of you," Maddoc tells her, his voice a little gentler. "I'm not going to separate you again."

Chloe relaxes, and Maddoc looks to me again, those gorgeous dark-rimmed gray eyes giving away the depth of emotion that he manages to keep out of his voice.

"Shit with West Point is gonna get worse before it gets better here in Halston. You won't be safe here, but now that McKenna got what he needed from you...?"

He turns it into a question even though I was right there when Austin told him I signed all the money over to him.

I nod, and Maddoc grunts, but then gives me the hint of a smile. "I guess it was too fucking much to hope he was lying about that shit, but at least it means West Point has no reason to care about the two of you anymore. You should be safe once we get you out of the city."

"Relatively safe," Logan murmurs next to me, a hint of dissent in his voice.

I lift my chin, narrowing my eyes at Maddoc. I don't care that he just made me all but promise not to put myself at risk anymore. If they're here, I'm here. If they fight, I'm fighting too.

"Logan set up a safe house out of state," Maddoc says, staring me down.

"I'm not going."

Across the room, Dante crosses his arms over his chest, giving me an apologetic smile. "We got some of our best people on the way here to take you right now, princess. The Escalade's been in the body shop, getting new glass and reinforced siding, and they're bringing it. Madd made sure you'll be safe on the way there, and we're going to leave a few guys and some serious firepower—"

I shake my head, my eyes never leaving Maddoc's gray ones.

"Quit being stubborn," he growls, looming over me like he thinks he can intimidate me into obeying him now. "You're going."

I spring to my feet, tipping my head back to glare up at him. "The hell I am."

"Do you really think I'm going to give you a chance to throw yourself into danger when we just fucking got you back?"

"Do *you* really think that's up to you?"

"Of course it's up to me. I *am* the Reapers. *I* make the rules here."

"And *I'm* not a Reaper."

My heart starts to pound and Maddoc clenches his jaw, neither one of us willing to look away.

I only said it to make a point, but I realize almost as soon as I say it that a part of me wants to hear him tell me I'm wrong.

Instead, he pivots. "McKenna's gonna be able to do a lot of damage with that kind of money. I already told you, Halston won't be safe."

"Which is why I'm not leaving."

He takes a half-step closer. "Yes, you fucking are."

I don't back down. "I'm not leaving town and hiding out while the three of you face down a fucking psycho—

"That fucking psycho is armed with enough cash now to—"

"I know! All the more reason I'm not—"

"Riley!"

"Maddoc!"

"*We can't fucking lose you,*" he roars, right in my face, so close now that we're toe to toe with my breasts all but flattened against his chest.

Our ragged breathing is the only sound in the room as the silence stretches out between us, taut enough to snap the second one of us breaks.

There's no fucking way it's going to be me, though.

I'm *not* leaving my men in danger.

Chloe leans out from the couch, poking my thigh. "Are you two about to fuck, or what?"

Dante laughs, breaking the tension, and Maddoc's arm snakes around my waist, his hand splaying wide over the top of my ass.

"Fuck, you're stubborn," he murmurs, the hunger in his eyes telling me just how much he likes that.

I flatten my hands against his chest, tilting my head back. "Pot, kettle."

Dante snickers again. "No lies detected, Madd."

The hint of a smile tugs at the corners of Maddoc's mouth. "Fine. You can stay. But I'm not playing around, butterfly. That only stands as long as you promise, and I mean fucking *promise*, that you'll be careful."

I arch an eyebrow. "I will if you will."

His eyes drill into me like he didn't just learn that I'll never break. Not when it comes to this.

"I'm always careful," he finally says, which I'll take for the promise that it is... which I know damn well is still no guarantee, not when Maddoc's right about how bad it might get now that Austin has the resources to do whatever the fuck he wants.

"I'll be careful too."

Relief flashes across Maddoc's face, so raw it lays him bare for a moment. "Thank you."

I want to kiss him right now, so badly I can taste it. But the clock is ticking and he isn't wrong about the danger that's about to slam through the city.

As if that connection between us has ratcheted up to a whole new level now that we're finally on the same page, we both turn as one and look down at Chloe.

"What?" she asks, her head tilted to lean against Logan's shoulder. Then she slowly figures out what we're getting at, and she straightens, her face falling. "Oh, hell no. Riley! You can't be serious."

"I am."

"That's not fair!"

"You really will be safer once the guys get you out of Halston."

And I refuse to feel like a hypocrite for saying so, because

I'm not. I'm her big sister, and it's still my job to take care of her, even though she's proven she can handle shit on her own if she has to.

She shouldn't have to. That's the whole point.

"But—" she starts, her chin jutting out defiantly.

"You're going," Maddoc cuts her off. Then he adds, a little more gently, "If you stay here, we'll all worry too fucking much. It will be a distraction, and distractions get people hurt."

It warms me to hear him say that. The Reapers care about my sister too.

"But if *Riley* gets to stay—"

I'm the one who cuts her off this time. "I'm in too deep with all this to stop now, and West Point has fucked with you too many times already."

"They just fucked pretty hard with *you* too."

"I know. And now that I've enjoyed that bastard's 'hospitality,' do you really think I could handle it if he got his hands on you again?"

Her eyes well up with tears. "Maddoc said West Point won't care about us anymore."

I drop down to my knees in front of where she's sitting on the couch, taking both her hands in mine. "Except we matter to the Reapers, and Austin already knows what they'll do to get either of us back. We've got no idea what he'll do with that money, but he gets off on hurting people, and I need to know you're safe. I need you out of harm's way. Don't fight me on this one, okay?"

I can see that she wants to, just like I can see that she knows she'll lose if she tries.

"Goddammit," she says with a sigh, her shoulders slumping. Then she lurches forward, wrapping her arms around me in a hug that makes my ribs ache. "Fine. You win. But I hate it."

"Me too."

All three of the guys' phones go off, and Chloe and I break apart.

"They're here," Maddoc says, all emotion stripped from his face as he falls into leader mode. "We need to move you fast, Chloe. If we're lucky, McKenna's people will still be thrown off from what went down at the warehouses. I want you outside city limits before they get their shit together enough to start plotting revenge."

Chloe nods, getting stiffly to her feet, then gives Logan a look of betrayal when he hands her a packed bag. "You just did this? You knew Maddoc was going to make me leave!"

"Maddoc is right. We've got to move you out of the city quickly," he says a little stiffly, which is basically a yes. Then he pats her shoulder awkwardly, one of the few times I've seen him voluntarily touch someone other than me. "I reconfigured a laptop for your use. It's in there with your clothing and toiletries and some... reading material."

Chloe sniffles, then grins. "That manga you got me hooked on?"

Dante grins at the two of them, then heads to the door to let in the Reapers who've arrived.

Logan looks slightly pained by Chloe's enthusiasm, but I fall for him just a little bit harder when he humors her. "You'll find a book on game theory, a complete Python reference manual, and... yes. I included the final three volumes of Death Note for you too."

Some of the sadness fades from her face as she murmurs, "Thanks, Logan."

He clears his throat. "Of course. As we discussed, game theory has many useful applications for strategic thinking, and Python is the simplest coding language to start with."

"*And* you knew how much it would suck if I didn't find out what Light decides to do in the final battle."

"And that too," Logan answers dryly.

I've got no idea what they're talking about but I'm beyond grateful that he's distracted her from the fact that we're about to be separated again. Of course, that only lasts until Maddoc takes her arm, steering her toward the four men waiting just inside the front door.

"We need to get you on the road," he says, taking the bag Logan packed for her and tossing it to one of his men. "While you're there, Nathan will take care of anything you need. I'm going to rotate out most of my people, but he'll stay with you for the duration." Maddoc tips her chin up, smiling down at her. "He'll keep you safe, Chloe. He's got all the skills to do it, and it's his one and only fucking job, okay?"

"Okay," she says a little shakily, looking over at the guy now holding her bag.

He gives her a brisk nod, so he must be Nathan, but it's like Maddoc's words have just reminded Chloe that this is all really happening, and that it's happening right now.

She whirls out of his grip and flings herself at me again. "Do I really have to go?" she asks me in a tearful whisper, clinging tightly.

"Yeah," I say, all I can get out before my throat closes up. I hate how often I've had to say goodbye to her lately, but hopefully this will be the last time for a long, long while.

And at least this time we *do* get to say goodbye.

Chloe and I trade one more long squeeze, then she nods and straightens her shoulders. "Love you, sis."

"I love you too."

She turns to my men, keeping a hold of my hand. "Thanks for getting Riley back. Please keep... keeping her safe."

No one laughs at the awkward phrasing, or comments on the thick tears we can all hear in her voice. Instead, all three men nod solemnly, vowing that they will, and then my sister is gone.

I stare after them until the Escalade disappears from view,

then close the door and turn back to my men. Except Logan and Dante have already left the room, and it's just Maddoc.

I stare at him, too much space between us. "Are you sure this Nathan guy is loyal?"

"I'd trust him with my life."

"You just trusted him with my sister's life."

His lips quirk up, the mask of leadership falling away and warm sympathy taking its place. "The way she matters to you?" he says softly, moving toward me. "Same thing."

Oh.

Oh.

This whole fucking day has been almost more than I can handle. The beating Austin gave me starts to make itself known, and a ton of confusing emotions swell up inside me as Maddoc stalks closer and closer.

"Thank you for sending her somewhere safe," I say, not sure how to handle everything else. I'm not sure if I want to jump him right now, ask him to hurt me enough that I forget all the ways Austin did, or beg him to just hold me.

I suspect what I really need is some fucked-up mashup of all of the above.

I definitely *want* something.

"I wish I could have sent you somewhere safe," Maddoc grumbles when he finally reaches me, the heat in his eyes at odds with the gentle way he cups my jaw, callused fingers holding onto me like I'm something precious, as delicate as the butterfly he's taken to calling me.

He knows I'm not.

He knows I'm strong.

And that just makes the moment all the sweeter.

"I can call them back," he murmurs, staring down at me. "You can still go to the safe house."

"That ship has sailed." I feel a little breathless as our gazes lock. "Didn't we already establish that I'm too stubborn to leave your fine ass?"

He smirks, his eyes dropping to my lips. "Yeah," he says huskily. "I'm pretty sure we did."

"And you like it."

His gaze snaps back up to meet mine. "Yeah. I'm pretty sure I do."

My breath hitches in my throat. I don't know who moves first, I only know that Maddoc's hands are suddenly on my ass, lifting me against him, and I've got mine wrapped around his shoulders as I drag him down where I need him.

I have to fucking taste him.

I want to do nothing but just *feel* for a while.

Logan walks back into the room before I get what I need.

"You're hurt," he says in a flat tone that I'm starting to understand is just another form of armor for him.

Logan is no stranger to inflicting pain, but when it's been done to me, done by someone other than him, he fucking hates it.

Maddoc's arms instantly loosen at the interruption, and he gently moves me away from his body, frowning as his eyes rake my torso. "That motherfucker hit you."

It's not a question and doesn't require an answer, but apparently both men are going to insist that we address it before anything else happens.

I'd rather not think about Austin at all right now, so I try to divert them. "I'm fine."

Maddoc shakes his head, pushing me toward Logan. "Take care of our girl," the overprotective bastard says. "And be sure to catalog every fucking scrape, bruise, and laceration."

Logan nods. "He'll pay for every one of them."

The two of them share a look, and even though the heat still simmering in my core makes me want to bitch about being cock blocked, there are worse things than being coddled by two overprotective bastards. Or three, since I've got no doubt at all that Dante would back them if he were here too.

As much as I want their hands on me for dirtier reasons right now, the feeling of being cared for by these men makes something just as sweet and addictive as the lust I feel for them unfurl inside me.

10

RILEY

LOGAN DOESN'T SPEAK as he leads me up to his room, but I'm used to his silences by now. He'll probably never be the most expressive person, but he wants me here. I can tell.

"You missed me, didn't you?" I tease him, something I never would have had the guts to do when we first met.

He doesn't answer, but he flashes me the small, private smile that's starting to come to mean the world to me as he opens the door and ushers me through.

His room is just as orderly and pristine as every other time I've been inside it, but this time, it doesn't feel as weird to be here as it has in the past. I don't feel like I have to walk on eggshells because of how volatile he can be. I'm not sneaking or snooping, and Logan's not just putting up with me, either.

"Sit," he says, nodding toward the edge of his bed where he's already got medical supplies laid out. He turns away to grab the chair from his desk, trusting me to obey him, and knowing it doesn't stress him out to have me in his space anymore tells me more than any words could how he actually feels.

He positions the chair in front of me as I pull my hair back and wind it into a knot to keep it out of the way. I get that tiny smile again in approval, then Logan grips my chin with his elegant fingers and starts carefully looking me over, his gaze skimming over all the aching areas on my face and throat from Austin beating on me.

I've finally figured out that the less expression Logan shows, the harder he's working to keep it suppressed inside, and as he catalogs each injury, his eyes go completely flat, his face as expressionless as stone.

He's furious at Austin, the kind of fury that only death and dismemberment will satisfy, and the darkness inside me responds to that fury with a rush of heat that makes me squirm.

"Be still," Logan says, tightening his grip to exert the control that's so necessary for him.

And that I find so damn arousing.

His fingers brush over a stinging cut on my cheek. "This one will scar."

I didn't even realize the cut was there until Logan touched it, but Austin was wearing one of those gaudy gold West Point Gang knuckle rings when he backhanded me, so I'm not surprised.

I can't hide my wince as Logan starts to clean it, and I feel the slightest tremor in his fingers as he closes it with a couple of butterfly bandages.

"It's fine," I whisper.

Logan nods, his touch becoming sure and firm again, and I tilt my chin back to give him better access as he methodically works his way down my throat, checking and disinfecting everywhere Austin touched me.

When he reaches the loose collar of my shirt, his fingers lightly skimming my collarbone. "I need this off."

I do it, removing my bra too, then I stand to wiggle out of my pants while I'm at it.

Logan frames my hips with his hands, his lips tightening so much that they turn white now that he can see the full extent of what Austin did to me.

Then he does his best to erase it, systematically examining every mark that bastard left and treating it in some way, even the ones that don't really hurt. It's like Logan can't handle the thought of any trace of that bastard's hands on my body, and I'm more than fine with that. His possessive determination feeds into all the emotions that have been so close to the surface ever since my men came for me at the exchange.

Logan stays seated in front of me, his blond hair perfectly combed, utterly silent and completely clinical as his hands move across my body. Every touch is precise and controlled in a way that affects me just as much as Maddoc's possessive aggression did earlier.

He runs his fingers over the outer curve of my left breast, then down over the angry red skin covering my ribcage. "This is new. The bruises haven't darkened yet."

"It just happened this morning."

Logan's lips tighten again, his fingers digging into my ribs a little.

I flinch, and his eyes snap up to mine, his hand going still. "Does it hurt?"

I nod. "But it's okay. They're just bruised, not broken."

He runs firm fingers over every single one of my ribs, as if he needs to prove it to himself. I take a deep breath in to show him, and it *does* hurt, but there's none of the sharp, stabbing pain that would mean Austin had managed to crack a few.

Finally, Logan nods, as if satisfied that I'm right. He's staring at one of the blooming bruises on my stomach, and he leaves his fingers pressed against it for another moment before abruptly pulling them away.

"A soak in the bathtub will help. I have Epsom salts." He looks up at me again. "What set McKenna off this morning? None of these injuries are older than that. Why did he beat you?"

I raise an eyebrow. "Because he's an asshole?"

That gets me the tiniest twitch of Logan's lips, then his eyes narrow in thought. "Of course he'd beat you this morning," he says softly, as if he's talking to himself. "He wanted us to see it."

I'm sure Logan's right about Austin getting off on that idea, but that wasn't why.

At least, it wasn't the catalyst.

"I don't know if he was just trying to fuck with my head, or if he meant it, but he started talking about keeping me for himself," I tell Logan.

A mistake, because it takes me right back to the moment Austin assaulted me. I felt worse than powerless, and my breath hitches at the memory, my pulse starting to race.

Of course I didn't want that motherfucker to touch me, but my bigger fear came from the realization that he's totally sadistic enough to have set up the whole exchange solely for the sick pleasure of taunting me with what I wanted before taking it away again.

Logan's hands go still on my body, and he looks up at me. Then he sets aside the disinfectant in his hand and stands. "We wouldn't have let him."

"I know." I grab his hands and bring them back to my ribs, my nipples tightening. "Austin kissed me. I bit his tongue."

Logan stares at me for a moment, then his lips tip up at the corner, just a fraction of an inch. "You should have bitten a little harder."

"I stopped when I tasted blood."

Logan's eyes flare again at that, but he turns me away from him and goes back to carefully cleaning my wounds, his hands trailing down my spine. Once he reaches my ass, he turns me back around to face him, reaching for the disinfectant again. There are at least half a dozen spots where Austin broke the skin, thanks to that fucking ring he wore.

Eventually, as if he's been processing it this whole time,

Logan gives a small nod and says, "That's why he hit you. Because you made him bleed."

It's not a question, and he's not wrong, but it wasn't just the blood. It was my defiance.

If I hadn't bit Austin, if I'd played at being a willing little wifey for him, he'd just have found another reason to hit me.

I *know* he would, because he enjoyed it too much.

But still—

"It was worth it."

Logan meets my eyes again and smiles, a rare one that spreads wide across his face, as slowly as sin... and looks twice as tempting.

"That's my wildcat," he murmurs, pride in his voice that does something to me, just like his touch does.

He lifts one of my arms and folds it across my chest, placing my hand on my opposite shoulder. The friction of my own arm against the tight nubs my nipples have become has me squeezing my thighs together tightly as heat pools between my legs. A heat that spikes hard when Logan pours disinfectant on a raw area he exposed under my arm, a spot Austin got repeatedly with that fucking ring of his.

I hiss out my breath at the intense sting, and Logan freezes, his eyes drilling into mine as tension builds between us.

We're standing so close that I can feel his breath on my neck and the roughness of the denim from his jeans against my hip.

And I feel something else too.

He's hard.

"I keep hurting you," he rasps, his gaze dropping to my lips for a split second before bouncing back up to my eyes.

"And you like it," I say, twisting to face him more fully... and to rub myself against his erection. Logan freezes again, and I lay my hand against his smoothly shaven jaw. "My pain turns you on, doesn't it?"

Just asking the question has me getting even wetter, and

even though he doesn't answer me, I see the truth in his face. He does like it... and he still feels like a monster because of that.

Logan hasn't fully embraced that he and I each carry a seed of true darkness inside us, and that that darkness isn't just one of the things that draws us together; it's something we both need.

He should never feel bad about that. It's not wrong. It's *us*.

I give his chest a little shove, and the chair he brought over hits the back of his knees as I rub his firm pecs, echoing the order he gave me when he brought me in here. "Sit."

He does it, humoring me, and I crawl onto his lap.

Logan's face is blank again, and I just know he's working to keep what he sees as his monster caged tightly inside. His cock grows even harder as I settle myself on top of him though, and a hot thrill rushes through me as the hard length strains against me.

"Hurt me," I whisper, rocking my wet pussy over his shaft.

"Riley," he starts, his hands twitching where he's got them resting loosely on my hips. "I don't want—"

I lean forward and kiss him before he can lie to me, not offended at all when he stays frozen and doesn't kiss me back.

"Yes, you do," I say when I pull away, taking one of his hands and bringing it back up to the wound he was just disinfecting.

It still throbs with a dull, burning pain from whatever it was that he treated it with. The whole area is tender, the bruising there starting to darken from angry red to a bluish-purple.

I press his fingers over the worst of it. "Hurt me. I want you to."

Logan's cock jerks in his pants, but he's still holding himself back.

I cover his fingers with mine and push them deeper into the bruise, hissing with the sharp ache. "It's okay. It turns me on too, remember?"

Logan gives me a long stare, then—never breaking eye

contact, and as slowly as he allowed himself that sinfully sexy smile earlier—he presses his fingers into my bruised ribs a little bit harder.

I let my head fall back and roll my hips over his cock. "Yeah, like that."

The pain moves through me like a wave, and that darkness inside me, that twisted part of me that was never satisfied before I met these three men, uses it to feed the craving I already have for him.

"I know you're in control," I pant, staring into his ice-blue eyes. "You'll never hurt me more than I can take. I'll use my safe word if I ever need to. Do you remember it?"

"Red," he says without looking away from me.

There was a time when maybe Logan truly did want to hurt me. Out of anger, not lust.

But everything is different now.

I know if it ever gets too much for me, he'll respect my safe word.

I just need him to understand how completely he has my consent, so that he'll respect that too.

I drape an arm around his neck, grinding down on his cock as I lean forward, whispering the words against his lips. "Don't ever feel bad about what turns you on. Not when it turns me on too. Not now that you've shown me what I was missing."

Finally, he groans, sliding his hand up my bare back and loosening my hair from its knot. The thick blue and purple waves fall around both of us, and he tunnels his fingers through it, gripping the back of my skull.

Then he tugs my hair.

Hard.

"Fuck," I gasp, rubbing my bare breasts against him as the sharp sting of pain in my scalp sends tendrils of heat winding down to my core.

"You do like this," Logan says, his voice full of wonder. "Every time. I hurt you, and you... take it."

"I don't just take it." I grind against him, my thong soaked. "I crave it. It adds something I didn't even know I needed. And I've finally started to accept that it doesn't make me a freak, not any more than it makes you a monster. It just makes us—"

"Good," he whispers, releasing my hair and gripping my ass with both hands. He's the one in control again now, and he rocks me over the thick shaft of his cock until I'm right on the verge of coming from that alone. "We're good together, wildcat."

"Damn right we are."

Logan pulls away, lifting me off his lap and spreading his legs so I fit in between them.

Then he puts me on my knees.

He fists my hair again, tipping my head back as he looks down at me with smoldering eyes. "But we'll be even better with my cock in your mouth."

Despite the smolder, he says the words with a careful precision that reminds me I'm probably the only one he's ever said such a thing to. And it's hot as hell.

I lean forward, holding his gaze, and mouth his shaft through the denim.

The tight grip on my hair never loosens, but Logan's eyes drop to half mast, the flush of arousal creeping up his neck and spreading over his cheeks.

"Unzip me."

His voice is husky, deepening as he gives in to his desire, and the rough sound heightens my own.

I pull his cock out, then lick a long stripe up to the head before sucking it into my mouth.

Logan makes an obscene sound, fingers digging into my scalp as a flood of his salty flavor hits my tongue.

"More," he rasps, hips snapping forward hard enough to gag me.

I moan and open wider, the effect I have on him like a drug I could easily get addicted to, but Logan catches himself and pulls back, wrapping a hand around his cock as it slides out of my mouth.

"You won't be able to use your safe word if we do this," he says, his fingers flexing and tugging my hair like he can't quite find his usual restraint, despite the concern in his voice.

I look up at him, rubbing my cheek against his throbbing length. "Please. I want it."

He starts to shake his head. "Riley..."

"I trust you," I say quickly.

A punched out sound escapes him, and he closes his eyes, a tortured look on his face as another spurt of precum spills from his slit.

I stay completely still, waiting, and when he finally looks back down at me, his pupils are completely blown in those eerily pale eyes of his. "Open," he grits out.

I do it, and he winds more of my hair around his hand, fisting it hard enough to bring tears to my eyes. It makes me moan again, heat flooding my pussy as he holds me firmly in place and guides his cock back to my open mouth.

I extend my tongue and he rubs his cockhead over it, feeding me more of his musky flavor.

"Put your right hand on my hip," he orders, his voice tight with control. When I do, he rewards me by letting his eyes drop to half-mast as his hips jerk forward in a series of short, shallow thrusts, plundering the heat of my open mouth.

I want to suck his cock.

I want to fucking *worship* it.

But I also want exactly what Logan wants: I want *him* to be in control, and I want him to use me hard.

His eyes drill into me as saliva pools in my mouth and starts to spill down my chin. "Tap my hip twice if you need me to stop. That's your safe word right now. Blink if you understand."

I blink.

Logan continues to stare down at me, his cock resting on my tongue. He's still holding back.

I need him to know I'm his and I want this.

I carefully close my teeth behind his frenulum, applying just enough pressure to make him hiss and suck in a sharp breath before I ease up.

He doesn't pull away, though. Instead, his hiss turns to a low, primal growl, and I can practically feel the darkness inside him start to bloom.

The changes in his demeanor are subtle but distinct. He's still holding the most dangerous, most violent parts of his desire in check, but just barely.

The only reason I can see it now is because I know what to look for. It's in his eyes, in the tight corners of his mouth, in the way he twists my hair in his fist until I gasp with the sharp sting... and then goes just a bit further.

He grabs my jaw with his free hand and pulls my chin down. "Open," he says sharply, then exhales in a long, tight, controlled breath when I do it, fully opening my mouth to him. "Remember what I said."

It's the only warning he gives me.

With his eyes locked onto mine and enough force to take my breath away, he slams into the back of my throat and makes me heave forward on his cock. He doesn't pause or let up. My eyes start to water as he thrusts even harder, his thick length blocking my airflow as he fucks my face for a minute, then lodges himself deep in my throat.

My body's natural, reflexive instinct is to struggle, to fight, to push him away. I tamp down on those reflexes, though, holding his gaze and digging my nails into his thighs—daring him to keep going. Or maybe begging him to.

I don't care that I can't breathe. I don't care that my throat is going to be just as sore as the rest of my battered, bruised body by the time he's finished. I crave it, and fall a little bit more in love with Logan for not coddling me right now and giving me exactly what I need.

My vision starts to dim at the edges, my whole world narrowing to this moment, in this room, with this man who understands parts of me I never would have dared acknowledge before I met him.

"I fucking love the way your throat spasms around my cock," he whispers, never breaking eye contact. "You really do trust me, don't you?" He asks the question as if he's being hit with that simple, honest truth for the first time, and I can feel something new open up between us. "I'm fucking choking you with my cock, but you aren't even struggling. I'm hurting you."

The heat in his eyes and the possessive, exquisitely painful hold he still has on me is at odds with the almost emotionless tone of his voice, and knowing we're in this together, and that we both crave the same dark, twisted things, is comforting in a way I'm not even trying to comprehend.

I want him to take whatever he needs from me, to use me.

I want him to *hurt* me.

It's everything Austin threatened me with, but it's completely different now that it's Logan. He's in control, but this is *my* choice, and I want him to push me to the very edge and then keep pushing so he can catch me when I start to come undone.

I start to feel lightheaded from lack of oxygen, and he grunts and pulls out until just the head of his cock is left resting on my tongue. It pulses in my mouth, the salty, bitter taste of his precum flooding my senses.

Logan flashes a look that's as sexy as it is dangerous. "We have to slow down. I'm not ready to come yet."

I moan and work the underside of his cock with my tongue, letting him slip completely from my mouth just long enough to admit, "I am. I need this. *Please.*"

My voice is just barely above a whisper and almost gravelly from the pounding he's just given my throat, but I still want more.

Without another word, he pushes back into my greedy mouth. He isn't as rough this time, but he's just as insistent, and he doesn't stop until he's stretching my throat again and sending another wave of wet heat rushing down to my core.

"Take it," he grinds out through gritted teeth, pushing even deeper as the iron control he always keeps on his emotions starts to crumble. "Every. Fucking. Inch. This is what you want, right? This is what you've been begging me to do. Fucking *take* it."

The tears that have been welling up in my eyes start to stream down my cheeks, and I'm not sure if it's the lack of air this time, or simply the weight of everything I've been through these past days and weeks, but I don't try to stop them.

I owe him my life.

I owe *them*. My guys. The Reapers.

And they've each put their lives on the line for me in return.

Willingly.

Eagerly.

The danger and adrenaline and the understanding that we *will* die for each other if it comes down to that has forged a bond between us that goes deeper than anything I've ever known. So much deeper than sex. Deeper than love, even—or what I thought love was before, anyway.

Everything in me, every fiber of my being, belongs to the three of them. Just like they belong to me.

There's a trust and a freedom that comes with that realization that's deeper than anything I've ever known. A trust that allows me to give my body to Logan right now without worrying about my own pleasure or well-being.

I know, without any words being spoken, that he'll take care of me. Not just my safety. He'll make sure I get exactly what I want, exactly what I need.

And he'll hurt me while he does it.

Logan will give me the pain I've been craving; the pain that will cleanse that motherfucker's touch from my body, mind, and soul.

My vision blurs again, and he pulls out slightly—just enough to keep me from passing out completely—but I keep my lips locked around his cock and I keep it buried as far down my throat as he'll let me. I'm dimly aware of my own hand between my thighs, even though I have no memory of reaching down there to touch myself.

"So close. So fucking close." The urgency in his voice makes me anxious to match his speed as I slip one and then another finger inside my wet, waiting pussy, grinding the heel of my hand against my clit as I chase what I need.

I'm rough with myself, imagining it's Logan's calloused fingers driving in and out, in and out, over and over again while his thick cock ravages my throat.

I don't think. I can't. I reach up with my free hand and feel his balls start to tighten. His cock throbs insistently against the back of my tongue, ready to spill over at any moment, and when I give his balls a not-so-gentle squeeze, it draws another hissing moan from somewhere deep in his chest.

He's losing himself inside me, and I fucking love it. Knowing he's willing to go to the very brink with me nearly makes me climax before I'm ready, and I have to squeeze my thighs tightly together as I try and fail to stifle another needy moan of my own.

"Together," Logan rasps out, pulling my hair back again —*hard*—as if he wants to ensure that my eyes are locked onto his as both our orgasms crest and overtake us. "Come with me, wildcat. Come *now*."

A fierce, violent pleasure rockets through me as my body

instantly responds to his command with a flood of wet heat that radiates out from my core, making my eyes roll back in my head and my toes curl as Logan's cock spills straight down my throat.

For a moment, a perfect split second suspended in time, nothing else matters.

Nobody else even exists.

Then the moment passes, and I slowly start to come back to my senses. Logan is still rock hard; still lodged deep in my throat as his shaft continues to swell and jerk with his release. My hand is clamped between my legs and my whole body is trembling from the force of the pent-up, intense orgasm I needed so badly.

"Fuck, fuck, *fuck*," he chants, unblinking as he holds me and finally pulls back enough for me to taste the last few drops as they hit the back of my tongue. "Swallow it all."

I do, and he exhales, his grip on my hair finally loosening slightly and his face more relaxed than I've ever seen it.

He gives me another of those small smiles that he seems to reserve just for me. "So good," he whispers, his grip on my chin keeping me in place and his hips lazily thrusting as he stares down at me like he's just as lost in the moment as I am.

I'm not sure how much time passes like this, with my blissed-out mind wandering and my lips still wrapped around Logan's cock. Long enough that I can't help but feel a pang of loss when his softening cock finally slips from my mouth.

"Logan," I whisper his name even though I can't say what, exactly, I need from him, or what I'm even asking for anymore.

"I've got you," he murmurs, pulling me to my feet as he rises and pressing his thumb into the scar he gave me between my breasts. "Are you okay?"

I nod instinctively, but I'm honestly not sure. Being with him feels perfect. The release we just shared? Mind-blowing. But reality is setting in again, and there's no denying that Austin has the power to hurt all of us now that he has my money.

Logan's eyebrows pull together in the middle, and I know he can tell that despite my nod, I've let my worries for what will come next intrude.

"Better now that I'm here with you," I say quickly, meaning it. I rest my head against his shoulder and take a deep breath, shoving those worries aside for now. "With *all* of you."

"You don't have to worry about being away from us again." He leans back and uses a finger to tip my chin up until I'm looking into his eyes. I can feel the sense of relief washing over him. I can see it in the way he's looking at me. "That isn't going to happen. We're all glad you're back. We all want you here."

There was a time when this conversation—in his room with just the two of us—would have been unthinkable. Knowing that Logan trusts me enough to share this kind of tender, intimate moment makes my heart do fluttery, floaty things that I don't dare mention out loud. Not yet, anyway.

For now, it's enough to know that he trusts me. That I trust him.

And that maybe he's learning to trust himself too.

"I'm glad to be back." I smile even though the endorphins are fading now and I'm more and more aware of each cut and bruise on my body with every second that ticks by. "I knew I'd be back. I wasn't sure how, but I knew it would happen."

Logan's arms tighten around me, enough that my ribs hurt again. It's the best possible kind of pain, though.

He doesn't say anything, but I'm used to that with him now, and he doesn't have to. The way he's holding me is telling me everything I need to know.

"Thanks for taking such good care of me," I say, smiling up at him when finally he releases me from that tight embrace.

He gives me a short, sharp nod. "Always."

The silence stretches out between us for a few more seconds, and I know—I *know*—we both want to say more. But again, we don't have to.

It's still the closest I've come to sharing my feelings out loud.

My feelings about him. About Maddoc and Dante. About all four of us together.

Not yet, though. Accepting these feelings is still too new, and all of my emotions are still too raw. There will be a time and a place for that conversation, but it isn't right now and it isn't right here.

Instead, I push my luck given all the liberties Logan has already allowed me, and go up on my toes to press a soft, chaste kiss against the side of his mouth. Then I reach for the door and slip out of his room before either of us can say anything else.

This is how it has to be for now.

But for now, this is enough.

11

RILEY

I SIT on the side of the bathtub and watch it fill up with water. I'm sore all over, the aches and pain from my time in captivity slowly overtaking the relaxation and relief I found with Logan.

Hopefully, the bath will help. With my body, at least. My mind is worn out too.

It's hard to believe that earlier this morning, I was still Austin's captive.

It's even harder to keep my thoughts from veering to the harsh, dark reality of what may be coming next.

We're all alive, so that's a plus. The way things had gone down when the men came to make the exchange, it's all too easy to imagine it having gone a different way, but we're still standing. Whatever Austin plans on doing with the money, at least Maddoc is still in charge, the Reapers have survived to fight another day, and we managed to get Chloe out before all hell breaks loose.

Knowing she's going to be far away and relatively safe when the fighting breaks out means a lot.

Knowing my men allowed me to stay here, with them, where I belong, means even more.

I stand up and slide my thong down over my hips, letting my

eyes flutter closed as I step into the mostly full tub and sucking in a sharp breath when the piping hot water laps at every cut, scrape, and bruise on my battered body.

I lower myself down, sinking as low as I can with my head still above water and letting the rush of sensation wash over me. The heat hurts like hell, but feels so unbelievably good at the same time, and slowly, one by one, my muscles start to relax.

I exhale the breath I've been holding and then inhale deeply. The realization that I *can* relax, that I can take as long as I want, sit here until the water cools if I choose to, hits me harder than it should.

I'm free now.

Free.

Once, this house felt like my prison. Now it's my sanctuary. Nobody is on the other side of that door, timing me and waiting to walk me back to that windowless little hell hole of a room Austin was keeping me in. I don't have to answer to anyone here, or worry about what kind of whim that sadistic fucker will want to exercise on me next. Taking a long, proper bath was the last thing on my mind while I was West Point's prisoner, but now I'm wondering how I survived without this.

I scoot down even further and lay my head back, letting the water come right up to the edge of my face before closing my eyes again and slipping completely under the water.

One second.

Two seconds.

Three.

Bringing my head back up out of the water, I open my eyes and take another deep breath. I'm not just washing away layers of dirt right now. I'm getting the stink of captivity off me. I'm letting go of piece after piece of mental armor, and brick after brick of the walls I built to keep myself sane.

And not just during my time of captivity with West Point.

Yes, I built those walls and put on that armor to keep myself alive until Maddoc and his Reapers could find me, or I could figure out a way to escape on my own. But I've been protecting myself my whole damn life, I've been the only one protecting myself, and now I'm not alone anymore.

Three men who used to be my enemies put their lives on the line to get me back today.

They weren't sure their plan could work.

They didn't know how many men Austin was bringing.

If anything—*anything*—had gone wrong, Maddoc would have been taken in exchange for my freedom.

And then he would have been killed.

I'm still shuddering from that thought when the door swings open on silent hinges. Maddoc. He stands in the doorway with his arms folded across his broad chest, his eyes locked onto mine, and a wave of such strong emotion goes through me that I'm not sure what to do with it.

He didn't knock, but I don't ask him to leave.

He takes a step toward me, then another. Finally, his eyes break away from mine and quickly roam up and down my body.

"Those cuts and bruises," he starts, frowning as his voice rumbles up from somewhere deep in his chest. "Did you get them looked at?"

I nod, my thighs squeezing together of their own volition. The inspection was deliciously painful, but what it led to has me feeling closer to Logan than I once would have thought possible.

Maddoc is still frowning, though.

"It looks worse than it actually is." I glance down at my own naked body and swallow hard. "Mostly."

It comes out as a broken whisper, the memory of being at Austin's mercy overtaking me for a moment.

Maddoc sits down on the side of the tub and traces a finger along a deep scratch on my shoulder, one left by Austin's ring.

I lean into his touch. Logan treated each mark. Cared for me and cleansed me. But I need this too. I need Maddoc's hands on me, staking a claim and erasing Austin's.

His eyes snap up to meet mine, almost as if he can sense it, and I bite back a needy moan, my pulse thrumming.

Without saying another word, Maddoc reaches for the shampoo bottle and squeezes some out into his palm, then rubs his hands together, lathering it up.

"I'm glad Logan took care of you," he says, his movements slow and methodical and his meaning clear.

He *is* glad... but it's not enough. He wants to take care of me too.

His strong hands are surprisingly gentle as he works the shampoo into my hair and massages my scalp. I know the kind of violence these hands are capable of, but the simple gesture is full of so much care and tenderness that I can't help feeling my throat start to tighten as he works his fingers from my scalp through the long waves that spill down my back.

I don't say a word. I don't want to risk opening my mouth and spoiling the moment we're sharing. It feels inevitable and almost sacred, reminding me of the way Logan bathed me and took care of me after Frank died.

Once, I never would have imagined that any of the Reapers were capable of making me feel safe, protected, or cherished, but that's exactly what Logan gave me then, and what Maddoc is giving me now. It's what I've found in Dante's art studio too. These men take care of me, always. It's never happened before, not really, and it feels really fucking good.

I lean into Maddoc's touch, watching his stern face as it softens, his focus completely on me.

I know him better now, and I can see right through that mask he wears as the Reapers' leader. I know his heart—all of their hearts—and they know mine. And it doesn't matter that we haven't exactly put those feelings into words yet, I—

No, it does matter.

Suddenly, it *really* matters.

Life's too fucking short, and these men mean everything to me. When I sacrificed myself by going with Austin, there was too much still unspoken, and in their world—my world now, too—everything can change, or end, in a moment.

Maddoc tips my head back and turns on the water, rinsing my hair and giving me no choice but to look up at him.

He smiles, a private one meant just for me.

I hold his gaze, my heart fluttering. "Why did you do what you did today?"

"You didn't want me to wash your hair?" The corners of his mouth twitch. "You didn't seem to mind while I was doing it."

I laugh and it feels good to let go for a second, but then I shake my head, my heart too full to stay silent about this right now.

"You know that's not what I meant." I swallow, then let myself fall into the black-ringed-gray of his eyes as his face gets serious too. "Earlier," I whisper. "Why did you risk yourself to get me free?"

He goes still for a moment, his hands a comforting weight as they rest on my shoulders. "You know why."

My heart beats faster. The look he's giving me is so intense I can practically feel the air crackle between us, but I need to hear it. I need the words.

"Tell me."

The silence stretches out, and the sound of my heart beating like a frantic, insistent drum in my ears is all I can hear. I know Maddoc isn't used to opening up like this any more than I am. He didn't flinch from the bullets flying around us during the exchange with West Point, but somehow, this feels riskier. More dangerous. Terrifying and exhilarating all at once.

"Tell me why," I repeat, the request more breath than air. "I want to hear you say it."

Finally, he speaks, his voice low and quiet, gravelly with emotion. "I did it because I couldn't stand the thought of you being hurt. Held captive. Kept from me."

A warm flush moves through my body.

For a moment, I think that's all he's going to give me, and it's... enough. It's not everything, but I know it's the truth, and it *is* enough.

"Thank you." I cover one of his hands with mine, holding his rough palm against my wet skin. "I—"

"Riley," he says, cutting me off. A muscle in his jaw works, and his eyes practically bore a hole through mine. "I did it because I'm falling in love with you."

I suck in a quick breath, and he catches my chin between his thumb and finger, pinning me in place more effectively than any captivity.

"Your turn. Why the hell did you sacrifice yourself to that son of a bitch?"

"Because I'm falling in love with you too," I whisper, the words hovering in the air between us. I swallow and, before he can say anything, before I can lose my nerve, I add, "And with Logan and Dante."

His brothers.

His seconds.

Maddoc's eyes burn into mine, and my nerves settle down even as passion flares in my blood from the heat in his gaze.

He already knows. He feels just as strongly about Logan and Dante, in his own way, as I do. And he doesn't seem possessive, or pissed off to hear me say it. He looks... satisfied. Almost smug.

Then he palms the back of my head and kisses me.

I melt into his touch, exactly where I want to be. My aches and pains are forgotten. My exhaustion replaced by something hot and needy and insistent that this man always brings out in me.

I reach up and tug him closer, water sloshing out of the tub, and he smiles against my lips.

"My butterfly," he murmurs, kissing me deeper, dirtier, as he leans over me, his free hand sliding down to my breast.

I arch up into his touch, splashing him again, and he squeezes just hard enough to make my breath hiss out in a needy whine, my nipple pebbling from the friction of his palm despite the warmth of the bath.

His lips are just as possessive as his touch as he moves his hand down my body, beneath the water, and emotions fill me hot and fast. Familiar, electric ones as I respond to his touch, but softer, giddier ones too.

I wrap my hand around the back of his neck and tug him even closer, then laugh into the kiss. "You're getting all wet."

He pulls back just enough to smirk at me, working his hand down between my legs and then dipping inside me and making me moan before I can catch myself.

"Pretty fucking wet yourself." His voice is like a growl, low and primal and so damn sexy I go from teasing to feeling so hungry for more that I can't help but whimper.

I only have to wait for a moment before he hauls me out of the bathtub and lifts me, dripping, into his arms. Neither one of us reach for a towel, and I wrap my legs around his waist and scrape my nails through his dark brown hair as I yank his head back to mine, greedy for him, as he turns without a word and heads out into the hall, toward my room.

Dante is walking toward us, and those vibrant green eyes of his immediately fill with appreciation.

"Damn." His voice is rough with all the same emotions that welled up between Logan and me; all the feelings Maddoc and I finally laid out in the open just now. "Best thing I've seen all day," he says, stepping aside as Maddoc starts toward my bedroom. "Hell, all week."

He lets his eyes roam over my naked body, but I know he means more than that.

He means the fact that I'm finally here. I'm home again. With them.

And I need *both* of them.

"Wait," I whisper as Maddoc walks past Dante. I look over Maddoc's shoulder and hold eye contact with Dante, my heart rate picking up yet again. "Join us."

Maddoc grunts, his arms tightening around me, and Dante licks his lips, his signature grin spreading over his face as his eyes flare with heat.

"I'd fucking love to, princess,"

Maddoc takes my mouth again as Dante follows us, and when Dante steps up behind me as we enter my room, boxing me in between them and kissing my neck, I know for sure that this is exactly where I'm meant to be. Where we're *all* meant to be.

Now, I just need them to get naked too.

12

RILEY

MADDOC'S HANDS tighten under my ass, and Dante's hot mouth on my skin sends delicious jolts of pleasure down to my core as he crowds up behind me.

"You fit us so damn well," Maddoc whispers as his cock swells, throbbing as it's trapped between us.

He holds my gaze like he's searching for something, and my breath hitches in my throat.

He said *us*.

Hearing him come right out and say that as he's sharing me with his brother means everything to me, almost as much as the feelings he finally confessed to me in the bath, because it means this is real. I can have everything I've dreamed of with these men.

I already *do* have it.

Dante brushes my hair to the side, baring the side of my throat, and sucks a fresh bruise into my skin.

It feels so good that I moan, but at the same time, I almost want to laugh. Austin, that sadistic motherfucker, thinks he won something, that he took something that mattered from me when he stole my inheritance. This moment right here proves him wrong.

Then Dante uses his teeth while Maddoc swoops in with a groan and seals his mouth over mine again, and laughing—just like any and all thoughts of the West Point gang's piece of shit leader—becomes the last thing on my mind.

Yes, I still want Maddoc and Dante stripped down, naked, and buried inside me, but something about being so vulnerable between them—my bare, wet skin pinned between their hard, hot, fully clothed bodies—makes me feel both aroused and safe in a way I can't remember ever feeling before.

"Take me apart," I beg with a gasp when Maddoc finally releases my mouth, my head falling back onto Dante's shoulder

"That's the plan, butterfly," Maddoc promises, the hard ridge of his cock jerking against me through his jeans.

I squeeze my legs around his waist and grind against it with a moan. Dante takes full advantage of the access I gave him when I tipped my head back, ravaging my throat with his teeth, lips, and tongue as he grinds against me from behind.

"That's it, brother," Maddoc says in a low growl, his eyes heating as he pulls back to watch Dante work. "Mark her up. Show the whole fucking world who she belongs to."

But then his eyes zero in on one of the stinging scrapes Logan treated on my cheek, and the heat in his eyes is replaced by a quick flash of rage.

Now *he's* thinking of Austin McKenna.

He's thinking of what that shithead did to me.

But Austin has no place between us—not now, and not fucking ever—so I bring my hand up and cradle Maddoc's jaw, rough with end-of-day stubble, and force him to look at *me*, not at the evidence of what Austin did to me.

"It's over. Make me forget." I throw his own words back at him. "Show me who I belong to."

I reach back and grab Dante's hip, including both of them in that plea, and Maddoc sucks in a sharp breath, then nods. But instead of taking my mouth again, he switches his support under my ass to a single hand and brings the other one up to skim over the damage McKenna left on my face, so fucking gently it makes my heart skip a beat. "We will. You're gonna feel us for days. But we don't have to do this right now if you're not up to it yet. You're not fucking going anywhere again. We've got time."

A hot thrill goes through me at that promise, but it's the way Dante goes utterly still behind me, both men waiting on my answer and proving their true feelings for me with actions that are a million times more meaningful than anything they'll ever say out loud, that really gets to me.

It takes me from simply turned on to completely desperate for it, ramping up my need for them in the space between one breath and the next. "It *does* have to be now. I need it. I need you both." I tighten my legs around Maddoc, rubbing myself against his erection. "I need *this*."

Dante responds immediately. "Fuck," he grunts, his hands roaming up my sides, rough fingers skimming the sides of my breasts. "Then we're gonna give it to you, princess. Gonna take such good care of you."

"Promise?" I gasp, holding Maddoc's eyes as they bore into me for another beat, like he's trying to dig the truth out of my soul. Then he smiles, hot and dirty, and grabs my hair, gathering it up and twisting it around his fist like an anchor.

"You heard him," he says, yanking me even closer.

Then he kisses me.

Devours me as he lets my feet slide to the ground.

Dante takes a half step back to make room for me, without taking his hands off my body, and the way the three of us move in perfect sync has my blood singing in my veins.

Dante reaches around to roll my nipples between his fingers as he whispers dirty promises into my ear, and when Maddoc's demanding mouth moves down my throat, his hands keeping a bruising grip on my hips, my desperation turns into an urgent need that I'll do anything to get them to hurry the fuck up and fulfill.

"*Off,*" I demand, shoving Maddoc's shirt up. "Get naked."

Maddoc knocks my hands away and whips the shirt over his head, tossing it aside, before he's on me again, dominant and hungry.

"Dante," I gasp, my hands roaming over hard muscle as I reach back for him, then shove him.

He chuckles, a low, dirty sound full of promise, and steps back to strip his shirt off too. "I'm on it, princess," he promises before wrapping himself around me from behind again, skin-to-skin.

His arms come around me, the hard planes of his chest a searing heat against my back, and I clutch Maddoc's shoulders as Maddoc thrusts his cock against my stomach with a groan, wrapping one hand around my throat as he stares down at me. "Is this what you want?"

"You know what I want." I tilt my chin up. "Tell me what I am."

"*Ours,*" he growls back instantly.

"Fuck yeah, she is," Dante grunts, the raw possessiveness in his voice making hot, liquid *want* pool inside me.

I squeeze my thighs together as my pussy throbs in time with my heartbeat, and for a moment, the two men stare at each other over my head, a fierce look on Maddoc's face that I swear to god I can feel mirrored in every hard line of Dante's body.

"I need you," I gasp, making Maddoc's eyes snap down to meet mine again.

I let my fingers flutter over the bold, black lines of the tattoo covering his chest while the heated press of Dante's skin sears into me from behind.

"You've got us, princess," he whispers in my ear. Then he reaches around and cradles my chin between his thumb and forefinger, turning my head to the side and meeting me there with his hot mouth.

I moan into the kiss, clinging to him as they both manhandle me toward the bed. It bumps my shins and Maddoc pulls my face back around and takes my mouth himself, his hands hot and demanding on my body as he maps it out like he's staking a claim.

When he takes his mouth away, Dante is there again, cradling the back of my head and kissing me hungrily again as Maddoc's fingers slip into my pussy. "This is Reaper territory."

I shudder with need as my body clenches around him, and Dante swallows the sound with a groan, his thick cock rocking against the top of my ass. "You always taste so fucking good," he mutters, his tongue twining with mine. "I can't get enough."

"She's addictive," Maddoc rasps, his teeth scraping down my throat as he puts his own marks on me. He sucks one into the pulse point at the base of my neck, then another into my collarbone before finally closing his lips around one of my pebbled nipples and sucking hard enough to make me scream.

"Love that fucking sound," Dante says with a groan, grabbing my hips hard enough to bruise as he grinds his hard length against my ass.

Maddoc's fingers are working inside me, thrusting and sliding and driving me fucking crazy, and I grab his head as he sucks hard on my tits, turning my head again so I can pant into Dante's hot mouth.

"Fuck, just, god," I gasp, helplessly grinding against Maddoc's hand as they keep me trapped between them. "Get inside me. Fuck me. Use me. *Please.*"

They've got their hands and mouths everywhere, and every inch of me throbs with the pleasure of being utterly possessed. They've got my skin tingling with a sizzling heat, and my core wound tight with a maddening pleasure that feels like it's going to break me.

I want it to.

I want *them* to.

My arousal scents the air around us with the desperation of my need. Every bruise on my skin is a visceral reminder of what I shared with Logan earlier, of the way he cared for me and hurt me and shared the darkness that connects us together, and each time Maddoc and Dante brush against one of my wounds, each time they awaken those aches with their rough, possessive touch, it feels like Logan's hands are still on me too.

"I need to come," I finally choke out, writhing between them.

Maddoc straightens up and stares down at me, his fingers still buried in my pussy and his eyes burning like gray fire. "You will. We're gonna fuck you so hard you won't be able to walk. Gonna pass you back and forth between us until you forget what it's like not to be full of Reaper cock. Gonna take you raw and mark you from the inside out, mark every inch of you to make sure you know where you belong. Is that what you want, butterfly? Is that what you're begging us for?"

"God, yes." My thighs clench as a rush of hot, wet heat floods my core, soaking Maddoc's fingers. "That's exactly what I need."

And when I catch sight of the three of us in the full length mirror near the bed, there's no doubt at all that this *is* where I belong. The contrast between the bright, vibrant colors decorating Dante's muscles and the bold, stark black lines all over Maddoc looks both dangerous and beautiful, especially with my smooth, pale skin trapped between them. But the sight isn't just hot as hell, it's also *right*.

The only way it could be more right is if Logan were here too.

Next time, though. Right now, no matter how much I fucking love the way Maddoc and Dante work me up and get off on dominating me, I'm done waiting.

And they've both still got too many clothes on.

"Take your dicks out," I demand, grinding back against Dante's while I reach for Maddoc's. "Get your pants fucking *off* already. Both of you."

A low rumble sounds in Maddoc's chest, something hot flaring in his gray eyes, and Dante's low chuckle behind me is laced with the same delicious heat.

They're both hard, dominant men, but I can tell it turns them on when I push them and challenge them... almost as much as it turns me on when they push back.

Dante steps away from me to do what I asked, but Maddoc doesn't move. He holds my gaze like he's trying to remind me who's really in control here, and my pussy clenches around his fingers as my body instinctively responds to the hard, primal strength that's attracted me from the start.

His lips quirk up. He's the leader of this gang for a reason, and his refusal to back down gets my blood humming even more.

I lift my chin in a challenge, daring him to remind me a little more forcefully.

A soft rustle comes from behind me as Dante toes off his shoes and kicks them aside, ditching his pants and putting on a hot-as-fuck show that I catch in my peripheral vision through the mirror. I don't tear my eyes away from Maddoc's, though. I can't. He still hasn't moved. He's still got his fingers buried inside me, and I've got his thick, throbbing shaft—still trapped by his jeans—pulsing against my palm.

I squeeze it, and he retaliates by grinding the heel of his hand into my clit.

I bite back a moan, pretending we can't both hear the hitch in my breath.

"Take your pants off," I repeat, the words coming out more like a breathless plea instead of a defiant demand this time. Still,

I refuse to blink first. It's too fucking hot to go toe to toe with him like this.

But instead of fighting me or forcing me, Maddoc suddenly grins, and it breaks me.

It reminds me that he fucking *loves* me.

I surge forward, and he slips his fingers out and catches me, wrapping one arm around my waist and hauling me up against him.

"Anything for you, butterfly," he murmurs against my lips, somehow managing to get out of his pants one handed while he kisses me.

Then both men surround me again, nothing between any of us but skin, ink, sweat, and desire. I'm pinned in place, their hot, pulsing cocks digging into me, thrusting against me, the air around us filling with heated, panting breaths and filthy, whispered promises while they start to take me apart exactly like they promised.

I'm so aroused it almost feels like I'm floating, and as they pass me between them, owning me completely, I'm transfixed by our reflections in the mirror.

We look even better like this.

We look fucking *perfect*.

Then Maddoc reaches for my hand and brings it down to his crotch. "Is this what you were so eager to get your hands on, butterfly?"

I stroke him slowly, letting the thick length slide through my palm.

Loving the way it jerks and throbs at my touch.

"That's right," I say, boldly meeting his eyes. "Because it's mine."

"Fuck yeah, it is," he answers with a low growl, thrusting forward. "Now show me what you want to do with it. Get me and my brother ready to fuck you. Make us good and hard to make sure you can feel it after we're through with you."

Both their cocks already feel like steel, but the promise of how hard he plans on using me has my thighs clenching together and my breath speeding up.

I reach for Dante's cock too, and he groans, grinding his hard length against my hip. "Ain't never gonna be through with her, Madd. You know that."

The growl Maddoc answers him with sends yet another flood of arousal through me.

"Damn fucking right I do," he agrees, thrusting into my fist as I start working both of them. "Never gonna be through, but she's still going to remember this. We need to make sure she feels it."

My men share a look, and it makes me want to spread my legs and beg them to take me right now.

He's not just talking about how hard they're going to fuck me. He's talking about the fact that they'll make sure I can feel *their* touch, not the echo of having Austin McKenna's hands on me.

Their ownership.

Their claim.

Their... love, even if Maddoc and I are the only two who have actually said the words so far.

"Go on, princess," Dante says when I rub my thumb over the wet slit in his cockhead and get a low groan of pleasure from him for my efforts. "Stroke us. Work us up. Just like that. Listen to Madd. You're gonna get fucked so good tonight. You wet enough to take what we give you?"

He knows I am, but I spread my legs a little wider so he can plunge his fingers into my pussy to prove it to himself. When he does, I moan, tipping my head back and begging for his mouth again too.

He gives it to me, then Maddoc's hand is on my pussy again too. Rubbing my clit. Pushing his brother's fingers deeper inside me. Adding his own.

"Fuck," I gasp, my hands tightening on both their cocks. "Yes, please, right there, god. Keep going, I... I... "

I'm trembling.

I'm on the verge of begging.

I'm barely stroking them anymore, just letting them both fuck my hands while they fingerfuck my pussy.

They're *owning* me, and I would've already crumpled to the floor in a whining, whimpering pile of need if they weren't still holding me up between their hard, straining bodies.

The invigorating rush of power I felt as I pushed Maddoc earlier and got pushed right back melts away into something that's both hotter and sweeter. I fucking love the feel of their cocks in my hands. The ragged sound of their breath and the filthy curses they drop as we all work each other up. But I've been strong for too fucking long, and like Maddoc said, I'm where I belong now.

I'm not alone anymore. I'm theirs, and I want them to take me.

I don't want to be defiant; I want to be dominated.

"Fuck, princess, you're so fucking sexy like this," Dante mutters, pumping himself into my hand as he holds me against him. "I need my cock inside you."

"Not before I taste her," Maddoc growls, sliding his fingers out of my pussy and shoving them into my mouth.

The flavor of my own sex overwhelms me. My eyes go wide and my core clenches tight, and the filthy smile Maddoc gives me when I clean my own arousal off his fingers, sucking them like a cock and stroking them with my tongue, is fucking everything.

"You can put your cock right here," he says to Dante, slowly slipping his fingers out. Then, to me, "Get on the bed."

He tosses me onto the mattress without waiting, then manhandles me into position with my head hanging over the edge and my body splayed out like a buffet on the mattress. I've been naked and on display for more men than I can count, but right here, right now, the way they both look at me makes me feel wanton and powerful and sexy as hell.

"Look at you," Dante says, fisting his cock as he lets his eyes roam over me. "Gonna remember this view right here forever, princess."

I turn my head toward the mirror, and he's right. The sight of the three of us sears into my memory forever. Especially when Maddoc crawls onto the bed like a fucking predator, spreading my legs apart to make room for himself, and settles between them with a look on his face like he's about to feast.

I grip the bedspread, my fingers digging into it, and then he does. He uses his thumbs to part my slick folds, meets my eyes in the mirror for a moment, and then fucking devours me.

"Shit, god, yes, please," I pant, my thighs shaking around his wide shoulders as he eats me out like he's been starving for it.

"Yeah," Dante mutters, licking his lips and stalking closer. "Fuck yeah." He keeps one hand on his cock and wraps his other around my throat, stroking it and anchoring me in place as Maddoc's sinful mouth makes me crazy. "Look at the way you move. Watching you come apart is fucking art, princess."

Filthy, obscene sounds tumble out of me as the rough rasp of Maddoc's jaw scrapes against my inner thighs, his insistent mouth pulling my orgasm closer and closer to the surface with every lick, suck, and bite.

"So fucking wet," he mutters against me, the vibration of his low voice sending a fresh shudder of need through me as he twists his head from side to side, inhaling my scent. "You're delicious."

"Damn right, she is," Dante agrees, his eyes roaming over me like a heated caress. He starts stroking himself again, his cockhead turning an angry red in his fist with every upstroke. "And like you said, Madd, she's fucking addictive."

I feel the same about him. I can't look away from his cock,

and when Dante grins down at me, no doubt reading me just as easily as he always does, my mouth starts literally watering for a taste of him.

He rubs his cockhead against my cheek like a fucking tease, painting me with his precum, but before I can chase his cock with my mouth, he uses it to nudge my face to the side, forcing my eyes toward the mirror again.

"*Look*, princess."

I obey him, and my breath catches in my throat as the desire already burning inside me turns into a white hot flame.

Dante is fucking gorgeous. He stands right over me, all muscle and ink and masculine beauty, his muscular ass flexing in the mirror as he slowly rubs off against my face. Maddoc looks like an alpha beast with his head buried between my legs and his naked body—covered in bold lines and brutal scars—a testament to the power he's carved out for himself in this city. And then there's me, spread between them like some kind of sacrificial offering on an altar, here for the two of them to use. Here for the two of them to worship.

Then Maddoc's lips close around my clit, sucking hard as he pounds his fingers into my pussy, and my eyes squeeze closed as a scream tears out of my throat, pleasure ripping through me so hard that I shatter.

I clamp my legs around Maddoc's shoulders as I come, my back arching so hard I almost fly off the bed. He makes an utterly filthy sound and laps it up, his wicked tongue working overtime as he pushes me even higher, making the aftershocks come hard and fast until it's almost too much. Until it feels like I'll never stop coming.

But then Dante fists my hair hard and my eyes snap open from the delicious burst of pain, my body still writhing as I pant through the waves of pleasure and stare up at him.

He stares down at me with the same burning intensity, and I

strain upward, chasing his cock. The angle is wrong and my body is still pulsating with pleasure, but I don't care. I want it.

Dante's grip on my hair is too tight for me to reach it though, and with Maddoc still holding me down, holding me in place as he laps at my pussy like a man obsessed, I can't do anything but writhe, pant, and beg.

"*Dante.*"

He shares a weighted look with Maddoc, and then, without a word passing between them, they're manhandling me again. Maddoc pulls back, his arms sliding under my thighs to lift me and push me forward, and Dante guiding my head, adjusting it to hang more fully off the bed.

I open my mouth, saliva pooling from how badly I want his cock, and he finally gives it to me, rubbing it over my lips a few times before finally sliding it in.

"Fucking heaven," he mutters, staring down at me as he teases us both with a few short, shallow thrusts. "Every part of you was made for this, princess. Made for us."

My eyelids flutter closed, my world narrowing to the taste of him, the feel of being filled like this, the heat starting to pool between my legs again as Maddoc dips a finger inside me, muttering dirty praise before pulling it back again and pushing my legs apart so I'm fully exposed to him.

"Who does this pussy belong to?"

Dante slides his cock out, staring down at me with hooded eyes as he slowly strokes it in front of my mouth. "Madd asked you a question, princess."

I meet Maddoc's eyes in the mirror. "You."

He pushes his fingers back inside me, and my hips give an aborted thrust upward. I'm desperate to be fucked, my pulse racing as I look up into Dante's vibrant green eyes.

"And you," I tell the beautiful, tattooed man.

Maddoc scissors his fingers inside me, grinding the heel of

his other hand against my clit, and I gasp as my arousal spikes into white-hot need.

"And Logan too," I blurt. "All three of you. It's yours. All of yours. I'm... I need—*ahhhh*."

Maddoc dives back in, his mouth devouring me again, and Dante grabs my chin and pushes his cock down my throat.

"That's right, princess. That pussy is ours. This mouth is ours. We're the ones you're gonna scream for. We're the ones who are gonna make you come, as many times as we fucking want."

My jaw strains to take his girth as the taste of him overwhelms me, and it's fucking perfect. I'm his to use right now, just like I'm Maddoc's to pleasure, and with Dante's balls pressed against my nose and his fingers lovingly stroking my lips as they stretch wide and tight around the base of his shaft, I can't breathe.

I don't want to.

It narrows my world and cuts everything out but this.

My pussy clenches with pleasure as Maddoc grips my thighs and holds them apart, eating me out like a starving man, and my eyes water, my vision blurring as I watch Dante's muscular ass flex and clench in the mirror as he grinds against my face, then pulls back to let me breathe for a moment before starting to fuck my mouth with long, languid strokes.

Then, when I whine, faster ones.

Rougher ones.

Until he's finally slamming down my throat and sending me flying. Awakening the darkness inside me that craves this.

The pain. The overwhelm. The bliss.

It goes on and on, my vision narrowing, then darkening at the edges as my body sings with a whole new level of pleasure from the way they ruthlessly dominate me. My throat feels raw and my clit is swollen and oversensitive from my first orgasm, but Maddoc forces my body to take whatever he gives it anyway, turning the delicious torture into another rising wave of dark pleasure.

Then Dante finally buries himself in my throat with a hoarse shout, holding himself there as his cock pulses on my tongue.

He's too deep for me to taste it, but knowing what he's giving me makes every single nerve ending in my body fire at once. I try to scream, but I'm choking on too much cock, and when Maddoc shoves his fingers into my pussy, nailing my g-spot while he sucks hard on my clit, the combination pushes me over the edge and a second orgasm crashes over me like a tsunami.

"Shit, princess," Dante grits out, his straining muscles standing out in stark relief under the bright, intricate artwork that covers his body as he grinds against my face like seeing my pleasure heightens his own.

Maddoc releases a low, primal growl and pulls me off Dante's cock, flipping me over and pushing me up to my hands and knees.

"Fuck, Madd," Dante says, grabbing his still hard cock, slick and wet from my saliva.

A trickle of cum hangs from the slit, and I fucking want it, my throat spasming from the sudden loss.

"I need to be inside her," Maddoc snaps, grabbing my hips hard enough to bruise.

My arms shake as the aftershocks keep hitting me, the intensity of that second orgasm doing its best to liquify my bones, and when Maddoc drives into me from behind, going balls deep in one thrust, they give out, and I collapse down onto my elbows.

Dante grips my chin, tilting my head up, and feeds me his cock again. "I'm not done with you." He threads his fingers through my hair as he holds my head in place, angling us so that I can see all of us in the mirror again. "Watch my brother fuck you. Look how well you take us, princess. See what you fucking do to me, even though you just made me come."

I do, and it's hot as hell. He hisses a little as I hold his cock in my mouth, no doubt too fucking sensitive to enjoy it... except that Dante has the same darkness inside him, and he's pushing it down my throat anyway. Getting hard as steel all over again. Holding me in place and fucking my mouth as Maddoc fucks into me like a machine, pounding into me from behind with a punishing rhythm that has my body greedily craving even more.

"So fucking good," Maddoc grits out, tilting my hips up to adjust the angle. "So soft and tight. Nothing else feels like fucking you, butterfly. You take my cock like a motherfucking dream. You're full of my brother's cum right now, but I'm gonna give you some of my own. Gonna mark you up."

He slaps my ass, and I see the two of them exchange a look in the mirror.

Something passes between them. It's not jealousy. They're both possessive as hell, but it's nothing like that at all. It's like they're feeding off each other's energy. Deepening their own bond as they work together to make me truly theirs.

They're perfectly in sync, tied together by the raw, rough, pounding sex and the emotions that simmer between all three of us. I lose track of time. I lose track of everything. And then, with no warning at all, I'm coming again, filled up at both ends and practically floating out of my body as it rolls over me in an unstoppable wave that has me seeing stars and shaking so hard that the only thing holding me up is my men.

"Fuck, fuck, fuck!" Dante shouts, pulling out of my mouth as he starts to come this time and stroking himself hard and fast, stripping his cock raw as he stripes my face with his cum.

Maddoc curses, low and dirty, slamming into me one final time. I can feel his warmth spreading inside me, fulfilling that promise he made to make sure I had his cum inside me too, and it's so fucking hot that it sets me off again.

"You see what you fucking do to us, butterfly?" Maddoc grits out, slowly fucking me through the second wave of aftershocks. "You're goddamn incredible."

What I am is worn out, sated, and feeling better than I have any right to be now that they've fucked all my worries about the future and all the ugly memories of the recent past out of me.

For now, at least. I collapse onto the bed, firmly blocking thoughts of anything *but* now from creeping back into my head. There will be plenty of time for that later, and no way to escape dealing with what's coming when it does, but no way in hell am I going to let it steal this from me.

These big, rough, dangerous men just used me as hard as they promised they would... and now they're showing me the more tender side of just how much they cherish me. They clean me up with a warm cloth and tuck me into the blankets, just as in sync as when they were both balls deep inside me. And when I grab their wrists and tug them down too, they prove all over again what they showed me today.

They'll always be here when I need them.

These men really will do anything for me.

"Stay," I murmur sleepily as they get in bed beside me, sandwiching me between them.

I nestle my ass against Dante's crotch as Maddoc pulls me close and cradles my face, staring into my eyes like he's willing them to stay open long enough to hear him. "Fucking always."

And the sound of Dante echoing that rumbling promise is the music I fall asleep to.

13

LOGAN

My EYES open with my alarm in the morning, my morning routine an ingrained part of my daily life that gives me a necessary sense of control. It takes me eight minutes to change into my workout clothes, handle what I need to in the bathroom, get down to the gym we've got set up in the basement, and prep the equipment I'm starting with today. I spend another two minutes stretching, then start my workout precisely at 4:10 a.m.

Most of the time, the physical exertion helps quiet my mind and focus my thoughts.

Today, the bruise I earn on my shin from the kettlebell I'm warming up with tells me I need to focus a little more.

I set it down, carefully lining it up with the seams in the industrial carpet we laid down here, and stare at my reflection in the mirror for a moment. I haven't been able to get Riley out of my mind since she left my room after fellating me last night. Since she begged me for pain and gave me her trust in return.

My cock starts to harden, pushing against the thin fabric of my gym shorts.

I ignore it and turn away from the mirror to load up the bar I'll be using for squats.

Arousal has no place here. I have a specific set of muscle

groups to work through, and limited time to do them in if I'm going to stay on track with my priorities today.

Staying on track isn't usually a problem for me, but ever since Riley came into our lives, things have been... changing. And as I clean the bar up to my shoulders and start working through my first set of squats, I realize that I'm not sure which unsettles me most—how much she's disrupted things and forced me to deviate from my comfort zone, time after time, or the fact that all of the changes she's brought about *don't* bother me more.

I like having her on my mind.

I like having my hands on her and my cock inside her.

Most of all, I like seeing my own demons reflected back, and even welcomed, when I look in her eyes.

Having feelings for a woman, any woman, after my mother showed me how evil they can be, isn't something I thought I was capable of, but I was wrong. I would have torn the world apart to get Riley back when McKenna had her, and now that we've got her again, I'll use every skill I possess to maim and dismember any man who hurts her again.

Except... that man is me.

I grunt, letting the bar drop to the ground with a clang, then load fifty more pounds on it. It's more than I've scheduled myself to work with this morning, but I need the exertion to turn off these thoughts for a few moments.

It doesn't work.

I fucking hurt her, and my cock turned to steel when she begged me to do it. I like her pain. I crave giving it to her, and find a release that feels far more than just sexual when I see the pleasure and satisfaction she finds on the other side of darkness.

My thighs start to burn, and I realize I've lost count of this set, rising and dropping in perfect form, over and over, with more weight than I should be using right now.

I force myself to stop, wiping down each plate as I remove it from the bar and stacking them back in the rack before breaking for water.

And still, I'm thinking about Riley. She isn't like anyone else I've ever known.

A part of me wonders if she really meant what she said to me. If she honestly likes the way I hurt her and the control I require when we're intimate. But I've never felt as close to anyone else in my life, not even my brothers, and when I review the moments we've shared, I can't find the lie.

She makes me feel like a different person. She makes me... *feel*.

I cap my water bottle and return it to the shelf near the door, then head to the corner where we keep the sandbags. It's time for deadlifts. But halfway there, I catch my own gaze in the mirror and freeze, a strange emotion rolling through my gut.

Something's different.

I lift a hand to my face, then let it drop. I still have my mother's soulless eyes. I still have the face of a monster, but I don't... see myself that way anymore. Maybe because Riley doesn't, even after I've shown her the worst of the things I keep locked away inside me. Her acceptance, her... feelings for me, make it harder to hate the parts of myself I used to despise.

"You're not a monster," I whisper almost soundlessly, staring into the eyes I inherited from one.

Then I blink, and force my feet to move again. To grab the handles of the hundred pound sandbag and start a set of deadlifts. To clear my mind once and for all so I can find the focus and control that my morning workout always gives me.

This time, it works, and when I finally finish up and head upstairs intending to grab a quick shower an hour later, I'm not surprised when my feet lead me in a different direction entirely.

Toward Riley.

When she first came to live with us, I thought that trusting her was a weakness and I fought my brothers when I saw them succumbing to that weakness.

I was trying to protect them. To protect us all. But I was wrong.

Trusting Riley makes me stronger. Somehow, she's become my anchor, the one person I can trust most in all the world. Not that I don't also trust my brothers. I trust them with my life. But Riley is something different. She's seen everything I truly am. I've exposed her to the darkness that lives inside my soul and come at her with my most depraved needs, and instead of shying away, she bares her soul right back.

I push open the door to her bedroom. She's still asleep... and so are my brothers, one on either side of her.

I heard them last night. I still have cameras in this room. Knowing what they did together after she left me had me aroused to a level that required all my self-discipline to ignore, but I know what it is to find release with Riley's body now, and now that I do, I no longer want it any other way.

I wanted to come join them last night, but I'm different than my brothers. There's still a barrier between what I want and what I can allow myself to have, and while I won't deny myself a relationship with her, the connection I have with Riley isn't the same as what she shares with my brothers. It's darker, and it would have changed what they did together if I'd brought that darkness into the pleasure they gave her last night.

Still, I let my eyes roam over the three of them hungrily. My brothers don't arouse me, but seeing Riley between them, knowing she's been filled and used and taken by them, that affects me in a way that makes me feel closer to all three of them.

I move toward the bed. They've kicked the blankets down, and Riley's naked body is on display, all subtle curves and dark bruises and skin so soft it's irresistible, made to be marked.

My eyes go to the scars I've left on her, a fierce pleasure flaring inside me as I take them in.

The scars are *my* marks, and while McKenna's will fade, mine are permanent.

There are new marks now too. Marks my brothers left last night that make her look even more beautiful.

When I reach the foot of the bed, drawn toward her like a moth to flame, her eyelids start to flutter, then slowly open, locking onto me. In the dim morning light, their whiskey-brown color becomes two pools of welcoming darkness, and I suddenly want, I *need*, to feel the unique connection I have with her again. The one that sets me apart from what she has with my brothers. The one that tells me I'm not what I once thought I was.

I need to remind myself it's real.

I place a knee on the bed, and she rolls onto her back, silently welcoming me. I crawl up over her, never breaking eye contact, the sex-drenched scent of her sleep enveloping me like a drug.

She stares up at me without saying a word.

She's truly not afraid of me.

I wrap my hand around her throat. Not hard enough to cut off her air, just... testing. Waiting to see if the fear will finally come. If this will be the time she finally sees me as a monster. If she'll use her safe word to save herself.

She doesn't, and something flares between us as her breath quickens, her pulse thrumming so insistently that it makes my soul ache.

"Logan," she whispers, my name forming on her lips without any sound.

My cock starts to harden, and I tighten my grip on her throat, needing more. Needing to feel the rapid flutter of her pulse beneath my palm. Needing to know she doesn't just trust me; that she craves this too.

She licks her lips, subtly lifting her throat to press against my hand, and a low groan rips out of me as heat surges between us.

She gasps softly, squirming beneath my body as I tighten my grip even more, and I know she's wet for me. I'm feeding the side of her that no one else will. She wants this, and this little wildcat is everything *I* want.

Every fucking time I give her a chance to hate me, she doesn't, and for the first time, I actually start to believe what I said to myself in the mirror this morning.

Maybe I'm not what I've always thought I was.

Maybe, for her, I truly can be something better.

"Logan."

Maddoc's voice is low and tense, and I blink, noticing for the first time that both my brothers have awakened.

They don't like the chokehold I have on our girl.

"It's okay," she tells them, keeping her eyes on me. "Logan and I are figuring it out."

She reaches up as she says it and wraps her hand around my wrist, holding it in place.

"You like it."

I don't make it a question. I know she does. But I still need her to say it. I need her to say it in front of *them*.

And once again, she doesn't let me down.

"I like it," she breathes. "I need it. I need you, Logan."

Something crashes through me, a feeling that's hot and shaky and bright, and I'm more grateful than I'll ever fucking admit that Dante jumps in, giving me a moment to deal with the swirl of unfamiliar emotions making my chest ache.

"Logan's pretty intense, princess. You're in for it now. You just gave him a free pass to—"

"To hurt me?" Riley cuts in breathlessly, her pupils dilating. "That's what I want. I like it intense. I like hurting a little bit."

123

Dante claps a hand on my shoulder. "Well, I'm pretty sure our brother here can help you with that one."

I roll my eyes, but he's not wrong. They know I'm broken. The strange thing is, I don't feel it as much with Riley.

She gives me a little smile, something private between just the two of us, and maybe that's it.

She knows I'm broken too. But all my broken pieces fit perfectly with her.

It's a good feeling, and those emotions swell in my chest when I finally release my hold on her throat and she turns her head to press a soft kiss to my palm.

Out of the corner of my eye, I can see Maddoc and Dante share a nod as they get out of bed, leaving the two of us in our own little bubble. We linger like that for a moment, our gazes still locked, and for the first time in as long as I can remember, I feel something almost like... contentment.

It's almost impossible to drag myself away from Riley, even though I know we need to get up. We have to buckle down and figure out what our next move will be. The thought of the danger she could still be in is what finally urges me into action, and I pull my hand away from her face and lean back.

Once we finally clamber out of bed and head down to the kitchen, Maddoc immediately gets us all back on track, reminding us that West Point has a serious advantage over us now that McKenna is in control of Riley's inheritance.

Dante starts up some coffee as we begin to discuss how to fucking deal with that, and I pull out meat, vegetables, and eggs to start an omelet for Riley and my brothers.

"He got all the money," Riley says as we review what we know, a stricken look on her face. "I signed everything over. Shit. Why didn't I fight him?"

"Because you needed to stay the fuck alive," Maddoc growls as Dante smooths his hand down her hair, the vibrant colors twining around his fingers.

"You did what you had to, princess," he adds. "That's all we fucking care about."

"Austin can do some terrible things with the money though, can't he?" she asks, her eyes flicking between us.

"He can fucking try." Rage flashes in Maddoc's eyes for a moment, then he slips his calm mask of leadership back on and scrubs a hand over his face. "He *will* try. But having a few more resources is about the only advantage that piece of shit has, butterfly. West Point will never take us out, because McKenna doesn't actually know how to build something that will last. He's got no fucking loyalty, and it's gonna come back and bite him in the ass at some point, when money can't help him."

I agree with Maddoc's assessment, but Riley doesn't need to be coddled. The facts are that McKenna isn't going to win here, but he can still do a lot of damage along the way.

I share a look with Dante, seeing the same thoughts brewing in his green eyes.

Maddoc catches it.

"Fuck," he says with a sigh, his expression grim. "Yeah, okay, he's gonna cause some problems. We need to do damage control and try to predict where he'll strike us first."

"And what his endgame is," Dante throws in.

We discuss a few potential scenarios as I crack eggs into the pan I just heated and whisk in the other ingredients, and the mood in the kitchen shifts to something grimmer with each one.

"What about the other gangs?" Riley asks, accepting a cup of coffee from Dante as I start to plate the omelets. "Will you lose allies over this? Or will Austin go after some of the others? Not to sound cold, but maybe that will buy you some time?"

"Us," Maddoc corrects her, taking the coffee out of her hand as she lifts it to her lips and grabbing her chin to hold her in place. His eyes drill into hers. "Buy *us* some time."

"Us," she repeats, smiling.

He dips down to steal a kiss, then hands her back her coffee.

"But yes," I tell her, "we'll lose allies, and McKenna will try to take over some of the weaker gangs' territories now that he's got access to so many resources, but he won't do it strategically."

Riley blinks. "Why not?"

Dante laughs, a dark sound that he's not suited for. "'Cause he fucking hates us. It will cloud his judgment."

Maddoc's lips compress into a thin line, and he nods sharply. "We'll do what we can to protect our holdings and set up some lines of defense, but we're flying blind until he shows his hand. Right now, we only know two things for sure. He's got a lot more resources than he used to, and Dante's right. McKenna hates the Reapers, so he's not gonna be strategic. He's going to make this personal."

"He already has," I say, my knuckles whitening as my hand tightens on the spatula I'm holding, picturing those marks he left on our girl.

She may like pain, but only *my* pain. Only from me or my brothers. If Maddoc doesn't kill him for what he did to her, I'll do it myself.

"He was trying to make it personal when he offered to trade for me," Riley says in a strained voice, looking at Maddoc. "He doesn't just hate the Reapers, he hates *you*."

Maddoc nods. "And now that he knows what you mean to me, butterfly, he's gonna become an even bigger threat."

She makes a strangled sound, her hand flying up to cover her mouth. "So, if I wasn't—"

"Don't," Maddoc cuts her off sharply. "That's not what I meant. That's not ever gonna be the answer. You're ours. That isn't negotiable."

"Having you here just gives us more to fight for, princess," Dante says, a deadly gleam in his eye as he grins at her. "And it puts things into perspective when it comes to the Reapers and West Point coexisting here."

"How can we?" Riley asks. "Austin will turn the city into a war zone."

"That's right," I say, slipping the omelet onto her plate. "Dante meant we can't coexist. It's no longer possible. This isn't just about territory anymore. We'll have to end it."

Maddoc's eyes flash. "It's gonna be him or us."

I meet his gaze and give him a sharp nod, understanding passing between us. Only one of those options is acceptable. Us.

Whatever it fucking takes.

14

RILEY

HIM OR US.

Those words hit me so hard I have to push back from the counter for a second, worried I might throw up if I try to eat the delicious-smelling omelet Logan just made for me.

Not that this is the first time I've realized how much danger we're in. It isn't. But it's a cold, hard dose of reality after letting myself get lost in the warmth and safety of being home, being *loved*, last night.

It's also the first time I've felt like I have so much to lose.

"If Austin wins this fight, this war—" I start.

"He won't," Maddoc says, cutting me off sharply.

"Eat," Logan adds, all the feelings he and I still haven't named to each other coming through in the single, flat word.

He pushes my plate closer, and I scoot the tall stool back toward the counter, knowing it's his way of caring for me, a counterbalance to the pain we both thrive on.

I force myself to pick up my fork as the men continue to discuss the war looming on the horizon. The one where Austin has all the firepower and resources my inheritance can buy.

"We need to incentivize some of our relationships in the

warehouse district," Maddoc says, rattling off some names and locations that seem to mean something to Dante and Logan.

"I'll talk to Ruiz about getting the 17th Street Gang to help us fortify a perimeter," Dante says. "Not sure he'll go for it, but it's worth trying."

Logan's lips turn down, his voice tight. "His gang is already spread thin. We'll need to supply them with weapons if Austin..."

I tune out the details for a moment, panic rising in my chest. I hate this fucking feeling. I want to be angry, not scared, but part of admitting my feelings for these three men means realizing how devastated I'll be if we lose.

If I lose *them*.

But the time I spent as Austin's captive and the callous way he and his men treated me speaks to a level of ruthlessness that's shaken me more than I want to admit.

I'll do whatever it takes to help defeat him, to help the Reapers wipe West Point from Halston's streets. I just wish I felt more confident that we'll be able to stand against him now that he has the power to do basically whatever he wants.

The thought makes my stomach turn, and I choke on the bite of eggs I just took. All three men immediately snap their attention to me, their conversation pausing in a way that tells me more than anything else how much I mean to them.

I recover as quickly as I can, taking a deep breath and schooling my features. I don't need them worrying about me more than they already do. I want to help, not be a hindrance.

"Everything okay, princess?" Dante asks, cocking his head to the side and studying me intently.

"I'm fine," I lie, offering a weak smile and forcing myself to take another bite of the omelet I can barely taste.

Maddoc shakes his head. "You might be fine now, but you weren't fine a few seconds ago." He pauses, then nods. "It's West Point. Talking about them upsets you."

"Their existence upsets me," I snap, then put down my fork when I realize my hand is shaking. I take a breath. "Sorry," I say, only half meaning it.

I'm not sorry I let my anger and fear show, I'm just sorry it came across as lashing out at them. But I'm done covering up the way I feel around these three men who would literally give their lives to protect me, and the way Maddoc's gaze softens for a moment, I know he doesn't expect me to.

It's Dante who breaks the tension, though. "We all are, princess," he says with a low chuckle. "So let's figure out how to fucking end it, yeah?"

"I'd like that," I say softly. "They..."

I close my mouth and shake my head as memories of my time in captivity suddenly well up and threaten to choke me. Stupid, because other than the beating Austin gave me at the end, they didn't actually hurt me.

"They what?" Logan asks, deadly menace in his voice. "You need to tell us. The wounds I treated last night were fresh. Were they the only ones McKenna will have to answer for?"

"Yes," I say honestly. Then I can't help but add, "But I know how dangerous Austin can be now. He really is a sadistic psychopath. He has no conscience. Hurting me, hurting *you*, excites him."

I shudder, and Logan's pale gaze sharpens, burning into me as he searches my face.

I hold it, putting my heart on display for him when I realize how that may have sounded. Austin terrifies me, but it's different. The sadistic pleasure that asshole takes in making others suffer is completely different than the darkness that binds Logan and me together.

Finally, Logan nods, his body subtly relaxing.

"You don't need to protect me from hearing your plans," I say, the connection I feel with him—with all of them—giving me strength. "Austin's going to be hard to beat. Harder now with all that money to work with. But I don't want to be on the sidelines. I'm in this with you. It's why I stayed."

Although I'm grateful as all hell that they got Chloe out of the line of fire.

"We are too," Maddoc says gruffly. "But I don't think that's the only thing bothering you right now. Fuck's sake, Riley," he pauses and scrubs a hand down his face. "You looked like you were going to pass out or throw up or—or I don't even know what. Tell me what's going on. Now. Did he touch you? Did he—"

"No," I stop him before he can finish asking the question that's twisting his features into something dangerously angry. "He felt me up a couple of times, but that's all. I swear. None of them tried anything more than that. Austin threatened to. You know he—" I swallow down bile but make myself say it, reminding myself it doesn't matter. Not really. "He married me. It's how he got legal access to the money. But no one raped me."

It's true, but my voice cracks and my skin crawls as I remember the fear that they would. And not just rape. I can survive fucking anything, and I'm no stranger to blocking off my emotions when men want to use my body for their pleasure. But the way Austin's men talked about me—talked about sharing me and passing me around before they finally killed me, and how sure they were that Austin would "reward" them that way—gets to me on a level I'm embarrassed to have my men see.

But of course they see it.

In an instant, Maddoc crosses the kitchen and pulls me up off the stool I'm sitting on, crushing me against him in a hug so tight it feels like he might break me in half.

"What else?" he demands.

I shake my head, closing my eyes as I lean into him.

It didn't happen, so I don't need to dwell on it.

Maddoc feels differently. He tips my chin up, forcing me to meet his eyes. "What happened, butterfly? We need to know."

"Nothing," I start.

His eyes darken so fast I shudder, a visceral memory of him belting me rising up inside me.

I almost beg him to do it again. To take me out of my head that way. To lash away these fucking fears that have burrowed into me before they can take root and turn me into someone weak.

But we don't have time for that, and I'm stronger than that anyway.

I go up on my toes and kiss him, then straighten my shoulders. "Nothing happened, but if I'd stayed there much longer, I think—" My voice breaks as I remember how helpless I felt and how frustrating it was, but I swallow and power on, holding his gaze steadily. "I think it would have been bad. The longer I was there, the bolder Austin's men got with me. Groping me and taunting me about what he'd do, what he'd let *them* do, once he had no more use for me."

I don't know which was worse, the way they threatened to use me, or the fact that Sienna implied Austin would simply kill me.

I don't want to bring her up, though. Not with the history Maddoc has with her.

"What did they say they would do?" he asks in a hard voice, his muscles tense and his jaw going tight.

"They wanted to break me. Degrade me. Pass me around and use all my holes. Draw it out and make me hurt, make me cry." It's almost too much, but it pours out of me in a cathartic rush, my breath growing short and my throat closing up as the words pour out. "They said he'd toss me to them like a scrap of meat after he got the money. He didn't let them touch me while he got all the legal shit in order, but they promised he wouldn't care how much they tortured me afterward, and I... believed them."

My voice fades away, my throat finally closing up

completely as I let the full horror of what the Reapers saved me from wash over me. Every fucking one of Austin's men was just like him. All of them getting off on the idea of turning me into a plaything that they'd be able to use and abuse with their leader's blessing.

The color drains from Maddoc's face, but his features stay hard and still as a block of granite as he searches my face. Then he leans in until his forehead is resting against mine.

"I'll kill him for that," he promises in a gravelly tone that's barely above a whisper. "I should have killed him a long time ago, butterfly, but I swear I'll make him pay this time. I'll fucking end him."

Then he captures my mouth in a hard, deep kiss that goes on long enough to make my head spin from lack of oxygen.

I don't care. My back is bowed from the force of it, my body held up by his arms, his strength, and the intensity of his feelings slicing through the hold the memories of captivity had on my mind, finally freeing me from them.

I believe him. Austin signed his own death warrant, and the darkness in me rises up and relishes every fucking bit of Maddoc's intensity as I kiss him back.

He finally releases me with a dark, possessive growl, his entire body still vibrating with emotion. For a moment, I think he's going to say something more. Instead, he pins each of his seconds with a dark look, then strides out of the kitchen, pulling his phone out as he goes.

A moment later, we all hear the front door slam as he leaves the house.

I blink, lifting a hand to touch my tingling lips, then looking to the other men to explain whatever it was that wordlessly passed between the three of them just now. "Where's he going?"

"He's going to make sure you're safe from McKenna," Logan says flatly, his pale gaze just as intense and lethal as the anger Maddoc took with him.

"He's gonna handle some shit with our people," Dante adds grimly, the easy demeanor I'm used to from him nowhere to be found. "He needs to make sure our territory is secure and fortify protection around our key holdings so that when McKenna comes for us, we can fend him off."

I suck in a deep breath and slowly exhale. It sounds like Maddoc's doing everything we were already talking about over breakfast, but the way he left... that's my fault.

"I shouldn't have said anything about what happened with West Point. I didn't mean to piss him off."

Dante offers a sympathetic look. "No, it's good that you didn't lie. We need to know this shit, princess. Madd will be fine. He just needs to work things out on his own for a bit, and putting things in motion to take control of the situation is gonna help him get a handle on his emotions."

"Okay," I say, forcing myself to stop twisting my hands together when I realize that's what I'm doing. I take a breath and repeat it, grateful for Dante's explanation. "Okay. Fine. That's... good. As long as he's going to be okay."

"He will be," Dante promises, pausing as he gives me an intense look. Then he lets out a gusty breath, his lips quirking in a faint imitation of his usual smirk. "Although speaking of getting a handle on emotions—" He jerks his head toward the stairs. "I'm gonna need you to come with me for a few."

I almost reassure him that I'm fine again, but something in his face stops me. I share a look with Logan as I follow Dante out of the room, and even though I can't say why, it settles me.

I follow Dante up to his studio.

"Do you want me to paint again to get my feelings out, like I did before?" I ask, not hating the idea even though I'm not sure I need to right now.

He chuckles, giving me a rueful look as he pulls me against him. "Nah, not this time." He cups my face, letting his thumb brush back and forth across my cheek in a gentle caress that reminds me just how much I matter to this man. "When I mentioned getting a handle on emotions, I was talking about me, not you."

My heart does a slow roll in my chest, and for an endless moment, I get lost in the vibrant green intensity of his eyes.

"Maddoc wasn't the only one who heard that shit you told us down there, princess," he says, getting more serious than I've ever seen him. "Having you gone was hell on all of us, and I—" His voice cracks, but his gaze never wavers, his entire soul laid bare to me. "I care about you, so fucking much. I want to paint you right now. A portrait."

"Are you serious?" I ask, feeling a little bashful at the thought. Portraits aren't his usual style, and it feels intimate, important in a way that transcends what he's shown me with his art in the past.

Dante nods, covering my heart with his hand. "I need to commit this shit to canvas," he says quietly.

15

RILEY

It's NOT a confession of love, not in words, but it feels so close to it that tears spring to my eyes, my heart stuttering in my chest as the enormity of the bond between us crashes over me.

I kiss him, giving him my own confession that way, and he grips the back of my head, tangling his hands in my hair, and deepens it.

This man does things to me. He has since the first. And it doesn't take long before the emotion between us sparks into heat.

"Can't ever fucking get enough of you," he growls against my lips, hauling me against his body. "That's... why... I want..."

His mouth on mine is hot and demanding between each word, but he trails off to tip my head back and suck on my throat, making us both groan.

I know what he wants. He wants to paint me. Keep me. Memorialize this feeling, this connection that's been between us from the start. But we're both distracted now, and when he tugs at my clothing I help him get me naked, I return the favor by yanking his shirt off, eager to reconfirm our connection another way.

"You're so damn beautiful," he says, stepping back for a

moment to run his hands down my sides. He frames my pussy with them. "This right here is my own personal heaven, princess. You know that, right?"

"Dante," I say, my throat closing up even as heat blooms in my core. "I—"

He surges up and kisses me again before I can say the words burning to get out, scooping me up into his arms and carrying me over to the couch he keeps in the corner of his studio.

"You what, princess?" he asks, his voice husky as he lays me down on it, trailing his fingers down my body and dipping them between my legs. "You wanna take me to heaven? You wanna remind me what the fuck we're fighting so damn hard for?"

I squeeze my thighs together, trapping his fingers inside me, and rock down to get them deeper.

"Fuck," I gasp when he obliges. The man knows exactly where my sweet spot is, and the cocky, sexy-as-fuck grin on his face tells me he knows it.

"Maybe I want you to get a little heaven too."

"This will get me there," I pant, reaching for his cock, the thick outline clearly visible through his pants.

He grunts when I rub it, then retaliates by grabbing both my wrists and raising them over my head, pinning them to the arm of the couch with one hand.

The other is still busy between my legs.

"Dante." I moan his name. "I fucking need you."

"I'm right here." He stares down at me with an intensity that makes it feel like he's already fucking me. "Always gonna be here for you, princess."

I spread my legs, writhing on his wicked fingers. "Please."

He smiles at me, slow and dirty. Then he pulls his wet fingers out of my pussy and rolls one of my nipples between them, then the other.

I arch up, heat shooting through me, but he keeps my wrists

pinned down and leans over me, eyes on mine as he sucks one of my nipples into his mouth, licking it clean. "Fucking delicious."

"Shit, Dante," I gasp, squeezing my thighs together around the flood of arousal that brings on.

"Love your tits, princess," he mumbles against them. "They're perfect."

He takes the other one in his mouth, sucking it in whole, and filthy pleas tumble out of my mouth, begging him for more.

He groans, then releases my wrists and straightens up, taking a step away. "Perfect," he repeats, his eyes roaming over me possessively.

I sit up with a gasp, my chest heaving, and reach for his pants. "I'll show you perfect," I promise.

He smirks and catches my hand before I can free his cock, bringing it to his mouth and pressing a hot, tender kiss against the inside of my wrist.

"You do every fucking day, princess," he says, his voice still husky with need. "But I told you, I want to paint you... just like this."

My jaw drops. "You want to paint me *now?*"

"'Course I do," he says, heat in his gaze. "This is exactly the way I like to see you best. Soaking wet and on the verge of begging for my cock."

I narrow my eyes and scowl at him, because he's right. I'm definitely on the verge of begging for it. He got me all worked up, and—

And damn, I can't be mad. Not when every word out of his mouth, every heated look and cocky smirk, makes me feel like I'm the center of his whole world.

I prop one leg up on the seat of the couch, lounging back against it. "This is what you need to work out your emotions?"

Dante sets up an easel, preparing his paints. "It's a start," he says as I slide a hand between my legs and circle my fingers over my clit. "But you gotta stay still for me."

I stop moving, ripples of desire making my pussy clench.

His eyes flare with heat again. "Good girl. Now spread your legs a little wider and get those nipples hard for me again."

They're still puckered into twin buds, tight and sensitive from the attention he already paid to them, but if he wants me to give him a show, I will. I'm used to it, fucking good at it... except this is nothing like stripping. As Dante murmurs more filthy directions, getting me to pose the way he wants, his eyes skipping between me and the canvas he has angled away from me, I feel sexier than I ever have before.

I love the way his eyes burn for me.

I love the dirty things he wants me to do.

I love... him. The emotion is almost overwhelming, and it makes everything hotter, the deep sound of his voice turning me on until I almost can't stand it as he uses it to guide me into the position he wants.

"Just like that," he murmurs, his hand flying over the canvas. "Like you're dying to be fucked."

"I am," I say, my fingers trembling where he wants them to rest, just inches from my pussy. I wiggle them closer. "Let me show you."

He laughs, low and dirty. "You bet your ass I expect you to show me," he says, the deep sound of his voice stroking over my skin like it's made of sex. "Later."

"Dick."

"You can have that later too."

I arch my back, rewarded with a flash of heat in his eyes. "You sure you want to wait?"

"I'm sure you're worth the fucking wait," he says, holding my gaze until it's all I can do not to launch myself across the room and climb him like a tree.

I'm either going to need his cock or a distraction, because the man is about to make me come with his words alone.

I definitely plan on holding him to the promise to give it to me later, but for now, I go with the distraction. "How did you get into painting in the first place?"

His brush pauses for a moment, just a stutter, before he continues painting. "I told you a bit about my dad, yeah?"

I nod. "He was a hitman."

Dante's lips quirk up. "He was a lot of fucking things, but yeah, he was that. Took me out and trained me up from when I was young, and one of the things about it was... you gotta understand, princess, his clientele meant we were often working in some shitty-ass conditions. Dark. Dank. Dirty places with people who'd never had any fucking color in their life, and didn't even miss it."

I let my eyes roam over his shirtless torso. His body is gorgeous all on its own, but even more so with the bright, vibrant ink he's covered himself in.

I already know the nature of his father's work didn't bother Dante, but I can't imagine him ever enjoying moving through a world without color.

"The world can be an ugly place," I whisper, knowing that fact firsthand.

"You got that right," Dante agrees. "Literally, and with all the shit people do to each other in it too. But you know what one of my favorite things about my dad's kills was?"

He doesn't wait for me to respond. He shifts away from the canvas for a moment, holding out his left arm and turning it to expose the veiny surface of his forearm, bright with interlocking designs.

"The blood," he says, touching the art right in the center. It's an amazing piece of ink that looks almost three dimensional. A bullet hole exposing chipped concrete underneath, surrounded by an explosion of red splatters that overlay his other tattoos like an explosion of blood.

I suck in a sharp breath, realizing what he means. I know killing doesn't bother Dante, but I also know it doesn't thrill him. He's good at it, but not a fucking psychopath. "It was bright. It added color to that fucked up world."

He grins at me, then goes back to his painting. "Got it in one. That shade of red is still my favorite color. There's nothing else like it. It's fucking *life*, you know?"

"So how did that get you into painting?" I press.

"That was a little later in life. One of the first jobs I did on my own. The target was a true piece of shit. Ran a sex trafficking ring that catered to pedos, but painted a target on his head when he failed to tithe enough to one of the gang leaders who let him operate in his territory."

I shudder, his words bringing to mind some of the fears I had when Austin first took Chloe. "I'm glad you killed him."

"Yeah, I didn't hate the job, that's for sure," Dante agrees, putting down his brush for a moment and picking up a tool that looks like some kind of scalpel. He works on the canvas with it for a minute as he goes on. "The thing was, he was an oily fucker, good at watching his back. I had to stake out the hole in the wall he was operating out of for a couple of days before I could get him. Spent the time in this rat-infested shit hole with a good view of the door he used, tucked into this back alley over in the warehouse district."

I grimace, picturing it all too clearly after all the searching we did for Chloe around there.

Dante sees me, and laughs. "Yeah, you know how it is over there. Fucking ugly, in every sense of the word. But then there was this alley that the target snuck in and out of..." His eyes go distant for a moment, the hint of a smile dancing over his lips before he shakes his head and returns his attention to the canvas in front of him. "You never would've known it, but tucked away in all the concrete and piss and grime of the place, someone had painted the whole thing with this vibrant scene. Like a... a mural. Transformed the whole wall into some kind of urban warfare fantastical shit, dragons mixed with rocket launchers, all in colors just like this."

He holds out his arm, and I suck in a breath, imagining what it must have been like to come across that in such a fucked up place, doing what Dante was there to do.

"Exactly," Dante says softly, clearly reading the emotion on my face. "It blew my fucking mind. I've still got no clue who did it or why it was there, but the best part—" He grins, sharklike and fierce. "The best part was when I took the target out, right there as he stepped out of the doorway. Seeing his blood splatter across the concrete wall behind him, it was fucking beautiful. It was like I'd added something, my own mark, to this other scene. Like the rush of the kill was right there, emotions written in bright, vibrant colors instead of hidden away inside."

He paints a picture with his words that's just as vivid as anything he puts on canvas, and I find myself breathing hard, the distraction I was after not exactly working. The passion in his voice is just turning me on even more.

"How did you get from that to paint and canvas?" I ask, Dante's eyes snapping up to meet mine at the husky, needy tone.

"I was hooked," he says, his hooded gaze making me even hotter. "I didn't want to wait for another kill to make that kind of art again, so I went out and bought some supplies. Started fucking around with them, and..."

He ends it with a shrug, gesturing around to all the canvases displayed and stacked in the room.

I laugh, shaking my head in awe of him. "You're really good for having gotten your start just 'fucking around.' Every one of your paintings feels like an explosion of raw emotion, like I can't help but feel things when I look at them. They move me."

He grins. "I like that, princess. And you know, it's probably the same with you and your dancing. You didn't have formal training, right? But you got good at it because you loved it, and since you loved it, you wanted to do it all the time."

I sigh, his words pulling up a different kind of emotion. "Yeah. I... miss it, you know? Not dealing with drunk shit heads. I don't need an audience or anything. But the dancing itself was a way to just let myself go. Nothing else is like it."

"Ain't that the truth," he says, his eyes boring into me with an intensity that has a flood of heat rushing through my core.

I press my thighs together, clenching my inner muscles with a little gasp, and Dante's eyes burn even hotter.

"None of that, princess," he says. "You need to stay still for me. Spread those pretty thighs wide and show me what you've got for me."

"Fuck, Dante," I gasp, hating him for the torture a little as I do it. The kind of hate that I'd really love him to fuck right out of me.

He grins again, a dirty promise on his face as he goes back to painting. "Seeing you on that pole for the first time was sexy as hell. Like you said, there's nothing else like it. The way you wrapped your legs around it was all about your pleasure, not the assholes watching you. That was crystal fucking clear, and it made me want to pull you right off that stage and let you wrap those thighs around me instead."

"You did," I remind him, squirming despite my best intentions as my arousal starts to peak again.

"The fuck I did," he says, his eyes glued to the canvas. "I didn't get my cock inside you until you finished on that stage, but what I wanted to do was bend you over it with all those colored lights playing over your skin. Eat that sweet pussy of yours that you kept teasing us with until you screamed louder than that beat they had playing. Let you dance on my tongue for a while and then show me how fucking good you are at riding a pole by impaling you on mine."

143

"Shit," I whimper, arching off the couch as I dig my fingers into it to keep from touching myself.

"What's wrong, princess?" he asks with an evil grin. "Having trouble holding still for me?"

"You know what's fucking wrong," I pant, my inner thighs slick with my arousal as I clench my muscles, forcing myself not to squeeze them together because the cocky asshole told me not to.

Because I *want* to be on display for him.

Because even though holding still is the opposite of dancing, the feeling I miss—letting myself go to the music, letting it take control and move me—is a hell of a lot like the feeling I get when I submit myself to Dante's demands. To Maddoc's and Logan's too.

I trust them to move me, manhandle me, or hold me down, and it's exactly the same kind of rush as surrendering to the beat of the music and putting my body under its command. It's addicting.

"Touch yourself," Dante says, his brush moving languidly across the canvas in front of him as he rakes me with a possessive look. "But don't come, don't even fucking think about it, princess. Not until I say so."

"Asshole," I pant, shoving my hand between my legs so fast my head spins.

Dante chuckles. "I definitely won't say no to some back door action, but we'll play with that another time, princess. Right now, just finger yourself for me. Make yourself feel good. Get that pussy ready for what I'm going to give it."

I want to glare at him, but his dirty talk is turning me on too much for that. Instead, I do what he said and grind the heel of my hand against my clit, squeezing my legs together and half expecting him to tell me I have to spread them again so he can get a good view.

Hell, not just expecting him to... wanting him to.

Or else wanting him to make me.

"Play with those hot little tits for me too," he says instead, his voice husky and low as he watches me. "Don't get greedy and give it all to your pussy."

"Both," I gasp, doing what he says and using one hand to roughly squeeze my breasts the way I really fucking wish he would right now. "I can do both."

"Prove it."

I dip between my thighs and thrust three of my fingers inside myself, letting my head fall against the back of the couch as I fuck myself on them until I'm shaking with the need to come, pinching my nipples so hard that the pain spikes down to my core and almost tips me over.

"Fuck, Dante, I have to—"

"No."

The single word is as hard as the thick cock I can see straining to break out of his pants, and it sends white-hot heat rolling through my body.

I'm panting as I ride on a razor's edge of arousal, teetering at the brink and ready to shamelessly beg for what I need. "Please. Fuck. God."

"Nah, it's just me," he says in a sex-soaked timbre, "but keep begging like that, princess. It's hot as motherfucking hell. And work that pussy a little harder. I know how you like it."

I moan, doing what he says. Abandoning my tits so I can be as rough as I need it between my legs. Rubbing my clit hard and fast while I clench around my fingers and wish they were a fucking cock. Letting my head fall back as desperate, obscene sounds tumble out of my mouth and my pussy... oh fuck, my pussy...

"Come," Dante snaps. "Do it, princess. *Now.*"

I scream, the orgasm slamming through me on his command and whiting out my vision. It goes on and on and fucking on, the most intense pleasure I've had by my own hand in—

Ever.

"Fucking Christ," Dante says with a groan, dropping his paintbrush to the ground.

He's across the room in a flash, his pants shoved down and that massive cock of his out and in his hand while the waves of bone-melting pleasure are still rolling through me.

"You've got no idea what you do to me," he mutters, pinning my arms above my head the way he did before as he fits himself between my legs.

Then he drives into me, impaling me on his cock and ripping another scream out of me when it sets off a second shockwave of pleasure.

"That's it. Fucking scream for me," he demands, fucking me hard and deep. He lifts one of my legs over his shoulder, bending me in half. "Give me everything, princess."

I cling to him, my body his to control. His to dominate. His to fill up and own completely.

"Yeah. Fuck, yeah," he grits out, like he's either read my mind or I've got no filter. "That's exactly what I'm gonna do."

He pounds into me so hard that the couch slams into the wall behind it, and nothing else exists outside the need for more of everything he's giving me.

"Please, fuck, make me—"

"Do it." He releases the hold he's got on my wrists and slips a hand between us, pressing down on my mound so that his next thrust hits my g-spot like a lightning strike. "Come for me again, princess."

I tumble over the edge, throat raw from the screams of pleasure he loves to pull out of me as I obey him. He follows right after, his hips grinding against me as he fills me with his cum and whispers filthy praise in my ear, fucking us both through to the other side.

Our chests heave together as the intensity finally starts to recede, our bodies locked as close as they can be. I drag my eyes open, getting lost in the vibrant green of his gaze. Neither of us speak, but finally, my heartbeat starts to slow, falling into sync with his.

I wrap my arms around him, not wanting to be anywhere but here, and he pushes the hair off my forehead with an achingly tender look in his eyes, then presses a slow, languid kiss to my mouth. "Heaven."

I don't believe in that shit. Not in the traditional sense. But Dante almost makes me feel like it might be real after all, working the same kind of magic on my body, on my heart, as he does with paint on canvas.

"Show me," I whisper, remembering what he brought me here for. "I want to see what you painted."

"I already told you," he says, gathering me close and then, with his cock still buried inside me, rolling to his feet with me in his arms. "I worked out my emotions. Put them where I could see them."

Before I can reply to that, we're already there. Standing in front of the easel. Looking at... me. Spread out and wanton on a field of swirling colors, my body looks ethereal and beautiful, and my face—

My heart squeezes.

"That's not what I look like," I whisper, emotion clogging my throat as I cling to him.

His hands tighten on my ass, and I can feel his heart kick in his chest, bumping against mine. "Yeah, it is, princess. You're fucking gorgeous."

I can't tear my eyes off it. Most of his paintings are abstract, and I had no idea he could also do this. Something so realistic and yet also somehow *more* than real.

It's not just my face, it's an emotion he and I still haven't named to each other, right there on the canvas, like he said, for anyone to see.

A choked sound escapes me, and my hand goes to my

mouth. Tears well in my eyes, making this amazing piece of art, this piece of his *heart*, blur in my vision.

Then Dante turns my face back toward his.

"I lied to you earlier," he says, his face as serious as I've ever seen it, raw truth in his eyes. "I told you I care about you, but that's a cop out. I'm fucking in love with you, Riley. I *love* you. I—"

"I know," I cut him off as all my own emotions surge up inside me, making me cling to him. "I know. I love you too."

He grunts like the words have hit him hard, a single, powerful shudder moving through his body. Then he wraps his arms around me so tightly that my ribs ache and kisses me, inhales me like I'm the oxygen his soul requires to survive.

He kisses me for so long that all the shit swirling around us —the danger from West Point and the volatile future we're walking into and the horror show of possibilities that no doubt wait for us there—all of that fades to the background, eclipsed by this one little slice of heaven. By the one thing that's solid and real in my life. The one thing that matters.

This.

Him.

Us.

16

MADDOC

I'VE BEEN GONE MOST of the day dealing with the business of securing Reaper positions and preparing for whatever McKenna might throw at us next, but I still haven't done enough.

I'm not sure if it's possible to do enough, now that he has such a big cash advantage.

I scowl, pushing that thought away before it can gain any traction. We'll do whatever it takes, and since we won't back down until we take him down, "whatever it takes" *is* gonna be enough, by definition.

Of course, the other problem to contend with is that we're trying to second-guess a fucking psycho. He's always been a wildcard, but now he's just as dangerous as he is unpredictable, and that's going to be a deadly combination no matter how much planning and reinforcing we do.

I park the SUV in the garage, suppressing my daily twinge of annoyance over the loss of our Escalade, and walk in through the kitchen, still silently cursing myself for letting McKenna get so far ahead.

Not that I had a choice. My focus was and always will be on keeping Riley safe. There's no amount of money that will ever change the way I feel about her.

At least I made some progress today. I touched base with several new informants that McKenna won't realize are on my payroll. Hopefully, they'll be able to pick up any rumblings about what he's up to before he figures that shit out.

I stop in the kitchen and look through to the living room. I can just see the top of Riley's head over the back of the couch, but that's enough to make my worries fade into the background for now. Just knowing she's here calms my nerves, soothing the side of me that's been agitated and raging all damn day.

She belongs in this house, and I don't ever want to know what it's like without her here again.

I still have shit to do, but my legs carry me across the room instead of toward my office, and I don't fight it. Next to her is the only place I want to be right now, and for once, just for a minute at least, I'm putting what I want before what I need to do as a leader.

My beautiful butterfly looks up and smiles, and dressed in comfortable clothes without any makeup on or one of the flashier nose rings she likes, she's still sexy as hell.

She's even more than just sexy, though.

She's what I want to come home to *every* fucking day.

I sit down next to her, but there's a slight hesitation in her eyes as she places a hand on the center of my chest. "How did things go today?"

I grimace, then drape my arm across the back of the sofa and pull her into my side, where she doesn't have to see my expression. I don't really want to talk about my day or the necessary preparations we all need to make right now. She has a right to ask, though. She's caught up in this shit as deep as the rest of us are.

"Maddoc?" she presses, starting to pull away, like she's gonna try to sit up and search for the answers she wants in my face.

I hold her tighter, needing her close just as much as I want to shield her from seeing the turmoil I'm feeling about what's coming.

"It went as well as it could." I pause. Apologizing, explaining myself, looking weak, opening up about shit like feelings, all of that is a dangerous move in my world, and I've been betrayed enough in my life to know how stupid it is to show any vulnerability. And yet, everything's different with Riley. Besides, she already knows how I feel about her, so I go ahead and add, "I'm sorry I left so abruptly."

She shakes her head. "You don't need to apologize for that. I could've picked a better time to tell you all those things about Aus—"

"No," I cut her off sharply. I don't want to hear her say that bastard's name. "I'm glad you did. We needed to know what happened while he... had you." I almost choke on the words, rage bubbling up from the darkest depths of my soul again. Then I take a breath and bare my soul to her. "It fucked me up when McKenna took you. I hated every second that he had that power over you, every second that you weren't here. But come what may, you need to know one thing. He is never gonna get the chance to hurt you again. Not while me and my brothers are alive to stand in his way."

It's the barest admission that I might not live through the storm that's coming, but that's the only concession I'm willing to make. I'll have to be dead and gone before I let that son of a bitch get anywhere near Riley again, and I know Dante and Logan feel the same.

"I believe you," Riley whispers, looking stricken. "And I know you didn't want me to go with him in that alley, but it felt like the only option I had."

"Maybe it was." The admission kills me, but I understand what she means, because I feel it too. "I love you."

She melts into me, her eyes turning glassy with emotion. "I lov—"

151

I put a finger over her lush mouth, stopping her before she says it back. Not because I don't want to hear it, but because I need her to understand what I mean.

"It fucking consumes me, butterfly. This love isn't like anything I've ever felt before. It's not just here." I pull her hand over my heart and hold it there. "It's in every atom of my being. It's sunk into my goddamn soul. I've never felt this way about anyone before."

She sucks in a sharp breath, her eyes going wide as her fingers tremble over my heart. "Maddoc..."

I kiss her, brushing those gorgeous waves of color back from her face.

"Yeah, baby. I know. And I spent too much fucking time trying to deny falling for you. That mistake gutted me when that bastard took you away. If I'd missed my chance, thrown it the fuck away because I'd taken too long to man the fuck up about these feelings—"

"You didn't," she cuts in right before I get choked up. "I'm here. I'm not going anywhere."

I stare into her eyes, seeing the same steely determination there that I feel in my own soul. "Good. You know, when Sienna betrayed me, it pissed me off. Picturing her and McKenna together used to be enough to make me want to annihilate something. But that was nothing like what it felt when he had you. That shit was..." Words fail me. Well, maybe I've got one. "Torture."

A small hint of a smile passes across her lips despite the heavy subject matter. "That 'torture' you were feeling? I'm pretty sure that's what love is."

I have to laugh because it's fucking true. "Yeah, okay. I guess you're right." Then I get serious again. "But I didn't know it before. I thought the shit I felt before was love—"

"For Sienna," Riley whispers.

I nod, but I'm not interested in talking about her. She means nothing to me now. "It wasn't. Not like this. After she left, I was pissed, and that turned the 'love' off. What I feel for you is different. There is no off switch, and I don't know how to love you with anything less than my whole heart. With my whole everything. I feel it in my head, in my gut, in my fucking pores. It's like a fire that's burning me up from the inside, but instead of hollowing me out, it just makes me stronger. The only thing that even comes close is what I feel for my brothers."

Those beautiful eyes of hers spill over, but she wipes the tears away with a fierce determination and grabs my face, her soft hands framing it as she stares into my eyes. "I love you too, Maddoc. And I love Dante and Logan, just as hard. I'm in this as much as you are. I'd fucking die for you. Any one of you."

"Don't," I snap, my heart lurching in my chest. I squeeze my eyes closed and suck in a sharp breath, then let it out slowly. I don't look at her again until I can do it calmly, and then I murmur, "Don't say that. Ever. Or even fucking think it."

She slowly smiles, a challenge in it that heats my blood even as it warms my heart. "Don't tell me what to do."

I narrow my eyes, loving her so much it hurts. "You fucking like it when I tell you what to do," I growl, tugging her onto my lap. "And you'd better get used to it. I'm gonna piss you off, but I'm not going to apologize for needing to protect you. I'm gonna be an overbearing asshole, and all you're gonna do is thank me for it, butterfly. Because the thought of anything happening to you—"

My throat locks. I can't have that thought, because I can't breathe if I do. And if it actually happened? I'd go feral.

"I won't ever ask you to apologize for loving me," she says softly, smoothing her hands down my shoulders, then back up again to wrap around the back of my neck. "Or for protecting me. I just need you to understand that I feel exactly the same."

She leans closer, her breath tickling the side of my neck and those pert little breasts of hers flattening against my chest.

"And not to give away my big secret," she whispers in my ear, pausing to nip the lobe like she's trying to goad me into fucking her over the back of the couch, "but sometimes, I like your overbearing asshole side."

I grin, then spank the sweet little ass she's rocking over my hardening cock. "I know. That's why this works so damn well."

She gasps, then rocks back and stares into my eyes. "I said *sometimes*."

I smirk. "I know what you said, but I also know what you meant." I squeeze her ass. "Just like I know what you really like."

"Oh? And what is it you think I like?" she asks, lifting an eyebrow. The hitch in her breath and the way her pupils dilate with lust give her away, though. My butterfly craves exactly the kind of domination that gets me off.

She really is fucking perfect for me. For all of us.

"I know you'd like it if I told you to get on your knees and suck my cock right now."

I start to swell just from the thought.

Her cheeks flush as she feels it, my cock pushing up against the soft heat of her core. And I'm not wrong. She licks her lips, her gorgeous eyes lighting up with all those feelings we've just been talking about. Then that tight little body of hers starts to undulate over my dick, and she slowly moves herself off my lap to sink down between my legs, her eyes full of filthy promises as she holds my gaze.

"Maybe you do know what I like," she says, stroking me through my jeans and then reaching for my fly.

She pops the button... and my fucking phone rings, the shrill tone freezing us both in place.

My heart wants to shut out the fucking world for this woman, and that greedy little mouth of hers is definitely worth letting the world burn. But I can't. Not right now. Too much is on the line, and McKenna's not going to just sit on that money.

He's going to do as much damage as he can with it, and most of the tension I walked in the door with today is from waiting for the other shoe to drop.

The shrill ringtone sounds again, and Riley gives me a subtle nod, and the fact that she understands exactly what's at stake here and everything I need to do just makes me fall for her even harder.

I cover her hand with mine, keeping it on top of my dick in the hope that we can pick this up where we left off and the call will turn out to be nothing, then I answer my phone.

It's one of our informants, and I immediately go tense as I listen to him speak.

Fuck. It's started.

That second shoe didn't just drop; McKenna fucking drop kicked it straight into our teeth.

17

RILEY

I FEEL the change in Maddoc immediately, and all the sexy, fun energy we had going between us drains from the room as his face hardens into stone.

He says a few terse words to the caller, and the whole conversation is over almost before it begins.

"What happened?" I ask when he ends the call.

He makes eye contact with me, and it's like the whole world slows to a stop for one single, quiet second.

Whatever it is, it's bad.

Then everything happens all at once. Maddoc surges to his feet with a grunt, hauling me up with him as the sound of Dante and Logan's heavy footsteps thunder down the stairs.

"There's an attack on Reaper territory," Maddoc finally tells me as his seconds burst into the room. He shoves his phone back into his pocket and buttons his jeans, his straining erection all but forgotten as he turns grim eyes onto the others.

"Isaac called," Logan says without preamble. "We're going to lose six months' worth of product if the warehouse goes."

Adrenaline surges through my veins. Even without really understanding the details of how the Reapers operate, losing six months' worth of anything sounds a lot like the kind of hit that would cripple a smaller organization.

Dante straps on a holster as he catches my eye. "One of our warehouses is under attack," he explains while Logan tosses Maddoc a bulletproof vest and then brings a second one to me. "They're trying to burn the place down, but it's not just product. They're also keeping our people trapped inside."

"West Point?" I ask, my heart pounding as Logan secures the vest on me

"Has to be," Maddoc says grimly, already heading toward the door. "And we need to get down there right the fuck now. McKenna obviously knows it's one of our main storage depots. I upped the protection detail on it this morning, which is how they caught on before all the exits were blocked."

"From what Isaac reported, the extra men aren't gonna be enough to hold this shit off for long, Madd," Dante says as he arms himself with additional weapons, making them disappear into his clothing like they're a part of him. "This is a full assault."

A muscle tics in Maddoc's jaw. "I know. So fucking *move*."

I hurry out to the SUV with them, my stomach in a knot but a small, secret ball of warmth underneath it all about the fact that none of them questioned my involvement this time. None of them tried to stop me, or acted like I was weak or had to be tucked away and protected.

The vest Logan zipped me into doesn't count. If anything, it makes me feel even more like I'm a part of them.

This time, Maddoc gets behind the wheel and Dante takes the passenger seat as Logan pulls me into the back with him. He turns to me once we're on the road and presses something cold and heavy into my hand.

A gun. Of course.

I swallow, the grim urgency permeating the car suddenly feeling all too real and immediate.

"Do you remember how to use it?" he asks, an intensity behind his pale gaze that reminds me just how much he cares about me.

It settles my nerves, and I nod. Then, hoping for one of those illusive almost-smiles of his, I say, "Just aim at anyone with one of those stupid gold rings and pull the trigger, right?"

The corner of his mouth twitches. "Exactly." Then all humor drains from his face, and he closes his hand around mine, gripping the gun's stock with me. "Let's review the basics."

He makes me run through it a few times, and once he's satisfied, I look up and find Dante's eyes pinned on me through the rearview mirror.

"Bottom line, kill them before they kill you, princess. That's non-negotiable."

I nod, my stomach clenching with nerves.

"Almost there," Maddoc says from the driver's seat. He turns to Dante. "Call and tell Isaac to open the big door for us. We're coming in hot, and Vic and Amari should be right behind us."

Dante is on the phone before Maddoc finishes speaking, and a few seconds later we're speeding down a side street toward a warehouse that wouldn't look out of the ordinary at all if it wasn't on fire.

"Shit," Maddoc snarls as a bullet ricochets off the hood of our SUV. "Hold on tight."

My knuckles are already white from gripping the door handle and the gun Logan gave me, but I squeeze both a little tighter and close my eyes as Maddoc barrels up a small service ramp, straight into the warehouse at a speed that would have taken him right through the door if his people hadn't managed to get it open at the last second.

"Stay down and stay away from the fucking windows," he shouts, shielding me with his body as we get out of the vehicle.

The all-too-familiar sound of gunfire ricochets around us,

and I've got no idea whatsoever what the game plan is here. I just know that I'm not letting my men get in the way of any of those bullets without doing whatever I can to take out the shooter.

"Vic's gonna hold this entrance," Dante says as Logan melts into the smoky interior, low and fast and deadly. "Amari will flush out the attackers and try to salvage the product."

"No." Maddoc grabs him, his face a stone mask. "People first. The fire's spreading. We'll take them out and deal with the rest once our men are secure."

Dante nods sharply, then shoves Maddoc to the side and fires off a series of rapid shots at a shape I can barely make out in the dim, hazy light. The shape drops, and gunfire erupts all around us as someone—the one they call Amari, I think—starts laying down cover fire for a group of men who look familiar.

Reapers, I'm sure of it.

There are at least a dozen of them, and they give us quick nods and a few looks of relief when they see us. The smell of smoke is almost choking me, and the oxygen rushing in from the open roll-up door behind us has the flames deeper in the building roaring even higher.

I haven't seen anyone from West Point yet, but their bullets are flying at us in a steady barrage, and I see why Maddoc had us come in. The warehouse doesn't have a lot in the way of solid cover, and the SUV is a shield as much as a getaway vehicle.

Glass shatters somewhere overhead, shards of it raining down from the windows near the rafters, and somehow, the Reapers keep coordinating with each other through the chaos. Trying to clear an exit route for some of the Reapers that are trapped on the far side of all that gunfire.

"Stay close to me," Maddoc says, his gun trained on the open garage door as he pulls me behind him. "They're ramping this shit up."

He's right. Even I can tell that the gunfire is steadier now, the thundering roar of it almost nonstop. Suddenly, out of the smoke, I make out two guys running toward us, then another and another after that.

These aren't Reapers. They're coming at us with guns blazing, moving together like a well-oiled machine as they escalate the attack and make my blood run cold with fear.

"Maddoc!" I scream, tugging his arm.

He doesn't duck; he moves in front of me. Lifts his arm and takes aim, moving in tandem with the Reapers arrayed around us.

One by one, the attackers fall back or go down, but each time, another is there to take their place.

My hand shakes, but I lift my own gun and flip the safety off, aiming past Maddoc's shoulder. Determined to do my part to be an asset, not a liability. To help hold them back long enough to make a difference.

I shoot, and a surge of vicious satisfaction that's almost sexual goes through me when my bullet clips one of the attackers in his shoulder, causing him to spin to the side.

But the shot he was about to take goes wild, hitting one of the Reapers near us.

Maddoc curses, and I gasp, then clamp my jaw closed and take aim again, firing at anyone and everyone with a gun pointed our way. Over and over and fucking over, until Maddoc finally drags me back to the SUV and shoves me inside.

"The roof is starting to collapse." He turns and shouts back toward his people, "Fall back! Everyone out! *Now!*"

I don't know how they hear him over the chaos of gunfire, smoke, and shouting, but they do it. Dante drags the guy who went down from that stray bullet into one of the other vehicles, and Logan dives behind the wheel of our car as Maddoc covers me with his body in the back seat.

Sirens sound in the distance, and neither Maddoc nor Logan say a word as we peel out and careen out of the parking lot, driving deeper into Reaper territory. I shove Maddoc off me and twist to peer anxiously out the window. "Dante?"

"He's in Vic's ride," Maddoc answers, his voice clipped. "Got Kyle with him."

That must be the guy who was shot. Shot because Austin felt empowered by all the money I gave him access to. Shot because my bullet threw that fucker's aim off.

I start to shake, and Maddoc hauls me against him, the smell of smoke and gunpowder almost overpowering. "Stop it," he says sharply, grabbing my chin. "We're here. We're alive."

I nod.

His jaw clenches as he stares at me, then, with the smallest twitch of his lips, he murmurs, "This is where I get to be the overbearing asshole and you thank me for it. You're not allowed to imagine what if. Stop. We're here, and we're alive. That's the only shit that matters right now. We'll deal with the rest in a minute."

I nod again, but this time, I mean it. I can't go down that what-if rabbit hole or let any kind of guilt take hold. Austin did this. He's to blame. And everyone I care about made it out safe, which really is all that matters right now.

We pull up at another nondescript warehouse, and Maddoc gives me a short, sharp nod, then flips into leader mode. He's out of the SUV in an instant, his shoulders subtly relaxing once he's counted the other vehicles that tear into the lot and accounted for all his people.

Dante is standing near a low-riding car that has one side riddled with bullet holes, helping bandage up a young guy who looks vaguely familiar.

"Just got grazed, boss," the guy calls out to Maddoc with a tired smile. "You should see what the weasel I took down looks like."

We head over there, and Dante nudges Maddoc. "It could've been a lot worse. Those weren't McKenna's—"

"I know," Maddoc interrupts, cutting him off sharply.

"That wasn't West Point?" someone asks, all the Reapers starting to gather around.

"It was," Maddoc says, his face smoothing out. "McKenna is escalating, so we're gonna have to get a step ahead of this. Before we talk about how, I need a report on injuries and losses."

A few of the smoke-streaked men who must have been working in the warehouse when it all started step up, and they quickly rattle off details that go over my head. Grim ones, based on Maddoc's expression, but at least they confirm that despite some injuries, none of the Reapers are dead.

I can still see that Maddoc is fucking pissed, despite the calm facade he puts on for his people. The stress shows in that telltale jaw muscle and the tension in his shoulders, but I can't help but admire how he holds it together and focuses on making sure his people are okay. It sounds like the loss to the Reapers' business is going to hurt, but that's not Maddoc's people's fault, and he makes that clear.

It's no wonder they're so loyal to him. It's exactly why I love him too.

"How are you doing, princess?" Dante asks softly as Maddoc starts to wrap things up after reviewing the gaps in their protection that allowed the attack through.

I lean against Dante, accepting his arm around my shoulder.

"Better now," I tell him honestly, only half listening as the men around us get their orders from Maddoc about coordinating with Logan to fortify their territory even more.

Dante squeezes me, pressing a warm kiss against my temple, then herds me into the SUV as soon as Maddoc dismisses everyone. It's not until we're pulling back into the garage at the house that I realize that the low thrum of tension that accompanied us on the silent drive home is about more than just the aftermath of the attack.

"We gonna talk about this?" Dante asks when Maddoc kills the engine.

Maddoc gives him a look I can't decipher, but gets out of the vehicle and heads into the house without a word.

"What's going on?" I ask as Dante and Logan exchange a look.

"Come on, princess," Dante says instead of answering me, pulling me into the house with him.

Maddoc is in the kitchen, pacing.

"You cut me off back there, but you know I'm right," Dante says without preamble. "Those weren't McKenna's men."

"That was a West Point attack," Maddoc bites out, spinning to face Dante with a dark look on his face. Then he lets out an explosive breath, shoving a hand back through his hair and leaving the brown strands messy. "*Fuck.* They weren't McKenna's usual shit-for-brains goons. You're right about that. Those were military formations and tactics, and if I hadn't had extra security on hand, they would have taken our people out."

"They were mercenaries," Logan says flatly. "Expensive ones."

"Well, shit," Dante says with a heavy sigh. "I was hoping you'd say I was wrong, but I guess that answers the question of what that son of a bitch is doing with all the money he stole. He's not planning on fighting; he's planning on rolling right over us. Strong-arming his way into our territory with a bunch of hired guns."

My stomach plummets. Dante was kind enough not to finish that sentence.

Austin is planning on strong-arming his way into our territory with a bunch of hired guns... using the money *I* gave him.

18

RILEY

DANTE'S WORDS land between us like lead, the weight of them affecting each of the men as much as they do me.

Seeing that shatters my guilt. None of them blame me for this, and as dangerous as today proved to be, I can't regret going with Austin that day in the alley when it meant saving their lives. I can't regret signing over that money, because it means that we're all here to deal with whatever Austin throws at us, no matter how bad it looks right now.

"The Reapers are strong, Maddoc," I remind him, resting my hand on his arm. "You've made them strong."

That muscle in his jaw jumps, and I swear it's like I can hear his thoughts. No matter how fierce of a street gang they are, the Reapers aren't some kind of elite mercenary unit. Strength is different than training, skill, and superior firepower.

I swallow hard, ugly images filling my mind as I imagine all the ways this could be bad for the Reapers. With Austin bringing in the kind of people who can outfight them, it will only be a matter of time before West Point starts pushing the Reapers out of their territory, picking apart the entire organization, and taking out the members, the *people*, who are so loyal to Maddoc.

And if it feels that daunting to me, it's no wonder Maddoc looks stressed.

But he's a natural born leader, and after a moment, he shakes his head, then straightens his shoulders, looking each of his seconds in the eye. "Riley's right. We're strong. It doesn't matter what that piece of shit throws at us. All the money in the world can't buy McKenna true loyalty from his people. That's something a pathetic little fuck like him will never realize, and it's exactly why we're going to beat him."

He says it with conviction and both Dante and Logan murmur their agreement, but even as he speaks, I can tell Maddoc is still worried. Logan is clearly stressed too. He's holding himself stiffly, his body tense and motionless the way I've noticed he gets when he's full of big emotions.

After a moment, the impromptu meeting breaks up, and Logan leaves, heading upstairs quickly.

"Is he okay?"

Dante pulls me close and kisses my temple. "None of this shit is okay, princess, but don't worry about Logan. He's taking it hard 'cause we didn't see it coming. He has trouble with things he feels like he can't control or fix, but he'll do what he needs to do to deal with it."

I nod my understanding, but as Maddoc and Dante put their heads together, going over some tactical planning that I can't be much help with, I decide it's not good enough to just understand how Logan gets. He shouldn't have to deal with his feelings all on his own. I want to help him the way he's helped me in the past.

I want to love him—not just the feeling that's already in my heart for him, but actively. Proactively. I want to fucking be there for him, because I know how insidious the darkness is. How those kinds of thoughts can spiral if you let them, turning into something that feels impossible to break free from on your own.

My steps slow a little as I near his room, but I can't second guess myself. I'm starting to understand him more, and I know it's not just my imagination that the walls between us have been coming down.

Even if he turns me away, I need him to know that I'm here for him.

But just as I raise my hand to knock on his door, I hear him.

He's moaning my name.

Heat races over my skin like wildfire. There's no way that sound can be anything but Logan pleasuring himself, and my heart stutters in my chest. I'm no stranger to using orgasms to relieve the pressure of fucked-up situations, but it kills me a little to realize he's still choosing to do it alone.

I want him to come to me when he needs that kind of relief.

I want him to know he never has to be alone again.

Another low groan sounds through the door, and it's hot as fuck. It also gives me all the courage I need to push it open and step into the room.

Logan may have his demons, but I'll never shy away from them. I fucking love him, even if I haven't been able to bring myself to say so to his face. His demons are my demons. His darkness is my darkness. And when he needs relief, there's nowhere I want him to go for it other than to wherever I am.

He's standing next to his desk, one hand braced on the wall as he jerks off, and the slick sound of his hand moving over his cock has me squeezing my legs together, a gasp escaping me.

His head snaps up, those ice-colored eyes of his widening in shock and his urgent strokes stopping as if a switch has been thrown. His pants are hanging open, his fly down just far enough to free his shaft, and even though I know I caught him off guard in a vulnerable moment and there's every chance he'll reflexively shut down or push me away, maybe even violently, I don't retreat.

If anything, the hint of danger turns me on even more,

making me even more determined to show him just how much I want to be here for him.

His breath is ragged, his cockhead almost purple from the grip he has on his shaft, but other than that, the only thing that moves is his eyes, following me with laser-like intensity as I step farther into the room and close the door behind me.

I go to him and drop to my knees, the musky scent of his sex sending another rush of heat through my body.

This isn't about me, though.

Logan's nostrils flare, but he still hasn't told me to leave... or released the grip he has on his cock.

I reach up and run my fingers lightly over the back of the hand he has wrapped around his thick shaft. "You have me now."

A shudder goes through his body, and his hand loosens.

I lift it away and place it on the back of my head, keeping my eyes locked with his. "May I?"

His hand tightens on my scalp, fingers tunneling through my hair as he stares down at me. "It's always better with you," he finally rasps. "But this is—"

"What I'm here for," I cut in, instinctively knowing that what he'd been about to say would have been something along the lines of "too much" or "too intense," both of which would have been wrong.

Logan will never be too much for me. I crave his intensity, his darkness, his pain and desire to inflict it on me.

I trust him to give me all of it without ever taking it further than I can handle.

Now I just need him to trust me enough to unleash it on me.

He twists some of my hair around his fingers, making my scalp sting, but he still doesn't push me toward his cock, even though it jumps, precum beading at the slit, every time my breath gusts over it. I lean forward, making the sting from the way he's pulling my hair even sharper, and lick away the slick moisture coating his cockhead.

"*Fuck*," he grits out, grabbing my chin with his free hand and pulling my mouth open farther.

Then he slams his cock into the back of my throat.

I gag, tears springing to my eyes and my pussy suddenly so wet that I can't hold still. I squirm, grabbing onto his legs and pulling myself forward, needing more. Needing him to use me just as hard as he wants to.

"Hands behind your back," he says sharply, making me moan around the cock he's still got stuffed in my mouth.

I do it, loving his rough domination just as much as I love the fact that he's accepted my offer to use me, that he's letting me in, letting me do this for him when he so clearly needs it.

And god, I need it too.

I need the way he stares down at me, intense and heated, as he adjusts his grip on my chin and my head, then starts fucking my mouth in a brutal, relentless rhythm that pushes me right to the edge. And I need the way he slows down, fisting my hair even harder, before either of us reach our peaks, like no matter how badly we both need this, he wants to savor it too.

"Open your eyes," he rasps, pulling back until just the tip rests on my extended tongue.

I do it, saliva pooling in my mouth and running down my chin as I stare up at him.

"I like it when you look at me. I like seeing you break down like this." He runs a finger from just under my eye down to my jaw, no doubt tracing the path of the tears his rough use has brought to my eyes. "I like knowing you're doing this for me, pushing yourself for me. So don't blink, wildcat. Don't blink until I come. Don't blink unless you need me to stop. Blinking is your safe word right now, do you understand?"

I moan, nodding as much as his tight grip on my hair will allow.

"Good," Logan says, his icy blue eyes bright with lust. "Now suck me."

He slides back into my mouth, the expression on his face so heated that I feel like I'm going to combust. My jaw aches and my scalp burns and the combination makes my pussy wet enough that it almost feels like I could probably take all three of my men at once if Dante and Maddoc were here right now.

I don't mind that they're not, though.

Only Logan can give me this perfect combination of carefully ruthless domination exercised with iron control, so just like he told me to, I keep my eyes open wide, until tears pour down my cheek and they start to burn.

"Fuck," Logan grits out, thrusting down my throat and grinding against my face. "You look even better in tears. I want all of them. They're mine, wildcat."

My eyelids start to flutter. Not because I want this to end, but because my whole body is trembling for him, my need to come getting to be as desperate as my need for air.

But I don't want this to stop. Not until I get Logan's cum. So I force them open wider again, staring up at him with my heart in my eyes.

He shudders, then jerks his hips back, pulling his cock all the way out of my mouth. "Breathe."

I gasp for air, refusing to move other than the heaving of my chest, as he strokes himself in front of my face and stares down at me like I'm some kind of miracle.

"You make me so fucking hard," he whispers, his voice getting choppy. "You make me want to ruin you."

I open my mouth and extend my tongue, begging him with my eyes. If he wants to ruin me, he can. He can do anything he wants to me. The way he touches me pushes buttons I never knew I had before I met him; he takes me places I wouldn't have felt safe going with anyone else.

Logan groans, his face contorting as if he's in pain.

He's not.

He's about to come.

I strain toward him, my hands twisted together behind my back and still held firmly in place by the hand he has fisted in my hair, and his cock starts to spurt. He paints a single hot stripe of cum on my face before he shoves it back down my throat, harsh, guttural curses falling from his mouth as he finishes.

My pussy throbs so hard I almost can't stand it. And even though he told me not to move, I need to. Maybe I even want to, just to see what he'll do about it.

His cum dribbles down my chin, filling my mouth faster than I can swallow all of it, and with his cock still in my mouth, I scoop some off my face with my finger and shove my pants down, my vision entirely blurred now as my eyes burn from the effort of obeying his order not to blink.

I rub my cum-slicked fingers together, then slide them over my clit.

I moan. I can't help it. And without my permission, my eyes drift shut.

"Riley," Logan snaps, slowly pulling away from me as I force my eyes open again.

I wasn't safe-wording, and I see the moment he trusts that. Then I suck hard on the end of his shaft, not willing to let it go. He hisses, no doubt overstimulated, as I start rubbing myself hard and fast.

"Don't come," he grits out, and I moan from the combination of sexual frustration and intense arousal that his demand wakes up in me.

I have to come.

I'm so close that there's no way to stop it.

Not unless I stop touching myself, but I *can't*.

Logan suddenly tightens his grip on my hair, making me cry out when he uses it to haul me to my feet.

"I said. Don't. Come," he repeats, and the exquisite pain

that shoots down my body from my scalp freezes my impending orgasm in its tracks.

I teeter on the edge. The tiniest whisper of any touch at all —his breath, my own hair drifting against my skin, the slow slide of his cum as it meanders down my cheek—could send me over the edge.

"Please," I beg, my voice shattered.

This is what I need. He's what I need. I thought I was here to help him, be here for him, and I am.

But Logan will never let me forget that there's a deep, dark well of depravity in me that only he can ever satisfy.

"That's it. Cry for me," he says, his eyes searching my face with a hunger and passion that have me shaking. "Get me hard again so I can fuck an orgasm out of you. I need to take it, wildcat. I'm a killer. A monster. I need to know you want that."

"I do. I want all of you. I'm yours, Logan."

It's nothing but the truth, and it rips a broken, almost feral sound from his throat. Then he hauls me over to his bed and pushes me down, face first.

I catch myself with my hands, arching my back to present myself to him. I'm his to use. His to fuck in whatever way he chooses to.

"You took my cum," he says, shoving his hand between my legs from behind and rubbing at my pussy with a rough, demanding touch that has heat flooding my core and my thighs shaking. "You took it, used it, without my permission. You need to ask. You need to let me decide where it goes and whether or not you've earned it."

The raw, dark heat in his voice is just short of a threat, and it turns me on almost as much as the rough, possessive way he handles me. I know he won't hurt me. Not in any way I don't want him to. I *know* it, down to my soul. And it's thrilling beyond words to flirt with the monster he always claims to be, the killer I was terrified of when I first arrived at the Reapers' house.

Logan curls his fingers, pushing them inside me as he leans over my back and whispers in my ear. "Ask."

"Please," I say instantly, my voice wrecked from his cock. "Please show me how to earn your cum."

I can feel his cock, still wet from my mouth and already growing hard again, pressing against my ass. I can also feel the soot and grit in the rough material of his shirt, scraping against my back, reminding me of where we just were. Of the danger we faced together and the shit show that's coming for us.

He straightens up, taking his weight off my back, and pulls his fingers out of my pussy.

"I'm going to fuck you."

"*Yes.*"

"It wasn't a question," he says as I feel his knuckles brushing against my most intimate place. He's gripping himself, lining up his cock. Then he slides it between my legs, thrusting between them without entering me until I'm shaking and desperate.

"I should take you here instead," he says, abruptly dragging the head of his cock upward and pressing it against my asshole. "Wreck you in a way no one else ever has."

A shiver rolls through me as my body instinctively clenches from the unfamiliar sensation, pulling away from him.

He drags me right back, not letting me escape.

"But you're not wet enough in that hole," he says, circling it with his cockhead and waking up a ripple of pleasure I'm not prepared for. "I need to fuck you hard and fast, wildcat. I need to give you what you've earned. I need to come in that tight pussy of yours. Make sure I've filled you up at both ends. Give you what you came in here for. Is your pussy wet enough for that?"

"Yes."

"Why?"

"Because I... you... *please*, Logan."

I can't think.

He yanks me up so my back is pressed against his chest and wraps his hand around my throat, giving me another taste of that heady rush I got when his dick cut off my air earlier as he whispers in my ear. "Because sucking my cock turns you on. Hurting for me gets you wet. Letting me use you almost made you come."

I nod, feeling lightheaded. I've got no idea if it's because he's restricting my air or because the way he's using me is such a turn on. I only know I don't want him to stop. Not until he makes me come.

Not until he gives me *his* cum.

"I'm going to fuck you now," he promises, as if he can read my mind.

He doesn't waste any time, guiding his cock to my pussy and slamming straight into me, fucking me with an intensity that sends me flying, anchored only by the hand he keeps wrapped around my throat.

I've never felt like this before. I'm full of so many sensations that I feel like I'm floating outside my body. And at the same time, the need to come is so intense that I'm whimpering incoherently as he croons filthy encouragement in my ear.

"That's it, wildcat. You're so fucking sexy when you're full of fear, high on adrenaline, fighting the monster in me, begging me to end this."

Then he reaches around and pinches my clit, releasing his grip on my throat at the same time, and pain and oxygen flood my system in equal measures, making me come so hard that I nearly black out in his arms.

He fucks me through it, and I finally come back to myself—boneless and loose—just as he pulls out and coats my back with his release, coming with a string of low curses that sound like they've been ripped out of his soul.

It drips down the crack of my ass, and he pushes me down onto my chest, using his softening cock to rub the cum into my skin.

"Thank you," I murmur, wanting to sink right down into the mattress. I feel turned inside out, fully exposed to him in ways that I didn't even know were possible, and so close to him that it's all I can do to keep my feelings from tumbling out too.

But "close" and "open" are two things I know push Logan's boundaries to the limit, so it really doesn't surprise me at all when I feel him stiffen and start to pull back.

It doesn't surprise me, but I'm also not going to put up with it.

I'm the one who opened the door and walked in. And I'll pull down every one of the walls he puts up between us, take everything the "monster" in him can throw at me, until he realizes the truth.

I'm not going anywhere.

He'll never drive me away.

I love this maddening, damaged man, and if I can't quite say that to him yet, I can at least show him that he'll never scare me off.

I roll over and get to my feet, advancing on him as he retreats. "Look at me, Logan."

"I am," he says in that clipped, closed-off and utterly factual way he has.

I smile, letting my expression lay bare all the emotions he's not ready to hear.

"Look at what you did to me," I whisper as I reach him, bunching up the material of his smoke-and-gunpowder stained shirt and pulling him toward me. "I'm a mess. Your mess. And if you can give me all of that, you can at least kiss me too."

His brow furrows. "I'm—"

"Mine," I interrupt softly, not so subtly stroking the scar he left between my breasts. "So kiss me and show me that I'm yours too."

Something shifts in his eyes, then he slides his fingers through my hair and palms the back of my head, bringing his mouth to mine. Carefully. Intentionally. Deliberately. Completely in control.

I give in to him, opening for him without any hesitation, releasing his shirt so I can slide both hands up his chest and wrap them around his neck as I press myself against him.

I'm *his*, just like I'm his brothers', and I feel it the moment he lets himself believe it, turning the kiss into a possessive claim that has none of the desperation of the sex we just had, but every bit of the dark hunger that fueled it.

It feels good. It feels perfect. And whatever comes next, whatever that bastard McKenna throws at us as this war escalates, it's something that no one can ever take away.

Not from either of us.

19

DANTE

I wake up on the couch downstairs, my mind still turning over some of the scenarios Maddoc and I were working on last night. It doesn't surprise me that I fell asleep down here. We were deep in battle planning mode, and the urgency of this bullshit with West Point meant that neither one of us wanted to let up until we came up with an idea of how the fuck we're supposed to protect what's ours now that he's bringing in mercenaries who could theoretically mow our people down without lifting a finger.

Theoretically.

Obviously, that didn't work out so well for McKenna yesterday at our warehouse.

I smirk as I sit up, but then lose the expression in the face of hard facts. Yeah, we got all our people out without any casualties, but we lost a fuck-ton of product and worse, showed them what we're capable of.

I've got no doubt at all that trained operatives like he sent after us at the warehouse are going to use what they learned from our response to hit us harder next time.

"Fuck," I mutter, needing some goddamn coffee before I deal with that thought. I smell some, and if I had to guess who's in the kitchen this early making it, I'd go with either Logan or Riley.

My bitch-ass mood evaporates in a wave of heat. I went upstairs to grab some shit Madd and I needed to look at last night from the library next to Logan's room, and there was no mistaking the sounds coming from behind his closed door.

I grin, adjusting my morning wood when things get a little tight in my pants as it reacts to that memory.

There will never be a time when Riley's pleasure doesn't get me going. The woman is the hottest thing in existence, and all this love shit between us just adds fuel to the fire.

Although I've gotta admit, so does what she has going on with Logan.

It's crazy as hell to see him opening up to her too. I'd lay down my life for him, but I never thought I'd see the day he'd admit to wanting someone. Or, hell, allow himself to get close enough to have someone, what with all his control issues.

I guess it just took finding a woman who meshes perfectly with all his jagged edges, and it's not even like she smooths them down, she just... fits. It's fucking incredible, and if I'm being honest, I don't think there's any way I could have the feelings for her that I do if she didn't have something just as deep with both my brothers too.

Would I still want to fuck her if she didn't? Sure.

Crave her pussy like a fucking addiction? I did, right from the start, after that first incredible fuck at the strip club.

But I had no idea at the time that it would turn out to be anything more than that. That she would become something essential to my existence, something as necessary to both me and my brothers as air. Something that honestly makes me wonder how any of us functioned before she got here.

Not that we had problems working together. We're fucking family. We've lifted the Reapers up to be a serious contender in the city. But until Riley came, all of that was still missing something that I'm pretty sure none of us realized was even possible.

She... completes us.

Something clatters in the kitchen, and the low curse that follows has me grinning.

It's her, and I scrub a hand back through my hair and shake the stiffness out of my limbs, then head that way to greet her.

Fuck, she's gorgeous. She doesn't see me at first, turned away and facing the counter, and when I come up behind her and move her long wavy hair aside to nuzzle her neck, I notice some light marks Logan must have left there last night.

"These look good on you, princess," I say as I lean down to nip one.

She jumps, then turns in my arms and blinds me with her beauty all over again. "Good morning."

"Morning." I kiss her properly. It's required. Then I run my fingers over the faint finger marks on her throat. Not love bites. Logan had his hands around her throat. "I'm glad you two are working your shit out."

"Me too," she says as her face flushes with color and she gets a faraway look in her eyes.

She lets out a soft sigh, her body moving against mine in a telltale rhythm that I easily recognize. She's thinking of what she did with him, and it turns her the fuck on.

My cock urges me to go with that, but I tell it to shut the fuck up for a second.

"I'm serious, princess," I say, cupping her face. "I mean it. You're so fucking good for him."

"He's good for me too," she says as more of that flush floods her cheeks. "He helps me understand a part of myself that I see reflected back in him. Not just understand it, but... be okay with it."

"Okay?" It comes out like a growl. "You'd better be a hell of a lot more than just 'okay' with yourself. Every part of you is fucking incredible, and you need each one, all the colors, to make the whole picture. The picture I'm fucking in love with."

I never thought I'd say that to anyone. Now, I'll fight every day for the privilege of telling her.

She sucks in a sharp breath, her eyes shining up at me, and I've got no idea who moves first, but our kiss is explosive. Fucking perfect. It's everything I need to get me going for the day.

And then it's fucking interrupted.

The sharp knock on the front door ricochets through the house, quickly followed by an insistent jab on our doorbell.

I loosen my arms around her as Maddoc and Logan come thundering down the stairs, then pull her along with me as we follow them to the front door.

When Maddoc answers it, I recognize the man on the other side instantly. We all do, even though I'm pretty sure my brothers don't know his name any more than I do. Not that it matters. What matters is who sent him.

The Six.

"They sent me with a message for you."

Logan goes still, and I push Riley behind me. Maddoc keeps his cool as per usual, but I can see the tension in his shoulders. "What is it?"

"They require your presence at Saraven tonight."

Madd doesn't push him for more, because that's not how this shit works. Once he gives us the time we're expected, he leaves, and it's Riley who breaks the silence.

"Maybe... they'll help?"

"That's not what they do, butterfly," Maddoc says gruffly.

She takes a deep breath, then puts on a determined smile. "Well, then they're not going to help West Point either, right?"

"Right."

I exchange a look with my brothers. Technically, that wasn't a lie, and damn, I love our girl even harder for trying to keep our spirits up. Still, I see my own gut feeling reflected back in Maddoc and Logan's eyes.

Whatever The Six want, it's ain't gonna be good.

We head to Saraven, the upscale club that's understood to be neutral ground, once it gets dark out. The four of us are silent as we're ushered through the ritzy front areas of the club to the same room we were summoned to last time. And just like last time, the six true leaders of Halston's underground are seated behind a long table on a raised dais, the only piece of furniture in the room.

Also like last time, shortly after we're brought in front of them, McKenna is shown in with a posse of his goons posturing behind him.

I scowl before I can help it, then school my face fast. But fucking hell. If we were anywhere else, I'd be tempted to end this thing permanently by putting that shit stain in the ground right now. Next to me, Maddoc suppresses a barely audible growl, no doubt having much the same thought. Even Logan twitches a little, the barest hint of the raging emotion we're all feeling about those assholes rippling through his normally impenetrable facade.

"Thank you for coming," says the dark-haired woman in the middle, her blue eyes piercing even from a distance.

Ayla Fairchild. If ever there's a woman whose spine of steel reminds me of our princess, at least by reputation, it's her.

Maddoc murmurs some platitude in greeting and McKenna proves he's as dumb as he is aggressive by failing to show her respect as he grunts his response.

Ayla doesn't call him on it. None of The Six do. But I can see on their faces that each takes note of his attitude.

It's almost enough to lighten my spirits for a second.

Almost.

"You've been called in because, despite our earlier warning, there was another large altercation that brought the attention of the police where it shouldn't be," Ayla starts without any further preamble. "That's unacceptable."

I hear Maddoc's teeth grind, even though he keeps his face outwardly calm.

Before he can formulate a response, McKenna jumps in.

"West Point is happy to follow your directive, ma'am," he says with an ingratiating smile. "All my people have been warned. But when the Reapers start shit with us, we gotta defend, you know?"

Ayla raises one perfectly groomed eyebrow. "No. I don't know. Are you saying that the Reapers are responsible for the shoot out and warehouse fire that drew so much attention last night?"

"That's right," McKenna says, puffing out his chest. "They fucking ambushed us."

"That's not what happened," Maddoc says, his voice hard. "The warehouse was ours. The attack happened on our territory."

Ayla turns her attention to Maddoc. "Attack?"

McKenna scoffs loudly. "That's not—"

"Be quiet."

Ayla doesn't raise her voice, or even look at him, but I guess the piece of shit does have a shred of self-preservation instinct after all, because he actually shuts the fuck up.

His face sure as shit doesn't like being treated like that, though.

I almost smirk. I've got self-preservation instincts too though, so I don't.

"What happened?" Ayla asks Maddoc. "Are you contradicting McKenna's account of this mess?"

He doesn't twitch, doesn't even look toward the West Point

delegation, and I get it. My brother has a lot of control, and right now, he needs it to navigate the treacherous waters we're stuck in, called on the carpet like this.

But some things—and Austin motherfucking McKenna is one of them—are enough to break even Maddoc's iron control.

Especially when I note the fucker eyeing our girl with a lecherous gaze that makes me want to pull out both his eyeballs and piss on their crushed remains.

I subtly shift my position, blocking his view of her as Maddoc gives The Six a clipped, succinct description of what went down with those fucking mercenaries yesterday. Not that he comes right out and says McKenna hired trained operatives, but he makes the details clear for anyone who knows how the dark underbelly of this city operates as well as The Six do.

Like we told Riley earlier though, they ain't here to help us, so it's no surprise that they take it in without much of an outward reaction.

On the plus side, I can tell they're skeptical of McKenna's version of events. They're too fucking smart not to be.

"Is that it?" Ayla asks once Maddoc's done.

"No," McKenna snaps. "He's lying. They lured our men there. Took some of them out. We demand retribution."

The look she gives him is so cold she could give Logan's heart-of-ice impression a run for its money. "You're not in a position to make any demands here, Mr. McKenna. And while we won't tolerate either of your organizations continuing to put what we've built at risk by drawing unnecessary attention to areas we'd prefer to keep law enforcement out of, at the end of the day, our job isn't to be arbiter in your disputes, or to dole out consequences relating to an individual gang's grudges. Our role is to maintain order in the Halston underground, and make no mistake, we *will* do that."

A vein starts to throb in McKenna's temple, but much to my disappointment, the fucker holds his tongue.

I would love to see what would happen to him if he actually forgot who we're speaking to. Especially when his body language draws a sharp look from Marcus Constantine, another member of The Six whose uniquely colored eyes make him unmistakable. Despite that, the grumbling agreement McKenna finally gives them has a lot in common with a middle finger when delivered the way he offers it, but Maddoc confirms our understanding on behalf of the Reapers without further incident, and they dismiss us shortly thereafter.

It ain't good, but it's not as bad as it could have been. Although I'd be lying if I said their final words, delivered by Marcus, aren't ringing in my ears as we leave.

"This will be your last warning," he says, no inflection in his voice.

He didn't need any. The aftermath of their rise to power here in Halston makes it clear what will happen to anyone who crosses The Six, and the look I share with my brothers just drives home the fact that staying off their radar while we do whatever we have to is gonna make it that much harder.

20

RILEY

I BARELY TAKE note of the ornate surroundings we pass through as one of The Six's attendants leads us out of Saraven. Earlier in the day, a small part of me had almost looked forward to coming before The Six again, if only because I wanted another chance to see that the connection I'm sure is there between Ayla and a few of the men—the one that gave me hope for the relationship I'm in now with the Reapers—is as solid as it seemed the first time they called us down here.

The minute Austin walked in the room, though, I forgot all about that, overcome with a sick shakiness that it took everything in me to hide from him.

Now, on our way out, all three of my men close ranks around me, and it helps. The minute we get outside though, with Austin and his entourage hot on our heels, I'm on edge again.

The club is neutral territory, but that doesn't apply to the street in front of it.

"Easy, princess," Dante murmurs, taking my arm and crowding even closer to me. "McKenna's not that stupid."

I give him a shaky smile, comforted by how easily Dante reads me even if I'm not sure I agree with him about Austin.

It's true that no violence flared up between the two gangs once we left Saraven last time, but Austin's cockier now. He's gained power along with the money he stole from me, and he knows it. Hell, he practically flung it in The Six's faces back there, the wins he's got under his belt now obviously going to his head.

So it's really not a surprise when he stops and blocks our way as soon as Saraven's doors close behind us.

He smirks, his eyes seeking me out even as my men use their bulk to try to block his view.

"I've missed you, wifey," he calls out, the faux endearment making bile rise in my throat. "But I'm glad to see you've still got a few mementos of our time together. I should've hit you harder, but don't worry—I'll have to be sure to give you a few more signs of my affection before those bruises fade completely."

I lift my chin, refusing to let his taunting words get to me. It's true that he did some damage with that beating, but Logan doctored every single mark the bastard left on me. They're healing well, and none of them will be permanent—unlike the marks Logan has given me, the ones I bear proudly.

"You ever lay another hand on her, and I'll cut it off," Maddoc promises Austin grimly as all three of my men bristle around me, their bodies going tense and their hands twitching toward the weapons that it would be suicide to draw here.

Austin laughs, then lunges toward Maddoc only to stop short, a hairsbreadth in front of his face. "She's my lawfully wedded wife. And after I pick apart your territory, piece by piece, I'll do the same to her. It's my right."

"It's your fucking death sentence," Dante says as Maddoc stares Austin down, his hulking body poised for violence.

On my other side, Logan's utter stillness promises the same thing, and I honestly don't know if we're going to walk away from this without any bloodshed, no matter how suicidal starting something right in front of The Six's base of operations would be.

I also don't know if I care.

I want Austin's blood to spill.

I want to see it spread across the concrete, adding some fucking color to this dark, dangerous world.

The tension is so thick it's almost choking, and for a moment, I picture it so clearly, exactly the way Dante described it to me when we spoke of his art, that I almost think it's actually happened.

A sound escapes me, not anything more than a faint puff of breath, but it breaks the stare-off between Austin and Maddoc, drawing Austin's eyes to me like a vulture to rotten flesh. His gaze turns lecherous, and he draws in a deep breath, like he's some kind of feral animal on the hunt.

"Wifey."

The bastard draws out the word like he can taste it, a sick hunger in his gaze, and Maddoc snaps, surging forward and slamming his body into Austin's. Somehow, Maddoc has the control and presence of mind not to draw his weapons, and his seconds follow his lead. It's still violent enough to send Austin stumbling backward, a look of unfiltered rage on his features as his men scramble out of the way, leaving him sprawled on his ass.

"She'll never be that to you, no matter what a piece of paper says," Maddoc says in a strained, raspy voice. Then he turns his back as Austin pushes himself back to his feet, cursing almost loud enough to drown out the pounding of my heart as it surges up into my throat.

"That's *your* death warrant," Austin hisses as Maddoc grabs my arm.

"We're leaving, butterfly," Maddoc says to me, ignoring West Point completely as he stalks toward the SUV.

Dante and Logan close ranks behind us, protecting our

backs, but I'm shaking with adrenaline, shocked to my core when we actually make it to the vehicle without anyone getting a bullet in the back.

Maddoc doesn't let go of me, sliding into the back seat with me as Dante takes the wheel. He doesn't speak until the engine starts up, and when he finally does, it guts me.

"I fucking hate that he married you."

I swallow hard, tears springing to my eyes, but I hold his gaze anyway and lift my chin, because we've already had the conversation about me doing whatever I needed to while I was West Point's captive—including marry their bastard of a leader.

I'm sure Maddoc knew that's what Austin was planning for me the second I agreed to go with him. After all, it's exactly what the Reapers planned to do before Maddoc and his seconds had a change of heart.

But a part of me is still disgusted that I allowed myself to be tied to Austin like that, even though I had no choice. To my shame, I feel tears sting my eyes before I can actually answer Maddoc.

His gaze instantly softens, and he pulls me into his arms. "It doesn't fucking matter, butterfly. You're not his."

"I'm not."

"You'll never be his."

I just nod, but he doesn't let go and I don't move away, and we pass the rest of the ride in silence. Once we're back at the house, Maddoc is still obviously in his head, sorting out his feelings, and after giving his seconds some quiet orders about things that they need to take care of tonight, everyone splits up.

Maddoc heads to his office, and I give him his space, needing a little bit of my own.

I thought I'd already come to terms with the darkness I discovered inside me here. I've even found a way to twist it into something good, something deep and true that I share with all these men, something that binds us all closer in three unique ways.

Tonight, with Austin's eyes moving over my skin like acid, I realized there's something deeper inside me. Something even darker. Tonight is the first time I wanted blood on my *own* hands, and it wasn't even about how sickened I am by Austin's fixation on me. It was the threat to my men. He was goading them, and if it had worked, if Austin had made the Reapers retaliate in front of Saraven, I have no doubt at all that The Six would have taken Maddoc, Dante, and Logan out without blinking an eye.

I wanted—I still want—to kill him for that.

Instead, I decide being alone with my dark thoughts isn't any better for me than it was for Logan last night, and I go to Maddoc.

He's in his office, his back to the door and his eyes locked onto the map he keeps on the wall, each gang's territory clearly marked out and a series of notations covering Halston's familiar streets to indicate allies, enemies, and other designations I don't understand.

He doesn't turn around when I enter, so I circle his desk and stand in front of him, the bloodlust inside me calming, receding, just by being in his presence.

This is what I need. The reminder that it's not our enemies that matter, it's the fierce, burning love I feel for these men.

"Butterfly," Maddoc says, his voice stiff and raspy from disuse. He reaches for my hair, twining the long strands of purple and blue around his fingers. Then he tugs me toward him.

I go willingly, settling on his lap. "He can do it," he says, his eyes moving past me to the map again. "He can take apart everything I built. Break up our territory, piece by fucking piece."

"You built it piece by fucking piece," I remind him, cupping his jaw and bringing his eyes back to mine. "He can't take anything apart that really matters."

A flash of anger surges across his face. "You're saying my territory doesn't matter? The gang I fucking bled for? The *Reapers* don't matter?"

"No. Never. I'm saying the opposite. The Reapers are the only thing that matters, but the Reapers aren't your territory, Maddoc. The Reapers are your people. Buildings are replaceable. People aren't. That's what he doesn't understand. He'll blow that money and he'll cause some damage, but you've got to play the long game. If you need to give up territory to keep the Reapers safe, you should do it, because he can't break that. He can't take it apart. They're loyal to you, not to the streets you've claimed."

He stares at me long and hard, his arms locked around my body like a vise. Then he lets out an explosive breath, some of the tension draining out of him.

He leans forward, resting his forehead against mine. "Where the fuck did you come from, butterfly?"

I twine my arms around his neck. "The real question is 'where am I going,' and you already know the answer to that."

"No fucking where."

I nod, repeating it like a promise. "No fucking where. *You're* my territory. And I'm yours. The only thing that's important is that we both, that all of us, live to fight another day."

It's always been my motto. It's how I survived. How I built a life for Chloe. How I made it through my captivity and how I'm going to make sure that my men and I make it through this shit storm, whatever McKenna throws at us.

Maddoc's eyes drift back to the map, and I can see that he's still feeling tortured by what's about to come at us. He's a powerful man, and it must be hell for him to realize that, in one area at least, McKenna truly does have more power than he does right now.

189

Still, my words seem to have bolstered him a little bit, and it helps ease the ache in my heart from all the weight he carries.

"Promise me you'll do that," I whisper, drawing his attention again. "Promise me that no matter what, you'll live to fight another day. That you'll be here for me, and for your brothers, and the Reapers. We need you. You're an amazing leader to your people, and I—"

My voice cracks, but he already knows.

"I promise," he rasps, burying his face in my hair and breathing me in. He squeezes me tight enough to make my ribs ache, and he doesn't let up, not for a long, long time.

And I don't want him to.

I'll always be willing to hurt for this man, and nothing on this earth will ever make me want him to let go.

21

MADDOC

I CLING to Riley for a long moment, just needing to be close to her while that gut-wrenching promise settles between us. Needing to feel her softness, her nearness. Her love.

There was a time that this need would have made me feel weak, but that's bullshit. Nothing about Riley is weak, and everything about her makes me stronger.

I don't know if she's right about me being a good leader, but I do know she's right about my people. It's the thing that makes me different than my father, the reason I've been able to build the Reapers, to earn their loyalty, when—for all his street smarts and connections—my father was never able to rise up in Halston's underground.

I learned a lot from him, but some of the lessons were what not to do. And one of those, the one that I've never wavered on, is people first, always.

Keeping the Reapers who've pledged themselves to me alive is more important than anything, and it's the worst fucking feeling in the world to know that I might have to give up what I've fought so hard for in order to make that happen, but I needed the reminder.

I fucked up. I'm not sure exactly how or where I could have

done shit differently to put us in a stronger position right now, but if I'd been the leader Riley sees me as, the one I want to be, I wouldn't be failing my organization the way I will be when I fulfill that promise I just made to my butterfly. I wouldn't be faced with the choice that isn't really a choice—to let Austin take what's ours, or to protect the whole reason we exist. Our people.

Riley makes a soft sound, shifting on my lap, and I realize I'm holding her too tightly. I relax my arms a little and lean back, tipping her chin up. "You're right. I hate it, but you're right. Thank you, butterfly."

"You never need to thank me," she says, the love shining from her eyes almost eclipsed by her faith in me.

It's almost painful to see, because failing the Reapers isn't the only thing fucking me up right now. I failed her too. I let that son-of-a-bitch fucking *marry* her. Hearing him call her "wifey" tonight was like a knife between my ribs.

"I fucking hate the idea of you being with anyone but me and my brothers," I growl, the truth bursting out of me as I dig my hands into her soft body, marking her, claiming her.

She gasps, and I know I'm hurting her a little.

I also know she'll welcome it.

"I never will," she promises, fire flashing in those bottomless whiskey eyes of hers. She doesn't fight the bruising hold I've got on her. She leans into it, cupping my face again and staring right into my fucking soul. "Do you hear me, Maddoc Gray? I only belong to the three of you. You, Dante, and Logan."

It's nothing but the straight-up truth, and I know she means it with every fiber of her being... but I'm still the fucking caveman who can't get over the idea that even if he didn't fuck her, McKenna still married her. *Is* still married to her.

It grates on me to the point that I can't fucking stand it, and I know I'm gonna have to do something permanent about that issue. Soon. But for now, what I need is something else. I need to fuck her, fill her up, mark my own claim on every goddamn inch of her gorgeous body. Wipe that word out of her memory and the taint of that bastard from between us.

I kiss her. It's brutal and savage and fills my mouth with the coppery taste of her blood as our teeth clash together, but my fierce little butterfly doesn't shy away from it. She meets me with a ferocity of her own, my perfect match in every way that matters.

"You're mine," I mutter against her mouth, smoothing my hand down that amazing hair of hers and then wrapping the strands around my fist and yanking her head back so I can suck on her throat. I want to claim her so goddamn thoroughly that no marriage vow to another man will ever keep us apart.

She arches into me, giving herself just as completely as she always does, and there's nothing on the fucking planet—not my territory, not the respect of my people, not even my vengeance on McKenna—that I want more than this, right here, right now.

I need the whole fucking world to know she's mine. That she belongs to me and my brothers, and that we'll destroy anyone who ever tries to take her from us.

"Maddoc," she gasps as I scrape my teeth over her collarbone and rip her shirt open, baring her for me the way I need.

Nothing can be between us. Nothing can block me from having her. Not fucking ever.

"You belong here," I growl, pushing the torn fabric aside and squeezing her breasts together so I can suck both of them at once. "You fucking belong to *me*. To *us*."

Her hands land in my hair, the filthy sounds I pull out of her turning my cock into steel.

She's straddling me, that hot pussy of hers rubbing over my shaft as she writhes in my arms, but there's still a barrier. Still something trying to stop me from taking what's mine.

"Up," I demand, digging my fingers into the crack of her ass.

She lifts her hips and helps me as I get rid of that barrier, yanking her pants off and tossing them aside before putting her back where she belongs. Right over my cock.

She's so fucking wet that my fingers sink right into her, the silky little scrap of her panties easily pushed to the side. "I need to be inside you. I need my cock right here, right where it belongs."

"Do it, please, fuck, *Maddoc*."

She's panting hard, just as desperate for this to happen as I am, and she lifts herself up, practically clawing at me, just enough for me to free my cock before I shove her back down on it.

The sounds she makes when my shaft spears into her shoots liquid fire down my spine, and I take her mouth and swallow it, claiming every fucking bit of her as her pussy clenches around me, gripping me like a vise, milking me until I'm in serious danger of busting a nut before we even begin.

It feels too fucking good, but it's not enough.

I need to fucking wreck her.

I need to push her over the edge before I get mine. It's the only thing I'll be satisfied with.

"Say it again," I demand as I grip her ass and lift her, dragging her up and down my cock as she pants into my mouth, her hands greedy and demanding as she pulls herself closer, clings to me and begs for more. "Tell me who you belong to. Tell me what you need."

"I'm yours," she gasps, her lips crushed against mine as we kiss wildly. "All of yours. I need your cum inside me. I need to be filled with you. Need to feel your claim dripping out of me. I need... I need..."

I groan, fucking her harder. Hard enough that she can't speak, her words trailing off into a whimper.

"Gonna give you all of that, butterfly. Fucking everything," I promise, breathing her in, licking into her mouth and letting the whole fucking world fall away as I take what belongs to me and drive into her until we're both on the edge of shattering apart.

Something cracks in the chair under my ass as I slam her down on my cock again, grinding up into her perfect heat as I rip her panties off, needing to get at her clit. Needing to send her fucking *flying*.

I thumb the little nub and slap her ass hard enough that my hand burns, and she screams for me. Coming apart on my cock, head thrown back and soul laid bare for me.

She's everything. Every fucking thing I could ever want, and I *would* die to keep her.

But only after I kill the motherfucker who dared to lay a claim on her.

"Madd. Oh god, I... fuck," she gasps brokenly, her pleasure rippling through her in visible waves.

It's the most beautiful fucking thing I've ever seen, and I grip her hips and drive my cock into her even deeper, greedy as all hell to keep it going. To get even more. To wipe everything but the bliss she's feeling out of her mind.

She drags her eyes open, cheeks flushed and mouth wet and panting, and stares down at me as I raise her up and drop her on my cock again.

"Maddoc," she whispers, her whole heart in the word.

"Fuck," I groan, my orgasm ripping through me without any further warning. My balls unleash like a fury, my cum pumping into her so hard that it blacks out my fucking vision for a second. "Riley, shit, baby, *Jesus*."

I'm holding her too tightly again. Squeezing her until her breath is nothing but short, sucking gasps.

I don't care. She's mine. I'm never letting her go.

"I fucking love you," I murmur, burying my face against her neck as my cock gives one final pulse inside her. "So damn much."

She strokes my shoulders. The back of my neck. Cups my face.

"I love you too. With my whole soul," she whispers, the words filling me with a sense of true peace.

It can't last. I know that. There's a battle to fight, and the worst is yet to come.

But when she sighs softly in my arms, melting against me, and presses a soft kiss against my throat, it's enough.

Nothing fucking lasts, but whatever hell we're about to wade through is worth it when it means I get this.

22

RILEY

Maddoc looks exhausted when we all gather in the living room the next day, like he hardly slept at all after we finally went our separate ways last night. But despite that, I see a new determination in him that sparks warmth in my chest. Especially once he starts to discuss his plans for the Reapers.

As grim as the subject is, I know that I helped him make his peace with what needs to happen, and being able to give him that after he's given me so much means more than anything to me.

"McKenna's going to come at us hard after you put him on his ass like that yesterday, Madd," Dante states matter-of-factly.

"He was always going to come at us hard," Logan says. "This has been personal for him from the start."

Maddoc nods. "You're both right, and starting now, every time he attacks, the standing orders are going to be to fall back."

It's a testament to their trust in him that the only reaction Dante or Logan have to that statement is a widening of their eyes and a tense silence.

I'm seated on the couch, next to Logan, while Dante stands with his arms crossed and one hip resting against the window sill. Maddoc paces in front of us, but comes over and squeezes my shoulder as he looks between his seconds and explains. "We don't have the resources to go head to head with him. Our only choice is to play the long game."

They both nod, and it feels good to have them validate what I told Maddoc last night, even though I don't know all the ins and outs of their operation.

"We can't waste our resources by trying to hold territory under West Point's mercenary attacks," Maddoc goes on. "We're going to have to give up ground." His hands clench into tight fists at his sides, his knuckles turning white, but he keeps his voice steady. "I'm not willing to throw our people's lives away on something we can't win."

I can tell it kills him to admit that. He's fought for every inch of territory that the Reapers have claimed in this city, and he's earned what he's built in a way that Austin's money—*my* money—never will.

I'm proud of him for choosing to put his people first, though. I never doubted he would once he made his peace with where things stand right now, but it makes me love him even more to have him move forward with that plan so decisively.

I can tell all of my men have feelings about Maddoc's decision, but none of them waste time whining about it. Instead, they jump into logistics planning, with Logan taking the lead on pulling some of their resources back, arranging for their people to transport as much of their equipment, product, and other material goods relevant to the Reapers' operations from locations closer to the perimeter of their territory to areas that will be more secure.

"This shit ain't gonna be sustainable long-term though, Madd," Dante says with a frustrated huff once they've shot off messages to key players and put some of that in motion. "We can't move everything, and if we give up too much territory, we're gonna lose the resources we need to continue to function as a gang. You know you've got your people's loyalty, but they also gotta survive, and if we can't protect them, can't provide for them..."

He trails off with a low curse, and when he looks away, the rage and grief that flash across Maddoc's face while he thinks his brothers aren't looking almost breaks my heart. But as quickly as his emotions break free, he shuts them down again, refocusing on what has to happen.

"If we let it go on too long, McKenna will eventually roll right over us anyway," he agrees. "This isn't a retreat." He grimaces, then corrects himself. "It's a short-term, tactical retreat, but we need to use the time it buys us wisely. He's got Riley's inheritance. That's just a fact, and we're never gonna match that. We need to come up with another way to beat him, and we need to keep everyone alive to fight another day if we want to keep that option on the table."

"It's not 'an option,'" Logan says, cold fury blazing from his eyes even though he keeps his voice steady. "We *will* beat him. We'll fucking destroy him. This isn't negotiable."

"Right," Maddoc says, his shoulders pulling back and raw power in his voice, like hearing Logan's utter conviction gave him strength and reminded him who he is. Who the *Reapers* are. "Okay, so let's get fucking proactive. Who else can we make alliances with?"

Dante frowns. "Depends? Who's McKenna likely to go after next? The Scorpions? Mathis?"

I wish I had something to offer as they toss around a few more minor gangs' names, weighing the likelihood of convincing them that they'll be able to hold West Point off if they all work together against the grievances and alliances that already exist, but for all that I'm in it now, I really don't know this world well. And I sure as shit don't understand all the ugly history that seems to exist between some of the players they mention.

I'll learn, though. Their world is my world now, and even though I know I'm missing some of the nuance as they discuss which strategic alliances to go after, I follow along as closely as I can, determined to gain as much knowledge as possible so that I can be a true asset in this relationship.

Without turning to look at me, Logan reaches over and covers my hand with his, twining our fingers together like he can sense my feelings somehow. It grounds me, and I remind myself that I do have something to offer. These men count on me too.

"You know, it's really too fucking bad that The Six won't step in on this shit," Dante says with a scowl.

Maddoc grinds his teeth together, then visibly forces himself to relax. "They won't, at least not yet."

"The disrespect McKenna showed them yesterday was a mistake," Logan says flatly.

Maddoc nods. "They're not gonna forget it. You know The Six keep a tally of everything that happens here in Halston. But McKenna acting like an ass isn't enough on its own to make them act. They didn't get to the position they're in by being impulsive, and West Point isn't a threat to them, no matter how much posturing McKenna does."

"But he's the reason the cops and fire department got involved at the warehouse," I blurt, pissed off all over again at how fucking unfair it is. "Isn't that what they're mad about?"

"Yeah, princess, but I don't know if 'mad' is quite the right word. There's always infighting amongst the gangs. Alliances come and go, and grudges can be held for fucking ever. Right now, the way The Six see it, McKenna's beef is with the Reapers, and they've got no reason to choose a side in this fight at the moment. Like that Ayla chick said, their only objective is to maintain order. They're not gonna police how we all operate, they're just gonna make sure that we *can* all operate, you know?"

I grimace. It does make sense, and I even feel a grudging respect for The Six for not being drawn into fights that aren't theirs. I'm starting to understand just how powerful they are, and that impartiality they insist on, even in the face of a complete asshole like Austin, shows why they've managed to stay at the top of the food chain in Halston.

Still, I wish we could have them on our side. Ayla Fairchild feels like a kindred spirit, in a way. I don't know her well, but that doesn't change the fact that she's one of the few women I've ever come across that I feel a connection, almost a sisterhood, with.

"We're gonna handle this, princess," Dante says, tipping my chin up and searching my eyes. "We're gonna come out on top. No need for the long face."

I blink. I didn't even realize Dante had crossed the room, much less that the men were finished talking already.

Shaking my head to clear it, I give him a smile. "I know."

I mean it, and I know Dante does too, but our conviction is put to the test an hour later when Maddoc gets a call from one of his people about another attack on a building in Reaper territory.

"You have your instructions," I hear him say grimly, once he's received the report.

We're all in the kitchen this time, Logan plating food for us.

"They're going to fall back," Maddoc confirms once he ends the call.

I can tell the admission tortures him, but it's the right call, and even though the mood is somber, none of us voice any doubts or second guess it over the next twenty minutes as the reports come in from the organization, confirming the retreat.

Dante was right earlier when he said we won't be able to do this forever, though. The Reapers are going to have to find a way to stop Austin once and for all, before it's too late.

My stomach knots, and I push the last of the meal Logan made around on my plate, my hunger fleeing.

Logan makes a small, disappointed sound, and I look up quickly to find him eyeing me with concern.

I smile despite myself. He's such a contradiction, his need to hurt me just as strong as his need to take care of me, to feed me and bandage my wounds and protect me from the real monsters in this world, like Austin.

I fork up the last bite of food and eat it despite the way my stomach is still twisted into a cramped ball of anxiety, willing to do anything and everything I can to show him that I appreciate it.

It works. He smiles back before turning away, that tiny, fleeting one that always gets me right in the heart, and I remind myself that if earning a smile from Logan is possible, then anything is.

Just like he said earlier, we *will* defeat McKenna.

That's not negotiable.

Even if I still have no fucking idea how we'll actually manage it.

23

LOGAN

It's taken us most of the day to organize contingency plans based on our best guesses of where Austin might attack next. Maddoc and Dante both agree with my assessment that McKenna will start whittling away at our territory at its most vulnerable points, the edges, and we've done our best to make sure our people who live and work in those areas have a place to bail to if things get hairy.

No, not "if."

When.

I tamp down my rage over McKenna's aggression, because it's not productive here. The mood in the house is tense enough already, and the lack of solid information—the lack of control over what's happening with our organization—has me feeling like ants are crawling under my skin.

It's a feeling I'm familiar with, but surprisingly, I don't feel the need to resort to any of my usual coping mechanisms. I'm self-aware enough to realize it's because of Riley, I just don't have the words to explain to myself or to her why exactly that is.

The sex has helped stabilize my mood, of course. Endorphins have predictable results. But it's more than that, and the "more"—this connection she and I share, the outlet she gives me for feelings that would otherwise fester inside me until they explode—is something that makes me...

Not uncomfortable.

I don't want to be rid of the feeling.

But I'm not entirely comfortable with it, either.

I push those thoughts aside since I'm not sure what to do with them, and don't even realize I'm searching the house for her until I finally come across her curled up on the couch in the living room and realize that I have no other reason for being here except for my desire to be close to her.

She looks up as I enter the room and smiles at me, and that thing I'm uncomfortable with flares to life in my chest.

I definitely don't want to be rid of it. I might even crave it.

"Hey, Logan," she says, one hand resting on her stomach and the other wrapped around a mug with steam coming out of it. "Did you guys get things set up at the perimeter?"

"We did." I frown, taking note of the way her knuckles are white around the mug, and the faint tightening of the skin around her lips and eyes. "Are you all right?"

She blinks up at me, those small signs of distress disappearing for a moment as a fuller smile graces her decadent mouth. "Yes, of course," she says quickly, then backpedals a little with, "I mean, I'm worried of course. We all are, right? God, I hate that Austin is able to fuck with us like this."

I nod absently, but then shake my head. She's not lying. But she's also not telling the whole truth.

"Something else is affecting you," I state, at a loss for the right words to define how her distress is affecting me.

I need to know what's causing it, though.

I need to understand the scope of the problem so that I can find a solution.

This time, when Riley smiles up at me, that feeling in my chest becomes almost painfully warm. I don't even realize how close I've drifted toward her until she reaches out and slips her hand into mine. I look down at our joined hands, then back into her eyes. She squeezes, and I'm surprised to find I don't mind the uninvited touch at all.

I maybe even... enjoy it.

"You're so observant," she says with a soft little laugh, releasing my hand to rest hers over her stomach again. "It's really nothing to be worried about, though. I promise. I just started my period, and the stress of everything is making the cramps kinda brutal right now. It will pass, though. It's just, you know, woman things."

I frown. No, I don't know about woman things. I know they exist, of course. But I've never been faced with them, and feel a frisson of anger at myself for being caught off guard by something I should have realized would become a part of our lives now that Riley is.

None of that anger is for her though, so I suppress it and give her a brief nod in acknowledgment, then head back upstairs so I can correct my oversight about this issue.

It takes more time than I anticipated given the ratio of anecdotal nonsense versus definitive research I find online, but eventually—and after contacting one of our runners to deliver certain items from the drug store—I'm prepared.

This time, I find her in her room, still curled around what I assume is another cup of tea, but this time on her bed.

She looks up in surprise when I walk in. "Logan?"

I set the supplies I brought with me down on her nightstand and remove the mug of tea from her hand, placing it next to the items I've gathered.

"Take your shirt off, please." I hesitate for a moment, then add, "And your pants too."

The pair she has on is high waisted, which won't do.

Her lips twitch a little, almost like she's laughing at me, but I don't feel offended. I feel something softer. And she does what

I've told her to without argument, which makes my chest ache again in that way that I'm quickly starting to crave.

I sit on the mattress next to her and guide her down onto her back, my body reacting to the sight of her smooth skin and athletic curves, clad only in a small pair of black underwear that barely cover the slit between her legs.

I have enough practice to make it easy to ignore the way my cock rises in response, but I can't help the way my eyes are immediately drawn to the marks I've left on her.

The thin scar between her breasts.

The neat line of dots from the stitches I placed along her waistline.

The barely there signs of my fingers, still present around her throat.

She's enchanting, but this isn't the time to become distracted by how appealing I find her. Despite her apparent pleasure at my presence, all the signs of discomfort I noted earlier are still present in her body language, and this sort of pain clearly isn't the type she enjoys.

I dim the lamp next to her to create a more soothing environment, then uncap the scented oil and pour some into my hands, rubbing them together to warm it.

"What are you doing?" Her eyebrows lift with surprise when I smooth the oil over her taut stomach, working outward from her navel in the appropriate formation for her anatomy.

"You know that I... enjoy hurting you," I start, my voice low and my thoughts strangely muddled as I struggle to answer her; to put into words why I need to fix her distress.

She doesn't flinch or deny what I've said, just looks up at me with a steady gaze, open and soft.

It's still hard to accept how readily she welcomes the pain I inflict on her, though, and I swallow hard, dropping my eyes back to her stomach; focusing on the sight of my fingers, pressing into her warm skin in a steady, outward-circling rhythm. The way her flesh drinks in the oil is almost mesmerizing.

"Logan?"

"I enjoy hurting you," I repeat, "but I enjoy taking care of you too. I like it."

That's not quite the right word. It's not big enough. But it's also not the wrong one.

I look up, meeting her eyes, and a soft smile spreads across her face that does something to me. "Thank you. I like both sides of you, you know."

I didn't know that. I'm still trying to come to terms with the fact that she cares about me at all.

Thankfully, she doesn't press me to discuss things like feelings, nor does she stop me as I continue to rub the oil into her belly.

Touching her like this makes my cock even harder, but I continue to ignore it. I know her body is available to me. She's made that clear. But this is about her, not me.

"Is it helping with the cramps?" I ask after a while, surprised at how husky my voice sounds. How intimate it feels to be with her like this.

"Yes." She trails her fingers up my forearm. "How did you know to do this?"

I blink. "I looked it up. Some of the available information couldn't be verified, but I found several methods with documented efficacy for menstrual pain relief."

She bites her bottom lip, her eyes sparkling. "Oh?"

"Yes."

She laughs, a low sound that sends heat spiraling through me. "What else did you find?"

I reluctantly remove my hands from her body, then meticulously wipe the oil off them before reaching for the bottle of whiskey I brought. "Apparently, a drink can ease the pain too."

She looks from the bottle to me, then reaches for it.

I pull it away, an impulse taking me over that I refuse to question. "No. Open your mouth."

She lets out a soft sound that I've heard from her before. She enjoys being dominated. And she's so fucking beautiful like this.

I uncap the whiskey bottle and tip it into my mouth, the liquid cool and smooth on my tongue. I hold it there, then lean over her and grip her jaw, letting it pour from my mouth into hers.

She swallows it, a heated flush spreading from her face and throat down to the beautifully delicate area beneath her collarbone.

"You're turned on."

"Can you blame me?" she asks, her breath quickening.

Her arousal heightens my own, but the way she's allowing me to fix this for her, to care for her and ease her pain, is even more satisfying right now than the idea of fucking her.

"What else did you learn about helping to ease cramps?" she asks, dropping one of her hands to rest over her stomach again.

Her skin has absorbed most of the oil.

It looks even softer than usual, rich and sensuous as she glides her fingers over it.

"Orgasms," I tell her, lifting her hand off her body and placing it on the mattress next to her hip instead.

I enjoy watching her touch herself, but I enjoy being the one to decide how she receives her pleasure even more.

"I've never tried orgasms," she says a little breathlessly, leaving her hand where I've put it and holding my gaze as she spreads her legs. "Not for cramps."

"Good."

The idea that I'll be the first to bring her this kind of relief, just as she's been my first for certain experiences, is more satisfying than I can properly express.

I slip my fingers under the silken scrap of material hiding

her pussy from me, watching her face carefully as I drag them through her folds. They're slick with her arousal, and there's a coppery tang to the scent of it that I'm not used to. But I don't encounter any blood, and it's clear that she enjoys my touch.

Even now.

Even like this. Without any pain.

I circle her clit, my fingers lubricated by her own body, and a gorgeous shudder ripples through her.

"You like this."

"Yes."

"You're going to come from this."

"*Yes.*"

Her fingers dig into the bedspread, her back arching as her hips undulate in response to my attention, but other than that, she holds herself still. She lets me give this to her. She submits to my control.

I rub her clit faster, harder. Feel it swell under my fingers as her breath quickens and her nipples harden, untouched, into twin pebbled nubs.

"Please." The word bursts out of her on an explosive breath, dripping with need, and I reward her by pinching her swollen button between my fingers, granting her a sharp, sudden burst of the pain that I know will send her right over the edge.

It does, the orgasm rolling through her body right before my eyes.

It's addictive, so I give her another one. And then another, pushing her until she's panting for me. Whimpering and begging as she writhes under my touch, her initial obedient stillness overridden by the intensity of her body's response.

She's incredible. I can't get enough. I've never been so focused on another person whom I wasn't in the act of killing before, and drawing her pleasure out of her consumes me until I lose track of my original purpose and exist only to hear her moans, to map the flush of arousal as it colors her skin, to feel her tremble under my touch and to taste her urgent, panting pleas as I push her to come, over and over.

I don't remember laying on the bed next to her. I'm not sure when I pulled the panties that had become soaked with her pleasure off and tossed them aside. I have no idea how I ever existed without the feel of her mouth on mine, without her hands clutching my shoulders, tugging on my hair, clawing at my back.

I know I never want to exist that way again.

"One more, wildcat," I demand, one hand buried between her legs and the other tangled in those long, jewel-toned waves of her hair. "Come for me."

She obeys. She's never disappointed me. But as her body comes down from the shuddering pleasure this time, her eyes drift closed and she sinks into the mattress, boneless and clearly exhausted.

She murmurs something unintelligible, and I press a chaste kiss against the corner of her mouth, a deep ache in my balls. I ignore it, just like I ignore the throbbing urgency in my cock, painfully hard where it's trapped in the confines of my pants.

I've taken so much pleasure from Riley's body tonight that the denial of my own is almost like a masochistic kind of fulfillment of its own. Or maybe it's simply that I'm satisfied on a different level now.

One I didn't know existed before her.

"Riley," I whisper quietly, gently tracing the delicate blue veins in her closed eyelids with the tip of my finger. "Wildcat."

Her only response is a soft exhale.

She's asleep. I've worn her out. And she's no longer in pain.

Warmth blooms in my chest, a deeply satisfied sense of pride at what I've accomplished here, and I carefully roll off the bed, then rearrange her body in a more comfortable position for sleep, tucking the blankets around her.

I've done what I came to, and there's no further reason for

me to stay, and yet I stand next to her, watching her, for longer than I can justify.

There's no sense to it. I could access the same view from the cameras, back in the comfort of my room. It's what I've always preferred in the past, but I no longer have any desire to keep her at a distance.

Finally, though, I press a kiss to her hair, carefully smoothing it back from her face, and leave.

24

MADDOC

"Shit, Madd," Dante says under his breath, rolling his shoulders back as he adopts a lazy-looking smile and chin nods at the representatives of the 17th Street Gang as they head toward us. "Not often we have so many outsiders this deep."

I grunt softly in reply, knowing the comment is just his way of relieving some nerves. Neither Logan nor Dante likes my decision to invite so many other gang leaders this deeply into our territory, but they do understand it.

Our perimeter is at risk. Just like we predicted, McKenna's been picking away at it every fucking day. We've done what we can to protect our people and our resources as we continue to give up ground, but now we need allies. We need a goddamn alliance to stand against him, and the only way to convince other gangs that we need it, and more importantly, that we'll honor it, is with a face-to-face meeting.

And as much as it pisses me off to admit, the only place I truly feel confident we can get that done without risking an attack from West Point that would disrupt these talks before they even get started is right here, in the heart of Reaper territory.

I nod at the familiar faces of the other gang leaders as they array themselves around us. Besides the 17th Street Gang, which we've always had a solid relationship with, we've invited the Cobalt Crew, who we definitely haven't, and a few other low-level players; organizations whose borders either touch ours or touch West Point's.

Gattrock, from the south side of the city. The Kraits, whose tiny-ass territory is crammed between the warehouse district and the neutral zone downtown that The Six enforce. The Stonebrew gang, led by an upstart who's too fucking bloodthirsty, in my opinion, but knows how to get shit done.

It's no surprise that he's the one who speaks up first. "What's this about, Maddoc?"

The cocky smirk he usually wears nowhere in sight as he shifts his weight uneasily, obviously no happier to be in the heart of our territory than we are to have him here.

Before I answer, I scan each group carefully, giving my gut one last chance to pick up on any potential treachery. On any reason not to share the information we have with them.

I don't find it.

Everyone we've brought together is clearly wary of each other and wondering why I brought them together, but none of them are outright enemies. Other than the 17th Street Gang, I wouldn't say any of them are actually allies, either—not with us, and not with each other—but I do know they've all made deals with each other before.

It's a start.

"You're all here because we have a common enemy," I finally say. "West Point."

That gets me a variety of reactions, from skeptical muttering to verging on disrespectful.

Victor Ruiz, the leader of the 17th Street Gang, is the only one who has the balls to respond directly.

"It's no secret that we're not on good terms with McKenna,"

he says carefully. "But I'm not sure I'd call him an enemy of 17th Street."

"And I'm sure you'll feel differently once I explain the situation. McKenna has recently expanded his gang's financial resources exponentially."

"I heard some rumors on the street about that," Gattrock's leader says. "The numbers that are being thrown around, though? Sounds like bullshit."

"It's not," I tell him grimly.

My brothers and I have already decided not to go into specifics, and we're sure as shit not going to give anyone Riley's name or let them know how she's involved. I confirm how much fucking money McKenna got his hands on, though, and assure the other gangs that we've verified it.

"No fucking way," says the Stonebrew gang's cocky-ass leader, scowling at me like he wants to punch something. "Are you shitting me? With that kind of money—"

"West Point becomes a massive, looming threat," I interrupt. "To all of us."

The statement shuts him up, but I can tell he's still skeptical. They all are.

This time, it's the Cobalt Crew's leader, Wolf Mathis, who speaks up. "All due respect, Maddoc, but you Reapers have history with West Point. We don't."

"The fuck you don't," Dante drawls, crossing his arms over his chest. "Who disrupted your business down by the tracks last year?"

One of Mathis's seconds narrows his eyes. "That was a misunderstanding."

Dante smirks. "Really? Because it looked a lot more like your people turning tail and running when McKenna decided he was going to take over some of your protection racket."

The whole Cobalt delegation bristles, but I've got enough of my people stationed around us to make them think twice about taking too much offense.

Besides, it's true.

"McKenna's always been a threat," I remind them all. "He just hasn't had the power to rock the boat too much before now."

"By rock the boat, do you mean push into Reaper territory? Because that's what it looks like from where we're standing," Mathis says with a sneer. "In fact, it sounds like this little meeting of yours is less about a 'common enemy' than it is the Reapers asking for help in your long-standing feud. The one you're now losing."

"We're not asking for anything," I say tightly. "We're offering an alliance that will benefit us all."

Mathis scoffs. "I don't see much benefit to joining up with the losing side in a war we've got no part in. How much territory have you lost so far, Maddoc? Heard one of your warehouses burned last week, and just the other day, West Point staked a claim to the entire 300-block over by the old transfer station. Didn't that used to be Reaper territory?"

"It did."

In other circumstances, I wouldn't put up with this shit. As it is, I exercise every bit of my self-control to keep my temper from getting out of hand. There's more at stake here than a little posturing, and it's no surprise that, out of everyone we invited, Mathis is being the most combative. Our history with them is a rocky one, but unfortunately, we need them.

More importantly, they need us, even if they don't realize it yet.

"We haven't lost any territory due to neglect," I tell them all. "McKenna hasn't been sending his people after us—"

Mathis snorts again, but I ignore him.

"—he's using some of that bottomless well of cash he's got now to hire unaffiliated mercenaries. Trained operatives who are employing strategic military tactics to advance into Reaper territory and dismantle it, block by block."

The other gang leaders exchange looks, even Mathis shutting up at that news. Every one of them is ruthless in his own way, but we've all come up through the streets. Not a single one of them has the knowledge or training to go up against the kind of people McKenna's brought in, not any more than the Reapers do.

"You sure about that, Maddoc?" the leader of the Kraits finally asks, scratching the back of his head. "That ain't usually how we do things in Halston."

"If I wasn't sure, you wouldn't have been invited here."

I don't just mean to the meeting. I mean into the heart of our territory, where we can be as sure as it's possible to be that we can still defend ourselves. Where we've only welcomed them because we've got no other choice.

"You're right that the Reapers have a history with West Point," I go on as I watch that sink in. "But if McKenna succeeds in tearing us apart, do you really think he'll be satisfied?"

The Kraits leader snorts, shaking his head. "Damn. No, I don't. He doesn't pay much mind to us since our territory is so far from his borders, but that piece of shit has never made a secret about how greedy he is when it comes to expansion."

"He'll go after all of you," Logan says quietly. "Once he gets a taste of winning, he'll roll right over every other gang who has territory he's interested in. Every operation whose business he wants to get his hands on."

A vein starts throbbing in Mathis's forehead, and I've got no doubt at all he's thinking back on what West Point's already taken from him. It's the main reason we invited him here, despite our differences.

I lay it out for them as clearly as I can, looking each one in the eye. "We either work together to stop him now, or he becomes unstoppable. It's as simple as that."

Tension rises in the room as each group digests that statement. Then the cocky little shit from the Stonebrew gang sums up the general feeling for all of us.

"Mother*fucker*."

Dante snorts, then shakes his head. "Yeah, he really fucking is. So what are you all gonna do about it?"

Their voices rise to a low hum, each gang talking quietly among their people as Dante's question reminds them that they each got where they were by being men of action, and I exchange a look with my brothers, trying to gauge their take on the mood.

Eventually, the other leaders have a few questions about what McKenna is planning, and I answer them to the best of my ability.

It pisses me off that the "to the best of my ability" isn't much more than a few predictions and best guesses, given that we haven't been able to get any concrete information from our informants yet, but we still share everything we've got even though it grates on me to be so fucking open with people whose loyalties aren't solidly with us yet.

But like Riley reminded me, the main thing is living to fight another day. And right now, we need strength in numbers to do that.

"Okay, Maddoc," Ruiz finally says with a respectful nod. "We'll take this back and chew on it, then be in touch."

"I appreciate you coming," I tell him, signaling some of my people to escort the 17th Street group to the edge of our territory, ensuring their safety as long as they're within our borders.

Once they leave, the other gangs quickly follow. None of them outright committed to allying with us, but it's clear that at least a few of them have reevaluated their perception of West Point and the threat that McKenna poses.

"It's a win, Madd," Dante says once we see the last of them off, obviously reading my frustration. "It's not like we can expect more right out of the gate, yeah?"

"Sure," I say, scrubbing a hand over my face. "But *fuck*. McKenna's not gonna wait around for them to get their heads out of their asses and recognize what's really happening here."

"No, he's not," Dante agrees, his expression somber. "But he's also not being that fucking subtle, so they'll see it, sooner or later."

Logan nods. "You've laid the groundwork. That's all today was about."

He's right. I know it, even if I wish we could make this shit happen faster, before more of my people are hurt or displaced by McKenna's vendetta and his insatiable greed.

"Let's head home," I say, more than ready to see our girl and not fucking shy about the fact that I want a little of the peace having her with us will bring after the stress of this meeting.

"Good call, Madd," Dante says, clapping me on the shoulder as we head to the SUV, waving off the security detail that offers to escort us back to the house.

The day we need them right on our asses, here where we should be the most secure, is the day we're well and truly fucked.

"Is Wolf Mathis going to be a problem?" I ask as we pile into the vehicle, needing to find out if my brothers' take on things matches my own.

"No," Logan says immediately. "It was the right call to include him."

Dante smirks. "Even though he's an ass."

"Even though he's an ass," Logan concedes with a small smile. "He's been burned by West Point before, though. He's not going to risk it happening again after the way McKenna humiliated him last year."

I nod. "I agree. And hopefully, the other gang leaders will see the writing on the wall soon enough to step up and help us take a stand before it's too late."

"Yeah, unless McKenna gets wind of today's meeting and tries to form his own alliances with them," Dante says, shaking his head. "Short-sighted fucks. I wouldn't put it past that little shit from the Stonebrew gang to make the mistake of thinking he'll have a better chance at survival if he throws in with West Point."

Logan frowns. "We should put surveillance on him and make sure he doesn't run to McKenna and initiate that."

"If he does, it's gonna piss me the fuck off," I admit, which is news to precisely no one. Then I exhale roughly, and let it fucking go for now, because we've done what we can, and given what's at stake, we already agreed reaching out like this was worth the risk.

Now, only time will tell if we were actually right.

25

RILEY

Something about knowing what my men are doing today has me all up in my feelings. Probably because even though they're mine now, nothing is guaranteed in this world. Even in the heart of their own territory, the fact is, they're not meeting with friends, and no matter how strong the Reapers are and how fiercely I know they'll fight for what matters to them, shit could go badly at any moment.

For some reason, that fact hits me hard when they walk in the door after their meeting with the other gang leaders. "How did it go?"

Maddoc grimaces. "As good as could be expected."

"That well?" I joke, not doing a great job of masking my jumpiness if the guys' expressions are anything to go by.

"We gave them something to think about," Maddoc says, pulling me into his embrace and gripping my chin. He stares into my eyes for a moment, then smiles. "It's good to be home, though."

The way he's looking at me, I don't think he means the house.

My heart gives an embarrassing flutter at how openly he's putting his feelings on display. He's the first man who ever told me he loved me and made me actually believe it, and it just gives me one more thing that I'm not willing to lose. One more thing I'll do anything to keep in my life permanently.

I feel that way about all three of these men, and when Logan heads off to do some sort of high tech badassery and Maddoc goes into his office to get some work done after kissing me hard, I want—no, I need—to do something about that.

"Is it safe for us to go out, as long as we stay in Reaper territory?" I ask Dante.

He tucks a loose piece of hair behind my ear. "Depends where you wanna go, princess. So far, McKenna's stuck with attacks at our borders, but we still need to be on alert. Where are you thinking?"

"I want to go to that tattoo parlor again," I admit, letting my fingers skim over his chest, tracing the shape of the ink he put there. "The place you got this one."

Dante's eyes flare with interest, and he covers my hand, holding it against his chest as his voice goes a little husky. "All right."

He ushers me out to the SUV, shooting off a quick text ahead of us and getting the heads-up that Nico, the artist who did his ink, can see me.

"Really?" I'm genuinely surprised. "I kind of figured I'd have to settle for someone else."

Dante smirks. "Not on my watch."

I bite my lip. I don't ask what he did to make it happen, but I'm pretty sure Nico isn't the type who'd have a last-minute opening in his schedule like this without a little nudge. I'm not going to complain, though.

"Has Chloe been in touch?" he asks as we drive.

I nod. "It sounds like she's got that guy you assigned to watch her out there, Nathan, hooked on the manga series Logan sent with her."

"That's like, what, a comic book?" Dante asks, chuckling. "'Cause I never did figure Nathan for much of a reader."

"He'd better not just be humoring her," I say, bristling a little at the thought since Chloe has been gushing about the guy a little.

"Nah, Nathan's a good one," Dante reassures me. "You know we wouldn't have sent him out there with her if we didn't trust him. And I've got it on good authority that he's taking his job seriously."

I want to ask him what he means by that, but when Dante parks behind the tattoo parlor, a rush of adrenaline kicks in and distracts me. I'm not sure if it's because this will be my first tattoo, or if it's because of what it means to me, but my body starts to thrum with excitement as we walk in, and Dante clearly notices.

"You good, princess?" he asks softly, his hand resting low on my back as he guides me back to Nico's station.

I smile up at him. "So fucking good."

Nico and Dante exchange greetings, then Nico kicks a rolling stool toward Dante and helps me into the tattoo chair.

"Tell me what it is you're looking to do today, princess," Nico says with a wink, rolling toward me on a second stool.

Hearing that word from him startles me.

"Her name is Riley," Dante growls before I can respond, a possessive bite to his voice I'm not used to hearing... and definitely don't hate.

Nico laughs. "My bad, bro." He turns back to me. "Go on now, *Riley*. Talk to me about the new ink we're doing."

I bite my lip, not sure how to put it into words now that he's putting me on the spot like this.

I can still see it in my memory, though, so I do my best.

"I need it in red," I start. "Blood red."

Dante's favorite color.

I drag my fingers over my chest, mimicking the slash of red

paint he put there once. It was bold and dangerous-looking and hopeful. More importantly, it was his, and I want it on my skin permanently. Just like the scars Logan has marked me with. Just like the claim all three men have made on my heart.

Nico nods. "We can do that. Like a true crimson, yeah? That'll pop nicely against your skin. What's it gonna look like?"

I try to describe the shape with touch, curling my fingers over the top of my right breast. "It needs to twist around like this."

I meet Dante's eyes, the heat of them making my breath hitch. I can see that he remembers.

I can also see that possessiveness flare up in his eyes when Nico nods and tells me to take my shirt off.

"You want to just guide me as I freehand it?" Nico asks as I reach for my hem. "Dante can hold this mirror for you—"

"No," Dante says, shooting to his feet. He pushes between me and Nico and bats my hands away. "I'll do the fucking stencil. I know what she wants."

Nico snorts, but I can't see what he thinks about that with Dante blocking my view.

Or, I suppose, blocking *Nico's* view.

"You do remember we met in a strip club, right?" I tease Dante once I realize that.

"I don't give a fuck," he says, his voice low. He peels my shirt off and cups my bare breasts. "These are mine now."

I squeeze my thighs together. "Just yours?"

"You know what I mean, princess." He pinches my nipples hard enough to send a bolt of arousal shooting through me that almost has me forgetting what we're doing here. "This is Reaper territory, and I only share with my brothers."

"That might make this whole tattoo thing kind of hard to do," Nico drawls from behind him. "You do know I need to work on her skin, right?"

Dante's eyes stay locked onto mine. "I know."

But he doesn't like it, and that possessiveness has me turned on enough that it takes a bit of effort to remember how much I want this tattoo too.

"You can keep me covered up," I say, sliding his hands down to cover my tits. "But I want this, Dante. I need your marks on me."

"Fuck," he mutters, squeezing my tits. "Okay, princess. We'll make it happen."

He snags the shirt he just took off me and flips it around a few times, turning it into something like a bandeau top for me that leaves enough of my breast exposed to allow him to follow through on freehand stenciling in the shape of the mark he painted on me when we fucked in his studio.

"This what you want?" he asks, his voice husky as he traces it with the tip of his finger, feather-light.

"Yes," I tell him, a lump in my throat. "It's perfect."

No one has offered me the mirror, but I still know it's true.

Actually, it's a million times more perfect than I'd imagined when I spontaneously asked to come here for some ink, because now it really will truly be Dante's mark that Nico inks onto my skin.

"Ready for this?" Nico asks once Dante finally steps aside.

He takes one of the rolling stools and puts a hand on my thigh that feels like one part possession and one part support.

I hold his gaze as Nico leans over my chest with his tools, and get a reassuring squeeze in return.

"I'm ready."

Nico grins, giving me another wink. "It's gonna give you a rush," he promises. "Here we go."

Then the needle finally bites into me... and it fucking *hurts*. The pain is like a thousand bees stinging me, all at once without letting up.

I suck in a sharp breath, and something deliciously dark flares to life in Dante's eyes.

"Looks so fucking good on you," he says in a throaty whisper.

I have no idea if he's referring to the bold red lines Nico is inking into my skin, or to what the pain is doing to me, but I get my answer when he slides the hand he's been resting on my thigh up between my legs and rubs his thumb over my clit through my pants.

Both. He definitely likes both.

"Oh fuck," I breathe out, spreading my legs for him a little as the pain starts to get even more intense.

Nico's totally focused on the tattoo, his back toward Dante as his hands move with steady determination over my skin, but there's no way he can miss the way my breath quickens or the tiny droplets of sweat beading up on my skin as I force myself to stay still through the addicting onslaught of pleasure and pain the two men are subjecting me to.

I've got no idea if he knows what Dante's doing to me or if he thinks those are just my reactions to the needle, but I also don't have it in me to care. Not when Dante's obviously bound and determined to wreck me.

"You're taking that ink so fucking well, princess," he says, his wicked fingers a counterpoint to the steady thrum of pain. "My mark's gonna be on your body forever."

"Yes. god, *yes*," I pant, then bite my tongue before I go any further even though the effort of working so hard to stay quiet when he's doing all he can to make me scream for him is almost more than I can stand.

Nico smirks. "Gonna do this center section for you now. It's a solid block of color there, so you're definitely gonna feel this next bit."

"She already feels it," Dante says in a low rumble, grinding down on my clit. "She feels it, and she fucking likes it. Ain't that right, princess?"

"Bastard," I whisper, fisting my hands until my nails dig into my palms as the pain twists around the pleasure he's got rising inside me, merging them together until I can't tell where one stops and the other begins.

Dante chuckles, low and dirty. "Love you too, beautiful."

"Shit," I gasp. I'm still not used to just *hearing* it like that, and the words push me over the edge, threatening to fuck up my tattoo as the orgasm rolls through me.

Dante smirks, but I can't even be mad. I can't be anything for a few minutes as the aftershocks shudder through me.

Thankfully, Nico pulls the tattoo gun away from my skin for a second, and I decide not to think about the fact that he obviously knows damn well how Dante was distracting me from the pain. Actually, when Dante rolls his stool forward and not-so-subtly nudges Nico to the side to lean down and kiss me, I don't bother thinking of anything at all, so high on endorphins that I barely feel the final few passes of the tattoo gun when Nico snorts and shoves Dante out of the way again to finish it up.

Once Nico gives me some care instructions and steps away, I look up at Dante. "What do you think?" I ask, feathering my fingers over the deep red ink visible through the clear wrap Nico covered my new tattoo with.

"Fucking gorgeous," Dante says, his eyes locked onto mine.

"Thanks, brother," Nico says dryly. "Glad you appreciate my work."

Dante laughs. "Okay, yeah. The ink looks good too. Your work is stellar, Nico, as per always."

"Damn fucking right it is," Nico says, clapping Dante on the shoulder. "I'll meet you two up front, yeah?"

"It really does look good, princess," Dante says more softly once Nico leaves us alone. He pulls me upright, then unwinds my shirt from around my breasts and shakes it out before easing it back over my head and brushing his fingers over the new ink. "I ain't seen anything yet that doesn't look good on you and doubt I ever will, but nothing is hotter than seeing this kind of proof."

"Proof of what?"

He stares at me, a slow, sinful smile spreading across his mouth. "You know what."

My breath hitches, and yeah, I do. But I lift my chin anyway, my heart beating in a deliciously quick counterpoint to the way the swooping lines of the new tattoo throb on the other side of my chest.

"Tell me."

He pulls me in, tipping my head back even farther for a searing, possessive kiss. Then, while I'm still reeling from that, he finally answers my question. "I'm fucking in love with you, and seeing you permanently decorate yourself with something I made, choosing my marks, my art, to go on your body like this? That's all the proof I need to know you're really mine."

The art may be abstract, but clearly, Dante understands exactly what getting this tattoo means to me.

Still...

"Is that what this means?" I ask a little breathlessly, goading him anyway, just a little, because this new possessive side of him that's come out now that he's finally admitted his feelings for me gets me fucking hot.

He grins, seeing right through me and giving me what I want anyway.

"Fuck yeah, that's what it means. And it's too late to back out now, wild thing. You belong to me and my brothers, and since this shit is permanent, I guess you always fucking will."

He's not wrong. And no matter how much uncertainty awaits us when we step out the door and back into the shitstorm brewing with West Point, having this one forever-thing to hold on to means something to me.

And having Dante understand that means even more.

26

RILEY

DANTE MURMURS something to Nico when we reach the front of the shop, then slips him some money.

"That wasn't the deal," I say, pushing my way between them. "I can cover my own—"

"I know," Dante interrupts, grinning down at me. "But let me." He runs the backs of his fingers down my cheek, leaning close to whisper. "And I can't wait to mark you up with a few more tattoos. Seeing you get inked like that was fucking hot."

I hide a grin of my own as he finishes up business with Nico, taking a moment to look at some of the art they've got on the wall. I might as well, since I've got a feeling Dante's going to follow through and convince me to get a lot more ink in the future.

An idea that I definitely don't hate.

"Ready, princess?" he asks, putting a proprietary hand on my back as we head out the door but then pausing before we exit to tug the low neckline of my shirt up a little higher, smoothing it over the new ink. "Gotta keep that shit out of the sun for a while."

"I know."

"Oh you do, do you?" he asks, a playful note to his teasing that I've really fucking missed.

We step out of the shop. "I was actually listening to the aftercare instructions." I tease him right back.

"Well, shit." He pulls me against him and presses a kiss against my temple. "Guess I didn't do a good enough job of distracting you then. Next time, I'll need to—what the *fuck?*"

He shoves me behind him so fast that I stumble, managing to keep a grip on my arm at the same time so I don't actually go down, but then immediately releasing me once I'm stable so he can surge forward and address the threat.

Sienna Morgan.

"What the fuck?" I repeat, echoing Dante as adrenaline surges through me.

I don't know where the hell she came from, since we're deep in Reaper territory. The last time I saw her, she was sneering at my captivity and telling me how her boyfriend, Austin McKenna, planned on killing me once he was done with me.

Dante recovers from the shock of her sudden appearance before I do. He lunges at her, shoving her into the alley next to the tattoo parlor and pinning her against the wall.

"What the fuck are you doing here?" he demands, his voice as cold and deadly as I've ever heard it. "Even if we weren't in the middle of this shit, you know you're not welcome. Did McKenna send you?"

"No," she whispers, her voice hoarse.

"Then you can turn around and get the fuck out of Reaper territory," Dante says before she can get another word out.

"Dante," she bursts out in protest, earning not even a hint of sympathy despite the fact that she looks like shit. Her hair is a hot fucking mess, there are puffy circles under her eyes, and the clothes she's wearing look just as unkempt as the rest of her, even though they don't do jack to hide the fading bruises visible on her face and body.

I can relate to how few fucks Dante gives, though. The bitch deserves none of them.

"I don't want to hear it," he says, pulling her away from the wall and spinning her body so that he can bend her arm up behind her back and use it to propel her forward. "Fastest way for you to be gone is to head toward 26th and Jefferson. Go."

He shoves her, but she stumbles and then turns back to face him. "Do you know how fucking hard it was to make it here? Fuck no, I'm not going. I need to speak to Maddoc."

Dante crosses his arms over his chest. "Nope."

Sienna flips her straggly hair and narrows her eyes at him. "Trust me, he's not gonna like that."

Dante usually operates at a much more even keel, somehow able to look out at the world from a laid-back place of humor and acceptance even during seriously shitty times. Not so much right now, though, and I love him a little bit harder for that, since I know it comes from a place of unshakeable loyalty to Maddoc.

But unfortunately, we can't ignore the fact that Sienna is probably right.

"Dante," I say softly, resting my hand on his bicep. It feels like coiled steel, and he's still got his body mostly angled to block me from Sienna, protecting me in case she turns out to be a threat. But as pissed off as he is, he doesn't ignore me.

We share a look, clearly both aware that whatever Sienna's playing at could very well be some kind of trick or a trap she's cooked up with Austin. But finally, Dante gives me a slight nod. "Maddoc will want to know about this."

I can see how much he hates giving Sienna her way in anything at all, so I whip out my phone and make the call.

Maddoc answers right away. "You okay, butterfly?" he asks, worry making his voice snap.

"Totally fine," I assure him. "Really, I am. But we've, uh, got a weird development here."

"Where are you?" he asks sharply.

"Reaper territory. I'm with Dante. I just got some ink from Nico, and—"

"You did, huh?" Maddoc interrupts, practically purring as his voice goes from hard to pure heat. "Then I'm definitely gonna need you to come back to the house so I can inspect—"

"Actually," I cut in, hating Sienna more than I already did for having to interrupt him. "We found Sienna Morgan here."

I get a split second of silence. Then he speaks again, his voice flat. "She's in Reaper territory?"

"She was waiting for us." I meet Sienna's eyes, keeping my voice neutral because there's no way in hell I'm falling for the little quiver in her chin. Even if it's real, I'm with Dante on this one. "She wants to talk to you."

This time, the silence goes on a little longer. I'm sure Maddoc's just as shocked as Dante and I are.

But I'm also not surprised when he tells me he's on his way.

"Tell Dante to bring her to Clancy's," he says in a clipped voice. "Logan and I will be there in ten."

It's the same dive bar I first approached the Reapers for help in. It feels like a lifetime ago, but this time, it also feels like I belong.

Sienna, on the other hand, doesn't.

Dante keeps a firm grip on her as he hustles her to a booth in the back, then pulls a weapon once he has her seated and keeps it trained on her under the table as we wait for his brothers.

I make a move to slip in the booth next to him, but he shakes his head.

"Keep a lookout at the door, princess. Let me know when Madd and Logan get here."

Since it's not like there's any way he won't know once they do, and it's definitely not like Maddoc and Logan aren't going to be able to find us in the tiny place, I'm pretty sure it's just

Dante's overprotective instincts kicking in to demand that I stay away from the potential threat.

I don't fight him on it, though. I fucking love him for it. I don't plan on letting my men see me as someone weak who needs protecting all the time, but I also don't mind giving in when it will give them a little peace of mind, either.

Maddoc and Logan roll up a few minutes later, and the way they each give me a quick once over, their relief at finding me safe and unharmed quickly masked once they turn their attention to Sienna, just confirms that I made the right choice.

Maddoc leads the way back to the booth, and Logan takes my arm much like Dante did before, keeping me not-so-subtly behind him. Once we get there, neither of them take a seat, and Maddoc crosses his arms over his chest.

"What do you want?" he asks Sienna without any preamble.

She starts to give him what looks like it might become a sultry smile, but whatever expression she sees on his face makes her sigh and drop it. Instead, she waves a hand, taking in Dante, Logan, and me with the gesture. "Can we speak in private, please?"

"We are," Maddoc says flatly. The bar is practically deserted, and the few patrons near the front are smart enough to ignore us.

"You know what I mean," Sienna snaps.

Maddoc doesn't react to the little display of temper. "You can say whatever it is you came for in front of my brothers and Riley, or you can skip it. I literally don't give a shit. But there's no way in hell you've got anything to say that can't be shared with my seconds."

Sienna raises an eyebrow, giving me a pointed look.

Maddoc reaches a hand back and tugs me forward, draping his arm around my shoulders possessively.

"Or with our woman," he adds, holding her gaze. A complicated series of expressions cross her face, but Maddoc

232

doesn't give her any time to sort them out. "Decide, Sienna," he adds sharply. "I've got other shit to do. Tell me what you came to say, or get the fuck out of our territory. Logan will make sure you get across the border."

Her face turns a mottled shade of red, her eyes darting between all of us for a moment, but there's really only one option here if whatever the fuck she came for is that important for her.

"Fine," she finally says, lifting her chin defiantly. "You want to know why I came? I'm here to help you take down West Point. I want to fucking *destroy* Austin McKenna, and you're the only one who can do it."

RILEY

MY EYEBROWS SHOOT up as Sienna locks eyes with Maddoc, as if daring him to believe her. I'm not sure whether or not I do, but I do know I don't trust her.

Or, for that matter, like her.

Around me, I can feel each of my men reacting with surprise too. None of us expected Sienna to say that, and even if their body language doesn't give them away, I can tell that they're just as shocked—and just as distrustful—as I am.

"Why?" Maddoc finally demands.

Dante snorts. "You really all that surprised she'd betray him too, Madd? We know her true colors."

"Fuck you, Dante," Sienna snaps. "He's gonna take you Reapers out, and *I'm* the one who walked in here to do something about that."

"He's not taking us out," Logan says flatly.

Sienna laughs, sounding a little manic. "Do you even know how much money this bitch gave him?" She flings an arm in my direction, and I hear Dante's gun cock under the table.

We all hear it... and Sienna's eyes go wide.

"You wanna rephrase that?" Dante suggests quietly.

She swallows hard, shooting daggers at me with her eyes,

then quickly looks away, taking a deep breath like she's trying to center herself.

"I just mean that getting his hands on all that money has got him getting a little too big for his britches now," she finally goes on, a little more subdued. "He's been making all these plans, like, ever since I threw in with him, but now he can actually move on them."

"We noticed," Maddoc says dryly.

"Yeah, well did you also notice that he's a power hungry psycho?" she snaps. "And the more power he gets, the more of an ego maniac that fucker becomes."

"Of course we've noticed," Maddoc says, starting to sound a little impatient. "None of this is fucking news, Sienna. Are you just here to whine, or do you actually want to take him down?"

"Of course I fucking want it."

He waits her out, and after a minute, she quits glaring, her shoulders slumping in defeat. "We had a fight."

"Okay," Maddoc says flatly.

"*Look* at me," Sienna demands, waving her hands in front of herself. "This wasn't just some minor argument. I told him I didn't agree with some of the shit he's planning, and he fucking snapped! He was supposed to marry me before that bi—"

All three men go rigid, and Sienna freezes like a deer in the headlights for a moment, then pivots quickly, wrapping her arms around herself and darting a quick look at me before staring down at the top of the table as she goes on.

"Before he got his hands on all that money, everything was good between us. He actually listened to me. Then everything changed. He's got big plans for his gang, and when I told him I thought he was moving too fast and taking too many risks, he just told me I needed to shut up and learn my place."

Dante snorts. "Well, your place sure as shit ain't here."

"I never said it was," she snaps, then quickly covers her mouth when her eyes well up with tears.

I legit don't know if she's playing us or having some kind of breakdown, but I'm pretty sure it would be hard to fake the way her voice cracks as she continues telling her story in a broken whisper.

"I pushed back when he said that shit, because hell no, you know? But he... he hit me. Not just a regular slap or something. The fucker beat me." Her eyes dart up to mine again, then away. "He wouldn't stop. Wouldn't let me get away from him. He tried to kill me, just for disagreeing with him."

"If he'd wanted you dead, you would be," Logan says flatly. "If he wanted you to come to us with a sob story, he'd give you a few bruises and send you in to win our trust."

"Oh, fuck you, Logan," she says, rocking back. "He knows none of you dickheads are ever gonna trust me. And he *did* try to kill me. I lost consciousness while he was hitting me, and when I came to, I was in the river."

"What?" I blurt out, an involuntary shiver of terror rocking through me.

I had way too much time to think about how Austin would get rid of me after I signed over my inheritance while I sat in that prison cell of a room, and I blamed Sienna for putting those thoughts in my head in the first place. But none of that changes my horror at hearing that he went and actually did it.

She nods, twisting her hands together in front of her on the table. "Yeah. I'm pretty sure he threw me in there while I was unconscious. Or I mean, he probably had Tony or Jackson do it, the sick fucks. But Austin definitely never meant for me to make it back out."

She stops talking, and after a couple of minutes of silence, Maddoc asks, "Does he know you're alive?"

When Sienna blinks, looking up with a lost expression that shows just how hurt and traumatized she is, it hits me harder than I'm ready for.

She's really not faking this. And I'll never like her, but I'd be lying if I said I didn't feel a little bit sorry for her too. She'll always be the bitch who betrayed Maddoc, and since she made that bed, she definitely deserves to lie in it... but not to be fucking dumped in a river and left to die for it.

No one deserves that.

Maddoc doesn't seem to be softening much toward her, though, and she definitely deserves *that*.

"Well?" he presses, his voice hard. "Does McKenna know that you're..." He stops and shakes his head. "You know what? I don't actually give a shit. I also don't see why you think this is gonna help us stop him or take West Point down."

"Oh, really? You don't think anything I've picked up over there might be useful?" Sienna asks, her snark killing off most of my sympathy.

"Doubtful," Dante mutters, leaning back in his seat... but not so far that he can't keep his weapon trained on her under the table.

She glares at him for a moment, then deflates, slumping against the back of the booth as if exhaustion has finally caught up with her.

"Fuck you too, Dante," she says tiredly, tucking some of her limp hair behind her ears before looking back up at Maddoc. "Austin may never have seen me as his partner, but that didn't mean he didn't talk about shit in front of me. I thought we were in it together, and I gave him some damn good ideas over the years that he took fucking credit for, but his current plan is suicide."

"Suicide?" Maddoc shares a skeptical look with his brothers. "You just said you wanted to destroy him. If that's true, you'd let him burn."

"Yeah, except what if it's not? Do you have any idea what you can buy with the kind of money she handed over to him? Fucking *anything*. Maybe even this."

"Maybe even what?" Maddoc asks. "Quit fucking around if

you really want to take him down, Sienna. What's McKenna planning?"

Her eyes flash for a second, like she wants to snap back at him with something else nasty, but then, to her credit, she sucks it up and just nods, straightening her spine. "Austin hates you, but this is bigger than you." She swallows hard, looking at each of us. "He isn't just planning to decimate the Reapers. He's set his sights as high as they can go here in Halston."

It takes me a minute to realize what she means.

It takes Maddoc a lot less.

"McKenna's planning to take down The Six," he says grimly.

I blink. "He... can't though, right?"

I wish I felt more confident about that, but there's too much I don't know. I can tell the Reapers are shocked to hear that McKenna is planning on it, though, so maybe I'm not too far off.

And maybe, *maybe*, this information is actually worth dealing with Sienna for too.

"Fuck," Maddoc mutters after a moment, scrubbing a hand over his face. Then he gestures to Logan, who guides me into a seat on the far side of the booth from Sienna before sitting next to me. Maddoc takes the seat across from her. "Fine. Talk. How does he think he can manage to take down The Six?"

Sienna hesitates, then shrugs. "I don't actually know."

"What?" Maddoc asks, his face darkening.

She winces. "I mean, I don't actually know all the *details*, but I'm sure that's his plan. It's all he's talked about ever since the first time they called the two of you in front of them."

"Okay, so we're done here," he says flatly.

"No," Sienna blurts, reaching for Maddoc across the table.

He pulls back so that her fingers don't do anything more than skim his sleeve. "Why? What else have you got to offer?"

"Really, Maddoc?" She looks up at him through her lashes. "You like a lot that I have to offer. I know you haven't forgotten."

The only thing stopping me from punching the sultry look off her face is the flat, uninterested stare Maddoc gives her.

"It sounds like that's just one more thing you're wrong about then," he tells her. "There's nothing memorable between you and me. There never was."

The bitch actually pouts. "I know you don't really mean that. I shouldn't have left you. I can see that now. You treated me better than Austin ever did, and—"

"And fucking nothing," he says, standing up abruptly. "I don't give a shit that he beat you, and the only problem I have with him dumping you in that river is that you crawled back out."

"Asshole," she hisses, glaring up at him. "I came to *you*."

"And now that you have, I should finish what McKenna started," Maddoc says coldly, pinning her with a look that has all the blood draining out of her face. "He's already gonna die for kidnapping Riley and forcing her to marry him, but you went along with it. You were there. You were a part of that shit, Sienna. Make no mistake, there's only one woman I care about here, and it's gonna be up to her whether you live or die today." He looks at me, his eyes full of simmering rage, barely held in check. "Butterfly?"

Sienna's eyes dart toward me too, true fear flashing across her face.

Maybe I'm the monster here, because I like it. Seeing it feeds the darkness in me, and I hope like hell that she's remembering the way she treated me, the way she taunted me, because I sure as fuck am.

"You can't be serious, Maddoc," Sienna says, her voice trembling a little.

He doesn't even bother to answer her. He's waiting on me. And I know just as well as Sienna does that if I give him the word, he'll do it in a heartbeat. Any one of these men will kill for me, no questions asked.

But the fact that they did ask, that Maddoc's giving all the power to me after that bastard, McKenna, took it all away, it's... enough. I hate Sienna, and I hate what she did, but I don't want more blood on my hands, and I don't need it. Not when I'm the one who fucking won here. She's a shitty person, but she already lost everything that matters. She lost one of the best men I know, and now she's lost everything she left Maddoc for too.

"I don't want you to kill her," I tell him.

He holds my gaze for a moment, and I can't tell if he's disappointed or proud, but there's definitely a lot of emotion in his eyes. Then he turns back to her. "You heard Riley."

"Okay, yeah," Sienna says, nodding quickly and scooting toward the edge of the bench seat, clearly ready to bolt.

Maddoc nods toward Logan, and Logan blocks her.

"The fuck?" Sienna spits out, glaring up at him.

Logan doesn't react, and Maddoc leans across the table, getting right in her face. "Right now, it's Riley's choice, and she's made it," he says, his gray eyes burning into hers, "but if you ever show your face in Reaper territory again, if you ever fucking *look* at Riley again, I'll end you, do you understand?"

She swallows hard, shrinking back. "I understand."

"Logan," Maddoc says without looking away from her.

Logan nods and steps back, letting Sienna out of the booth, then he taps something into his phone as she slinks away.

"I've got Greg and Vic on it," he tells Maddoc after a moment. "They'll escort her to the border."

Maddoc nods, then tugs me against him, practically pulling me onto his lap. He buries his face against my neck, taking a few breaths as his hands dig into my hips.

After a moment, he looks up at his brothers, not addressing the fact that he's still holding me so tightly that I'm guaranteed a few new bruises. "What do you think about that bitch's intel? Have either of you heard any word on the street about this shit with The Six?"

"Fuck no," Dante says, snorting. "Sienna's right about one thing. That would be fucking suicide."

"And not good for the city," Logan adds, his eyes flat.

Maddoc sighs, then pinches the bridge of his nose. "But since McKenna's a narcissistic fucktwit, none of that shit's gonna hold him back, and like Sienna said, he's got the money to actually make a go at it."

"Fuck," Dante says. "We're all gonna suffer if he does, win or lose."

Maddoc nods. "But none of that means Sienna's wrong." He pauses, then curses. "She's a lot of things, but I don't think she's that. Not about this."

Dante and Logan nod, and even if I don't know all the factors they're probably taking into consideration, my gut agrees. Austin really is going to come gunning for The Six.

"That could change things," Maddoc says grimly. "If they see McKenna as an actual threat to their power, they'll have to step in."

Dante drums his fingers on the table. "That could help us."

"They still won't take sides though, right?" I ask.

"That's right, wildcat," Logan says, giving me one of those small smiles that make me feel so damn in love with him. "But the enemy of my enemy is my friend."

"I think they could become very good friends to us," Maddoc says slowly, like he's contemplating strategy. "But we'll need to get proof of what Sienna said if we want to take this information to The Six and make that happen."

Dante nods. "They won't act on rumor or hearsay alone, that's for damn sure. Especially not when it means starting some shit that could destabilize Halston's entire underground."

"The Six exist to keep order, right?" I ask, looking between the three of them.

"That's right, butterfly," Maddoc says, turning to press a

thigh-melting kiss behind my ear. "They do, and they're ruthless about it."

"I like ruthless," I say, earning three matching looks, each hot enough to curl my toes.

"We know you do, princess," Dante says, those vibrant green eyes of his promising me that they'll give me *exactly* what we like once we get home.

"But first," Maddoc says, pinning us each with a look. "We need to get some actual evidence of McKenna's plans. How are we gonna do that?"

None of them have a quick answer to that, and I bite my lip as they start throwing around ideas, realizing that the information Sienna brought was both good and bad. On the one hand, she's finally given us the first real chance we have to fight back with something concrete; to really find a way to stop that motherfucker once and for all.

But on the other hand, the Reapers don't have anyone on the inside in Austin's organization, and with no reliable allies or informants to lean on for this, in some ways, being able to finally end this thing feels farther away than ever... especially if we don't figure it out fast enough.

Because if Austin actually starts something that pulls Halston's underground into an all-out war that involves The Six? Everyone's gonna suffer, and I can tell by the serious looks on my men's faces that even they aren't sure the Reapers could survive that.

RILEY

"Quit scratching that thing, princess," Dante says, catching me in the act as he passes my room.

I jump, dropping my hand from my healing tattoo, startled more than I should be since I know all three men are home right now. We've all been on edge though, and I know Dante gets it. West Point has been getting more and more aggressive, and just yesterday he attacked us again, getting a lot deeper into Reaper territory than he's dared up until now.

Worse, this time, a few of our people got hurt. It's not just Austin who's getting more aggressive; the mercenaries he's hiring seem to be getting more bloodthirsty by the day.

"That motherfucker," I whisper, appreciating it when Dante frowns and steps fully into my room, pulling me against him.

"We're gonna end him," he says, not needing me to explain where my mind just went since he feels it too.

"I know. Are we making any progress, though?"

"You know what Logan says." He pushes some of my hair back, smiling down at me. "It's coming together."

I'm not sure that's exactly what Logan actually said, but I go up on my toes and press a kiss to Dante's mouth, happy to take his reassurance in the spirit he means it.

For now, at least.

He's got to be just as stressed as I am, but for the first time in a few days, he doesn't look it. I don't know how. We've all spent every waking hour since Sienna dropped the bomb on us about Austin's plans, working to make the most of this information... and it feels like we're stuck on step one. Namely, we're still trying to dig up evidence that Austin is planning to move against The Six, while also fending off his attacks and fortifying our position as he continues to fuck with us.

Logan's been mapping out all the spots Austin's been attacking so far, and just like Maddoc predicted, most of them are on the edges of Reaper territory, but he's also started going after a few of the gangs who've allied with us now too. We've been tracking anywhere and everywhere that West Point gang members or his mercenaries show up around the city, trying to spot patterns, and so far, nothing useful has come of it. Certainly nothing that we can bring in front of The Six.

Dante pulls my fingers away from my right breast, letting his thumb brush over the bright red of my new tattoo. "Itchy?"

"Not too bad."

"You should get your mind off it."

My breath quickens. We've all been so damn busy that I haven't been with any of my men the way I'm craving them for the last few days. At least, not enough to satisfy any of us. But if Dante thinks we have time...

He laughs, low and sexy, and laces our fingers while taking a step backward, toward the door. "Come on. That's not what I meant this time."

"Where are you taking me?"

"I've got something to show you," he says, pulling me out into the hallway and heading for the stairs.

"Is it safe?" I ask, my breath stuttering for a different reason this time. One I fucking hate. "The last attack—"

"Has been fucking dealt with," he says firmly, cutting me off. Then he blows out a gusty breath and pushes me up against the wall, kissing me deep enough that I manage to stop worrying about it for a moment. "Quit thinking about that shit for a little while, okay?" he murmurs once he finally lets me come up for air. "I'm taking you somewhere safe. We're not even leaving the house. I just want you to come down to the basement with me."

The guys all work out religiously in the gym they've got set up there, but I haven't spent much time down there even though I admit it's a great way to blow off steam. Just not my favorite way.

"Please tell me we're not doing laundry right now," I tease him, pretty sure that's the only other thing they use the basement for outside of the kind of gang business that they've kept me out of so far.

"No laundry," he says, leading me down to the gym. He slides his hands down my hips, pressing himself against my back as he leans down to whisper in my ear. "You might be a little overdressed, though."

"Feel free to help me with that problem," I joke-but-not-really, not even noticing that he's using his grip on my hips to steer me around until I'm facing the far corner. Then I blink as I realize why I'm overdressed.

There's a stripper pole in the corner.

"Holy shit," I breathe out, a visceral thrill rolling through my body, a sense memory of something I haven't even let myself acknowledge I've been missing. "Where did that come from?"

"I had it installed for you," Dante murmurs, letting me go without a fight when I move toward it. "You know I deal with my shit by painting, and I fucking love having you up in my studio, sharing that. But it's not really your thing, is it? You need to dance."

"I've missed it," I admit, running my hands up the pole and feeling it like a stroke on my own body.

"I know," Dante says, his voice full of all the emotions that give me something to fight for. "And I want you to be able to dance anytime you want it. Anytime you fucking need it. Right here at home."

I don't know if it's hearing him calling this my home, which it is, *he* is, or if it's how touched I am that he thought to do this for me. That he understands me so well. Whatever it is, he's right. I do need this, it's how I've always worked out my emotions, and right now, I'm full of them.

I kick my shoes off and wrap a leg around the pole, letting my body weight pull me around it in a move that feels so familiar, so fucking right, that it's crazy to think I haven't danced in so long.

Well, it feels *almost* right. It's easier to dance with skin to the pole, so after trying out a few moves and shaking off the rust, I strip down to my bra and thong, then keep going.

"Fuck, you're gorgeous," Dante murmurs from somewhere behind me, breaking through the trance I've let myself fall into as I work my body around the pole.

It's the perfect amount of slick, and sturdy enough to take all my weight without shaking, and when I twist around it, turning my body so I can face him, a hot thrill goes through me at the heat I find waiting in his gaze.

I slide one hand up the pole until my arm is at its full extension, then let myself slowly undulate around the metal as it starts to warm a little from the heat of my body. "This reminds me of the first time I saw you."

"You remember that?" Dante asks, his voice dropping low and husky in a way I can never help but respond to. "Because I do."

"I remember the feel of your eyes on me that night." I let myself turn around the pole again, dropping low and feeling a delicious burn in my thighs as I slowly work myself back up it. I twist to look back at him over my shoulder. "It felt just like this."

There isn't any music, but somehow, it feels like there's a rhythm moving through my body anyway.

I close my eyes and arch my back, rolling my hips as I let it take over; as I let myself enjoy the feel of my hair brushing against the top of my ass while I swing myself around the pole.

I run my hands up my sides to cup my tits and throw my head back with abandon, instinctively using all the moves that used to make me so much money on stage, but this time, dancing purely for myself, the way I've always loved best.

Although maybe this time, I'm loving it just a little bit more with the sensual weight of Dante's eyes on me, too.... and not *just* his. At some point, a low bass beat starts up, one I feel more than hear at first.

I drag my eyes open, not even sure when I let them drift closed, and find that Maddoc and Logan have joined us.

Having all three of my men watch me dance does something to me that's completely different than when I used to strip for cash. The air thickens as I feel their heated gazes on me, and I let my body go, dancing out every bit of anger, stress, frustration, and fear that I haven't had an outlet for. Letting them fuel the other things these men make me feel. Loved and cherished and so fucking aroused that it scents the air and flows through my blood.

None of them try to touch me or join me.

And none of them take their eyes off me, not even for a second.

Pole work has always been my favorite. Sensual and fun and freeing. But nothing has ever turned me on the way their eyes on me do right now. I strip my bra off, making a show of it. A private show, just for them.

I'm tempted to lose my thong too. I want to dance for them naked and then beg them each to fuck me, but as the heat builds between us all, it's almost too much. I'm so wet that my thighs are slick with it, and my pussy throbs with arousal as I wrap my legs around the pole, forcing me to grind against it in a desperate bid for relief.

I drop low, one hand on the pole and the other running down my body, then slowly work my way back to my feet, rocking against the hard steel between my legs, driven on by the intensity of my men's expressions and the bass that feels like the beat of my own soul.

All three of them are hard, their thick cocks straining against their pants and their eyes devouring me as I moan, working myself against the pole faster and faster.

I wish it was them.

I *need* it to be them.

But it's so fucking hot to give them this show, to see how much my getting myself off turns them on, that I can't stop. I can't look away. I can't help but rub against the rigid pole until I finally fall apart.

"Oh fuck," I gasp as I start to come, gripping the pole tight and fucking myself against it because it feels too good to ever stop. "Fuck, fuck, *fuck*."

Dante is suddenly right in my face, faster than I even realized he moved.

"Exactly what I was thinking, princess," he groans before grabbing the back of my head and kissing me hard enough to set off my orgasm all over again.

29

RILEY

I GASP into Dante's mouth, wrapping my legs around him when he lifts me up and presses me back against the pole.

"You're so fucking gorgeous," he mutters, swallowing my moan and squeezing my ass as he grinds against me. "So damn sexy like this. I want to fuck you right here, with my brothers. I want all three of us to fill you up, princess."

My stomach flips. "Yes," I breathe out.

Dante groans, slipping his fingers under the thin strip of my thong. "You want that, beautiful?"

"*Yes.*"

They've all fucked me before. Each one of them has filled me up—with his cock and with his cum—and I've fucking loved it. But this time, I know Dante doesn't mean one at a time. He wants to truly share me with his brothers. He wants me to take all of them at once, and the idea turns me on so much that the orgasm I just had feels like nothing but foreplay.

"Say it, princess."

"I want that." I grind against him, kissing him harder. "I want all of you. I want to feel nothing *but* you. I want everything else to disappear."

Dante pulls back and gives me a wicked look. "I think we

can make that happen." He shifts his weight, getting my legs to slide down until my feet touch the ground. Then he turns me around to face the pole. "Grab it."

I do, arching my back to press my ass into his groin. I rub it against the thick ridge of his cock, moving like a slow twerk and getting a low, sexy-as-fuck groan for my efforts.

The groan is followed by a hard smack that has me gasping as the sharp sting fades into a sweet, delicious heat across my bare ass.

"Fucking hot," Dante mutters. "Keep a hold of that thing and bend over for me, princess. That's it. Go all the way down."

It's a move I've done a thousand times on stage, and I know how good it looks. This time, it feels good too. Wanton and sexy and filthy as fuck.

My hair sweeps down to the floor, hanging around me like a purple-and-blue curtain, as Dante rubs the spot he just spanked. "That's it. Perfect." He gropes me a little, then slips my thong down. "Lift your feet."

I do it, letting him pull it all the way off and toss it away. But then, instead of feeling his hands or his cock on me, I hear the faint chink of metal followed by a soft, unmistakable *whoosh*.

"Fuck," I gasp, goosebumps erupting all over my body.

His belt is coming off.

"Gonna help everything else disappear for you," he promises, his hand sliding between my legs from behind. "Remember that night Maddoc belted you? We could all see how wet you got." He drags his fingers through my slick folds. "Do you want that again? Before we all claim you?"

I nod, too turned on for words right now. Because I *do* want it. I want the pain. I want the release and the promise Dante just made me—that it will take me out of my head and make everything disappear. But as much as I love Dante for knowing that, it's not him that I want to belt me.

"I want Logan to do it. He knows how to give me what I need."

Just enough pain. Even better, he'll get off on it too.

Logan lets out a low noise. The fact that he's turned on enough to let it slip out tells me more than anything else just how much he wants this too.

Dante chuckles and takes a step back. "Gonna be hot, princess. Gonna get you panting for us."

I close my eyes, the blood that's rushing down to my head starting to make me feel a little lightheaded.

Somehow, that makes it even better. I feel safe enough to let go completely around these men, especially here, secure in this protected space. I don't want to think.

And I love that they're not going to let me.

I hear the men muttering to each other for a moment, then firm hands smooth over my ass, kneading my curves with a deliberate, almost clinical precision that's becoming as familiar to me as breathing.

Logan. I spread my legs for him.

His fingers trace lines across my ass and thighs, each touch making me shiver. "You'll have welts."

My core throbs, my pussy clenching as the image excites me.

I hated Maddoc for belting me when it happened… in part because of what it did to me. But this time there's no mistaking it. This time, it's not a punishment. It's pure sex.

Logan isn't warning me. He's not even asking me. He's just stating a fact… but I know him well enough now to hear the yearning desire simmering under his flat delivery, and it ignites my own.

"Mark me up again," I beg, pressing back into his touch. "Do it, Logan."

"I would do anything for you," he says, so low I almost miss it.

But I don't... and it feels a hell of a lot like he just said *I love you*.

Before I can do anything with that, he rests one hand on my lower back and nudges my legs apart, forcing me to spread them wider. "Stay still. Brace yourself."

It's all the warning I get before he cracks Dante's belt across my ass.

The shock of the impact shoots through my whole body and takes my breath away so I can't even gasp. Then the bright, hot sting sinks into me, and I moan.

Logan drags his finger along the first of the raised welts he promised me, his touch like a fiery brand. "That's one, wildcat. If you want more, you'll have to be the one to count them off. Do you want two?"

"Yes," I whisper, my body clenching with anticipation.

Logan doesn't make me wait.

"Two," I gasp with the second strike. Then, "*Three.*"

I'm panting, and Dante was right about what this would do to me. I was already flushed and wet from the private pole dancing show I gave my men, but with every crack of the belt, my pussy gets even wetter.

A hand strokes my back, following the curve of my spine.

Not Logan's.

"You take this shit so fucking well, butterfly," Maddoc murmurs. "Nothing looks better on you than the signs that you belong to us."

"Nothing feels better than being reminded of it," I breathe out just as Logan snaps the belt against the backs of my thighs.

Pain blooms under the strike, eclipsing almost everything. I clutch the pole for balance, letting it roll through me and push my arousal even higher. Then firm hands slide between my legs, stroking my clit with a touch that makes me shudder so hard I almost come.

"More?" Logan asks, bringing me back to myself a little.

"Please," I whisper, forcing my eyes open even though I'm not sure when they drifted closed.

Maddoc's shoes are to my left. Dante's to my right. I have no idea which one of them is rubbing my clit, and when Logan whispers filthy words of praise from behind me and belts me again, I don't care, either.

"Five," I mouth, the fresh stripe stealing my breath. "Six," I pant when he gives me that one. Then, "Seven. Oh god. Oh fuck, *Logan*."

"You're beautiful," he says, slowly dragging the leather over my new welts.

I start to shake, the pain not even feeling like pain anymore. It's just licks of fire, each one burning a new mark of ownership into my soul.

"Enough?" Logan asks.

I shake my head, but that's not enough. "Please." My voice sounds hoarse, my mouth too dry. "Another."

"Fucking incredible," Dante murmurs next to me as a rough thumb brushes over my clit.

One of them pushes thick, callused fingers into my pussy at the same time, making my body clench hard as pleasure rocks through me, and this time, when Logan gives me what I asked for and belts me again, I forget the count, filthy sounds escaping me instead.

"That was eight," Logan says, smoothing his hand over my ass. "The pattern isn't complete. You need two more."

I nod, and he gives them to me.

"Nine... *ten*."

I'm right on the edge by the time the last blow falls, shaking and breathless and so desperate to come that I almost feel disconnected from my body. I hear the belt drop to the ground behind me, but I can't get my fingers to unclench from the pole.

Dante does it for me, and then Logan pulls me upright,

turning me to face him and staring into my eyes like he's searching for the secrets to the universe.

"Logan," I pant. My head feels floaty and my body is on fire.

He smiles, brushing my hair back from my face in the most tender gesture I've ever known from him. "You did so well," he says softly. "I..."

He pauses, then pulls me against him and takes my mouth, kissing me with all the emotion he normally keeps under lock and key.

I gasp, clinging to him, and let him have me. Let him push me back against the pole and *devour* me.

"Is she ready for us?" Maddoc asks, his voice like gravel.

Logan slips a hand between my legs without coming up for air, sinking three long fingers into my pussy and grinding the heel of his hand against my clit... then swallowing my scream when I come so hard that my vision whites out.

He holds me through it, his cock an iron bar trapped behind his pants that pulses against me as he locks his arms around my body to keep me upright. "She's ready," he tells Maddoc, slowly sliding his fingers out of my pussy as I pant against his neck. "She's wet enough to take us all."

I'm not just wet. I feel almost boneless, and it's fine, because my body is completely theirs.

They pass me between them, groping and kissing me, murmuring filthy promises in my ears as each of them strip down to their skin and take turns bringing me back to the edge of desperation.

I'm in Maddoc's arms when Dante spreads himself out on the floor. He lies on his back, feet flat and knees bent and spread wide, slowly stroking himself as he watches me with hooded eyes. He looks like a god made of muscle and ink, and just like he always does, he reads me like a book.

"Give her here, Madd," he says with a sexy smirk. "I need to feel that sweet pussy of hers on my cock."

Maddoc lowers me down to straddle his brother with a dark chuckle, and as I sink down onto Dante's shaft, Dante grips my hips, guiding me where he wants me.

"You know this is my favorite fucking view in the world, right, princess?" he says, giving me a smile hot enough to scorch me once I'm fully seated.

"Same," I gasp, because I can honestly say that about each of them.

I run my hands over the vibrant swirls of color that bring so much depth and beauty to the hard planes of muscle in Dante's chest, rocking my hips against his just to feel that thick cock of his rub against my g-spot, and his eyes turn dark with lust.

"Yeah? That's what I like to hear," he says, low and husky. "Now quit teasing and ride me hard, princess. Dance on this fucking pole for me. I know what those hips can really do."

I laugh, but the sound turns into a hot, filthy moan when his grip tightens enough to bruise and he slams up into me, spearing my core.

"Fuck," I gasp. "*Yes.*"

Dante grins, then slaps my ass, making me suck in a sharp breath when it wakes up the fire from Logan's welts. "That was me doing all the work just now. I thought I told you to ride me. Give my brothers something to keep them interested."

"I don't think that's going to be a problem," Logan murmurs, looking down at me with so much heat in his eyes that my body reacts without my permission, clenching hard enough around Dante's cock to make us both groan.

"Princess," he grits out, all the teasing in his voice from earlier replaced by pure sex. "Work that gorgeous body of yours."

It's like he flips a switch inside me. I've already come for them today, but it will never be enough. I ride him hard, just like he told me to, losing myself in it just as much as I ever do dancing.

"I fucking love this," Dante mutters, letting his hands roam all over me. "You belong on my cock."

"And mine," Maddoc says from behind me, the primal need in his voice sending a shiver through me when he grabs my hips too, then starts to knead my ass.

"I want both of them," I gasp, catching Logan's eyes as Maddoc starts kissing the back of my neck. "*All* of them."

Logan's pale gaze burns into me as Dante and Maddoc start to take me apart, the two of them stroking my stomach, my thighs... cupping my breasts and then pinching my nipples hard enough to put me right on the verge of coming again.

"I need to be inside you, butterfly," Maddoc murmurs in my ear, pushing me forward until my breasts flatten against Dante's chest.

Dante's arms go around me, and I hear a little snick, turning my head to see Maddoc slicking his fingers with clear lube from a small bottle.

Then he drags those fingers down the center of my ass and presses them against my little hole.

"Fuck," I gasp as something hot and wicked shoots through my body, making my inner muscles clench hard enough around Dante's cock that he curses too.

"Do that again, princess. Milk me."

Maddoc chuckles, low and dirty, and starts to finger me open from behind. "You're tight as hell."

"I've never... oh god. Fuck, Maddoc," I pant, shivers wracking my body as he adds more lube, and then another finger, making the burning stretch start to feel like it's going to overload me.

I want it to. I want to be overwhelmed.

They don't disappoint.

Dante smooths some of my hair back from my face, the long strands darkened and damp from sweat.

"You're ours, princess," he murmurs, his gaze hooded as he

holds me in place for his brother. "You've never let anyone have this ass before, but you're gonna have to start." His lips tip up in a sexy smirk. "All three of us are greedy as fuck when it comes to you, and we ain't always gonna want to take turns. You ready to give it to us? You ready to give us everything?"

"*Yes*," I gasp.

"Good," Maddoc growls, easing his fingers out of me and replacing them with the fat tip of his cock. "Because nothing's better than being inside you, butterfly. I fucking need this."

The pressure is almost too much, an indescribable burn as he slowly pushes forward, forcing my body open in a way I've never experienced before. It hurts, but even though the pain is totally different from what I felt while being belted, it still fulfills the same promise my men made to me—it's so intense that the rest of the world disappears. Nothing else exists except the way they're filling me.

"*Motherfucker*," Dante hisses as Maddoc breaches me, his fingers digging into my hips. "I can feel you right through her, Madd."

"That's just the fucking tip," Maddoc grits out, starting to pump his hips in slow, shallow thrusts that push his cock deeper, inch by torturously slow inch. "Let me get inside. Don't fucking move, Dante."

Dante laughs, the sound as strained as his rock-hard muscles, bunched up into tight knots. "I can't, brother. Jesus *fuck*. Never felt anything like it. You're making our girl's perfect pussy feel even tighter."

Not just tighter. As Maddoc works his cock into me, it lights up nerve endings I didn't even know I had. It also does something to my g-spot that has a long, low whine escaping me. It hurts and feels incredible and completely overwhelms me. And Dante's right. I can feel both of them, and it's almost perfect.

I look up, panting hard as waves of heat roll through my

body, and lock eyes with Logan.

"Beautiful," he whispers, stroking himself as he stares down at me. "You really are made for this, wildcat. I can see the pain on your face. You love being split open by my brothers."

I do. It's so much, and I never want it to stop even as I wonder if I can really take it.

"Every single way of fucking you makes me want to lose my goddamn mind," Maddoc grits out, fisting my hair in one hand and slowly thrusting a little deeper into my ass. "But this is everything, butterfly. Taking you with my brothers. Taking your ass as my own. Taking... *fuck*."

His words heighten my own arousal so much that my body clenches down around him, around both of them, and he curses hard as Dante grunts beneath me, his hips slamming up and driving his cock deeper into my pussy.

I whimper, the feel of both of them surrounding me, owning me like this, making me feel like I'm about to shatter. "Please, just, god," I gasp, no idea what I'm begging them for.

"Fuck her, Madd," Dante says, his voice hoarse with the strain of holding himself still. "Quit fucking around and take her hard. I need to move, or I need you to, but this is killing me."

Maddoc growls an inarticulate response, then pulls back and palms my ass, waking up the burn from the belting again, and spreads me wide. "Love seeing you take my cock. Your hole is stretched to the limit, isn't it?"

I shudder, panting as I nod. "Please."

He runs a finger around the sensitive ring of skin he's so enthralled by, and I only realize after a moment that he's applying more lube.

Then he fucks me.

"Oh god," I gasp, trembling almost uncontrollably as he works up a rhythm that lets Dante thrust into me every time he pulls back.

"That's it, princess," Dante rasps, his hands guiding my

hips. "Fuck, yes, just like that."

"I want you full of our cum. Marked as a Reaper. Dripping with it," Maddoc grunts, the heat of his body behind me lighting me up inside. "I want you marked inside and out, in every hole."

I gasp, the dirty words almost more than I can take. But I want that too, and I can't have it without Logan.

I look up at him, too overwhelmed to speak.

I don't need to. He stares at me like he can see right into my soul, and when my eyes beg him to come closer, he does, running his fingers through my hair in a tender, loving gesture that makes tears spring to my eyes... then tangling them in the long strands and wrapping them around his fist so he can tug my head up hard enough to make those tears pour down my cheeks from the sudden, stinging pain.

"Open," he says, guiding his cock to my lips. "Tongue out."

He rubs the head back and forth over my extended tongue, the scent and taste of him like a drug. Then he thrusts into my mouth, not stopping until he hits the back of my throat.

I gag, and he groans, pushing his cock in even deeper and crooning sweet, filthy words to me as my throat spasms around his shaft.

"Shit, Logan," Dante grunts, his rhythm faltering for a moment. "Our princess looks hot as fuck with a mouth full of cock."

"She does," Logan says, pulling back until just the tip rests on my tongue again. He twists his hand tighter in my hair. "You don't want to think, do you? You don't want anything but our cocks."

I can't even nod, but I don't have to. He already knows the answer. They all know me so well that there's not a chance in hell I could ever doubt how they feel about me. Not even Logan, despite the way he's withheld the actual words.

I don't need them. Not right now. Not when he looks down at me like I'm everything to him as he starts slowly fucking my throat, his rhythm syncing up with his brothers' as they take me just the way Maddoc promised. Filling every one of my holes. Owning me. Surrounding me. Overwhelming me in all the ways I didn't know how to ask for; all the ways they instinctively knew I needed right now.

I dig my fingers into Dante's chest, relaxing my throat and surrendering my body to them. All I know is their cocks, their hands, their filthy, tender words as they fuck me until nothing else exists. Until the pleasure coiling inside me, tighter and tighter, finally snaps in a blistering explosion that rocks through me so hard it feels like I really have shattered.

I scream as I come, the sound choked off by Logan's cock, and it's like a domino effect, each of my men cursing as their releases overtake them.

"Fuck, fuck, *fuck*," Dante grits out, his cock pulsing inside me as he grinds up against me.

Maddoc is right behind him, and as they each fill me with their cum, Logan yanks my head back as he starts to come too, pulling away enough that instead of going down my throat, it spills out of my mouth, dripping down my chin.

He jacks himself through the last of it, spraying it across my face, then reaches down to rub it into my skin, dragging his fingers across my lips. "Suck."

I do, and I can still taste him as he pulls me up and kisses me, Dante and Maddoc's cocks sliding out of me as my body goes boneless in his arms.

"Fucking incredible," Dante murmurs, rolling to his feet and taking me from Logan to kiss me too. Then he smiles, pushing my hair out of my face, and dips his fingers between my legs. "You're a filthy mess."

Maddoc comes up behind me, gripping my throat and tilting my head back. "Our mess," he murmurs, taking my mouth as I melt back against him.

I feel too empty but completely sated, and I already know

that I'll need to do this again... and again... and again. But for now, even though I know we all have to go back to the real world, I feel calm and relaxed for the first time in days. Closer to all of them, with unbreakable bonds between us that, for the first time, really make me believe we're going to win this thing.

We have to. I've never been so fucking in love, or felt so loved in return.

My stomach growls as the three of them are helping me get cleaned up, and Dante laughs. "Come upstairs and let's get you fed, princess. You definitely put in the work for it."

"You're incredible," Maddoc says, his eyes shining with emotion and his voice serious. Then he cracks a smile and smacks my ass. "But Dante's right. You burned some calories just now. Gotta replace them before the next round."

I shake my head, laughing along with them as we head up to the kitchen and Logan starts pulling things out of the fridge. I honestly don't know if I could go again. But I also know how much I love the way they push me past my limits.

If they want me again, I'm theirs.

"Whatever you're thinking right now, stop," Maddoc growls, pulling me against him as whatever Logan's making starts to fill the room with mouthwatering scents that have my stomach loudly rumbling again. Maddoc smirks, resting his hand on it. "See? This is why you can't start looking at us like—"

He cuts off mid-sentence, his focus shifting in an instant when Logan suddenly stiffens.

"What is it?" Maddoc demands sharply.

Instead of answering, Logan drops the spatula in his hand and lunges for us.

No, for Maddoc.

He shoves him sideways, making me stumble back into the counter as Maddoc slams into the wall next to the fridge.

A bullet whizzes through the space Maddoc was just occupying, slamming into the cabinet door.

30

LOGAN

Riley screams as Maddoc grunts from the force of my tackle.

I barely have time to register either reaction. I noticed a strange flicker of light outside the window that faces the back of our house, a disruption of the order that we've set up a strict security perimeter to maintain—and I moved on instinct. An instinct that instantly shifts my priorities to protecting Riley as someone dressed in black bursts into the room, firing at Maddoc again.

A bullet grazes him, painting a bright red line across his torso before it buries itself in the wall behind him. I lunge for Riley and take her down to the floor, covering her with my body while Maddoc scrambles behind the island, cursing up a storm as he takes cover.

"Oh, *fuck* no," Dante shouts as the attacker slithers to the left, still fixated on getting a clear shot at Maddoc.

Dante barrels into him before he can, knocking his aim off and sending the bullet into our coffee maker instead.

Shards of hard plastic explode outward, one of them nicking the back of my neck as I twist around to shove Riley under the counter, out of the line of fire. It only takes a split second, but that's also all it takes for the attacker to turn on Dante, viciously forcing my brother back with a series of close combat moves that give away his training.

He's a mercenary. Probably ex-military; definitely deadly.

I dive for them, kicking the back of the attacker's knee in a move that should have dropped him.

Instead, he grunts and rolls with it, pulling a knife out with what should have been his non-dominant hand when the roll traps his gun arm underneath him for a moment.

He slashes upward, forcing Dante to jump back, and Maddoc slams into him from the side.

They both go down, but the attacker's training shows when he manages to evade a potentially lethal headlock I've seen Maddoc use before, and twists out of his hold completely, rising up to his knees.

"I don't fucking think so, motherfucker," Dante says, kicking the gun out of his hand before he can take aim with it.

The attacker pivots, driving his fingers into Dante's throat and rolling out of the way when I try to take him down again.

He comes up with another weapon in hand, and this time he gets a shot off.

He aims for Maddoc again, but Dante clocks the guy in the back of the head with one of our bar stools, and the fucking bullet goes wide, shattering the edge of the counter right above Riley's head.

Chunks of marble rain down on her, and the terror in her voice when she screams again fills me with a dark fury that eclipses anything I've ever felt before.

"Riley, get the fuck out of the kitchen," Maddoc shouts, diverting his attention from the attacker.

Mine narrows, all my senses converging on the intruder with a single-minded focus that's only possible because I trust my brothers with my life. More importantly, with Riley's life.

Maddoc's got her. I need to take the attacker down.

Dante has the same idea, but even two-on-one—three-on-

one a moment later, once Maddoc gets Riley out of the fucking room—it's an all-out brawl with the guy. He's more than good. He's lethal.

He gets another shot off that rips a line of fire across my hip, the bullet digging into the oven door behind me, and proves he really is ambidextrous when he shreds the shirt Maddoc threw on downstairs, leaving bloody slashes all across his chest before we finally wrestle the fucker down and disarm him and toss both his knife and the second gun out of reach.

"Who fucking sent you?" Maddoc demands, all three of us holding the attacker down.

Maddoc kneels on his thighs, keeping his legs down, while Dante pins the fucker's right wrist to his chest in a position I know will allow him to break it if the guy is stupid enough to fight it.

His left wrist already broke when we finally managed to get the knife from him, and it lies limply by his side as I keep his head down. But when Maddoc flicks a look at me, I ease up on the chokehold so the piece of shit will have enough air to answer Maddoc's question.

He doesn't, which I'm sure Maddoc lets him get away with only because none of us actually have any doubts about who sent him here. There are still things we need to know, though.

Maddoc's eyes narrow. "Who are you?"

The attacker meets that one with a silent sneer, obviously trained not to give any information up.

Dante's eyes flicker over him, then go hard. "He's an assassin."

I go still, letting that sink in. Not just a mercenary. This is someone who's trained specifically to kill, and who came here with a laser-focus on taking Maddoc out.

Of the three of us, only Dante was formally trained in that art. I have no idea what he sees, but I trust him implicitly. Which is why I become hyper-vigilant as Maddoc continues to question the man and notice the small, twitching movements he's making with his left hand.

His broken one.

I take a split second to admire the way his training trumps the pain it must be causing him, but the moment I see him extract something small and metallic from his sleeve—a weapon clearly meant to be accessed even when he's pinned down—I move before he can, twisting his neck in a sharp, practiced motion as he palms it and starts to jab the thing toward Maddoc.

His spine snaps with a clean break, his body instantly going limp as he dies.

Maddoc stares down at him, the room quiet around us for a moment. Then—

"*Fuck*," Maddoc yells, slamming his fist into the side of the island next to us. Then he sighs, scrubbing a hand down his face.

"I had to," I explain, turning the assassin's left hand over to reveal the weapon he held there.

Dante sits back on his heels, shaking his head, and Maddoc nods. "I know," he says, giving me a grim smile. "Thank you."

Riley pokes her head around the corner. "Oh god."

"It's fine now," Dante says, tugging her closer. "He's dead, princess."

"Fine? This isn't fucking fine!"

She's right, but the way she immediately stops herself, taking a deep breath and shutting down her freak out, makes me admire her even more.

She stares at the body for another moment, then dismisses him, taking the three of us in instead. "Are you all okay?" she asks, trapping her lower lip between her teeth as she looks at the bullet graze along my hip, then reaches tentative fingers toward Maddoc's bloody chest.

"Nothing a few stitches won't take care of," Maddoc says, his eyes softening for a moment as he captures her hand before

265

she can touch his wounds. "Don't worry about that, butterfly. We really are fine."

She nods, her eyes skittering back to the assassin and then away again. "He died before you could get him to tell you anything, didn't he?"

"It doesn't matter."

She looks up at me. "Of course it matters! He was trying to kill us!"

"He was trying to kill Maddoc," I correct her. "That alone tells us everything we need to know."

"McKenna sent him," Dante says, rage washing over his face for a moment. He springs to his feet, then lands a vicious kick against the corpse's ribs. "That piece of shit tried to take Madd out."

A grim cloud settles over the kitchen, and Maddoc breathes out a quiet curse. "He's getting bolder."

I nod, tightening my hands into fists to contain my rage about that.

"He's not just picking away at your territory anymore," Riley says, wrapping her arms around her middle as her body starts to shake. "He's coming *here*."

Dante pulls her against him, kissing the top of her head. "*He* ain't coming here. He'd never make it this far. But yeah, princess. This was an open, direct attack on our leadership. This was personal."

Then he smiles.

Maddoc's eyes sharpen, and a calm settles across the violent fury boiling in my soul.

"What is it?" Maddoc asks, clearly recognizing the dark hum of ferocity behind that smile just like I do.

"It's a fucking opportunity," Dante says. "Could be exactly the one we need."

"Maddoc almost dying is an opportunity?" Riley spits out, turning on him with rage in her eyes. "What the *fuck*, Dante?"

"I didn't almost die, butterfly," Maddoc says with a smirk, pulling her away from our brother and tucking her against his side. His body language becomes a little looser the moment she's in his arms, and I allow myself a small smile, a warmth in my chest from the sight that not even the grim circumstances can extinguish.

"You fucking did," Riley grumbles, ducking her head and dashing at her eyes. Then she punches him in the chest, his blood smearing on her knuckles. "Don't do it again."

"Okay," he promises, holding her even closer. He tips her chin up. "I love you."

She glares up at him, then sags against him. "I know," she whispers. "Don't let him take that away from me."

"Never gonna happen." Maddoc looks back at Dante. "What are you thinking?"

"We need proof that Austin is gonna go up against The Six, and the best way to get that proof is from the inside." He pauses, making eye contact with each of us. "This could be our chance to do that."

"This... dead guy?" Riley asks, her forehead crinkling in confusion. "How?"

"I'll use it to get in with McKenna myself," he says. "He wants Maddoc dead? We'll give him that. Except I'll pretend I'm the one who did it when his assassin failed, and the piece of shit will buy it, because he doesn't fucking understand loyalty."

I blink. Dante was trained as an assassin too. Except he wasn't *just* trained as an assassin. He was originally sent here to infiltrate the Reapers, and he almost succeeded because his training also taught him to be ruthless, deceptive, and strategic.

"McKenna will think Dante made a power grab when the opportunity presented itself," I say, the pieces falling into place in my mind.

Dante is right. If this works, it really will be a way to finally end this thing.

"What?" Riley blurts, her panic almost palpable. "No. He's not going to believe that, Dante! No one would. You and Maddoc are like brothers."

Maddoc wraps his arm around her middle, holding her against him. "We are," he says, his eyes locked with Dante's in grim understanding. "But like Dante said, McKenna can't wrap his head around that kind of allegiance."

"And he already knows that Dante defected from the Crimson Crows to join us," I add, ignoring the fact that the plan bothers me on a purely emotional level that would be dangerous to let myself indulge in. Strategically, it's brilliant. "It won't take much for Dante to convince him that he's just been leveling up."

"And that I want to do it again," Dante says with a grimace.

Riley's expressive face makes it more than clear that she doesn't want Dante to risk himself like that, but she holds her tongue while Maddoc thinks it through. I can see him running scenarios over in his mind as he runs a hand down her back, smoothing the long, colorful waves of her hair over it, over and over.

Riley must not believe he'll go for it, though, because when his hand goes still, she whips her head up to glare at him. "No."

He sighs. "Yes."

"You can't ask him to do that!"

"He's not asking, princess," Dante says quietly.

She opens her mouth to argue some more, and Maddoc's face goes hard. This isn't about his feelings for her. This is about Maddoc doing what he was born to, which is whatever it takes as the leader of the Reapers.

Including making the hard decisions.

Riley chokes back whatever she was intending to say when she sees his expression. "I hate it," she whispers.

"And I fucking hate what he did to you," Maddoc answers fiercely, holding her gaze. "This is how I'm gonna end it, butterfly. This is how we get retribution."

She stares back at him, and we all see the moment she accepts it. Her spine stiffens and her chin lifts, and a feeling I've been avoiding examining up until now crashes through me hard. It's almost overwhelming, but if we're doing this, it has to be now, so I carefully set it aside to deal with later, and refocus on logistics.

"He'll need proof," I point out.

Dante nods, then grimaces. "Yeah. *Fuck.*"

Riley looks between us. "Proof of what? The... the dead guy?"

"No," Maddoc says grimly. "We have to make McKenna believe Dante killed me. He's gonna need some kind of confirmation."

She swallows hard, her eyes flicking down to his bloody chest. "Like a video?"

"No," Maddoc says flatly. He flexes his hands, extending his fingers and then pulling them into tight fists, and Dante scowls hard before he tucks that emotion away and forces his face to smooth out.

He's good at wearing a mask. I have complete faith in him.

Riley still doesn't get it, though. And then—her eyes widening in horror—she does. "You don't mean... you're going to bring him a... a finger or something?" she asks, all the color leaching out of her face.

"That's easiest," Maddoc agrees grimly. "Something more vital would be better, but—"

"But that's not going to happen," I cut in flatly, silently vowing to make McKenna suffer for my brother's sacrifice, along with all the slow, painful suffering the piece of excrement has already earned for his other sins against my chosen family.

Dante meets my eyes. "You still got the pipe cutter we used when we had to clean up that mess at the chop shop over on Maine?"

I nod. It's a quick, efficient way to handle minor dismemberments.

But when it's finally time for retribution, I won't allow it to be either quick or efficient for McKenna.

Not after this.

31

DANTE

I CAN'T REMEMBER a time when I wasn't able to stay detached about death and violence. Dad started teaching me the art when I was so fucking young that some of my earliest memories are of helping dismember and dispose of some of his hits. It never bothered me, and this isn't any different.

It's fucking necessary.

So I snuff out the fact that it damn well *is* different and refuse to let myself feel what I'm feeling about my brother, the man I'd fucking die for, or the way Riley looks so fucking shell-shocked right now.

I want to remember her the other way. Blissed out and stuffed full of cock, down by that stripper pole she loves so much.

I want a lot of fucking things, but if I'm going to pull this off —and I am—then right the fuck now is when I need to start keeping those things on lockdown so I can do everything I need to do.

"Wait, you guys are going to do this right now?" Riley asks, her eyes going wide when Logan leaves the room to get the pipe cutter.

She's still too fucking pale, looking like she's about to be sick, and her voice rises with the kind of panic I'm not used to seeing on her. At least, not since we finally got Chloe back.

"Yeah, it's gotta be now, princess," I tell her, wanting to take back the last word the moment it slips out.

I'm so damn in love with her I'd burn down the world for her, but from this moment on, I need to cut myself off from my heart and trust my brothers to take care of her so that I can take care of business.

I turn to Maddoc, a little part of me dying inside over not taking Riley in my arms when she so clearly needs it. Hell, I need it too. There will be time for that shit later, though. I'll make sure of it by getting the intel we need to take this motherfucker down.

"Who are we going to bring in on this?" Maddoc asks, his eyes flicking back and forth like he's mentally reviewing our entire organization to figure out who we can trust.

I'd like to say all of them, and to some extent that's true, but there's trust and then there's what it's gonna take to pull this off, and that definitely means keeping the truth limited to just a few key players.

I name my top picks, and when Maddoc nods, I add, "We gotta keep the lower-level members out of the loop completely. All of them. We can't slip up or it will get back to McKenna."

He narrows his eyes, but I can tell he's thinking through all the ramifications of that, not doubting my call. Part of the reason he's the kind of leader and man I burned all my bridges to follow is because he knows when to rely on the strengths of others, and one of mine has always been the planning and execution of what my old man used to call "strategic deceit."

"Agreed," he finally says with a decisive nod. "We'll let the organization think I really died."

"What? No!" Riley bursts out, glaring at us both before focusing her outraged panic on Maddoc. "If they think you died, they're going to think Dante betrayed you!"

"That's right," Maddoc says calmly, holding her gaze. "We need to be careful about who knows the truth. That's how this works. It's the only way it works."

She's always been strong, and I'm so fucking proud of her for not breaking down.

I also don't blame her one damn bit when she finally says, "I... hate that. God, that *fucker*. I hate this!"

"I know, baby," Maddoc says, palming the back of her head and staring down at her. "But it's necessary, and we'll make McKenna pay for it. That's what this is all about."

She swallows hard, then nods. "Who will... um, who will step up if you can't act as the leader anymore? Logan, right? What if there's, like, a power struggle? Will the rest of the Reapers follow him?"

"Yes."

"Are you sure? What if they don't?"

"They will."

"But—"

"Butterfly." Madd doesn't get loud, but he gets his point across. This is happening, and it's happening now. Life doesn't wait for any of us to be ready before fucking us over. The bitch never has. "They'll follow Logan. He's my second. No one will challenge him. We'll put the word out there that he's taken over. No one's gonna question that."

"Okay." She takes a shuddering breath before straightening her spine and repeating it. "Okay. I get it."

She looks so fucking gorgeous that my resolve to keep my distance, necessary for getting into character, almost cracks. Logan returns before that happens, handing me the pipe cutter without a word.

And handing Maddoc a bottle of whiskey.

Maddoc's face turns to stone, but he takes a healthy swig, then turns to Riley and kisses her hard, fortifying himself.

He's got a lot of good ink on his body, all of it in stark black with none of the color that I'm so fucking addicted to. It suits him, though, and it's also really fucking distinctive, especially the twisting, bold lines that cover the backs of his hands and curl down over his fingers.

One of those bold lines ends in a set of stylized numbers that wrap around his left pinky. The date of his father's death. No one who matters in our world isn't gonna recognize that particular tattoo.

He holds out his left hand to me, pinky extended, and I fit the pipe cutter over it, holding his gaze.

Then I cut it off.

Madd doesn't make a fucking sound, but his lips press together tight, turning white as the pain flashes over his face. It's only there for a split second before he masks it, and none of us comment on it.

I take the finger to the sink to ice and wrap it while Logan quickly cauterizes the wound, then bandages up Maddoc's hand.

Madd is already on the phone while Logan takes care of that shit, getting in touch with the key people we agreed to bring in on it to help us deal with the assassin's body, get word of Maddoc's "death" out, and make sure this whole fucking thing works.

Once he finishes that up, Logan hands him the whiskey again.

Maddoc doesn't say no.

He also doesn't let it slow him down as we coordinate our plans, though. "You'll need to keep us informed, Dante. If shit goes south, we're gonna pull you out."

"It won't."

He levels me with a hard stare. "It can't. But if it does, we need to be able to move fast. We also need to be able to move as soon as you've got something we can bring to The Six."

I nod. "We can use some of the drop protocol."

It's an old-school communication system we use for some of our less-than-legal business ventures.

"That will be a last resort," Logan says, tucking away the last of his medical equipment and setting the case aside. He pulls out something else, holding it out to me. "This tech is small enough to be hidden on your person. It will let us keep in touch, and West Point won't be able to detect it."

Riley looks on while he gets it set up, then we do a quick test after he explains the instructions.

"It works," Logan confirms, stepping back. "And the battery is good for a lot longer than you'll need it, so you're good to go."

"How long?" Riley blurts, speaking up for the first time since before I took Madd's finger off. "How long will this take?" she asks, her voice strained. "What if the battery *does* fail?"

"It won't," Logan says flatly.

No one answers her other question, because we can't and our girl knows it.

After a moment, she gives a sharp nod and looks away.

Logan hesitates for a moment, then grasps my hand in both of his. "Be smart."

I grin at him, my detachment cracking for a second. "Love you too, brother." I tug him against my chest, thumping his back once and then letting him go fast, before I accidentally exceed his touch threshold. "And don't worry. If Madd couldn't see through me when I was here for the Crows, you know there's no way in hell a waste of space like McKenna is going to figure this shit out."

"Damn fucking straight," Maddoc says, pulling me in for a slightly longer hug than Logan put up with. "Do what needs doing."

"I always do. Take care of our girl."

He smirks. "I always will."

I turn to Riley.

"I can't," she whispers, reaching up to cup my face. "How the fuck am I supposed to just let you go?"

"The same way Madd let me take his finger," I tell her, harsh but true. I can't quite manage to keep my heart out of it with her touching me like this, though. "I'm sorry tonight's ending like this." I turn my face to kiss the palm she's got pressed against my cheek. "I had a lot more plans for you tonight, and most of them involved you coming on my face, not me heading out to infiltrate the fucking weasels."

Her chin lifts, showing that defiant spirit I fell so fucking hard for. "I don't care about plans being changed, I care about you being careful. I love you, Dante. Don't fucking... don't let anything happen. Promise me you'll be all right."

"Fuck, princess," I breathe out, resting my forehead on hers.

I want a taste of her more than I want just about anything, but I know I can't. The way to sell my defection to McKenna is to turn off anything that stops me from believing it myself, at least on the surface.

I can at least give her this, though, even though I know it's a promise I can't guarantee to keep.

"I'll be all right."

She holds my gaze, searching for the truth. "And you'll come back," she finally says.

"And I'll come back," I promise, pressing my hand to the ink she put over her heart before stepping away.

Logan tosses me the keys to the Escalade we finally got back from the body shop. It's Maddoc's ride, as distinctive as the tattoo on the finger I've got in my pocket, and driving out in it is one more way we'll signal to the world that Madd is gone.

I take one last look at the three of them, then head out, choosing the most direct route to West Point's territory.

I use the drive time to get my game face on, letting the last of my emotions drain away so I can focus on what I need to do. All I care about is moving up in Halston's underground. The Reapers were on the rise when the Crows sent me in, and befriending Madd was just a means to an end. I felt nothing when I took him out; nothing except the rush of finally having a chance to get ahead after being stuck as his second for all these years.

I sink into the story, making it my own as I navigate to a strip club where McKenna's men are known to be seen on the regular.

I've got no doubt that the minute the Escalade crossed into West Point territory, about three miles back, I was on their radar, and it's no surprise at all that the minute I walk into the strip club, all eyes are immediately on me.

"Reaper," one of the bouncers grunts as he moves in front of me, blocking my way and spitting on the floor at my feet. "You got a death wish?"

"I've got something." I smirk. "Not for you, though. Where's McKenna?"

"Funny you should ask," he says with an ugly smile as two other bouncers grab me from behind and rough me up a little, not even pretending it's about me resisting—which I'm not— before they take me prisoner.

And then, just like I asked very fucking politely in the first place, they finally take me to see McKenna.

"What the fuck were you doing in West Point's territory?" he asks when his goons finally throw me down in front of him about ten minutes later, after offering me a luxury ride in the trunk of one of their cars.

They've zip-tied my hands behind me and weren't gentle getting me in and out of that trunk, and the way McKenna smirks down at me as I get back to my feet tells me he's actually stupid enough to think the low-budget intimidation tactics can hide what an incompetent piece of shit he is.

Case in point, he doesn't wait for me to actually answer and provide any useful intel before trying to swing his dick around a little more.

"I should kill you right here," he threatens, getting up in my face. He slowly draws a finger across the front of my throat. "Send you fucking Reapers a message in your blood."

He has a few familiar faces in the room with him. His own seconds, and a couple other high level weasels.

It's like he's showboating for them.

I snort. "A message in blood? Come on now, you're gonna have to do better than that. Especially when you can't seem to hire a decent assassin. Seriously, how the fuck do you expect to get anything done with losers like that on your payroll?"

McKenna's smirk turns into a murderous scowl, and he sucker punches me in the gut. "Watch it, Reaper."

I straighten back up. "It's Dante, actually."

"I know who you are." A vein starts throbbing in his temple. Then he gives me a slow, sadistic smile. "I also know how much Maddoc Gray will enjoy getting you back in pieces."

It takes everything I have not to grin.

Seriously, though, could the asshat have given me a better opening?

"Kinda hard for him to enjoy much of anything since I just took him out."

Chatter erupts amongst McKenna's people, cutting off abruptly when he shoots them a hard look. Then he turns back to me, his eyes narrowing as he studies my face. "Do you want to repeat that, Reaper?"

I glance down at myself, then look up with a smirk. "Your boys roughed me up pretty good, but not all this blood is mine, McKenna."

His glances at the strip club bouncers who brought me here, still hovering by the door. "They look fine," he says dismissively.

"'Course they are. I didn't fight back. I asked to come see you."

His eyes narrow again. "So whose blood is it?"

I do grin this time, selling myself as the man I created on the drive over. "I already told you."

McKenna stares at me long and hard, then turns to bark at the bouncers. "Get the fuck out."

The expressions they quickly mask as they jump to follow his orders tell me everything I need to know about how he runs his organization... and what's gonna bring it down.

Not that it comes as a surprise.

There's no fucking loyalty here. It's why I already know he'll fall for the story that I don't have any, either.

"Explain," he snaps once they're gone.

"I've been thinking about it ever since I realized you got all that bitch's money from her. You sent her back to us fucking penniless."

McKenna smirks, and I don't want to carve the expression off his face and see what color his blood will turn the teal of his shirt once it soaks into the silk. I can't. Those kinds of feelings will give me the fuck away.

Instead, I shake off the last of the real me, the part that's still imagining how fucking good he'd look with a bullet hole between his eyes, and step fully into the roll I created on the drive over. I'm a self-serving shithead who only cares about being on the winning team, quick to switch allegiances if that's what it takes to make that happen, and I grin, cocky enough to gloat a little, as I tell him how it went down.

"It took some work for me and Logan, Madd's other second, to take down that shitty-ass excuse for an assassin you sent over to the house, I'll give you that. But I ain't fucking stupid. I can see the writing on the wall. As soon as we offed your man, I went ahead and did what he came to do. A little present, from me to you."

"*You* killed Maddoc Gray?" he asks, his voice dripping with disbelief. "Bullshit."

"I brought proof, if you want to cut me loose." He makes no move to do it, and I laugh. "Your people are fucking incompetent, McKenna. None of them even frisked me. You don't want to cut my hands free? I can tell you where to find it instead, including all the weapons they left on me. But fair warning before you go shoving your hand down my pants. You're not my fucking type."

His face mottles with rage for a second, and I'm fully prepared to take a few more hits for daring to insult his ego, especially in front of his seconds. But for once, the bastard surprises me.

"Brett," McKenna snaps, waving one of his people forward. "Give me a knife."

The guy lumbers over and hands him one as McKenna looks me over, a calculating look replacing the rage... or, more likely, just painting over it for now, while he weighs his options to see what's going to best serve his self-interest.

"Turn around," McKenna orders, slicing through the zip ties once I do it. He grabs my shoulder and roughly spins me back to face him, holding the knife to my throat. "Now show me."

I reach in my pocket and pull out Maddoc's finger, handing it over.

"Take it, Brett," McKenna says, pressing the knife against my Adam's apple as a sadistic light flares to life behind his eyes. The steel bites into me, stinging enough that the warm trickle of blood I feel flowing down my neck doesn't surprise me. "Tell me what the Reaper brought," McKenna says to his man without breaking eye contact with me.

He wants to see fear, but he's shit out of luck. I'm damn good at role play when I need to be, but I can't fake that bullshit no matter how deeply I've buried my true feelings.

"Shit," I hear his second say with a low whistle. "He's not lying, boss. He killed Maddoc Gray."

I smirk. "Is this the part where I say you're welcome?"

McKenna's eyes narrow, then he abruptly lowers the knife, turning to snatch the finger from his second. He turns it over, frowning down at it while he examines it from every angle. Finally, he traces the stylized numbers inked onto the skin with his nail, then looks up at me.

"This is Maddoc's."

"I took it on my way out. I would've brought you his head, but I kind of had to make a quick getaway."

"Did you kill Logan Adair? The girl? My *wifey*?"

"No." I don't let myself react. I'm not that person right now. "I saw an opportunity and I took it, then I got the fuck out."

"And you came here."

That one isn't a question, but I give him the explanation anyway.

"I wanted to move up, but that was never gonna happen with Maddoc running the show. Even with him out of the way, why would I waste time fighting off Logan to take over the Reapers when they're already losing territory to you every fucking day? I cut ties with the Crimson Crows once I realized that the Reapers were expanding faster, and now I see the same thing happening all over again, and I want in." I point at the finger he's still holding. "Not sure how to show you any clearer than that."

McKenna still looks skeptical, as he fucking should if he had any brains to go with his overinflated ego, but he doesn't, and I keep quiet now that I've made my play, knowing damn well that his arrogance, greed, and sadistically vindictive nature will win out in the end.

He doesn't disappoint.

"See?" he says, turning to his men with a sudden grin. "I told you we wouldn't have trouble recruiting. Everyone wants to be on the side that's more powerful. This Reaper is only the first. Pretty soon, West Point will start absorbing all the people who defect from the other gangs who try to stand against us."

"Does that mean I'm in, boss?" I ask as his people murmur a bunch of bullshit in response to his little speech, all of them nothing but power-hungry yes men.

McKenna turns back to me with a self-satisfied smirk. "You're in, but you'll still have to prove yourself, Reaper."

I glance at the finger he's still holding. "I thought I did."

"This?" He sneers at it, turning it over in his hand. "This was just your ticket in the door."

He drops it on the floor, then stomps down on it hard, sending bits of flesh and bone splattering over the carpet as he greedily watches for my reaction.

I don't give him the one he expects. I don't let him see what the contempt and disrespect he's showing my brother does to me. Instead, I just glance down at the mangled finger and lift one shoulder in a shrug. "Then how about I start proving myself right now, by cleaning that mess up for you?"

He grins, slow and ugly. "Not a bad start... Dante. Get it done. And welcome to West Point."

32

RILEY

It's late and I'm exhausted, but I stare up at the ceiling of my bedroom in the dark, unable to close my eyes without seeing the horrifying pictures my mind keeps supplying. Dante in a body bag. Dante with a bullet hole in his head. Dante—

I shut the images down. I can't let the worry I'm feeling eat me up inside. I love him, but the only way to survive this world is to be harder and tougher than anything it throws at me.

That doesn't mean I manage to stop thinking about him, though.

He hasn't checked in yet, and we all knew he might not. We talked about it. I know he has to be super careful about keeping up his lie and pretending to be on Austin's side.

But what if Austin saw right through it from the start?

What if Dante never even made it that far? What if he got taken out the minute he crossed into West Point's territory?

"Riley, don't."

I jackknife up in the bed, my heart pounding at the sound of Maddoc's voice. I've done a decent job of keeping my emotions in check since Dante walked out the door, but something about Maddoc's gravelly tone and the way he used my actual name instead of one of his usual endearments breaks something open inside of me.

"Don't what?"

It's a reflexive question. I don't know how long he's been standing there, leaning in my doorway, nothing more than a silhouette backlit by the light out in the hallway, but I'm sure he can read every worry I have on my face.

I'm sure he has his own too.

But it's not concern over Dante that makes my stomach twist into an even tighter knot when I look at him. Even in the dim lighting, the bandage on his hand is obvious.

And what it covers is... horrible.

There's no denying that shit has gotten serious now. That this situation is dangerous to everyone who matters to me. I guess it always has been, but now it feels like we're all standing at the edge of a cliff, looking into an abyss of darkness, one slip away from total ruin.

"Don't do this to yourself," he says, finally pushing off the doorjamb and coming closer. "Don't torture yourself with what ifs."

"I'm not," I lie quickly, wanting to be strong for him when he's given so much. "I'm fine."

He comes close enough that the light from the moon, shining in through my window, finally lets me make out his face. He smiles. "I know you too fucking well to believe that, butterfly. Don't ever lie to me."

Despite everything, the pain he must be in and the weight he's carrying on his own shoulders already, he says it tenderly, and it breaks through the tissue-thin barrier I put up between us, tearing down a wall that I never wanted to be there in the first place.

"I'm worried about Dante," I admit quietly.

He nods, taking a seat on the edge of my mattress and tipping my face up with his good hand. "He's smart, butterfly."

"I know," I whisper, a deep, soul-twisting agitation inside me despite the truth of what Maddoc said.

He stares into my eyes like he can see it there. "Dante is one of the strongest men I know," he finally says. "Physically *and* mentally. He's capable of just about anything, and he was raised as an assassin by his father, so he's deadly as fuck too."

"I know," I repeat, twisting my nightshirt in my hands. "I don't know why I'm being such a fucking..."

I make a vague, frustrated gesture, not even having words for what I'm feeling.

I believe in Dante. I know he's capable of pulling this off, but I also know that some shit will always be out of our hands, and I've had a whole lifetime of learning how to roll with the fallout of an unfair world that doesn't care about the things that matter most to me.

But the silence from him, not fucking knowing, all the worst-case scenarios that fill my head...

"I know he can handle Austin," I whisper, willing myself to believe it.

"He can," Maddoc says. "And you may 'know' that, but you don't *know*. You haven't seen him in action the way I have, not outside of taking that fucker down in the kitchen today. You've seen him be sweet with you. Playful. But you haven't seen him deadly and ruthless, and believe me—trust me—that's part of who he is too."

I take a deep breath, letting it out slowly as some of the worry twisting my stomach into knots starts to slowly unwind.

"Do you know how he first came here?" Maddoc asks, twining our hands together and raising them up. He kisses my knuckles, his face serious as he watches mine for my response.

"To the Reapers?"

He nods.

"Yes," I say a little cautiously, not entirely sure how Maddoc feels about the fact that Dante was able to fool him so thoroughly, even though he chose to join him instead of betray him in the end. "He told me about the Crimson Crows."

Maddoc smiles, and I realize that that's not true. I do know how he feels. I see it in his face right now, and I've seen it every single day since I arrived, in the bond of brotherhood the two of them share.

"Then believe me when I tell you that he's good at this kind of thing," he says, squeezing my hand. "I don't trust easily, and I'm a damn good judge of character. I'd like to think that that's why I let Dante get so close, because I saw his true character under the bullshit he was selling when he first arrived, but the truth is, it wasn't that. Not at first."

"Why did you decide to trust him when he first showed up?"

Maddoc shakes his head ruefully. "I don't know if 'decide' is really the right word. You gotta understand, he didn't just come here playing a role to infiltrate us. He..." Maddoc stares into the distance for a minute, then huffs out a breath. "Fuck, butterfly. I'm not even sure how to explain it, and I was right there living it. But it's like he can completely put himself aside. His true self, I mean. He doesn't just play a role, he fucking becomes it. And he reads people so damn well that whatever he becomes is exactly what they most want to see."

I take that in and sit with it for a minute, and yeah, I can see it. Dante's always been able to read me like a book, and for all that he and I share a connection—something special and unique —I know that the way he gets me isn't only because of that. It's also part of his own special skillset.

"How did he ever earn your trust for real?"

Maddoc grins, sudden and fierce, a bright flash of white teeth in the moonlight. "By telling me he'd been lying. Once he stopped doing that, he wasn't giving me exactly what I wanted to see every day anymore. He was being authentic, and he started pissing me off now and then instead of just telling me what I wanted to hear." Maddoc's smile fades. Not to sadness, but to a sober intensity that spears me right to my soul. "We've shared shit with each other, butterfly. The kinds of experiences that break most people, and the kinds of confessions you kill to keep secret. He became my family, my brother, and he's not just one of the only people in the world I'll ever say that about, he's also the only one who ever could have fooled me like he did in the first place."

I take a deep breath, letting it out slowly. "So, you're saying I don't need to worry about him while he's busy infiltrating West Point."

Maddoc pulls me close, kissing me hard before resting his forehead on mine. "I'm saying he was made for this kind of shit. If you didn't worry, you wouldn't love him the way you do, but if something goes wrong, butterfly, it's not gonna be because he fucked up or McKenna figured out the ruse. I trust Dante to get this done. I trust him to come back to us."

I love Maddoc for giving me something to hold on to that isn't just empty platitudes. For not reassuring me that nothing could possibly go wrong when we both know that will never be true.

I'm not stupid. Sometimes, bad luck just happens to strike at the worst possible time and life fucks you over even when you did everything right. But Maddoc is right about this; I know it. If anyone can pull it off, it's Dante.

"Thank you," I whisper, my voice breaking as the tight band of worry that's been locked around my chest, making it impossible to breathe, finally loosens a little.

Maddoc nods, then kisses me again, a little deeper this time. Like he needs the reassurance too.

Then he flinches and pulls away

"What?" I ask, reaching for him and then pulling back. "Your hand?"

"No," he digs his phone out of his pocket and frowns down

at it, then looks up and gives me a grim smile, turning the screen to face me. "Dante's in."

"Oh god." A wave of relief rolls through me.

Maddoc smirks, but I can see that he feels the same. "I told you it would be all right."

Neither of us point out that this is just the beginning. For now, it's enough to know that the plan is working. That Dante is...

He's not safe.

"No, he's not," Maddoc says, making me realize I said it out loud. He looks at me seriously. "I want you to be, though. As much as it's fucking possible to make that happen in this fucked-up world. Tonight, when that assassin showed up..."

He presses his lips together tightly, rage flashing across his face again.

"You beat him. We won," I remind him quickly, cupping his jaw.

He nods, holding my hand against his face. "We did, and if he'd hurt you, I'd fucking drag his corpse back here and kill him all over again."

"He wasn't after me. He was sent here for you."

Maddoc's face darkens. "He didn't give a shit. You were in the way. I need you to know how to defend yourself. It's important."

"Okay."

"No, this isn't negotiable, I—"

I cover his mouth with my fingers, my heart swelling with love for this fierce, ruthless man who puts his love for me before everything. "I said okay, Maddoc. You're right. I'll learn to defend myself."

He stares at me for a minute, then chuckles. "Right. Good. I want you to work with Logan. He's the best when it comes to fighting and self-defense."

"Okay."

He keeps staring at me for a minute, heat kindling in his gaze. Then he shakes his head with a rueful laugh and gets to his feet. "Quit fucking tempting me. You make me want to fuck you right through this mattress when you're a good girl and do what I say like that, butterfly."

"And that would be a bad thing?" I tease.

"That's never a bad thing," he says, his voice husky as he leans down and kisses me again. Then he straightens. "But you need to get some sleep, and I need to go update Logan on Dante's communication, so it's gonna have to wait."

"Okay," I say again, partly just to fuck with him.

He laughs, shaking his head at me, and leaves, taking a piece of my heart with him and leaving me with something even better. Something I'll need to hold onto with both hands, because tomorrow is another day to try to survive.

And not a single tomorrow is guaranteed. Not for any of us.

EVERYTHING FEELS off kilter with Dante out of communication, other than a few small updates here and there, over the next week or so. Maddoc's hand starts to heal as he stays out of sight, and as far as everyone else knows, Logan runs the Reapers now... which he actually does for the most part, despite still discussing all the important decisions with Maddoc whenever possible.

Still, he's running himself ragged, and not just because of the extra time it takes to be the public face of the organization, but because it pushes him out of the routines and sense of order he requires. And on top of that, he's training me in self-defense and combat, just like Maddoc wants.

"Again," he insists when I fumble the move he's been making me work on for the last forty minutes—a brutal but effective way to use my smaller body weight to break out of a chokehold and incapacitate my attacker.

He reaches a hand down to help me to my feet, and I glare up at him for a moment before I remind myself that I *want* to do this.

It's not fun, and it's definitely not the release I get when I dance, but I've thrown myself into all of it anyway—the hand-to-hand, the various weapons Logan's made me practice with, the defensive and offensive maneuvers—because it makes me feel powerful. Because Maddoc wants it. And because a part of me will always love it when Logan pushes me.

But thank fuck for a lifetime of athleticism and stamina, because he's the most demanding, uncompromising teacher in existence. He won't accept 'just okay' ever. I have to be perfect, every fucking time.

The minute I'm on my feet, he shoves me against the wall, no sign of strain on his face as he puts me into a chokehold again, using his greater strength, height, fucking all of it, to totally dominate me.

For a second, I scrabble at his wrist, clawing at it as an instinctual panic sets in despite all our practice.

"Come on, wildcat," he snaps, the faintest hint of impatience in his tone. "You know what to do. A real attacker would already have choked you out by now. *Survive.* Then make him pay."

He's right. It doesn't matter how tired I am or how exacting Logan's requirements are. Panic is no excuse.

I dig deep and move, throwing myself into the motions as the muscle memory he's trained into me battles with my exhaustion and wins.

Yes, Logan pushes me hard, but I've gone at this training even harder. It's the one thing I can do that makes me feel useful right now, and the only outlet I have for how fucking worried I am the more deeply enmeshed Dante gets inside Austin's organization.

And I know I'm not the only one. Maddoc and Logan are just as worried as I am, even though they both show it in different ways.

Or, usually, *don't* show it, which is fucking maddening... a fact that I use to fuel my frustration right now, knowing Logan won't just be able to take it, he'll praise me for channeling my emotion into pure, physical brutality.

I lift my arm and jab my elbow downward as I twist my upper body, breaking Logan's hold around my throat and moving immediately into the attack he taught me.

It should work. It *would* work if he didn't already know exactly what I'm about to do since he's the one who fucking trained me on it.

"*Fuck*," I scream, adrenaline surging through me as I kick and claw at him in a frenzy. He doesn't hold back or make it easy on me, fighting just as dirty as a real attacker would and making it almost impossible for me to break free from him no matter how many times we've gone over this fucking move.

It only takes a few seconds for him to have me flat on my back, pinned to the floor and in a position that puts me completely at his mercy.

He springs to his feet and holds out his hand to help me up. "You need to stay focused. Let's go again."

I bite my tongue hard enough to taste blood, holding in the rude words that spring to mind.

He's right. I can get this, and I need to. Life isn't fucking fair, and if he didn't go hard at me, I won't be prepared for it when shit goes down for real.

He slams me against the wall, putting me in a chokehold, and I lift my arm and jab my elbow downward as I twist my upper body, breaking his hold around my throat and—

He slams me back against the wall again. "You're moving

too slowly," he grunts. "You're telegraphing every move with your eyes. It will get you killed."

I pant for breath, staring back at him. Hating him just a little right now.

No, hating him a lot.

"Again," he demands, his hands going around my neck as he puts me back in a chokehold.

I lean into the pressure, hard enough to cut off most of my air and not giving one single, solitary fuck.

"Fuck... you," I hiss, narrowing my eyes at him. "I'm not telegraphing. You know because you taught me."

He blinks. "That's not true. You—"

I bat his hands away so suddenly that it actually works, slamming my fists into his chest hard enough to make him stumble backward.

The look on his face is almost comically surprised, but something's snapped inside me. I can't fucking take this anymore. I'm not amused. I don't find it touching. I'm pissed the fuck off, growling something at him that even I can't understand as I launch myself at him, beating at him with my fists, my feet, with no finesse at all and none of the techniques he's spent so many hours teaching me.

"Wildcat..." he says, sounding almost bewildered as he grabs my wrists and incapacitates me, so damn easily that I feel like a total failure.

I burst into tears, suddenly and without any warning, everything I've been trying to hold together for so long spiraling out of control all at once.

"Fuck," I gasp as if I'm drowning. "Goddammit. I'm so..."

Logan's eyes are so wide I can see the whites all the way around his pale, icy blue irises. When my knees give out, he drops my wrists and yanks me against him, spinning me so my back is against his chest and wrapping his arms around me tightly. It's a move he's showed me before, and one that I should be able to break free from.

Is this another test?

I don't know. And I'm so lost in the looming darkness of my panic that I can barely see straight, let alone think right. All I know is that I have to keep going. If I quit pushing, if I quit trying even for a moment, everything could come crashing down. I could lose these men. I could lose any one of them, everything I love, no matter what I do.

No matter how hard I fight.

"Riley," Logan says, his arms like a steel cage around me as I struggle, kicking and scratching and panicking so hard I can barely breathe. "*Riley*. What do you need? Tell me. What is this?"

"I don't... I don't know," I gasp. I can't put it into words. It's bigger than me. It's terrifying and overwhelming and too fucking much. "I don't know what's wrong with me."

He crushes me against him, stilling my movements a bit as he holds me tight. "Breathe with me. Tell me what you need."

I stare blindly ahead, my vision blurred from tears. Nothing seems real, except for the feel of his chest, rising and falling behind me. His steady breaths slowly force mine into a matching rhythm until I finally start to feel just a little calmer, a little more in control.

No, I'm not in control. *He's* in control.

I can't move. I can't break free. And I don't want to.

This is exactly what I need.

"Please," I whisper, the realization rolling through me. "Please. Don't let me go."

"I won't," he promises, his hot breath playing over the sensitive skin under my ear. "I'll do anything you need, wildcat. Always."

I shudder, sagging back against him as the choking, crushing pressure I've been under releases its hold on me all at once, his dark, determined, relentless brand of love driving it away.

Not that he's ever said that word... but he doesn't need to. I know how he feels, and *this* is what I need. I need to just completely let go for a moment, but nowhere is safe to do that right now.

Nowhere but here. Nowhere but with him.

"Take control," I whisper, twisting around to look up at him. "Let me be yours right now. Let me belong to you. Take *all* the control, Logan."

He stares down at me. "Is that what you need?"

"Yes," I breathe the word out like a prayer. "I need you to fuck me like you own me. Fuck me like I have no choice. Fuck me like it's all real. *Make* it real."

It's the one thing that's missing when he trains me. I always know he'll let me go in the end.

Deep down, I know he'll let me get away from him.

And I don't fucking want to.

33

RILEY

Logan stares at me so long that it feels like I really will drown in his blue eyes. He holds himself utterly still, but I know him now. It's what he does when he's the most intensely focused. When he's restraining everything I want him to unleash. The darkness in him is hungry for this, just like I am, and the only thing keeping me from spiraling into a full-blown panic attack is the unbreakable restraint of his arms around me.

But I need more. I need him to be my tether right now, and I let him hear every bit of that desperation in my voice as I beg for it.

"Please," I gasp, my breathing ragged as the dark place within me threatens to suck me under.

"Are you sure?" he asks, his voice strained.

"I am. I need you."

He brings a hand up to wrap around my throat, holding my head in place as he keeps it turned to look at him. I can feel the tension in his muscles, his entire body pressed against mine. "*Everything* is real between us," he says deliberately, not letting me look away. "You're mine, wildcat. I won't ever give you up, and I'll never let you get away. You belong to me."

His eyes are like pale windows to his soul. He means it... and that means fucking everything to me.

"Thank you," I whisper, my voice breaking.

"You have a safe word."

I nod, even though it's not a question.

His lips tighten for a moment. "All you need to do is say it, and I'll stop."

I nod again. "I know. I trust you."

He searches my face, and I can see the war inside him as the part of him that may always wonder if he's more monster than man clawing at the walls of this thing we've built between us.

The trust.

The need.

The feelings that bind us together and turn our darkness into something we can both thrive on.

"I trust you, Logan," I repeat in a broken whisper. "I need this. I need you."

His cock starts to harden against me, but he still takes a moment, holding me tight. Then he gives in to what we both want, giving me one sharp nod before pushing me away from him.

"Run."

The rasping command falls between us, full of dark promise, and my body reacts on pure instinct, turning away from a dangerous predator and bolting toward the door of the room.

I almost make it.

"*Mine*," he growls as he catches me, taking me down to the rubber mats they've lined the basement gym with. "What did I fucking say?"

I gasp, fighting him hard. Squirming to get away.

He reaches a hand between my legs, grabbing my pussy as he flips me over and restrains me completely. "I'll never let you get away. You belong to me."

I whimper, squeezing my thighs around his hand and grinding against it, relief and arousal slamming through me so hard I start to shake with it. He's got me face down, his body weight keeping me pinned down. It's a position he's taught me to break free from, but I don't want to.

And I trust him not to let me.

"You're mine to do whatever the fuck I want to," he whispers in my ear, rubbing his fingers right where I need them. "And it's making you wet, isn't it?"

So wet.

"Get off me," I pant, bucking hard. Trying to roll. To jab back with my elbows. To throw him off.

None of that is my safe word, and Logan does everything I asked, letting me fight him as hard as I want without giving me an inch. It's as if he's inside my mind. He overwhelms me. Takes all the control, disabling each of my attacks with his greater strength, with his size and iron will and total domination.

It's a kind of freedom I've never known before. I can let everything out, scream and thrash and release every bit of the choking anxiety that I was drowning in, and he'll take it all... and still force me to submit.

He rolls his hips against my ass, grinding his rock-hard shaft against me as he teases me with his hand. "You don't want to get away. You want to be owned. You want to be dominated. You want me to prove how far I'll go to keep you where I want you. You want me to use you until you break."

My voice cracks. "The whole fucking world wants to use me until I break."

He drags me up to my knees, controlling my body with pressure holds that guarantee I can't move in any way he doesn't want me to.

"The whole fucking world doesn't get to," he growls into my ear, positioning me where he wants me and then grabbing a rubber exercise band off the wall and binding my hands behind my back with it. "Only I get to decide how to break you."

"Do it," I whisper, the sick, helpless feeling of worry that's been swirling in the pit of my stomach ever since Dante left trying to inch up my throat and choke me. "Please."

"That's not up to you," Logan says, dragging my pants down around my thighs and pushing me back down to the mats. He pins me in place and caresses my bare ass, pushing my restrained hands up to the middle of my back so I'm fully exposed to him. "This is mine."

"Yes," I breathe out, closing my eyes and turning my face to the side, so my cheek rests against the firm rubber of the flooring.

"How do you know? You've let all the marks fade."

From when he belted me.

I shiver, arousal and a dark, twisted need for pain overtaking the worry that I haven't been able to let go of. "I'm sorry."

He pushes his hand between my legs again, rough and without any mercy. "How sorry?"

I whine, panting against the mats, already so wet for him that I can't help but spread my legs wider in invitation.

He curls his fingers, dragging through my slick folds, and delivers a single, stinging spank to my left cheek. "I asked how sorry you are, wildcat. You can either tell me, accept your punishment, or use your safe word."

But my safe word is the last thing I'm going to say right now. I pant for breath, rearing back just to force him to pin me down again and then struggling against his hold so that he'll restrain me even more.

He doesn't disappoint.

"Bad girl," he growls into my ear, holding me down hard as he snatches another exercise band from the wall.

He doubles it up, then snaps the thick rubber against my ass.

"*Oh fuck,*" I gasp. The sting of it is far gentler than the belt, but still enough to get my attention.

Logan yanks my bound hands up to the middle of my back, then lays into me with the rubber band. Every strike gets me wetter, making me squirm and writhe as heat spreads out from my core.

"I want your ass red. I want it bruised and covered in lines. I want my marks on every... fucking... *inch* of you."

His breath is ragged and my whole lower body feels like it's on fire. It takes me over, spreading everywhere and obliterating everything in its path. Turning me on so much that I don't even know what I start begging him for, just that I need more.

"Fuck, *Logan*, please, don't stop, take me, show me, just... just... "

I'm panting, barely able to get the words out, helpless to do anything but take what he gives me and desperate for everything he's promising. I want to feel utterly and completely owned.

And he knows it.

Logan tosses the exercise band aside and shoves his pants down to his thighs, pulling my hips up and driving his cock into me in one rough thrust that bottoms him out. "*Mine.*"

I gasp, a soul-deep shudder going through me as his hips slam into the new welts he just laid into my ass. He grabs my bound hands and yanks me up, grinding his cock even deeper as he wraps his free hand around my throat and licks a hot stripe up the side of my neck, stopping just under my ear.

"Did you hear what I said?" he rasps. "Your pussy was made to take my cock. Your ass was made to bear my marks. Your body exists to hold my cum. You're mine to fuck. Mine to dominate. Mine to use."

"Yes," I whisper, my inner walls rippling so hard it almost feels like I've come.

He groans, his cock swelling inside me, then shoves me back

down and holds me there, giving me no time to think, react, or resist before he's fucking into me from behind with a raw, primal intensity that shatters me completely.

And I'm not the only one.

The tight control he always keeps himself in check with is totally gone. The sex isn't just sex. It's total domination, and it's messy and intense and completely overwhelms me, ripping an orgasm out of me almost before I know what hits me.

I scream, my pussy milking his cock hard as I break apart for him.

"Fuck, fuck, fuck," he grits out, adding finger-shaped bruises to my hips as he fucks me through it. Then he pulls out and flips me over, throwing my legs over his shoulders and wrapping a hand around my throat. "Again."

It's not a request, and he drives back into me like a man possessed, his eyes burning into me until I give him what he demands and come for him again, the intensity so high that it wrecks me completely.

Logan follows right after me, coming with a hoarse shout. Pumping me full of his cum, just like he promised, until I'm overflowing. Pistoning his hips into me, over and over, like he wants to fuck it right into my soul and brand me from the inside out.

"Please," I whisper as he loosens his grip on my throat. I wrap my legs around his waist to hold him against me, my hands still bound behind my back.

He watches the word form on my lips, then drags his eyes up to meet mine. He doesn't say a word, but when he pushes my shirt up to expose the scar he gave me between my breasts, then lowers his head and presses a possessive, claiming kiss on top of it, I've never felt closer to him.

I've never felt more seen.

My thighs are sloppy with his cum and his cock is still buried as deeply as it can go inside my well-fucked pussy, and there's nowhere else I want to be right now. Despite the slight strain on my shoulders from my bound hands, I swear I can feel each and every one of my muscles melting in the aftermath of what he just gave me, all the tension I've been building up ever since all this started draining away.

That horrible, sick, helpless feeling of worry drains away too, leaving me completely at ease in a way I honestly didn't think was possible.

And maybe it isn't. Not without someone who understands the darkest parts of me to help me let go.

I let out a little huff of disappointment when he finally pulls out and tucks himself away. He gives me one of those small, barely there smiles that I know are just for me, lifting me up like I weigh nothing and carrying me into the small bathroom just off the room they converted into the gym.

He unbinds my hands and strips me completely, each movement careful and precise as he massages the tightness out of my hands, wrists, arms, and shoulders, then methodically cleans me up, thoroughly removing every trace of cum, sweat, and sex from my body.

"The rubber doesn't leave welts," he says, making a small, frustrated sound of disappointment as he runs the damp washcloth over the over-sensitized skin of my ass, still reddened and hot from the beating he gave me with the exercise band.

"But it still stings," I reassure him, letting my head fall to the side, giving him better access. "And next time, you can use the belt again."

He leans down, brushing the hair away from my shoulder and kissing me there as he continues to clean me. Once he's finally satisfied, he turns me around to face him, looking down at me with serious eyes. "I like to mark you."

My heart thumps, doing another one of those slow rolls in my chest. "I know."

He circles my wrists with his hands, a wrinkle of concern

forming between his eyebrows as he lifts them, displaying them between us. There are marks there, each wrist encircled in red.

"I bound you too tightly."

I smile. "No, it's because I was struggling."

The wrinkle gets deeper. "You wanted to."

The flat statement isn't a question, but I can see he's worried that he might have gone too far.

"You didn't hurt me." He hasn't let go of my wrists, and I use that to my advantage. Tugging him closer. Close enough that I can go up on my toes and kiss him. "You never hurt me in any way I don't want."

I can feel him relax a little at that, but not all the way.

"It was all right?" he presses.

"It was perfect." He finally releases my wrists, and I cup his jaw with both my hands, staring into his eyes and willing him to believe it, because it's the truth. "It was exactly what I needed. Thank you. I—"

I hesitate, and the wrinkle comes back, his concern a palpable presence between us.

"You what?" he asks sharply.

I take a deep breath, not sure why it's harder with him than with the others.

But I'm completely sure that it's worth it.

"I love you," I whisper, then smile despite the way he stiffens at the words. He doesn't need to say it back. I'd never expect him to. But it feels so fucking good to finally say it out loud that I do it again. "I love you, Logan Adair."

His entire body goes still. He even stops breathing. But when I go up on my toes to kiss him again, he finally moves, stopping me before I can.

He grabs my hair, gathering all of it into his hand in a quick move that traps me in place. He wraps it around his fist tightly enough that I can't move while he reaches up with his other hand to trace my throat, my jaw, my lips with his fingers, all the while staring into my eyes.

"You love me," he finally says.

I smile, turning my head a fraction of an inch, all that his tight hold allows, to kiss the tips of his fingers. "So much."

"I..." His fingers tremble against my mouth. Then something shifts in his gaze, and a fierce intensity overtakes him. "I love you too."

The hot sting of tears prickles behind my eyes, and I suck in a sharp breath, shocked despite myself.

I know he loves me. I do know it. But he's so much more closed off to his emotions than his brothers are—and with good reason—that I never truly expected to hear it.

He watches my reaction with the intense focus he always has on me, then the secret smile I love so much slowly spreads across his mouth. He uses his hold on my hair to tug my head back, then leans down and kisses the corner of each of my eyes before the tears get a chance to fall.

Then he takes my mouth.

"I love you, Riley Sutton," he whispers against my lips, delivering the words with the unique combination of tenderness and pain that only he can give me.

I smile as he kisses me, my heart swelling as I pull myself against him and let this one perfect moment of something good edge out all the fear and worry I've felt lately, all the fear and worry he just fucked out of me, and hold it at bay for a while.

I never meant to, but somehow, I managed to fall thoroughly and completely in love with three men, and despite what's waiting for us outside these doors, I refuse, utterly refuse, to let any of them die.

They're *mine*. And I'll do whatever it takes to keep them.

34

RILEY

"What's the status of that shit Isaac's handling for us?" Maddoc asks Logan a few days later, his back to both of us as he sets up the new coffee maker one of the lower level gang members delivered to the house today.

Logan's lips tighten. He's plating the food he just cooked for all of us while I sit at the counter cleaning a gun they've started insisting I have on me at all times now. "Isaac has run into a few setbacks."

When he doesn't elaborate, Maddoc gives the new coffee maker a frustrated thump, then turns to face him. "What does that mean?"

I need my caffeine, so I set the weapon down and go nudge Maddoc out of the way to figure out how the damn thing works as the two men continue talking about all the ways McKenna is fucking with us.

"He's doing more than just hiring mercenaries to go after us," Logan says. "He's clearly fucking with our suppliers behind the scenes too. Maybe we should ask Dante if he can find out—"

He's interrupted by Maddoc's phone.

We all tense up, recognizing the custom notification Maddoc set up. It's Dante. He hasn't been able to communicate with us very regularly, but whenever he can sneak a private moment where he's certain he won't be watched, he takes the chance to reach out and get us up to speed.

"Report," Maddoc says as soon as he answers the call, not wasting any time with niceties. "We're all here."

He puts it on speaker so Logan and I can hear as Dante starts talking. We never know how long we'll have. More than once, Dante has had to abruptly drop a call mid-sentence to preserve his cover.

"Shit's going well over here," he starts off, his voice strained and a little muffled as it comes through the speaker. "I'm working my way into McKenna's inner circle pretty quickly." He snorts. "Not like back when I first came to the Reapers."

Maddoc's lips twitch for just a second. "You know I don't trust easily, but you got in faster than most."

"I guess it's a good thing McKenna ain't as cautious. I've been acting like a fucking sycophant over here. Praising everything the fucker does. You wouldn't have fallen for that bullshit, Madd, but he's eating it up."

I nod. I can hear the disdain in Dante's voice, and it definitely checks out with everything I saw while Austin had me captive too. Then Dante's tone switches to a more serious one, with a hint of exhaustion coming through.

"He pulled me in as part of another attack on Reaper territory yesterday. I'm pretty sure it was a test to see if I'd really turned."

"The packaging plant?" Maddoc asks grimly.

I blink. I hadn't realized there was an attack yesterday, but it doesn't sound like it's news to Maddoc.

"That's the one." Dante sighs. "I know what that's gonna do to our finances, but I had no choice. It won me McKenna's trust, though."

"You did good," Maddoc says, exchanging a look with

Logan. "We didn't lose any people. That's what matters. I thought it was luck, but it was you?"

"Yeah, I managed to convince McKenna to time it so it was off shift for our crew, but the bastard went in a little early, so we still had a few trapped in there. Jay, Kieran, Greg... a few others I think. Luckily, McKenna doesn't know the layout like I do. I was able to get in and get word to them so they could escape before shit actually went down."

"Are you sure that didn't compromise your cover?" Maddoc asks tightly.

I lean my head on his shoulder, rubbing his back to try to ease some of the tension that locks up his muscles as he waits for Dante's answer.

It's got to be a painful question for him to ask, because it means he has to weigh the big-picture value of Dante's mission against the potential lives of other Reapers, and for Maddoc, there's no acceptable way to justify losses on either side of that equation.

It's one of the reasons I love him... and luckily, this time, Dante made sure we didn't have to.

"I covered it all up," he says. "McKenna thinks the place was empty the whole time. Trust me, Madd, I made sure there's no way anyone from West Point will realize there were Reapers there when we took it down."

Maddoc nods, his shoulders relaxing a little. "You did good," he repeats.

"I always do," Dante quips with a hint of his usual cocky humor.

It's not quite enough to make me smile though, because while it's great news that he's finally getting in with Austin, the longer he's with West Point, the more risk he takes... and the more Austin manages to pick away at everything the Reapers have built.

"Have you found out anything we can use?" Maddoc asks,

switching focus to the mission. "Do you know what he's planning to do, or have any evidence that he has plans to go against The Six yet?"

"How will he try to take them down?" I blurt.

It's hard to imagine, even with all the money Austin has access to now. The Six seem formidable, and there's no way they got to the position they hold in Halston's underground without having the ability to protect themselves.

"Fuck," Dante mutters, his frustration coming through clearly. "I don't know yet, princess. I haven't been able to get anything solid at all so far. I walked in on McKenna and a couple of his inner circle talking the other day, but they changed the subject the minute I showed up."

"I thought you said McKenna trusts you now?" Logan asks sharply, his concern for his brother tightly masked behind the abrupt question.

"Yeah, but that happened before we hit the packaging plant. I'm hoping the trust I built with that shit will get me some more access around him, but I'm not going to just sit around twiddling my fucking thumbs here."

"What do you mean?" I ask, my heart suddenly in my throat. "Don't..." I swallow hard. I can't tell Dante not to put himself at risk. That's literally his job right now. "Don't do anything that will make me hate you," I finish in a choked whisper.

He laughs. "Never, princess." Then his voice gets serious again. "I've finally figured out where McKenna keeps most of his important shit now. He's got a house that serves as his home base, just like we do."

"Will you be able to get inside?" Maddoc asks.

"Yeah. Gonna have a chance real soon."

Maddoc smiles grimly, exchanging a look with Logan. "Good. Anything else to report?"

"Yeah." His tone takes on a playful, husky timbre that makes my chest ache with missing him. "I'm going through some serious withdrawals over here. Got an addiction I need a fix for, but these fucking weasels don't have what I'm craving. Think you can help me with that when I get back, princess?"

I laugh, but the knot of worry in my stomach twists a little tighter. I want him back more than anything, but it almost feels like talking about it might jinx it.

I know that's bullshit, though. He's coming back, or else we'll burn the world down to get him.

"When you get back, I'll help you with anything you want," I promise, brushing my fingers over my new ink; my only ink.

Dante's ink.

He laughs, low and dirty. "Gonna hold you to that, princess. And I think we'll start back down on that new pole of yours." He pauses. "If I can wait that fucking long once I walk in the door."

I bite my tongue to keep from asking him to promise that he *will* walk back in the door, and soon, and he goes on to tell Maddoc and Logan which targets in Reaper territory McKenna is planning to go after next.

"Just don't make too many obvious moves to protect that shit," he finishes, sounding tired again. "I'm tight enough with the planning now that it could blow my cover if everything's suddenly fortified when they hit it."

"We—" Maddoc starts.

"Someone's coming," Dante cuts in abruptly before the line goes dead.

The weight in my chest settles like a lead balloon, but when I look up at Logan, then Maddoc, it grounds me.

"He's fine," I say, willing it to be so.

Logan gives me that small, private smile. "He's good at this."

"And I know shit's not moving as fast as we'd like, but his report is good news, butterfly," Maddoc adds. "He's on the right path and getting closer to finding what we need to finally take that fucker down. In the meantime, we still need to keep up the fight."

"And protect our people," I say, squaring my shoulders and taking a deep breath to center myself.

My worries aren't going to help Dante, and they're not going to help the Reapers. So they need to wait.

Maddoc smiles at me. "And protect our people," he agrees. "The question is, how do we prepare for those attacks Dante mentioned without giving away that we already know they're coming?"

Maddoc and Logan throw around a few ideas while we finally eat the breakfast Logan made for us, then they head into Maddoc's office to do some more focused planning.

I follow, staring hard at the map Maddoc keeps on the wall there as they start discussing logistics.

"What is it, wildcat?" Logan asks quietly, startling me out of my thoughts.

I blink, then walk over and trace a few lines on the map, then tap a shaded area just inside Reaper territory. "This is where he said Austin will send the mercenaries next, right?"

"That's right," Maddoc says, coming up behind me while Logan's gaze sharpens, following the path I just traced.

"I don't know that part of the city well," I say slowly, scanning the map again, "but if this is accurate, then they've got to take Jefferson Boulevard if they're coming in force. Otherwise, they won't have access." I tap another part of the map. "It looks like there are no through-streets here, so Jefferson is their only option. What if we put some kind of construction equipment in the way here, or even damage the road so that the city has to send a crew to fix it, cutting off the whole route?"

"That would either force them to advance on foot—"

"If they're trained the way we think they are, they're not going to do that," Logan cuts in. "It puts them at too much risk of retreat if they run into more resistance than they expect."

Maddoc nods as Logan's comment sparks another idea in my mind.

"True, it could definitely help protect the first target. The question is, will McKenna waste time regrouping, or just attack the secondary target?"

He taps another area of the map.

"If he does, we should do what Logan just said," I blurt.

Logan blinks. "What did I just say?"

"That we should make sure they run into more resistance than they expect. Look, we already know everywhere they're going to hit, right? So why don't we smuggle extra weapons into those areas beforehand? That way, we can make sure that wherever Austin diverts his mercenaries to when he runs into the roadblock on Jefferson, our people have the firepower to withstand it."

Maddoc nods slowly. "It wouldn't implicate Dante. It will just look like we're taking extra precautions as a response to all the recent attacks."

"We don't have the resources to fortify everywhere he might hit. It would spread us too thin," Logan says, his eyes out of focus, as if he's calculating things in his head. Then he centers his gaze on Maddoc again. "But he doesn't know that."

Maddoc smiles, a slow, sinister one that promises trouble for anyone who threatens the Reapers... and kindles a delicious heat, low in my belly.

"No, he doesn't." He tips my chin up, stroking my jaw. "You're good at this, butterfly. You've got a mind for strategy. Do you know how fucking sexy that is?"

I flush with pleasure at the compliment.

It's one thing to know he loves me, that he desires me, but knowing he respects me too, hits me somewhere even deeper. Still, as we keep discussing the details of how we'll use the information Dante gave us—both of my men including me as an equal, valued partner in every step of the planning—I can't help the feeling that it's not enough.

We're good together, but it feels like something is missing. Like we're incomplete.

Because we are.

And this *has* to fucking work, because we won't be whole until Dante finally comes home.

35

DANTE

"He give you any incentive to go easy on him, Tre?" one of the weasels I'm with, a young guy named Duke, asks with a snicker as the three of us head to McKenna's house.

We just finished a bullshit job, a shakedown that's gonna burn more bridges for West Point than it's gonna build, but neither of the two idiots in the car with me seem to see that.

I'm not surprised. The way McKenna does business doesn't really leave room for the type of followers who know how to think for themselves. He'd only see them as a threat.

Instead, he seems to collect dumb pieces of shit like these two, who truly don't seem to give a shit that fucking with the supplier they just threatened is gonna backfire if they ever have to follow through on their blackmail threats. If they take him out, a whole supply chain breaks down here in the city, and I'm not talking about the kind that city officials are gonna care about.

The Six, though? This ain't the type of intel I'm looking for, but when we do get a chance to bring McKenna's plans to their attention, I'm for damn sure gonna use it too. Even if McKenna wasn't gunning for them directly—which I'm now fully convinced Sienna was telling the truth about, even though I still haven't been able to get my hands on anything incriminating enough to bring in front of The Six—if left unchecked, his shoddy business practices are gonna destabilize Halston's underground.

And that's a threat to all of us, *including* The Six.

"What about you, Dante?" Duke asks, nudging me with his elbow as he gives me a knowing grin. "You grab a little bonus for yourself while we were working him over?"

"Nah," I say, giving him a lazy smile. "I'm still new here, remember? And that shit would have gotten me some repercussions with my last gang."

Duke makes a rude sound. "Good thing you got out then before you went down with them."

"No shit," I say with an easy grin, burying my true feelings down so deep it'll take a fucking excavator to extract them again. "But for real, Boss doesn't mind if we skim a little here?"

"Boss doesn't give a shit about what he doesn't know, you know what I'm saying?"

I laugh along with him, but what I actually know is that they've got about as much loyalty to McKenna as he does to them, and about as many smarts too. Not only did McKenna send these two out to shakedown a supplier he actually needs some loyalty from if he wants to keep running a profitable business, but he obviously doesn't take care of his own people well enough if they're this excited about taking a little extra for themselves on the job.

Duke and Tre aren't actually bad guys, just dumb as fuck and stuck with shitty leadership. Doesn't mean I want to spend any more time with them than I have to, of course, but luckily for me, I've got a gift for blending in with people and getting them to trust me, so none of that shit shows on my face.

The two of them think we're all tight, which works for my

purposes. But if I hadn't already hated these weasels before I was stuck masquerading as one of them for the past couple of weeks, I sure as shit do now.

None of them will ever truly get me the way my brothers and Riley do, but instead of letting my mind go there, I do a little fishing.

"Guess you gotta be here for a while to get one of those, yeah?" I ask, tapping the gaudy gold knuckle ring Duke's wearing. I play up a hint of jealousy just to stroke his ego, but I wouldn't be caught dead in one of those signature "W-P-G" monstrosities that West Point treats as a point of pride.

And sure enough, Duke holds up his hand, twisting it so the light glints off the three stylized letters. "Definitely gotta pay your dues for one of these," he says with a grin. But then he frowns. "And fuck, you'd think the boss would put more faith in those of us who've earned them, right, Tre?"

"Not lately," Tre grumbles, keeping his eyes on the road as we wind through the ugly neighborhood McKenna's house is in.

It's all the encouragement Duke needs to keep bitching, so I just nod and keep quiet and let him. All information is potentially a weapon, and I'll be damned if I'm gonna miss out on anything that could help us here.

"Damn right," Duke huffs. "He's been treating us like expendable grunts lately. What even was this bullshit today? He could have had a couple of runners handle it. There weren't even any... any..."

He flaps a hand around, scowling.

"Good shit," Tre offers from the driver's seat, flicking his eyes back in the mirror. "There weren't no good shit. Boss should've just sent some runners to handle it today."

Duke nods. "He's been giving all the good jobs to the new people he brings in." He nudges me with his elbow again. "Fucking noobs."

"Hey now, I may be new, but I don't know what all these 'good jobs' are you're talking about. He sent me along with you today."

I keep my smile bland as all fuck to mask how sharply I'm listening now. I'm sure by "new people," Duke actually means the hired mercs, and any specifics I can get about what kinds of jobs McKenna's been giving them is gonna help.

"Yeah, I guess that's true," Duke says as we finally pull into McKenna's driveway. Then he smirks at me and adds, "Then again, he didn't *bring* you in, you came begging, the way I hear it. Maybe that's the difference."

"I don't remember begging. I just offered my services," I say, giving him a lazy smile and refusing to rise to the bait. "I mean, come on now, a man's gotta look out for himself. Isn't that what we were just talking about?"

"Damn straight," Tre says as we all pile out of the car. "Which is why next time, you gotta make sure you get a little something for yourself when Boss sends us out on one of these supply maintenance runs."

He gives me a fist bump in solidarity, and I see my window of opportunity closing, so I push a little.

"Is this really as good as it gets, or were you guys shitting me about some of the other new guys getting better jobs lately?"

"Fuck no, we're not shitting you," Duke says, scowl back in place but voice hushed as we're ushered into McKenna's house. And, unfortunately, straight to him to report on the job, so I'm out of time to pump Duke and Tre for anything else.

"Did Wilson give you any problems?" McKenna asks Duke, some big-chested bitch hanging off his arm who I've got no doubt is a replacement for Sienna that he purchased with some of Riley's money.

"Of course not," Duke answers him, stifling all that attitude he was displaying in the car and playing the part of the fawning minion to a T.

He gives McKenna a quick rundown of the job we just finished, then we waste another ten minutes while McKenna asks some pointed questions about a few of the details, looking to me and Tre to verify them, as if he's half expecting to catch his own man in a lie.

Once he's finally satisfied—and has made it crystal clear with his shit attitude that he doesn't trust his own people, so is it any fucking wonder that they're not loyal to him, either?—he thanks us and dismisses us.

McKenna's new bitch hasn't said a word this whole time, and we haven't been given any further orders for the rest of the day either, so I'm about to suggest that Duke and Tre and I all go shoot the shit at a bar the weasels like to hang out at so I can steer the conversation back to what McKenna has the mercs doing, when another group of McKenna's people burst into the house.

"The fuck?" McKenna snaps as his front door slams open, a weapon in his hand before the echo fades away. His girl makes a fuss, but he ignores her, shoving her aside and tucking the gun out of sight once he recognizes the people. "Why the fuck are you bleeding all over my fucking floor, Benny? It's goddamn Brazilian Cherry, and I just had it refinished! Do you know how much that shit costs? What the fuck happened here?"

He stomps over to them, ranting the whole way.

Jesus, it's a shit show. Madd would never handle an incident like this. Of course, we'd never be caught off guard by Reapers bursting in on us when one of them pretty fucking obviously needs medical attention, either. We would have heard about that from the source, and nine times out of ten, Maddoc would be in the Escalade heading to them.

"This is a fucking bullet wound," McKenna shouts, jabbing his finger into the gore. The one he called Benny goes bleach-white, and almost drops. One of the other weasels keeps him upright, and McKenna spins around to shout at another. "Does this mean you fucked up the job I sent you to do? Who the fuck was shooting at you? Did you deliver my message, or not?"

McKenna's people can barely get a word in edgewise, but they sure as fuck try, chaos and shouting filling the room. Duke and Tre get right in the middle of the commotion, although whether that's because they give a shit that this Benny dude looks like he's trying to bleed out all over the floors McKenna is so fucking attached to, or just because they're bored pieces of shit who won't say no to a little excitement is anyone's guess.

I don't bother to guess. I know an opportunity when I see one, and I use their distraction to slip away, heading deeper into the house.

I've already managed to get an idea of the layout and eliminate a few areas during previous visits, including McKenna's office, so I move quickly and stealthily to the one area I'm sure I'll find some gold.

His real command center seems to be a pimped-out space off his bedroom that looks more like that strip club I first found Riley in than a place to actually get work done, but has a bunch of electronics and some locking safes that say otherwise.

I've got no doubt that Logan would wreak some serious damage here if he got a chance to hack into all the shit stashed in this room, but I'm banking on the fact that McKenna was raised more old school, like me, and will keep certain information in its original form.

I snap on a pair of gloves I've got on me for exactly this purpose, then make quick work of the locks he's got in place and rifle through his shit. It's more organized than I'd have given him credit for, a fact I appreciate when I finally hit pay dirt.

"Well, fuck me," I whisper with a shit-eating grin on my face, keeping my voice down, but—for the first time since leaving Reaper territory—feeling my spirits lift. "Thank you, asshole."

McKenna has basically dug his own grave by laying out his

plans in perfect fucking detail for us, and there's nothing better than destroying an enemy with his own hand... unless it's utterly fucking *annihilating* that enemy for hurting the ones I love.

I skim through quickly, pretty sure it's goddamn Christmas morning and Santa forgot my coal. The records I'm looking at couldn't be any clearer that he's already making machinations against The Six. Getting these into their hands will fucking end him, especially when they see the lengths he's gone to in order to stay under their radar.

I know for a fucking fact that McKenna's vendetta against Maddoc is real, but based on what I'm seeing, the fucker is a little smarter than any of us have truly given him credit for, and there's more to the war he's waging on us than just taking the Reapers out. He's been trying to kill two birds with one stone when it comes to attacking our borders, and while one of those birds is definitely laying waste to everything Maddoc's put his blood and sweat into building, the other... well, from the look of things, part of the reason McKenna's gone at us so hard is to make sure shit gets messy enough to keep all eyes on the conflict and deflect attention from what *else* he's doing with Riley's money.

He's been laying groundwork not just to take out The Six as his endgame, but to position himself to do it with a lightning strike—quick and deadly—the moment they finally fucking realize what he's up to.

He knows he can't keep them distracted forever, so he's been hauling ass behind the scenes trying to fortify his strike force and position his organization, so that by the time they do realize the threat, it will already be too late for them to stop him.

"I don't think so, motherfucker," I mutter as I quickly snap pics of all the relevant documents, then replace the originals where they were.

Living with Logan and his particular need for order all these years serves me well, and once I have everything back in its place, I guaran-fucking-tee that no one will be able to tell I was even in here.

Which means that once I get this information into The Six's hands, McKenna is gonna be fucking blindsided when they take him out.

I grin, then send the file to the secure server Logan set up for this exact fucking purpose and slip out of the room quietly. Raised voices confirm that the bullshit up at the front of the house is continuing, so I head in the opposite direction to get in touch with Maddoc real quick. As volatile as the situation has become, he needs to know about it now, not when I can have the pleasure of telling him in person.

"Report," Madd says, answering on the first ring.

"I got what we need," I murmur, backing into a little alcove that has some kind of decorative statuary shit in it. I turn my back to the artwork—it's ugly as shit—and keep one eye on the hallway that leads toward the front of the house everyone's congregated in while I fill Maddoc in. "It's just what we thought. He's planning to go against The Six. I just sent the file."

I get silence back for a split second. No doubt Madd is having his own Christmas morning moment as he imagines the utter fucking glory of bringing this bastard down and protecting our people. But he moves past it fast, because none of us have the time for that. Not yet.

"That's great," he growls. "Never doubted you would. Now get the fuck out of there."

I chuckle. "Yeah, that's the plan. I'm on my way as soon as we ha—"

I shut my mouth with a snap when I hear a door open behind me.

I whirl around, dropping my phone to reach for the gun I keep in the back of my waistband.

There's a motherfucking *door*, cut into the wall right next to the statue at the back of the alcove, in such a way that it was totally fucking disguised. I had no clue it was there and sure as shit don't know where it leads, but I do know I'm completely fucked, because Austin motherfucking McKenna steps out of it before I can get my weapon out, a gun already in his hand, pointed right at my head.

"Not smart," he says, a savage glint in his eyes that tells me I should have been a bit more suspicious about how fucking easy it was to move "undetected" through his house. "Were you just about to pull a weapon on me, after pledging your allegiance?"

The sadistic bastard is fucking grinning, practically salivating over the hole he thinks I've dug for myself here and the psychological warfare he thinks he's about to wage. He's too fucking easy to read. He wants me to claim I was all turned around, lost and confused, that going for my weapon was pure instinct. He wants that shit just for the rush of watching me realize he's onto me, the sick fuck.

Fuck that.

I make a break for it, shoving that ugly-ass statue into him as I turn to sprint down the hallway. The string of curses he lets rip as he trips over the broken pieces are music to my fucking ears, but I'm already reaching for my weapon again as I run, because I know that shit won't delay him for long.

I don't get far before I'm jumped by a whole contingent of these fucking weasels, including Duke and Tre. McKenna probably made them leave that Benny dude to bleed out for real, and I feel zero remorse about that as I take first Tre out, then some bearded asshole who goes for a chokehold before someone knocks the gun out of my hand.

"Take him the fuck down!" McKenna screams from behind me as I break someone's knee cap with a satisfying crunch when he makes the mistake of trying to sweep my leg.

I get in one more good hit, my vision obscured by blood

although with all the adrenaline in my system, I've got no fucking clue if it's mine or not, but there are too fucking many of them. They overpower me by sheer numbers, doing what their boss man said and taking me down fast.

I fight hard and I fight dirty, right up until they get me fully restrained, but the minute it's clear that I'm well and truly caught, I quit resisting. If I can keep breathing long enough to find a way to get out of here and rejoin Maddoc and the others, I need to take it—no matter what it costs me.

"Get him up." McKenna's voice throbs with rage as he prowls closer, but the way he keeps his distance while his men do it tells me what a fucking pussy he actually is.

"Scared I'll bite?" I ask, spitting out the blood in my mouth near his feet.

McKenna's face mottles with rage, and Duke gets in a vicious little kidney jab when he twists my arms up behind my back. "Show some fucking respect," he hisses in my ear.

I laugh, because there's *nothing* here I respect... and I can't help but keep grinning when I notice the big-ass bruise already forming on McKenna's forehead and the scuff marks on his knees.

It's not much. Nothing like what I'm sure he's about to do to me. But he tripped hard over that statue and no doubt looked like a flailing fool in front of his men when he got himself back up, and I'll take it.

My grin seems to flip a switch in McKenna. He replaces all his rage with a slow, sick smile that tells me I actually have something to worry about here.

"That's right, *Reaper*," McKenna says as my grin falls away, pulling a knife. "You've got nothing to smile about. But if you'd like me to give you something..."

He steps closer and digs the tip into my skin, right at the base of my throat. The sting is sudden and severe, and warm blood trickles down my chest as he slowly twists it, watching for my reaction like a hungry shark.

I let the breath out of my nose in a slow, deliberate release, slowing down my nervous system and reaching for that place in my head my father trained me to go early, the one that lets me stay focused and alert when I need to, no matter what's happening around—or to—me.

McKenna's eyes flash with a bit of that rage when I don't flinch or start begging him for my life or whatever reaction it is the sick bastard is looking for, and he drags the knife from my throat, down my chest, to my bicep, leaving a trail of blood and stopping when he finally gets to exposed skin.

"I like art too," he says, using the tip of his knife to trace a few of my tattoos. When he gets to a gorgeous tribal design I had done a few years ago, he digs the blade in, carving the lines deep. "How about we recreate every one of these tattoos in blood?"

"It's my favorite color," I murmur, letting my mind drift a little further inside itself, going back to the night I spent with Riley, telling her the story of my art.

I smile at the memory, and McKenna snaps, raging again. "I never should have trusted you!" Then he laughs, a little manic-sounding. "Oh wait, I didn't. But *you* thought I did. You came into *my* territory, into *my* house, thinking you could fool me? For that, you're gonna pay."

His eyes go hard again, and he jabs the tip of his knife into the left eye of the colorful Calavera skull inked in the center of my forearm, hard enough to make me grunt when I feel the tip hit bone.

"Oh, that's just the start," McKenna gloats. "I'm going to make you hurt."

I don't respond. He's not lying, but I won't give him the satisfaction he wants any sooner than I have to. Training or not, I've seen too much death, too much torture, to doubt that he'll be able to get more of a reaction out of me eventually. Hell, he can probably make me scream myself hoarse if he goes at it long enough.

But he'll never make me beg.

And he'll never make me betray my family.

RILEY

Maddoc puts Dante on speaker each time he manages to reach out to us, and I crave those small moments of connections like air. But this time, I'm frozen with fear from the moment we hear Austin's voice cut Dante's whispered report off until the sounds of fighting turn to... torture.

"No," I whisper, my heart in my throat and my stomach churning to acid as my brain tries to feed me a dozen different horrifying scenarios to go along with Austin's words and the ragged breathing and harsh grunts he pulls out of Dante.

I only realize I've got a death grip on Logan's arm when he covers my hand with his. It's the only movement any of us make, all of our attention locked onto Maddoc's phone.

Then the connection cuts off.

Maddoc slams his fist down. "*Fuck.*"

"We have to get him out of there," I gasp, panic rising in my chest. "We can't let him—"

"We won't," Maddoc says, yanking open one of the many drawers they've got around the house that they use as a weapons stash. He starts arming himself, handing over a few of the guns to Logan as he speaks. "We're going in now. We're gonna get him the fuck out. *Fuck* the plan.

Fuck the long game. We're not letting McKenna kill Dante."

He looks up, the drawer empty, and Logan nods, holding Maddoc's gaze as silent resolve passes between them. Then they burst into action.

Maddoc snatches his phone back up and starts calling in reinforcements, and Logan latches onto my arm, pulling me with him as he heads to the main armory.

"I need to grab more equipment," he mutters, moving like a man possessed.

"I'm coming too," I blurt, racing to keep up with his long strides. "You *know* I can be an asset, Logan. You've taught me well. I shot at least one of the mercenaries West Point hired when we first tangled with them. I wounded him! And now I know way more about weapons and fighting than I did then!"

We reach the armory, and when he stops to unlock the door, I crash into his back.

He turns and catches me when I stumble.

"I won't be a liability, Logan. I am *not* staying behind while Dante is in danger! I can't."

I feel sick, my throat closing up as the sounds Dante made while Austin tortured him reverberate through my mind.

Logan pulls me close and kisses me hard, swallowing my ragged, gasping breaths. Then he cuts me. Just a small one on my palm. I didn't even realize he had a knife.

No, he always has weapons on him. But I didn't realize he pulled it.

The pain centers me, pulling my panic in and giving it a focal point.

He finally releases my mouth, keeping a firm grip on the back of my head. I squeeze my hand closed around the small cut, my breath evening out as I anchor myself in his pale gaze.

"I know," he finally says. "You're coming with us."

I suck in a slow breath, then let it out. "Thank you."

I hope he knows I don't just mean for saying yes, for not even questioning that of course I'll be coming along. But also for how well he knows me.

I follow him into the armory, clenching my hand around the bright spot of pain again. I was spiraling, and he knew exactly what I needed.

"Strap this to your thigh," he says, handing me a leather holster and then, once I've done it, a sleek gun to slip inside it. He quickly arms me with two more guns, a knife, and a garrote, then once he's added a handful of additional weapons to his own arsenal and loaded two bags with extra firepower for the people Maddoc's called in to meet us there, he fits a bullet proof vest on me.

"Was this..."

"Was it what?" he asks when I pause, stopping mid-zip.

I shake my head. "Never mind."

He gets the tiny wrinkle between his eyebrows that means he doesn't like not knowing, and finishes zipping me up before turning me back to the door and ushering me out.

"Tell me," he says as we lock up.

I sigh. Of course he won't let it go, and it's stupid, and matters not at *all* right now.

But of course I tell him anyway. "I was just wondering if this was originally Sienna's. It's obviously too small for any of you."

For the first time since Dante's call, Logan's lips twitch in that familiar, tiny smile I love so much.

"No," he says as we head to the foyer to meet Maddoc. "Maddoc had it made just for you."

"I what?" Maddoc asks as Logan tosses him one of the weapons bags.

His phone rings almost immediately, and I brush off his curiosity, letting him know that it's not important as he answers the call.

It *is* important. It's everything. But right now, getting to Dante is all that matters.

Maddoc slips into the passenger seat of the sleek little Audi that Logan prefers, reviewing a couple quick details with whoever is on the phone. I have no idea if it's one of the few Reapers who've been trusted this whole time with the secret that he's still alive, or if word had already spread throughout the organization since Maddoc undoubtedly called in everybody, but either way, I trust him to do what's best, what's necessary, to get Dante out alive. If we lose out on the element of surprise when Maddoc shows up alive and in the flesh, we'll more than make up for it by sheer numbers and fury.

When he ends the call, we're already on the road with Logan pushing the speedometer to the limit.

He glances over. "Was Isaac able to confirm Dante's location?"

"No," Maddoc bites out, his jaw tight. Then, his control snaps and he punches the dashboard hard enough to crack it. "Why couldn't that fucking thing you gave him include a transmitter?"

It's not a real question, and Logan doesn't take offense. "We know he was taken at McKenna's house. Has the plan changed, or are we all converging there?"

"Nothing's changed." Maddoc clenches his fist, the knuckles bloody and the cauterized scar at the base of his missing pinky standing out in stark relief.

"We have no reason to think they would have moved him," Logan says, his eyes flicking toward a landmark that I recognize as we roar past it. We've just crossed over into West Point's territory.

"You mean, we're fucking *hoping* they didn't." Maddoc scrubs a hand down his face. "We should have had people tracking that shit."

But we all know that wasn't possible. If we could have

gotten our people that deeply inside West Point's territory, Dante never would have had to put on this act in the first place.

None of us speak for the rest of the ride, and my terror over what's happening to Dante right now starts to make me feel sick.

Or maybe it's the knowledge that there's a good chance I could die. A good chance we *all* could.

I'm in the back seat, and I take a minute to look at the strong jawlines and sharp profiles of two of the three men I'm so fucking in love with, then I close my eyes, taking a couple of long, deep breaths.

Logan is racing us toward hell on earth, and we *could* all die, but I don't want to, so I need to be as calm as fucking possible. And if we die anyway, I... don't care.

My eyes fly open, the knowledge hitting me like a freight train. I don't care if I die. Not for this. I don't have a death wish, and yeah, I'd feel like shit for leaving Chloe behind even though I know the Reapers would take care of her, but everyone fucking dies, and I already made the choice once before to sacrifice myself for these men. It's what love is, and I love them with every fucking cell in my body, every breath, every beat of my heart, every dark shadow and bright hope in my soul. I'm theirs, and I would walk into hell for them.

The certainty settles around me like a coat of armor, and when we rendezvous with all the Reapers who came to help get Dante out, it keeps me calm as we go over the plan.

At least, it does until I realize one crucial detail.

"No," I rasp, when I realize that the whole point of the way they're dividing up to go in from various points as we attack the house is to draw fire and provide a distraction while Maddoc goes inside.

Just Maddoc.

"We're not splitting up," I insist, my voice hard. "We *can't*."

It's one thing to walk through hell for my men. I just made my peace with that.

But it's another thing entirely to ask me to watch Maddoc go there without any backup.

He takes my hand and kisses my palm, his eyes burning into mine. "You're brave as fuck and more than capable of helping to save him, butterfly. But there's no fucking way I'm letting you go in to try to get Dante out. It's not happening, and we don't have time for this. I'm going. *Alone.*"

I can't agree. It will fucking kill me. But I have to, because I see the same all-consuming love that hit me in the car staring right back at me from his eyes, and I get it. I hate it, but I get it.

"Fine," I mutter, biting my tongue from saying anything else.

I will *not* remind him that I love him right now. He already fucking knows, and saying it would be like saying goodbye.

I refuse to do that

Besides, like he just said, we're out of time. We have to do this right the fuck now, before we lose the element of surprise.

We have to move before they do anything to Dante that we won't be able to save him from.

37

MADDOC

I KISS RILEY, hard and fast, then force myself to put her out of my mind. Logan will keep her close, and with everyone moving into their positions I need to find a way into McKenna's house so I'm ready when they signal.

I move quickly and stealthily around to the back, staying behind cover as much as I can. McKenna's security is for shit, and I've got no doubt at all that his arrogance makes him think he doesn't need as much since this place is in the very center of his territory.

If I ever had any respect for him, that level of stupidity would have lost it right there.

Of course, I never did, so it's not an issue.

I finally spot a promising window near the back. From what I can see, it leads into a utility room or some shit. Even better for me, some fuckhead has it cracked open, and periodic plumes of cigarette smoke escape. It means I'll have to take him out when I go in, but if he's stupid enough to screw with security measures just to sneak in a smoke, then it's safe to say that isn't going to be much of a problem.

We didn't have long to plan, but I'm not worried, because the plan is really fucking simple. My people will attack the house from every fucking angle, and once that shit starts, I'll go in and get my brother.

My phone vibrates with the signal to start the attack, and all hell breaks loose in the quiet residential neighborhood McKenna's holed himself up in.

I move the moment the chaos starts, shoving the cracked window open and taking the smoker out in the blink of an eye. Then I'm in, and my focus sharpens.

We don't know the layout of this place.

We have no idea how many men McKenna has here.

We don't even know if Dante fucking *is* here, but I can't worry about any of that shit, and I sure as hell can't let my fears for my family cripple me. The only way forward is to close my mind off from worrying about each of them. I can't change what's happening to Dante until I find him, and I can't afford a single thought for Riley or Logan right now. All I can do is what I came to: push forward, step by step, and do what needs to be done.

I was right that this is some kind of utility room, and I crack the door open to find utter chaos.

My lips pull back. Not quite a grin, just an expression of feral satisfaction born of primal rage.

All through the house, Reapers are wreaking havoc, but shouts in the distance let me know that more mercs are on the way for backup, so the tide's gonna turn on us fast.

I can't let that happen.

I need to get this shit done before McKenna's mercenaries flank my people and outnumber us.

I pull out my trench knife, fitting my fingers through the brass knuckles and ignoring the ache as the final hole rubs against the stump of my missing one, then pick a direction and move, rounding a corner to find two of McKenna's people in a firefight with mine.

I duck low, coming up behind them, and take the one on the left out just as one of my Reapers finally drops the other.

But not before the fucking weasel clips his shoulder with a bullet.

"*Fuck*," he grunts, spinning backward from the force of it.

It's Isaac.

He slaps a hand over the wound, blood seeping out between his fingers, and meets my eyes.

"Don't fucking die," I growl at him, getting a tight-lipped nod in return. Then he jerks his chin back in the direction he was coming from.

"Saw a door through the kitchen," he pants. "Could be the basement."

I nod my thanks and sprint past him. We all know it's the most likely place for any wet work, but before I can find the door he mentioned, I run into another one of McKenna's men.

Not a mercenary, thank fuck. This one is just a fucking kid.

He's facing the wrong way and holding his weapon like he's got no fucking clue how to use it. I slam him into the wall before he even realizes I'm there, disarming him quickly, then delivering two quick strikes with the brass knuckles before I force his head back with the blade of my knife.

"Where's Dante Channing?"

The kid's eyes roll with terror, the whites visible all around his irises, and he fucking pisses himself.

I ignore the stench and rock the blade over his throat, digging the tip in just under his ear. "Last chance. One push and this goes into your brain. Is he here?"

"Yeah," he finally croaks, his eyes flicking to my left, toward that door. He swallows, his Adam's apple bobbing. "B-B-Boss had him taken downstairs."

Relief slams through me. There's no time for even that, though. The mercs are coming, and I need to get Dante the fuck out.

I hesitate for a split second, then slam my augmented fist into the kid's temple, dropping him like a stone. I probably should have just gutted him, but Jesus. He still has fucking acne and peach fuzz over his lip.

I shove his body aside and get to the door, then slip down to the basement, my rage threatening to boil over when I smell the distinct tang of copper and steel overriding the earthy odor of wet cement.

West Point will pay for every drop of Dante's blood they spilled here.

I make my way through the total fucking maze of rooms the area is cut up into, heading for the only one that has light spilling out from its door.

Lights, but no sounds.

No thuds or grunts or screams.

I ruthlessly shut down the knowledge that silence is what's left behind if they've killed him, and quickly duck my head around the door frame to assess the situation.

Two guards. No sign of McKenna. And my brother, tied up, bruised and bloody, but fucking breathing.

Neither of the West Point shitheads saw me, and I keep the trench knife on my left hand through the brass knuckles, but pull two weapons, taking the safety off both. Then I barrel through the door and catch them completely unawares, gutting the one closest to the door with the knife and then ripping upward before finishing him with a bullet to the chest, the gunshot muffled against his body.

His partner knows what he's fucking doing, rushing me while I'm taking the first guard down and fighting dirty enough that my plan to keep this shit quiet to avoid drawing attention goes out the window.

He manages to knock one of my guns out of my hand, then makes the mistake of lunging for it.

I'm on him fast, rabbit punching his kidneys with the trench knife to slow him down before finally managing to get the other weapon up under his chin.

He rears back with a wet gasp, trying to buck me off. "Motherf—"

I pull the trigger, then kick his body out of the way and roll back to my feet and rush over to Dante.

He's unconscious. A fucking mess of blood, sweat, and other shit I don't want to contemplate.

"Jesus, brother," I mutter, quickly checking his pulse.

It's there.

I pull his head up and lift one of his eyelids. No response.

I know what it is to work someone over. I know a dozen fucking ways to do it, and I know what the aftermath looks like when it's been done to extract information, and what it looks like when the purpose is to send a fucking message.

This isn't either.

McKenna, that piece of shit, straight-up tortured him.

I slap his face a few times and get nothing, then quickly cut through his bindings, catching him when his body lists to the side.

He's completely out, and I drop the trench knife so I can lower him to the floor... then grit my teeth to hold in my rage when my arms come back covered in his blood.

But I've seen worse. Dante's breathing. That's enough.

And if I'm lucky, the chaos upstairs will have masked the sound of me taking out the guards here, because Dante's no fucking lightweight. It's gonna take some work to get him out of here if he can't do it under his own steam.

I'm not that fucking lucky.

I whirl around when I hear someone burst into the room behind me, reaching for my weapon a second too late. It's McKenna, a gun already leveled at my head and pure fury distorting his face.

"The fuck? Maddoc Gray... you're supposed to be fucking dead. *He* said you were."

He's practically spitting with rage, and when his attention veers to Dante for a second, the rage intensifying as if he actually thought my brother would break under torture, I move.

McKenna moves faster, jerking the gun back up and freezing me in my tracks when he clicks the safety off. "No," he says, a manic gleam appearing in his eyes. "I am fucking *sick* of this shit. I'm going to rule Halston. You fucking Reapers have been standing in my way, but once you're totally stamped out, the city is mine."

"It's never gonna happen," I growl, adrenaline surging through me as I balance on the balls of my feet, ready for an opening. All my senses are focused on the bastard, alert to every twitch, every breath, as I watch for it.

"It's already happening," he sneers. "And it starts right here."

He starts to curl his trigger finger, and I bum rush him, ducking low to avoid the bullet and catching him off guard enough that I'm able to knock the gun away. He twists like a fucking eel, cursing up a storm as we grapple.

"I took your woman," he spits as he drives his elbow into my gut. "I'll take fucking everything."

"You didn't... take... the woman who matters," I grunt, head butting him hard enough to get the upper hand for a moment.

McKenna fights just as dirty as his men do, but I grew up sucking at the teat of Halston's criminal underground. Pain and violence are in my blood, and I don't just fight dirty. I fight to fucking win.

I put McKenna in a headlock, my muscles straining as I try for an angle that will let me snap his neck.

"It's fucking over," I growl as he jerks against me, thrashing to get free. Grabbing for my arms like he thinks he has a fucking chance in hell of breaking loose after what he's done to my family.

I forget about my fucking finger, though.

McKenna doesn't. Instead of trying to yank my arms away, he goes right for my hand, driving his thumb into the partially healed stump, then using the shock of pain to twist around and gain the upper hand.

"You sacrificed this for nothing," he hisses, digging his blunt nails into the stump as he pins me down. "I'm still going to win. I'm going to take you apart, piece by fucking piece. Your finger was just the first. And once I'm done with you, I'll do the same thing to the Reapers."

"The fuck you will," I grit out.

His knee is in the center of my back, my arm twisted behind me as he rants.

"You're already dead," he says, lunging for his gun.

I buck hard, managing to keep him away from it even though it means he slams me back against the concrete, sticky and rank with mingled Reaper and West Point blood.

I grunt, reaching deep to block out the pain, and try to throw him off me again.

I fail, but when McKenna grinds my cheek into the rough concrete, I realize that my brother is awake.

Dante lies where I left him, his face swollen from the beating but his eyes cracked open now as he groggily tracks the fight. I hold his gaze, willing him to push through the disorientation a beating like that will have left him with. He blinks slowly, his breath quickening when he finally manages to focus on me.

I flick my eyes toward the trench knife I dropped near him, and the twitch I see as he readies himself is all the confirmation I need.

I coil my muscles under me and shove off hard, rolling toward my brother.

McKenna drops my maimed hand and drives a vicious punch into my ribs as I knock him in Dante's direction, but as if we'd fucking choreographed it, Dante surges up the moment I start the roll and knocks McKenna off me with a brutal jab to his throat.

I bounce to my feet, and before McKenna can recover, Dante snatches up the trench knife and follows his attack up by driving it into McKenna's side.

McKenna jerks back, hissing with pain but so amped up on adrenaline and rage that he doesn't let it slow him down. Instead, he grabs the chair Dante was tied to and swings it around, slamming it down onto the gory red lines he carved into Dante's shoulders.

Dante lets out a choked shout of pain, the blow taking him to his knees, and I see fucking red, ripping the chair out of McKenna's hands and giving him a roundhouse to the jaw that has blood spraying out of his mouth and his body spinning back in Dante's direction.

Dante lost the knife when he got knocked down, but he's already back on his feet, pale as fuck under all the blood and bruising, but all-in the way he always fucking is, beating McKenna back with a rapid-fire series of strikes that has McKenna retreating toward me and finally going down.

I drive my knee up into his face as he falls, knocking him backward, onto his ass, but when I surge forward to stomp his chest and put him down for good, the fucker scrambles backward, managing to gain his feet before we can get to him and then rush back at me with a primal yell.

He grabs my head, ignoring the blows I drive into his stomach, and digs his thumbs into my eyes, doing his fucking damnedest to twist my head all the way off.

I tighten my traps and squeeze my eyes closed as pain shoots to the center of my skull. I don't give a shit. I refuse to let him have the satisfaction of either snapping my fucking neck or blinding me, and I drive my fist up, clipping McKenna's chin.

He retaliates by twisting my head around hard enough that I have to spin to avoid breakage, and McKenna cackles like the sadistic bastard he is.

"That's right, I'll take you apart one fucking body part at a time, you worthless piece of—"

His threat ends in a pained grunt when Dante pulls the motherfucker off me with a hoarse shout, throwing himself into the fray again despite his injuries.

"Oh, fuck no," I grit out when McKenna digs his fingers right into my brother's flesh, trying to pull it apart where he already sliced into it.

I slam into him, knocking him away, and it turns into an all-out brawl between the three of us. With Dante already fucked up from the beating he took and McKenna just as ferocious when cornered as he is power hungry, it gets far fucking uglier than it should for two-on-one.

"Fucking end him," I grunt, when I finally get McKenna into a headlock. "Get that fucking knife, Dante. Find a goddamn weapon!"

The weapon I brought is on the other side of the room, too fucking far away, but I catch sight of McKenna's, the butt of the gun half buried under the remains of the broken chair.

"There." I jerk my chin toward it, and Dante lunges for it.

McKenna turns into a live wire, thrashing hard in my hold and managing to hook his foot behind my knee. It throws me off balance, and when he follows it up with a brutal jab to my ribs, it's enough for him to rip out of my hold and scramble toward the gun.

He shoves Dante out of the way a split second before Dante can snatch it up, and Dante goes down hard, a tide of red soaking the side of his shirt as if some of those pieces of flesh McKenna carved out of him have decided to offer up even more of his life's blood on the altar of McKenna's manic quest for power.

"Fuck," Dante grits out, trying to lever himself back up but collapsing with a pained grunt.

McKenna dives right over him and gets the gun, raising it in a smooth, practiced move as he rolls and comes up on his back with a crazed grin on his face and the promise of death in his eyes.

Too fucking bad for him, their scuffle bought me some time, and I used it to get to my weapon first.

"You're both dead," McKenna spits out as he rises to his feet, swinging the barrel between Dante and me. "You're both fucking de—"

I lift my weapon and shoot.

McKenna's body drops, a bullet between his eyes.

The sharp retort of the gunshot echoes off the concrete walls, leaving Dante and I in a ringing silence broken only by the ragged sound of our breathing. It's over.

Austin McKenna is dead.

RILEY

"This is bullshit," I pant as the fight escalates around us, the Reapers who've showed up storming McKenna's house with a brutal ruthlessness that has the West Point gang members fighting back in a panic. "What's taking him so long?"

Logan yanks me back behind the thick tree trunk we're using as cover, leaning around me to fire three rapid shots that take out one of McKenna's men before he can deliver a killing blow to the Reaper he just put on the ground.

"Maddoc will get Dante out," Logan says as the Reaper he just saved rolls back to his feet and shoots Logan a quick nod of thanks before attacking another group of men trying to hold fast at a set of French doors whose glass was shattered in the first wave of attack.

"I know, I know, I just—"

A fucking tsunami of gunfire suddenly erupts behind us, and Logan lets out a long string of curses as he roughly shoves my head down, then quickly scans the area and jerks his chin to the left. "There."

He ducks low and urges me ahead of him, running toward a low-slung sports car riddled with bullets.

"What the fuck?" I gasp, adrenaline making all my senses

feel like they're on overdrive. "I thought we had the house contained!"

"He called in the mercs," Logan says grimly, lifting his head up for a moment to scan the area before gripping my arm in an iron hold. "We need to move."

He lays down cover fire as we rush toward a shed next to the house, taking cover again, but not before I see that he's right. A wave of hired mercenaries start moving in on the Reapers who surround McKenna's house, forcing them—*us*—to go from attacking to defending from both sides.

"They're boxing us in," I gasp, panic rising. "How are we supposed to fight through them when Maddoc finally gets Dante out?"

"First things first, wildcat." Logan says grimly, nudging my gun arm. "Take that fucker by the rose bush out."

He turns the other way, picking off two of the mercenaries. Trusting me to do my part.

It settles me. I take aim, falling into the training he's given me, and take the shot.

The bullet slams into the siding behind the West Point bastard Logan just told me to aim for, and the man ducks down with a curse, trying to take cover.

He has none. Just that fucking bush.

I force my breath to stay even, and chamber another round, taking aim again. My heart feels like it's trying to pound out of my chest. It feels like everything is moving way too fucking fast, like I can't keep up as Logan forces us to shift positions over and over, sensing threats before I even notice them.

But it also feels like Maddoc has been in that house for *way* too fucking long, as if time somehow slowed down in there, even as it runs roughshod over all of us out here.

Sun glints off the gaudy gold ring on the West Point gang member's hand as he swings his weapon around, trying to figure out where my shot came from. The scowl on his face is as dark as the devil and my heart freezes up for a second when I recognize his face.

He was one of the guards on me when Austin held me captive.

He wanted to use all my holes and pass me around like a broken fucktoy.

Fear tries to rise up and choke me, but I force it down hard, breathing out as I push that shit aside and focus on the moment. All that matters is here and now, and clearing a way for Maddoc to get Dante out of that fucking house.

I pull the trigger again.

This time, I hit the fucker, and a triumphant burst of violent satisfaction explodes in my chest.

It's cut short when Logan slams me back against the shed wall. Hot lead tears a chunk out of the spot right next to us, a mercenary advancing on our position with what looks like a military-grade weapon spitting fire in our direction. Logan's mouth goes tight. He shoves me over, then shoots to his feet and puts a bullet through the man's eye.

He drops, and Logan yanks me up. "*Move.*"

A trio of mercs are right behind the one Logan just took out, and we sprint across the lawn, heading for alternate cover. As we reach it, Logan slams into me with a grunt.

"*Fuck,*" I pant, my grip tightening on my weapon. "Are you hit?"

"I'm good," he says gruffly. "But Maddoc had better do whatever he's going to do in there fast, or we'll all be dead. The mercs are overpowering us."

Another volley of gunfire comes from the house, forcing us to shift positions again.

"Run!" Logan shouts, right before punching me in the chest.

I go down to my knees hard, and only realize it wasn't him—of course it wasn't him—when I look up and see him covering me, shooting back at yet another group of mercs with a look of deadly rage on his face. He spares me one glance, his eyes scanning me up and down to make sure the bulletproof vest did its job, then nods sharply and pops up to his feet.

He takes out the guy who shot me with a single headshot, then mows down the three other mercs who were in formation with him.

I suck in a wheezing breath, forcing air into my lungs as I scan our surroundings. We're too vulnerable here. We have to move. We have to—

"*Riley!*" he shouts, swinging his weapon around to cover me from the other side as an upper floor window is abruptly flung open.

All the breath I just fought so hard for rushes right back out of me as a body is hurled through it a moment later. It lands in the middle of the lawn with a sickening crunch, and I realize in a flash who it is.

Austin McKenna.

The gaping bullet hole between his sightless eyes makes it obvious that it wasn't the fall that killed him.

All around us, the fighting pauses as Reapers and McKenna's people alike stare in stunned silence at the corpse sprawled on the lawn. Maddoc stands in the window, his blood-streaked face a stone mask as he stares down at the body of his enemy, then looks around, scanning the chaos and destruction.

"McKenna is dead," he finally calls out, his voice carrying to all of us. "For those of you who are here because he was paying you to fight, you can stay and die for a dead man, or you can stand down and the Reapers will pay you double whatever West Point promised."

The mercenaries shift uneasily, glancing at each other as they mutter amongst themselves about the offer. I hold my breath, the air thick with tension as everyone waits to see whether or not they'll back off.

Finally, one of them spits on the ground, lowering his

weapon. "Not like we'll be able to extract payment from a corpse," he says in a gravelly voice, walking up and nudging Austin's body with the toe of his boot. He looks up at Maddoc in the window. "How do we know you're good for it?"

Even from here, I can see Maddoc's jaw tighten. "I'm a Reaper."

The merc locks gazes with Maddoc for a tense moment, then makes some kind of hand gesture that has his men slowly start to melt away, one by one, covering each other as they go.

The surviving West Point gang members immediately start cursing them out, shouting threats after the mercenaries as they silently retreat.

"What the fuck!" one of them shouts, shooting to his feet from behind the bed of a truck near the curb. He points his weapon at a group of retreating mercenaries. "Boss already paid you good money! You fucking pussies! You can't—"

Gunfire from one of the Reapers near the house splits the air, shutting him the fuck up. He dives back down for cover, but the tide has totally turned against West Point, and the surviving members all seem to realize it at once. Every fucking one of them who can still move makes a break for it, Reapers helping route them out of the house and hurry them along with a deafening spray of bullets that tears the ever-loving fuck out of the neighborhood as they go.

I add some lead of my own, running out of bullets long before I run out of rage.

"It's over," Logan says, reaching out to lower my gun arm when the trigger keeps clicking. He glances around, then nods at me, giving me that tiny smile of his. "There are no more threats here, wildcat. But we've got to move. We need to clean up the mess here and get out."

I swallow hard, really looking around for the first time. The aftermath is exactly the kind of thing likely to draw the attention The Six keep warning us about, but Austin is dead and Dante is alive, so it was worth it.

Logan wraps an arm around me, leading me away from cover, toward the house. Despite having just told me there were no more threats, he keeps a wary eye out, reminding me that we're still in the heart of West Point's territory.

"Logan," I blurt, my heart suddenly in my throat again as I realize I don't actually have confirmation that all the men I care about are okay. "Dante *is* alive, right? Maddoc would have—"

"He did," he cuts me off, his wary alertness replaced for a split second by a smile so blinding I have to blink. Then his usual mask drops back into place, and he nudges me forward. "He's right there."

My breath hitches, and I shove my way past a couple of Reapers just as Maddoc and Dante step out of the front door.

A low rumble of approval comes from the surrounding Reapers, but I've got eyes only for Dante.

He looks like shit.

Maddoc is basically holding him up, and Dante honestly looks more like a creature stitched together from blood and bruises than a man.

It makes my heart ache.

It also makes me want just one more fucking bullet, so I can put another one into Austin's corpse.

I rush up the stairs and then stop, needing to reach for him but not wanting to add to his pain. He gives me a little half grin that reassures me, the vibrant green a little dulled but still potent enough to make my breath catch.

"Princess," he mumbles as Logan comes up behind me and Maddoc addresses the crowd, gathering them around. "We got the fucker."

Fierce pride swells in my chest. Damn fucking right we did.

"Report," Maddoc says to his people, his face hard as he scans the crowd.

Various Reapers call out, confirming merc and West Point kills and detailing the Reaper wounded.

And the dead.

Maddoc takes it all in stoically, but I can see how much it affects him. It's why they all showed up for him. Why they'll follow him to hell and back, and just proved it. His people are and always will be the main thing that matters to him, and his voice is so tight it sounds like it's going to snap as he demands the name of each Reaper who fell.

"They wanted to be here, just like you did, Maddoc," Logan says quietly once the accounting has been made.

Maddoc's fists clench, but then he nods. It's part of the price every single person has to be willing to pay in this world, and this time at least, the cost was worth it.

"Round up our wounded and dead," he finally says. "Get them out of here so we can finish this thing."

The Reapers move into action, making quick work of taking care of their own. Maddoc pulls a few men aside and directs them to drag all the West Point bodies out of the house, then douse every fucking inch of it with the accelerant the Reapers brought with them.

Sirens start to wail in the distance before they're done, but Maddoc doesn't move. "We're seeing this thing through."

Dante answers with a fierce, bloody grin, and Logan's pale eyes blaze with approval.

The last of the Reapers tasked with dousing the property finally dashes out of the house, tossing the empty gas can he used back through the front door.

He gives Maddoc a nod. "It's ready. It'll go up fast and take everything down to ashes."

"Good," Maddoc says. "Now go."

His people clear out, leaving just the four of us. The sirens are closer now, their urgent wail piercing through the air, but for a moment, no one moves.

Then Maddoc hands me a matchbook. "Burn the fucker down, butterfly."

I give him a savage smile. West Point hurt everyone I've ever loved. They tried to take everything from me. And they failed.

"With fucking pleasure."

I strike a match, the sharp tang of sulfur cutting through the scent of blood, sweat, and pain that surrounds all four of us.

Then I toss it into Austin's house, and with a loud *whomp*, flames erupt everywhere.

39

RILEY

THE PEOPLE MADDOC sent in to douse Austin's house obviously knew what they were doing, because it only takes moments before the whole house is engulfed.

"Fuck, yeah," Dante murmurs under his breath, speaking for all of us. But as satisfying as it would be to watch the whole place burn, the sirens are getting louder, and we can't afford to be here when they arrive for a whole host of reasons.

We hurry to Logan's Audi, Dante still leaning heavily on Maddoc as we cross the bullet-ravaged lawn. Logan slips behind the wheel, starting it up fast, but when Maddoc tries to ease Dante into the passenger seat, he shakes his head.

"I'm with Riley."

Maddoc huffs, almost smiling for the first time since all this shit went down, but quickly helps Dante into the back with me without any protest.

Dante immediately tugs me onto his lap.

"*Dante*," I say, horrified. He could barely walk on his own.

I try to squirm off him, doing my best not to cause any more damage, but his arms stay locked tight.

"Come on now, princess," he rasps, his voice a little slurred through the swelling on his face. "I could be dying right now. You really gonna deny a dying man his last wish?"

My heart plummets, ice filling my veins.

"What?" I whisper, my gaze jerking to the front. "I thought..."

My throat closes up.

Maddoc twists around, meeting my eyes. "Dante's not dying," he says with a smirk. "He's tough as shit, and he's been through worse than this. Shane will meet us at the house and patch him up, but he's fine. Trust me."

I do. With my body, heart, and life.

"Asshole," I mutter, scowling at Dante and gently shoving him in the chest.

"Love you too," he says with an unrepentant grin, capturing my hand and keeping it there. Then he grows serious. "Holding you would definitely be my last wish if I were actually dying, princess. Not gonna lie, I thought it might happen a few times while McKenna worked me over, and it was this right here that I was thinking of. You glaring at me. The feel of you in my arms. Loving you. Holding you."

He reaches up, brushing a tear off my cheek.

He captures it on the tip of his finger, turning it this way and that, so it glints like a diamond. He stares at it as if he's mesmerized, and when he finally looks up at me, I can see his entire heart in his eyes.

"But since I ain't dying, I've got another wish."

"What is it?" I whisper.

"I want to live to a hundred fucking years old, so I can hold you every day until then."

"Dante..."

I stop thinking about trying to climb off his lap and cling to him, holding him just as tightly as he's holding me. Breathing him in. Feeling his heart beat against mine. I close my eyes, letting the rhythm soothe the part of me that wasn't complete without him.

"I missed you," I murmur.

And I want the same thing he does. I want to give him those hundred years, and then take a hundred more.

He tips my chin up, smiling down at me. "Me too, princess."

He doesn't comment on the tears that keep sliding down my face, and I don't comment on the tight lines of pain next to his eyes. We just exist together for a while, and even though we've just opened up a shitcan of worms by taking out a major player in Halston's underground in such a visible way, it feels like the first moment of true peace I've felt since all of this started.

It's perfect.

But of course it doesn't last.

As soon as we arrive back at the house, time speeds back up. Maddoc made promises to some dangerous people today, and after a quiet word with Dante and a hard kiss that takes my breath away, he heads straight back to his office to deal with the fallout as leader of the Reapers.

"What's going to happen now?" I ask, torn between worrying about what exactly that fallout is going to look like and my concern for Dante.

I believe Maddoc when he says Dante's been through worse —I hate it, but I believe it—but that doesn't mean he doesn't need medical attention, and the Reaper who usually handles the things too serious for Logan to patch up, Shane, isn't here yet.

I wring out a soft cloth in the sink. "Sit."

He snorts, but doesn't argue when Logan eases him down onto one of our kitchen stools.

"Maddoc has to get the word out that the offer he made to the mercenaries is legitimate," Logan answers me.. "He needs to make sure we don't get any who try to retaliate against us for McKenna's death."

"Who, the mercs?" I frown, then glare at Dante when he

tries to wave me off, keeping it up until he finally lets me start to clean up some of the blood on his... everything.

Logan makes a distracted sound of affirmation, his attention obviously divided between this conversation and the constant barrage of incoming notifications he's been getting ever since we left West Point's territory. I know that as one of Maddoc's seconds, he has a ton of stuff he needs to deal with right now too, but everything feels like it's happening in a blur, and I can't let it go.

"Why would any of the mercs give a shit that we killed McKenna? They were only in it for the paycheck, right?" Then another thought occurs to me. "Send word to whom? Who does Maddoc need to notify? The Six?"

"The mercs got their own code, princess," Dante rasps, his face too pale and the damage that fucking sadist did to him more and more obvious as I clean him up. "They'll only care about Maddoc offing that piece of shit if their deal falls through with us. If they think they were suckered into backing off a contract, then they'll retaliate."

"But that won't happen," Logan says firmly, finally looking up from his phone. "Maddoc has a network of contacts in Halston's underground. Once they realize he's still alive and that he's good for the payment he offered, none of that will be a problem. He just has to make sure they hear from him directly, and fast, and then he needs to take care of our own."

He means the Reapers who were injured, and the bodies—and families—of the dead.

I swallow hard, but know it's always going to be a price for some in our world.

"And The Six?" I ask again.

Logan shakes his head. "Best if we clean up our mess a bit more before it's brought to their attention, if possible. Which is what I need to go do."

"You gonna be able to cover our tracks and keep the cops

351

from sniffing around when they investigate a whole fucking house full of charred bodies, brother?" Dante asks.

Logan actually smiles. "Yes."

No doubt. No hesitation.

God, I love this man.

Dante laughs, then grimaces, clutching his stomach. "Never... doubted it," he wheezes. "Go on now. Make the magic happen. Shane will be here in a sec. You don't have to babysit. It's fine to leave me alone."

I smack him, *very* lightly, on the shoulder. "Hey! What am I?"

His eyes heat up, far more than should be possible for a man in his condition. "Definitely not my babysitter, princess."

We share a long look as Logan heads up to the computer setup he keeps in his room, only interrupted when Shane finally arrives.

I hover as he checks Dante's vitals. "Is he okay?"

"Better than okay," Dante says before Shane can answer, holding my gaze with such intensity that I feel it in my soul. "I thought we discussed that in the car."

"I'm not sure I'd say 'better' than okay," Shane says, oblivious to the heat throbbing between the two of us, "but I can definitely patch you up."

He handles that with quick efficiency, reassuring me that Dante really is in good shape overall. He doesn't need too many stitches, and even though he's bruised all to hell and will be feeling the beating he took for a while, like Maddoc promised me in the car, none of it is life threatening.

Shane insists on checking me over quickly as well. Someone obviously tipped him off about the bullet I took with the vest, but while there's some bruising, he reassures me that none of my ribs are cracked.

I'm just glad the bullet hit me in the back. The possessive look of barely contained aggression on Dante's face as Shane examines me leaves me no doubt that, hurt or not, Dante would have done himself even more damage going all caveman on the guy if I'd had to bare my breasts to him.

Once Shane finally checks in with Maddoc and leaves, I help Dante up to his room and stay with him, the two of us talking quietly about nothing in particular, just enjoying being together. A few times, he almost drifts off, and I do what I can do to make him comfortable while he spends the majority of the day trying to assure me he already is.

I try not to let myself feel anxious about all the shit Maddoc and Logan are handling, or feel guilty for not offering to help with it. The truth is, I still don't know enough about their world or the inner workings of the organization to be much use today, even though I'm determined to learn those things.

But more than that, I need this time with Dante. It's something I'll never take for granted.

Not with any of them.

Once it gets late, Logan finally comes in.

"Got everyone off our trail?" Dante asks, wincing as he tries to prop himself up against his headboard.

I've been sitting next to him on the bed, and gently push him back down. He hasn't said anything, but he's definitely in pain.

He lets me, then keeps hold of my hand and strokes it while Logan walks over to join us, nodding in answer to Dante's question. "Law enforcement should have enough information to keep them satisfied now. None of which points to us."

"Fucking magic," Dante says, his voice still strained. "And I bet you've got all the tech in the city set to ping you if that changes."

"Something like that," Logan says, frowning. "When's the last time you took a painkiller? Didn't Shane bring you something?"

"Got all I need right here," Dante says, squeezing my hand.

Logan's eyes go soft. "Yes, but maybe add in some Percocet too. There's no need to suffer more than necessary. Not now that you're home." He pauses, then. "I'm really glad you did make it home, Dante."

He gets up to grab the drugs before Dante can tease him for being all emotional, and when he comes back, Maddoc is with him. He makes a beeline for the bed as Logan hands over the pills and a glass of water to Dante.

"All good?" Maddoc asks Dante, giving him a quick once over, like he needs to reassure himself that the report Shane gave him before he left was true.

"Never better," Dante says, lifting the glass in a salute.

Maddoc's body language subtly relaxes, and when I lean against him, he runs his fingers through my hair.

Dante's eyes track the movement, then he looks up at Maddoc with his trademark smirk. "You can do better than that, Madd."

Maddoc's hand stills on my head, then he pulls me off the mattress and kisses me like he's starving for it.

"Fuck," Dante murmurs. "Yeah, that's it."

I wrap my arms around Maddoc, pouring everything I have into the kiss. All my fears, all my relief, every bit of the gratitude I have for what he pulled off today, and all my anger about the damage that fucking monster did to my family.

Maddoc takes all of it and gives it back to me tenfold, and when he finally lets me come up for air, Logan is right next to us, watching with a level of heat in his eyes that I never would have believed possible in the beginning.

I reach for him, and he takes me. Tipping my head back and claiming my mouth with a different kind of intensity than his brother. One that's darker, but just as demanding.

I love it. Being able to kiss him like this, to revel in our connection and share the moment with all three of the men I love, it's night and day from our beginnings, and it was worth every moment of pain, suffering, and heartache to get here.

"I'm never giving you up," I tell Logan, running my fingers over the end-of-day stubble turning his jaw rough. I look at my other men. "Not any of you."

"Same, princess," Dante says with a groan that clearly has nothing to do with pain. "And that was hot as hell. I really wish I could fuck you right now. I missed you so damn much."

I suck in a breath and squeeze my thighs together as arousal slams through me hard. I've been low-key thrumming with it all day, but I've been ignoring it because I know it's not possible.

Not for Dante. Not until he heals a bit more.

He sees everything I'm feeling on my face, though. The man can read me so damn well. And he gives me a wicked smile of pure temptation in response.

It's almost enough to make me want to forget the doctor's orders.

"No," I say breathlessly, resting my hand on the middle of his chest to keep him still. "You can't."

"I really fucking can't," Dante agrees regretfully, wrapping his hand around my wrist. "But the next best thing would be to watch my two best friends fuck you, princess. You up to giving me that? You want Maddoc and Logan to take you here in front of me?"

My breath quickens, my body instantly responding to him the way it always does. "Yes."

"Good," he growls, tugging me down on his chest and kissing me hard. "Show me, princess. Show me what I fucking lived for."

40

RILEY

DANTE'S LIPS are firm against mine, and I put everything I have into our kiss. I want this man to know exactly how much I missed him.

And I want everything else he just asked me for too.

"You're killing me, princess," he mutters into my mouth, his cock rising under me when I finally end the kiss and carefully roll off him. He drives the heel of his hand against the thick bulge, chin-nodding at his brothers. "Now give me what I asked for, yeah?"

Heat fills the room as Maddoc and Logan look at me. I don't need to ask if they want this too. We're all on the same page, and the energy between us feels combustible.

Maddoc reaches for me, pulling me up into his arms while Logan carefully helps Dante sit up, propping him against the headboard with plenty of space left on the king-size bed for the rest of us. Maddoc doesn't lay me down there, though. Instead, he holds me against him, kissing me rough and dirty, until Logan's done.

Then he passes me over.

Logan fists my hair and stares into my eyes. "You want to be fucked."

It's not a question, and he doesn't need an answer. He says it just to make me squirm; I can tell by the way his pale eyes flare with desire.

"God, yes, please," I gasp, wrapping my arms around him, straining toward him for a kiss.

He pulls my hair harder, keeping me from reaching his mouth. Giving me a hot sting of pain that wakes up my body like nothing else.

Then he smiles, and it's so fucking dirty that my panties flood with arousal. "Beg me again."

"Please. God, Logan. Kiss me. Fuck me. Use me."

He groans, or maybe that's Maddoc, and finally takes my mouth. His kiss is all-consuming, and I'm panting for air when he passes me back to Maddoc.

His shirt is off now, and I run my hands up the bold, dark lines of the tattoo covering his chest and wrap them around his neck. "Kiss me like Logan did."

He laughs, low and dirty, and squeezes my ass. "You know better than to tell me what to do, butterfly."

My breath hitches. "Right. You like to be in charge."

"No, I *am* in charge," he corrects me. Then he proves it, owning me completely.

Logan comes up behind me while Maddoc is busy taking me apart, and when I feel his mouth—hot and demanding—on the back of my neck, I gasp, rolling my body against Maddoc's.

He rips his mouth off mine. "You've got too many fucking clothes on."

I don't get a chance to respond. As soon as Maddoc lets my mouth go, Logan twists my head around and claims it. They pass me back and forth, working my clothes off between hot, demanding kisses and filthy, whispered promises, until I'm finally naked, sandwiched between them, with Dante looking on.

"You too," I demand, tugging at Logan's shirt. He whips it

over his head, and pulls me against him again, flattening my breasts against the hard planes of his chest.

"Your skin feels like satin," he murmurs, running his hands over me as Maddoc shucks off his pants. "So soft. So clean."

"Dirty me up," I beg, totally shameless. "Paint me with your cum."

Heat flashes across Logan's face, and the iron bar of his cock —still trapped in his pants—jerks between us. "No." His hand dips between my legs. "I want it all inside you this time."

"I want that too," I gasp, grinding against him, wet and ready. "I need your cock. I need you and Maddoc to fuck me."

"Fuck, princess," Dante mutters from the bed, his voice dripping with lust. "You look so fucking good when you're desperate for it."

Logan spins me around, trapping me against him with my back against his chest and his shaft grinding against my ass. "Look what you do to my brothers."

Maddoc's cock juts out from his hard body as he watches us from the side of the bed, fully naked now, and Dante has his cock out too, a thick, angry pole in his tight fist as he watches the show I'm giving him with hooded eyes.

His body glistens with a bright sheen of sweat, his injuries standing out in stark relief, but he's here, he's alive, and he's one of the sexiest sights I've ever seen. They both are.

"Can't wait to get this in you again," Dante says, slowly stroking himself. "Best fucking pain relief there is."

"I've got some pain that needs relieving," Maddoc growls, dipping his fingers into my pussy while Logan keeps me pinned against him. Maddoc fingers me, staring down into my face until he has me panting. "You wet enough to ride me hard?"

"Yes," I gasp, my inner muscles clenching around his rough fingers. "I need more."

He gives me one of those predatory smiles, then backs off, lying down on the bed next to Dante. His cock is so hard it lies flat against his stomach, and he runs his hand over it a few times, just the palm, then circles the base with his thumb and fingers and lifts it high.

"Come on then, butterfly," he says, the thick shaft standing tall in his hand. "Come and get it. Give me some of that sweet-ass pain relief."

"You heard him," Logan murmurs in my ear, finally releasing my arms. "Go fuck my brother."

My core tightens, desire like a coiled spring inside me, and I don't waste any time crawling onto the bed between Maddoc's spread legs, prowling up his body on my hands and knees to get what I need.

I get as far as his cock when he stops me, grabbing the back of my head and rubbing his shaft against my cheek.

"I'm gonna sink this straight into your pussy," he promises, using his grip to turn my head so the tip rubs across my lips instead.

His slit leaks with his arousal, and I open for him, lapping some of it up. Moaning as the musky flavor of his sex turns me on even more.

"Get my cock ready," he says, rocking up with short, shallow thrusts to push the tip deeper into my mouth. "I'm gonna fill that sweet, wet hole of yours with everything I've got. You want that, butterfly? You want my cum planted deep inside you? You want to be full of the men who love you?"

I can't answer with my mouth full, so I suck him harder, pulling his cock deeper into my mouth and laving it with my tongue, then working his shaft down my throat until Maddoc starts cursing and grabs my hair, yanking me off.

"Don't tempt me to shoot my load into that hot little mouth of yours," he growls. "Get up here and get on my cock. You made a promise to my brother, and he deserves to get what he asked for."

"Fuck," Dante groans as I move up to straddle Maddoc. "I'm

not quite sure what any of us have ever done to deserve a pussy like that, but I'll fucking take it."

Maddoc grips my hips, and I sink down onto his cock, letting it fill me to my core.

"I'll fight for it," he grits out, holding my gaze. "Every fucking time."

"And I'll kill for it," Logan says with dark intensity, running his hand up my back, under the long waves of my hair, as I start riding Maddoc's cock.

Being the focus of all their attention is like a drug, and I brace my hands on Maddoc's chest as I fuck him, almost losing myself in the rising pleasure.

Logan brings me back to the present moment as he presses a palm between my shoulder blades, pushing me down until I'm lying chest to chest against Maddoc. Maddoc's big hands cup my ass, working me up and down on his cock while Logan grips the back of my neck.

"You're so beautiful," Logan murmurs. "You're radiant when you let yourself go like this."

"For you," I gasp, an orgasm rising hard. "Only for you."

They know I mean all of them. They're the only ones who get me like this. The only ones who understand what I need, and the only ones I ever want to get it from.

They're my forever.

The realization crashes over me, and before I know it, I'm coming on Maddoc's cock, panting against the crook of his neck as my pussy clenches around his shaft, over and over, in rippling waves of pleasure.

"Not yet," he grits out, smacking my ass hard enough to sting. "You're not milking my cum out of me yet, butterfly. You made a promise to Dante."

"Yes," I gasp, the aftershocks still rolling through me. It doesn't matter. It's not enough. I'm desperate and hungry for every piece of these men I can get, so grateful none of us died today that I just want to be reminded we're all still alive.

"You gonna take Logan, too?" Dante asks, his voice husky with lust. "You want to feel his cock inside you, princess? You want to be stuffed full?"

I push myself back up, still impaled on Maddoc's rock-hard cock, and turn to look over my shoulder at Logan. His eyes are blazing with the pale fire of his arousal, his attention completely focused on me with that unique intensity of his that I'm already addicted to.

"Fuck me," I beg, making all three men groan. "Help me give Dante what he asked for."

He got naked at some point, and his cock jerks against his abs, his muscles taut and rippling as he reaches for me.

"You want me inside you too." He palms my ass cheeks, then pulls me open and drags his thumbs down my crease, massaging them over my asshole.

It sends a wild jolt through me, the tight little pucker sensitive in a way I never realized before Maddoc took me there. I fucking love it, already addicted to the new sensation, but right now, I crave something different. Something I'm not sure I can take, but that the darkness in me, the part that hungers for pain, finds irresistible.

"I want to feel you both," I pant, rolling my hips as Maddoc's fingers dig bruises into my hips. "But not... there. Fuck me, Logan. Fuck me exactly the way Maddoc is."

Logan goes still, dark desire coming off him in a palpable wave, then he pushes me forward again, laying me flat on top of Maddoc.

"So wet," he murmurs, running a finger around the ring of my pussy, already stuffed with Maddoc's cock. "Is this where you want me?"

Maddoc cups the back of my head, keeping one hand on my ass, and pulls me up to his mouth. "What are you asking him for, butterfly?" he murmurs against my lips, holding me against him as he grinds against me, forcing his cock in as deeply as it will go. "Are you saying you've got room for both of us?"

I don't know if I do. I don't know if it's even possible. But I do know one thing.

"I *need* both of you," I gasp. "I need you both to take me."

"Like this," Logan says, sliding a finger into my pussy alongside Maddoc's cock. "Is this what you want? You want me in here, too? With Maddoc?"

I nod, my heart racing and words failing me. It's intense, just shy of pain, his single finger already stretching me to the point that I feel overwhelmed by the sensation.

It's perfect. And even if it's more than I can take, I want it.

"Please," I beg as Maddoc groans, slowly thrusting in and out alongside Logan's finger.

Then Logan adds another one, and tears spring to my eyes as it pushes me to my limit.

I start to shake, gasping and ducking my head against Maddoc's chest, panting against him as he rubs his hand up and down my back.

"That's it, butterfly," he mutters, his voice tight with strain and his muscles like heated iron underneath me. "You can do it. Gonna remind you that you're ours. Gonna share you with my brothers the way shit is meant to be between us."

Logan pulls his fingers out, and I whine, clamping my internal muscles down on Maddoc's cock, desperate for the overwhelming sensation I just lost, hungry to be filled in a way I never imagined before falling for these men.

Maddoc's hands palm both sides of my ass, and he rocks me forward, spreading me wide while Logan lines himself up behind me.

Logan uses one hand to rub his hot cockhead against my entrance and holds me flat with the other splayed across my lower back. "You're already stretched around Maddoc," he says, an undercurrent of dark excitement to his voice. "Can you take it?"

"Yes," I breathe out, already overwhelmed but craving more. "It will hurt."

I shudder, my whole body tightening at once. "*Yes.*"

Maddoc fists his hand in my hair, pulling my head back and giving me a look so hot it almost pushes me over the edge. "You're hungry for it. You want to be totally owned, don't you, butterfly? You want us to show you exactly how much you can take."

It's true. They're the only ones I've ever trusted to do it.

"Breathe," Logan says, slowly pushing the head of his cock against my entrance until the pressure becomes almost unbearable. Just before it breaks me, his cockhead breaches my pussy, sliding in just far enough to make him grunt.

Maddoc curses, his hips jerking upward before he catches them and forces himself still.

I can't breathe. Tears spring to my eyes. It *does* fucking hurt. It aches in a way that demands all of my attention and awakens a deep, desperate hunger for more.

"The things you fucking do for us," Dante murmurs. The slow, slick sound as he works his cock almost makes it feel like he's inside me too. "You're incredible, princess."

I shudder, making all three men groan. "Love you," I whisper, my senses completely overwhelmed.

"Use your safe word if it gets to be too much," Logan says, his voice strained as he starts to work his way deeper inside me, a slow, delicious kind of torture that pushes every limit I have.

It's the most intense sex I've ever had, and the closest I've ever felt to the men that I love.

"Look at me," Maddoc demands when I start to shake again, my body just as overwhelmed as my spirit. He yanks my hair hard enough to draw a gasp out of me, centering me with the balance of pain.

I open my eyes, and his burn into me with a fierce, primal devotion that calls to my heart.

"That's it," he says, his voice like gravel. "There you are."

Logan slowly rocks against me from behind, driving himself a little deeper, then a little deeper again, each short, shallow thrust making my body vibrate with rising tension, the best kind of tension, the kind that's bound to wreck me completely when it snaps.

"You have all of me," Logan says, carefully leaning over my back and grinding his hips against my ass in a slow roll. The movement makes Maddoc curse quietly and draws a moan out of me as it puts pressure on my g-spot. "You took my whole cock, wildcat."

"I feel him inside you," Maddoc grits out. "We're splitting you open. Claiming this territory. Can you feel it? Can you feel that you're ours, butterfly? Do you know who you belong to?"

"Oh god," I gasp, the two cocks inside me making that truth inescapable. "*Yes.* You. All of you."

They start to fuck me together, finding a perfect rhythm, like we really were meant to be.

They keep me tightly sandwiched between them, their hands holding me firmly in place and our three bodies moving in a slow dance as they alternate thrusts. Slow, but intense. Being stuffed so full has my world spinning on its axis and pushes my body to its limits, and when I lock eyes with Dante, using his hungry, vibrant green gaze as my anchor point, an orgasm rolls through me without any warning.

I gasp, my inner muscles tightening with the intense wave of sudden pleasure.

"Fuck," Maddoc grits out, his body locking up underneath me as his cock swells in my pussy, making Logan hiss, his hips stuttering to a halt.

Then Logan *moves*, fucking into me just enough to take the

pleasure and explode it into something deeper, and I scream, the sensation sending me flying.

"Oh, fuck yeah. You've never looked more fucking beautiful, princess," Dante says, his voice hoarse. "You were made for this. Made for Reaper cock, made to take what my brothers give you. I wanna see their cum dirty up that greedy pussy of yours until it runs down your thighs. Show me how much you can take. Show me how it feels to let my brothers fuck you raw."

Every word out of his mouth drags my orgasm out even longer, and even though neither Maddoc nor Logan is able to fuck me deep or go hard, I've never felt more thoroughly taken in my life. It's fucking intense, and just when it starts to settle into a bone melting afterglow, Maddoc's fingers bite into my ass, holding me in place as he slams his hips up.

"*Fuck*," Logan grunts, his hard body shuddering above me as Maddoc's hot release fills my pussy.

"Oh god," I gasp, the feel of it setting off a chain reaction that has me coming again almost before I know it.

Logan curses again and starts to fill me with his cum too, continuing to slowly fuck me through it as my pussy gets sloppy, just the way Dante wanted.

"Such a filthy mess," Maddoc murmurs, dipping his hand between my legs and rubbing his fingers through it, holding his cock inside me even as it starts to soften. He gives me a possessive look full of pure male satisfaction. "Dante's right. You're fucking beautiful when we dirty you up."

"You are," Logan agrees, pushing my hair off the back of my neck and leaning down to kiss me there.

It makes me shiver, causing me to clench around both of them again and sending another hot gush of cum down my thighs.

Both men groan as they slowly pull out of me, trailing hot kisses over my skin as they go.

"Fuck, that's it. Spread your thighs and let me see, princess," Dante grunts, jerking himself hard as he stares at my pussy with hooded eyes. "That right there is the only heaven I'll ever need. If I had to, I could die fucking happy from seeing you like this."

"Don't you fucking dare," I say, the bruises and lacerations covering him making that hit too close to home. "Not without giving me your cum too."

I crawl over to him and push his hand away from his cock, then dip mine between my legs, using what was inside me as lubrication as I take over.

His abs ripple with tension, and he throws his head back, the muscles in his neck standing out like thick cords. "Fuck. Princess. *Jesus.*"

"Give it to me, Dante. Don't make me beg."

He sucks in a ragged breath, his eyes hot as he grabs the back of my head. "You fucking love to beg."

"Only for you," I whisper. "Only because I love you."

He groans, then starts to come, shoving my head down just in time for me to open my mouth and swallow down his release.

"Fuck, that's it, take what's yours princess, *fuck.*"

His hand finally relaxes on the back of my head, and I slowly let his cock slide out of my mouth, then rest my head on his thigh, feeling boneless and complete and so fucking in love I have no words for it.

I don't need any. This day has wrung everything out of all four of us, and my men are just as ready to collapse as I am. Maddoc and Logan clean us all up a little, then surround me as I curl up next to Dante, acting like a protective shield, their presence all the proof I need that they're feeling it too.

This is where we belong.

This is what we were fighting for.

And whatever the fallout is now that West Point has fallen, this is how we'll get through it. Together.

41

RILEY

Sunlight pouring through the window from the blinds we never closed last night wakes me up the next morning, and it's not just the sun that's light. I feel amazing. Sore, but amazing. My entire spirit is light, and it doesn't hurt at all that I'm surrounded by hot, male bodies.

Sleeping male bodies. One of which is still healing from a beating.

My eyes pop open, a frisson of concern that I might have hurt Dante bringing me all the way awake. But to my surprise, it's not him who has me sandwiched against Maddoc's side.

It's Logan.

A warm contentment steals over my heart when I see him next to me. I know how much he needs order and routine and the ability to retreat to the cool isolation of his own personal space. He didn't go back to that last night, though. True, I can see that he took some time to align all the things on the nightstand next to him in neat, orderly lines, but he stayed here in the colorful, chaotic explosion of Dante's room last night.

For me.

For us.

I'm facing him, and he has one arm around me in a firm,

possessive hold and the other tucked under his pillow. His gorgeous face, usually kept so deliberately emotionless during the day, looks... not soft while he sleeps. But gentler. Calmer. I'm sure he'll always have some of those old tendencies and a strict need for order and control in his life. That's who he is, and I wouldn't want him to change. But it means everything to know that he's become comfortable adjusting his routines enough to include me, and what we all have together.

A gentle puff of breath on the back of my neck makes me shiver, and I nestle back, my ass firmly tucked against Maddoc's groin. The feel of his thick morning wood, hard and insistent as it presses against me, almost makes me wish I could take him again.

My pussy aches with a deep memory of how thoroughly he and Logan fucked me last night, though, and as much as I crave them, I might need a minute before we go again.

I roll over to face him instead, his face softened a little by sleep too, but still so full of purpose.

I lean in, pressing the whisper of a kiss to his parted lips, then ease myself up, trying not to wake either of them.

Dante is asleep behind him, breathing evenly. A fierce surge of satisfaction hits me with the knowledge that the man who beat him like that is dead now, but then I push Austin McKenna out of my mind once and for all. Fuck him. The only thing that matters is that Dante is here, now, alive and whole.

I watch him sleep for I don't know how long, just grateful to have him back. Grateful to have all of them here. Finally, his breathing changes, those amazing green eyes of his slowly drifting open. I'm not even sure he's fully awake at first, and for a moment, we just look at each other, my heart filling with so much love that it nearly overwhelms me.

Then he smiles. "Princess."

Maddoc stirs next to me, the light hold he has on my hip tightening into something more possessive as he starts to come awake. He stretches a little before his eyes open, his elbow clipping Dante's side.

His eyes fly open, and he sits up, shoving a hand through his bedhead. "Shit, sorry."

Dante grins, pushing himself up with only a minor wince. "I'll survive."

Behind me, the loose, relaxed feel of Logan's body changes between one breath and the next, a sudden tension to his muscles telling me he's awake now, even though he doesn't move. Somehow, it doesn't surprise me that he wakes up to a still, silent alertness, no doubt taking a moment to assess his surroundings by force of habit. And when all that tense alertness flows back to a comfortable looseness as he sits up, my heart swells even more.

This isn't what Logan is used to waking up to, but he's okay with it. More than okay, if the way he tugs me back onto his lap and plants a soft, sleepy kiss on the side of my neck is any indication.

"Good thing you have a king," Maddoc teases Dante, trying to stretch again and settling for just rolling his shoulders. The bed is big enough for the four of us... but barely.

Dante snorts. "Yeah, gonna have to find something better for the future."

I bite back a smile, a giddy happiness rising up inside me as it settles in my heart. These men are mine to keep. This isn't the last time we'll all wake up together. They're really mine.

"The size of the bed isn't as important as how it's maintained," Logan says, the stern reprimand in his voice ruined by how rough with sleep his voice still is.

Dante obviously thinks so too, since he tosses a pillow at Logan's head with a shit-eating grin on his face. "Maintain *this*."

Logan tugs me out of the line of fire and bats it away. "I had the bedding in good order and completely wrinkle free when we fell asleep last night. Look at it now."

Maddoc disguises his laugh behind a cough. "Looks slept in. Nothing wrong with that."

Logan huffs lightly, but the teasing glint in his eyes gives him away. He'll never say so, but he's enjoying this. "It looks like chaos. You're both going to have to learn to sleep more neatly in the future. The blanket is wrinkled, and there are two pillows on the floor."

Maddoc grins. "There's only so much room here, and, you know... gravity."

Dante picks up another pillow and holds it over the floor, then opens his hand and lets it drop.

Logan makes a dramatically pained sound, and Dante laughs. "Madd's right. Fucking gravity. Who invited it to this party?"

"You're just messy sleepers." Logan shakes his head. "None of this would happen if you two learned to sleep more neatly."

"Just the two of us, huh?" Dante teases, throwing me a heated smile that has all the emotion inside me bubbling up at once, making my throat close up as the love I have for these men almost chokes me.

I want this.

I want them.

I want it forever.

"What's up, butterfly?" Maddoc says, his eyes going gentle as he looks at my face. "Everything okay?"

"I want to marry you," I blurt. "All three of you."

Surprise flashes in his eyes, and behind me, Logan goes utterly still. Dante's green gaze drills into me with a heart-stopping intensity, but none of them say anything for a moment.

Then Maddoc clears his throat, his voice gruff. "No. That's not gonna happen."

My heart falls a little. It hurts to hear that, and I don't understand why he's so against it if we love each other.

Maddoc's hand shoots out, capturing mine, and he pulls me

off Logan's lap onto his. "Marriage isn't just about what we feel for each other," he says, almost like he's reading my mind. "It's a contract, a legally binding one. It's how McKenna got his hands on your money, and you know that was my plan in the beginning too. I don't ever want that to stand between us, butterfly. I never want you to wonder, or think we're trying to use you for your money. Marriage puts that in doubt."

"I... what? No, it doesn't." I shake my head, even more confused, even though his tender words soothe the hurt. "I don't have any money. Not anymore."

Something fierce flashes across his face. "You're Austin McKenna's widow. His fortune, the one he fucking stole from you, will all pass back to you. You're his legal next of kin."

I shake my head again, my stomach roiling at the thought of being Austin's, in any way, shape, or form. "I don't want *anything* of his."

"It ain't his," Dante says harshly. "It's yours. Your grandfather wanted you to have it, and that bastard had no right to it, no matter what that farce of a marriage made 'legal.'"

My grandfather. He means William Sutherland, a man I didn't even know I was related to until recently. But... he's right.

I take a deep breath, then let it out slowly, a determination settling in my chest. "Do you think I can get it back?"

This time, Maddoc's grin is fucking predatory. "I know you can. I made sure of it yesterday, with the help of some legal counsel Logan hooked us up with."

Logan nods, and my eyes fill with tears of gratitude. "Thank you."

"I love you, Riley Sutton," Maddoc says, cupping my face. "I'm so fucking in love with you I'd burn the world down. It's why I *won't* marry you."

He takes my mouth before I can argue for it, and I sink into the kiss, letting that be enough for now.

I believe him. I can feel the depth of his love, and while I don't agree—what's mine is his, all of theirs, forever—I do understand his feelings, and I love him even harder for caring so much.

When Maddoc finally lets me come up for air, he rests his forehead against mine for a moment, breathing in sync with me. "You're still mine, though. That won't change."

"Never."

He smiles, kisses me hard again, then lifts me onto Logan's lap so he can leave the bed. I can't even imagine all he has to do in the wake of taking down Austin, so I let him go, happily falling into another deep kiss with Logan, and also not surprised when he gets up afterward too.

"Is there anything I can do to help?" I ask.

Logan gives me that small, private smile. "Take care of our brother."

Dante snorts as Logan leaves the room, leaving the two of us alone. "I still don't need a fucking babysitter," he mutters, pulling me against his side.

I roll into him—carefully—and lightly trace my fingers over the bruises on his face. "Good, because I said I wanted to marry you guys, not babysit."

He captures my hand, kissing my palm before staring into my eyes. "If it were just me, I'd marry you in a second, princess. But with the way shit works, it's probably best if it's Maddoc when it comes to the legal stuff."

"He said no," I whisper, my heart still a little bruised from that even though I do understand.

Dante's smile turns wicked. "Yeah, well, he once said none of us were allowed to touch you, either. Don't fucking give up on that. Logan and I will marry you in spirit and fuck you just like real husbands, but I haven't seen you give up on something you want yet, so don't start now."

My breath catches, a warm glow spreading through my chest. "Oh?"

"Yeah." He tips my chin up and kisses me. "Just keep asking him until he says yes. You know none of us can resist you."

It's exactly what I need to hear, and when we finally get out of bed a little while later, he gets me laughing about how sore we each are. He's still moving slowly, and as we make our way to the shower, I'm limping a little too.

I wince as the hot water runs between my legs, reminding me how well used my pussy was last night.

"Look at us," Dante teases, supporting himself against the slick tile with one hand while carefully soaping me between the legs with his other one. "You took a good beating too."

I smack his chest. "That's not funny. There's no comparison."

"You got that right," Dante says, his voice husky as he turns me away from him and lathers up my hair. He drops a kiss on my wet shoulder. "Nothing's ever gonna compare to you."

It's not what I meant, but I let it go.

What happened, happened, and the biggest *fuck you* we can ever give an arrogant sadist like McKenna is to truly forget about him. Something that's easy to do when we head downstairs to find Logan cooking and Maddoc fighting with the new coffee maker again.

I grin, my heart lifting at the cozy domesticity of the scene, and go nudge him aside so I can actually get some caffeine out of the thing. Maddoc's hopeless with it, and that doesn't even take into account how many of these things have taken a bullet for the man since I first met him. But for the first time since I arrived here, things feel peaceful. Settled, even though I know there will still be repercussions on the horizon from what went down yesterday, and in this world—the dark, criminal underground that the respectable parts of Halston like to pretend doesn't exist—words like "settled" and "peaceful" won't ever truly apply.

But that doesn't mean I can't enjoy it while it lasts.

Which, as it turns out, isn't all that long.

I'm not even surprised this time when the doorbell rings a little while later and it's The Six's representative, summoning us to see them down at Saraven later tonight. Nervous, but not surprised.

"It'll be okay, princess," Dante murmurs, leaning heavily against the door jamb once The Six's representative leaves. He'd held himself upright, stoic and tall, while the man was here, but he still has a lot of healing to do, and it shows.

Just like his love does, since his first instinct is to reassure me.

"I know," I say, nodding jerkily. It's a lie. I don't *know*. After all, this will be the third time we've been called before The Six after breaking their first cardinal rule. Even though Logan deflected the authorities' attention from Reaper involvement, the incident itself has been all over the news.

Still, we have no choice but to go. We can't defy The Six by not showing up. Whatever consequences come from the showdown with West Point, I've got no doubt that they'll pale in comparison to what would happen to us if we chose to outright defy The Six.

I distract myself from that by turning my attention to Dante. "You should lie back down."

He grins. "Is that an offer? Because I wouldn't say no to a little company." Then he sighs, scrubbing a hand over his face. "But actually, princess, we've got work to do."

"You're hurt!"

He lifts an eyebrow. "A few bumps and bruises? Nah. This shit ain't gonna slow me down." His face turns serious. "Besides, we've got a shit-ton of work to do to reclaim our territory and make sure no one else rises up to take McKenna's place, right, Madd?"

Maddoc nods. "There's a lot of cleanup to do to deal with the fallout from yesterday, and we need to move fast. West Point is fractured and leaderless. Something or someone will have to step in to bring order to everything McKenna built, and if we leave that to chance, we'll regret it."

He's right. I may have woken up feeling euphoric, but this isn't a honeymoon. We've got work to do.

"How can I help?"

"By claiming what's yours," Maddoc says, giving me a hard kiss. "Logan's got some time-sensitive paperwork for you to deal with that will probably make your eyes cross with boredom, but it has to be done to reclaim your money now that McKenna is dead."

The fact that I'm going to get it all back still hasn't fully sunk in, but it turns out Maddoc's not wrong about how mind-numbing the process is. With Logan's guidance, I manage to get through it all before we have to leave for Saraven, and when we finally head to the upscale club in the evening, it turns out that, this time, it's just us who have been summoned before them. There's no West Point representative, or any other member of Halston's underground, in sight.

I hold my head high as we're led back through the club, to the room we've met them in twice before. They're waiting for us, faces grim.

"There was a fire yesterday," Ayla Fairchild starts without preamble. "One that apparently resulted in the deaths of..." Her eyes flick down to a small screen in front of her, as if she's reading from a headline. "'Several notorious members of a criminal gang, including its leader, Austin McKenna.'"

She pauses, her gaze raking over each of us before settling on Maddoc. Her eyes flick down to his missing finger for a moment, then return to his face.

"This isn't what we meant by staying off the authorities' radar," she says, no inflection in her voice. "What happened?"

"McKenna had plans to take down The Six," Maddoc responds. "We stopped him."

All six members react with low murmurs and angry expressions, but Ayla's gaze never wavers from Maddoc's.

"Explain," she demands.

Maddoc does, laying out the whole story, including how Austin married me in order to steal my inheritance, which he was using to fund his plans against The Six.

"We're no strangers to threats," one of the men says, his voice calm and his gaze assessing. "And for all Austin McKenna's arrogance, West Point has never been one."

"Not before he got his hands on Riley's money," Maddoc says. "But the resources that gave him were... formidable."

He names the dollar amount, and The Six all mask various expressions of shock.

"And these assets are still in the hands of what's left of West Point?" Ayla asks sharply.

"No." Maddoc gives her that predatory smile that always makes my heart trip. "It's in the hands of McKenna's widow."

Her attention snaps over to me, and the sharp intelligence behind her gaze strikes a chord in me. "You?"

I lift my chin. "Yes."

A faint smile graces her mouth, and she gives me a small nod, then turns back to Maddoc. "Go on. What makes you so sure that McKenna was planning on coming after us?"

"We were tipped off." He nods toward Dante. "My second infiltrated West Point to confirm the details. We were going to bring the proof to you once we had it, but McKenna caught Dante on his way out."

Ayla raises an eyebrow. "This was yesterday?"

"Yes."

She looks at Dante. "And did you find proof of his plans?"

"I did. He was setting himself up to take all six of you out in one fell swoop."

Her face goes hard. "Show me."

Dante transfers the digital files to her, and they direct us to wait out in the club while they review them.

My nerves return with a vengeance while we wait. "There's no way they can bring repercussions on us for this, right? We were doing them a favor!"

Dante snorts, and Maddoc chuckles, shaking his head. "That's not quite how it works."

"We were covering our own asses," Dante adds. "They know that, but that ain't necessarily a bad thing."

Logan nods. "They'll respect it. They were already impressed that we found out about McKenna's plans. I got the impression they would have been blindsided."

Dante nods. "They were definitely surprised. Now we just gotta see what they're gonna do about it."

"What's there still to do?" I ask. "He's dead." Then I shake my head before the men can answer, remembering what they told me this morning. Austin's death will leave a hole in Halston's underground that's going to be filled, one way or another. The Six may not involve themselves directly in gang activities, but they're also not going to ignore something like that when it's bound to cause even more chaos.

When we're finally summoned back into their chamber, they don't waste any time.

"You were right," Ayla tells Maddoc. "McKenna's plans were very... thorough. The resources he was pouring into overthrowing our power definitely elevated him to a true threat." She pauses, sharing a look with the rest of The Six before turning her attention to me. "Resources which now belong to you, Riley Sutton."

I'm not sure what to say. Does she think *I'm* a threat to them now?

I swallow hard. "I don't have any interest in overthrowing your power."

377

Ayla smiles, a genuine flash of warmth in her eyes. "That's good, because we'd like you to join us."

"I... what?" I shake my head. I don't understand. "Join you where?"

"Here." She uses her prosthetic arm to gesture to the table they all sit at. "We want to offer you a place among us, Riley. We want you to become one of The Six."

42

RILEY

I'm STUNNED. The offer isn't what I was expecting when we were summoned here tonight. Hell, it isn't something I would have come up with, even in my wildest dreams.

Especially because it's clear she means *me*. Not the Reapers, not all of us, just me.

Unlike Maddoc, Dante, and Logan, who grew up in Halston's criminal underground, the way things operate in this shadowy world is still new to me. I'm not sure what The Six think I can bring to the table, but one of the men—Marcus, if I remember their past introductions correctly, the one with heterochromia—clears that up right away.

"You have the resources to become a powerful player here in Halston now," he says. "We'd like to work with you, not against you. The file the Reapers gave us proves that he had ambitions of wiping us out and taking all of the power for himself." A sour look flashing across his face before he schools his features. "We should have seen the threat coming."

Ayla rests her hand on his wrist in a silent show of support; a reminder to me of the relationship I'm almost sure she has with some of these men, and how it opened my eyes to the love that was possible for me to claim with mine. It may be overstepping to think so, but she feels like a kindred spirit.

Marcus subtly relaxes at her touch, giving me a warm smile. "We didn't see it, but you and the Reapers did. That alone tells us we need someone with a fresh perspective to help us run things."

Maddoc shifts closer to me, resting his hand on the small of my back and next to him, Logan comes to attention, standing tall with that unique stillness he gets that tells me he's here to support me, no matter what.

On my other side, Dante's fingertips brush against mine. "Do you need a minute, princess?" he murmurs quietly. "This is huge."

I stifle an almost manic laugh. Huge is an understatement. I feel like I'm reeling from the sudden, unexpected turn of events, and I honestly have no idea if I should say yes or not.

I take Dante's question to heart, and the answer is yes. I do need a minute. I have no idea what joining them would actually mean for me, or what kind of effect it would have on the Reapers.

"Riley?" Ayla prompts me, her confident presence something I'd like to aspire to.

"Can I... consider your offer?" I ask cautiously, a little in awe of the woman and not sure what the protocol here is.

"Of course," she says instantly. "But let me ask for something too. May I have a moment to talk to you in private?"

Maddoc's fingers flex against my back, but I don't get the sense that he sees her as a threat to me. It's just his natural inclination to protect me.

"Of course," I tell her, following her into a small, comfortably furnished room off to the side.

The door stays open, and we have a clear view of the rest of The Six as they converse quietly amongst themselves. Something about the cozy space, or maybe about Ayla herself, puts me at ease. She's poised, but addresses me with a genuine openness that says a lot about the sincerity of The Six's offer.

"I understand your hesitations," she says once we both take a seat. "Do you know much about how we came to power here in Halston?"

"The Six?"

When she nods, I shake my head.

"Maybe I'll get a chance to tell you about it sometime, but for now, I'll just say that being a part of all this isn't something I ever expected, either. I never could have predicted that my life would take the turns it did. Falling in love with three dangerous men and ending up as part of a group that oversees and controls the city's criminal underground is not what I ever imagined for my future, but..." She trails off, a faraway look on her face. Then she shakes it off and shoots me a small smile. "But maybe you can relate?"

I laugh, an unexpected feeling of camaraderie bubbling up in my chest. Before the Reapers, Chloe was the only person I was ever close to. I'm not used to feeling understood, or understanding where someone else is coming from so well.

"Definitely relatable," I admit, hesitating before I add, "But I'm not sure if that means I'm cut out for The Six. I've spent most of my life trying to steer clear of this world."

Ayla gives me a knowing look. "But you're a part of it now, and forgive me, but I don't think that's an accident."

My heart starts to pound. "What do you mean? Have you heard something?"

"Oh, no, nothing like that. Nothing nefarious," she says, chuckling. "I just mean that it seems like sometimes things fall into place in ways we never could have predicted, but that turned out to be perfect. Painful sometimes, but still... perfect."

I swallow hard, her words resonating with me more than she can possibly imagine. "I understand that."

"Do you?" She smiles. "Because I really do believe that life leads us toward who we're meant to be, even if we don't see it at first. Even if we actively resist it." She pauses, then adds, "But when we quit resisting, when we embrace it, there's nothing more liberating than finally becoming the person we were always meant to be."

I understand exactly what she's saying, and it puts a lump in my throat. I remember doing everything I could to keep Chloe away from all gang activity in Halston, and now here I am, being offered a spot at the top of the criminal food chain. From one perspective, it doesn't make any sense. But at the same time, it feels like my time with the Reapers didn't force me down that path or shape me into something new.

It feels like it helped me discover not just who I truly am, but also the person I *want* to be.

I bite my lip, hesitating. I'm still not sure if that person should be part of The Six, though.

Ayla sits with me without any sign of impatience while these thoughts tumble through my head, giving me all the space I asked for to really consider things.

"I've fallen in love with three men too," I finally tell her, the words coming slowly as I try to put my thoughts into order. "And after all the shit that went down with Austin..."

I swallow hard, reliving those moments of terror again, when we heard him start to torture Dante over the phone. When we arrived at his house and didn't know if Dante was dead or alive. The soul-deep relief and joy I felt afterward, having all of my men home and safe and whole.

It's that last one that has me hesitating. I can't give that up. I won't.

"We barely came through it alive. I know this world I'm a part of now is dangerous, and that loving them means accepting that. But that doesn't mean I'm willing to invite more of it into our lives."

"I don't think we always have a choice about that," Ayla says, giving me a sympathetic smile.

She's right. I know she is. But still, "Getting even more deeply involved the way a position with The Six would require seems like I'd be inviting even more danger into our lives. I'll be honest, I'm just not sure if I can handle constantly living under that kind of threat and uncertainty. Losing them, any one of them, isn't something I think I'd survive. Along with my sister, those three men are my everything."

Ayla nods. "I get that, I really do. And the truth is that you're right. Being at the top of the food chain means there's always a target on your back. This thing with West Point proves that in spades. But Riley, have you ever heard that saying, *with great power comes great responsibility?*"

"Yeah, of course."

She smiles, and this one rivals some of Maddoc's for sheer predatory dominance. "Well, the reverse is also true. With great responsibility comes a shitload of power. When you're at the top of the food chain, you have the means to protect yourself. And more importantly, the people you love."

She glances through the open door at the rest of The Six. No, at *her* men, Marcus, Theo, and Ryland.

The deep, open love on her face gives me a moment of understanding and a sense of sisterhood with her that goes even further than her poignant words. The two of us really are more similar than I ever would have expected, and the epiphany settles all my doubts, freeing something in my spirit.

For so long, my purpose was simply to keep Chloe safe and to give her a better life. Through all the chaos of the last months, I never stopped to ask myself what my purpose will be going forward. Now, Ayla's just showed me that it doesn't have to change. Instead, it can expand to include *all* the people I love.

I smile at her. "Yes."

Ayla's eyes brighten. "Yes, you're accepting our offer?"

I sit a little straighter. "I am. I'm ready to become part of The Six. I'm ready to protect my family."

When we rejoin the others, each of The Six gives me a genuine welcome, but thankfully, don't seem to expect anything else from me for now. They tell me that more information will be forthcoming, then dismiss us for the evening.

I'm still in shock when we get home, but under it is a bubbling sort of excitement about the future that I've honestly never had before.

"I'm so fucking proud of you," Dante says as all three of them surround me, the fine lines of strain around his eyes from being on his feet all day eclipsed by the warmth in his eyes.

He pulls me close, kissing me thoroughly, then passes me to Logan. I get equal treatment from him before he captures my throat in his hand, stroking it softly as he looks down into my eyes.

"They made a good choice," he tells me seriously. "You'll be an asset to this city."

"The darker parts of it, at least," I tease him.

His lips twitch up, his grip tightening for a moment in a shared reminder of the connection we share. "The darker parts of it," he agrees.

"And what do you think?" I tease Maddoc when he tugs me out of Logan's hold. I wrap my arms around his neck and sway against him. "Did you know this was happening?"

"No," he says, gripping the back of my head and kissing me hard. When he lets me come up for air, he smirks, "But I told you that you were good at this, so I'm not surprised."

Dante snorts. "You were totally surprised." Then he sways a little. "Fuck, maybe I do need to lay down."

"Is that an invitation?" I tease him.

He grins. "Always, princess. Fucking always."

43

RILEY

It takes a couple more days for the guys to get things squared away enough in the organization that they finally feel comfortable bringing Chloe back from the safe house, and when they tell me it's time, I can barely sit still.

Chloe must feel the same, because the moment we arrive, she barrels out of the house, tackling me almost before I make it out of the Escalade.

"*Riley*," she squeals, hugging me tight enough to make the bruise from the bullet my vest took at McKenna's place ache like a bitch.

I'll take it. I'll take anything to have her back with me again, and I squeeze her back just as hard, laughing as we both try to talk at once. We've kept in touch as much as it was safe to, but even though she's up to speed on almost everything that's happened to me—*almost*—I suddenly feel like there are a million things I need to share with her.

She's the same way, and we could probably stay right here in the driveway giggling with each other all day—but then I catch sight of the indulgent smiles on my men's faces as they bring her bags out of the house, which reminds me what we actually came for.

"Are you ready to come home?" I ask Chloe, tenderly running my hand down her hair.

It's longer now, and the roots are all grown out.

She looks beautiful.

She grins. "Hell yeah, I am." Then her smile falters a little, a bashful look coming over her face. "Um, let me just say goodbye?"

"Of course."

Dante nudges my shoulder as Chloe runs back toward the house, giving me a conspiratorial look that I don't get at all. "We asked Nathan to stay a few more days and handle some shit in the area for us. He'll be back in Halston soon."

"O...kay?" I say, trying to remember if they've mentioned what kind of business the Reapers have an interest in way out here. Then I see Chloe saying her goodbyes to Nathan and realize it's not the business Dante was giving me a heads-up about.

It's Nathan.

My eyes narrow, my sisterly instincts instantly going on high alert.

Nathan is a young, hard-looking guy I vaguely remember meeting when Chloe left, and have definitely heard a lot about while she's been out here. Right now though, I'm picking up major vibes between them, and his badass, hard-eyed look has totally softened as he brushes something off her collar and tucks a strand of hair behind her ear.

I hold my tongue as they hug, and wait until we're all piled back in the Escalade and on the road back to Halston to ask her about him. Maddoc's driving with Logan in the passenger seat, and Dante dozes in the middle row, leaving Chloe and I to huddle together in the back.

"So," I start. "Nathan?"

Chloe's eyes widen, her cheeks turning cherry red. "Um, what?"

I raise an eyebrow. "What's going on there?"

"He's nice," she says, suddenly extremely interested in the boring scenery out the window.

I laugh. "I doubt it. He's a Reaper. He's probably a ruthless gangster who's tough as shit."

Chloe turns back to me with a grin. "Okay, he totally is." She looks down, twisting her hands together in her lap. "But he really *is* nice. I've... kind of got a thing for him."

"Kind of?" I tease gently.

She peeks up at me. "Okay, I've got a huge thing for him. Oh my god, Riley! He's the best."

She starts to gush about all of his amazing qualities, and I do my best to keep my protective instincts in check. A part of me still sees her as the little girl I have to stand guard over, and that part wants to warn her away from getting involved with a dangerous man.

Because yes, Nathan's young, and yes, I saw him being sweet with her. But I meant what I said. If he's a Reaper, he's dangerous... although even I have to admit that that doesn't mean he's dangerous to my sister. That kind of thinking would be hypocritical of me, given that one of my own men has killed for me, and any one of them would do it again if they had to.

There are a lot better ways to judge someone's character than just whether or not they're a criminal, so it's easy to be sincere when Chloe finally winds down her glowing list of Nathan's best attributes and I tell her that I'm happy for her.

"But that doesn't mean I won't kick his ass if he hurts you," I warn her, meaning every word of it.

Chloe grins, her eyes shining. "I know. God, it's so good to have you back."

"You mean, to have *you* back," I tease her. "You're the one who was tucked away in the safe house."

Her expression turns serious. "I didn't like being separated, but I understand why you wanted me to go." She grabs both my hands, squeezing them tight. "Just... don't do it again, okay? I want us to be together. It's one thing to hear about all your news secondhand, but I want to *be* there. I want us to have a life together."

My throat closes up, and I squeeze her back. "I do too."

Although I can't say I'm sorry she wasn't with me for everything that went down when she was gone. But that's over now, and with my new position... well, like Ayla said, with great responsibility will come great power, and I'll use every fucking bit of it to give Chloe the life I've always promised her. Chloe *and* my men.

Which reminds me, "There is one thing I haven't had a chance to tell you about yet."

"Yeah?" she asks, going a little tense. "Please tell me it's not more bad news."

"No, nothing like that." I hesitate, then just blurt it out. "I've been asked to be part of the group who oversee Halston's criminal underground. The Six."

"The Six?" Chloe's eyes go wide. "Um, I've heard of them. From Nathan. Are you *serious*?"

"Dead serious."

I bring her up to speed on the details of their offer and why they made it, and she gets a thoughtful look on her face after the shock drains away.

"It fits, you know."

"What?" I laugh, shaking my head. "Yeah, right. I'm sure you always thought your stripper sister would end up ruling over the local gangs I always warned you away from."

"No, I'm serious. You're not my stripper sister. You're my badass sister. The one who's always been there to save me. To fight for me." She blinks fast, then scrubs at her eyes when they start to spill over. "Dammit, I love you, Riley. I've always believed in you. And yeah, it *does* fit. I always knew you were destined for something way bigger than just shaking your ass in front of a bunch of leches to pay our rent."

"Thanks," I say, my throat tight. I clear it, then give her hair a playful tug. "And you know it wasn't just to pay our rent. I had to keep us looking good, so what the hell is *this* all about?"

Chloe laughs, then flicks her hair over her shoulder with some of the sass I remember from before life shit on her so hard. It warms my heart to see it. "Well, Nathan did offer to help touch up my roots, but I didn't trust him not to over bleach them. You remember what happened when we were living over that deli."

"Oh god, *don't* remind me."

We both laugh, then Chloe suddenly lights up. "Hey, does this shit with The Six mean we get to stay in Halston now? For good?"

"Yes, if you want to," I say cautiously, not sure how I'll handle it if she still has dreams of starting over in a new city.

Her squeal and the enthusiastic hug I get kill those worries before they can take hold. "I *definitely* do."

"This wouldn't have anything to do with Nathan coming back to Halston soon, would it?" I tease her.

"I don't know what you're talking about," she lies, flipping her hair again and then grinning at me.

Happiness fills my heart to overflowing. This wasn't the future I fought for so many years to give my little sister, but it's still exactly what I've always wanted for her.

She's safe, she's secure, and she's happy. *Truly* happy. And finally being able to provide that for her is worth all of it.

THE NEXT FEW weeks go by in a bit of a blur, and by the time I attend my first meeting as part of The Six, I'm feeling a lot more confident about my right to be there. Maddoc, Logan, and Dante have been educating me about all things Reaper-related, and I feel much more knowledgeable about the world I've stepped into.

The few nerves I do still carry into the meeting with me smooth out pretty quickly, because for all the power they wield, The Six are just people. People who it turns out I really like.

At first, it's a bit strange to see them outside the formal setting of their headquarters at Saraven. The meeting is actually held in the house that Ayla shares with Marcus, Theo, and Ryland, and seeing them in a more comfortable setting makes the love between the four of them even more obvious.

I can relate. The relationship with my own men gets deeper, better, every single day.

"Have you successfully reclaimed your entire estate now?" Marcus asks me before we get down to official business.

"Yes," I say with a vengeful surge of satisfaction.

I'm Austin's widow, and since that fucker forced me to marry him, I haven't just reclaimed my inheritance. I've exercised my right as his legal heir to *all* his assets.

"And the status of the new territorial borders?" Theo asks, slinging his arm around Ayla's shoulders as he takes a seat next to her on one of their plush couches. "Have the Reapers gotten those straightened out?"

I nod. "We'll be taking most of the former West Point territory. The small contingent of holdouts who wanted to continue operations for the organization have realized how difficult that would be without resources, and agreed to stand down."

"We had a report from Wolf Mathis that some of that last group swore fealty to him."

"That's right," I confirm. "And Maddoc is making a point to keep strong alliances with Mathis and all of the other gangs whose territory used to share borders with West Point, so that they all know the Reapers aren't gunning for their territory too."

"*All* the other gangs?" Marcus chides me gently.

I grimace. "You heard about the Scorpions."

"We heard that when they attacked, thinking the Reapers would be too disorganized to protect what was theirs, they tried to claim it was a defensive move when you tried to expand into their territory."

"They lied," I say flatly.

All six of them give me shark-like smiles, but it's Ayla who speaks. "We know. And the thorough way the Reapers put down their aggression sends a clear message to any other organization who might be thinking the same thing."

I bite back a grin. "I thought The Six didn't take sides."

She gives me an innocent look belied by the steel in her eyes. "We don't. We simply maintain order. And the support we're providing for the orderly expansion of Reaper territory is part of that. A smooth transition of power allows us all to profit."

"And on that note, let's get down to business," Theo says, leaning forward. "There have been some city zoning changes in the warehouse district that are putting certain operations at risk."

I listen intently, learning all I can as they efficiently go through their agenda. They're incredibly organized, ruthless and intelligent, and while I'm definitely a little bit out of my depth, they don't treat me that way.

Even better, I'm able to contribute a little bit here and there, which gives me the confidence that I won't feel that way forever. The more time I spend with The Six, the more my new role does feel like a good fit, just like Chloe said. It's just one that, like a good pair of heels, I'll have to break in a little before I'm completely comfortable in.

"Riley, a minute?" Ayla calls out to me when the meeting breaks up. I've already said my goodbyes and am more than ready to head back to my men, but I wait for her to catch up to me, silently admiring the red roses inked onto her arm above her prosthesis.

They're Dante's favorite color, and they make me want more ink of my own.

"What's that smile for?" she asks once she reaches me, a knowing gleam in her eye. "One of them in particular, or all of them at once?"

"What?"

She laughs. "Never mind. Although, I'd be happy to have *those* kinds of conversations over some good whiskey someday. Right now, I just wanted to check in with you. See if there's anything I can do to help you settle into... all this."

"Being part of The Six?"

"Sure, that too. But really, I just meant all of it. You're taking to your role with us like a duck to water, but I know how overwhelming it can feel when you really start to understand everything happening behind the scenes with these organizations."

I nod. "It's like a whole second city overlaid on the Halston I grew up with."

"Exactly."

We share a look that makes me think we're going to be more than just peers someday. I can really see us becoming friends.

"Thank you," I tell her for now, looking forward to that. "I'll take you up on that. And I appreciate it."

She gives my shoulder a friendly squeeze, then goes back into the house, and I head home.

Maddoc is on the couch down in the living room when I get back, going over some reports that have him frowning. I glance down at them and recognize them for what they are—important, but not urgent—so I tug them out of his hand and toss them onto the coffee table, then curl up on his lap.

He grins at me. "Welcome home."

"Thanks for waiting up for me," I tease, knowing that's not what he was doing.

He runs his fingers through my hair, letting the colorful strands curl around his wrist. "I'll always wait for you."

"Sweet talker." It touches me though, because I know it's true. "Tell me about your day."

He does, making me laugh a few times before he cups my face and gives me a serious look. "Shit is going so well for the organization right now that recruitment is up. With that and the new territory we've claimed, it's..." He pauses, his voice taking on an emotional rasp. "It's what I've been working toward, butterfly. What I've dreamed of. And you being part of The Six now is only helping that."

"Are you thanking me?" I ask, feeling emotional myself. "Because you know you never have to do that. Everything I do, I do for us. For the Reapers. For my family."

"I'm telling you I'm proud of you. I'm so fucking proud of you, Riley Sutton."

I kiss him. I have to. And then I can't resist saying, "How about we make that Riley Gray? Marry me, Maddoc."

He huffs out a laugh, shaking his head. "You're stubborn as fuck."

I narrow my eyes, because him calling me stubborn is definitely the pot calling the kettle black. "You're worth it."

It's not the first time I've posed the question to him, and even though he won't admit it, I can tell I'm slowly wearing him down.

I should be. I've been asking him nearly every damn day.

Today isn't the day he's going to say yes, though. I can already tell. But that doesn't mean I'm ready to admit it. Especially not when it's so much fun to push him a little.

"I guess I'll just have to be more persuasive then."

I let my hand slide down his chest and over his abs, then cup his bulge.

Heat burns in his eyes. "What do you mean?"

He knows exactly what I mean, but just in case there's any doubt, I slide off his lap, going to my knees between his legs, and press a hot, open-mouthed kiss over the outline of his shaft.

Maddoc groans, the sound sending a frisson of hot need through me.

I look up at him through my lashes, dragging my nails up the growing outline of his erection to toy with his zipper. "I mean that I love you. It's why I want to marry you. Are you going to let me make my case here?"

He cups the back of my head, giving me a filthy smile. "I'll let you do anything, butterfly. You know that. But it's gonna be pretty hard to talk about this while you're choking on my cock."

"Try me," I dare him, knowing I've already won.

Not about marriage. Not yet. But when it comes to being persuasive, who ever said anything about talking?

Sometimes, actions really do speak louder than words.

And this is definitely one of those times.

44

LOGAN

Sweat trickles down my back as I lower myself into a squat, then brace my core and tighten my glutes to drive the weight I've got racked across my shoulders back up. The metal of the bar is warm in my grip, the feel of it as familiar as breathing. I'm on my third set, and—

I freeze at the top of the motion, my form perfect but my count off.

I blink. *Is* this my third set? I'd been replaying a moment from the night before in my head, when Riley had helped me prep toppings for the pizzas she'd insisted we all make from scratch, and I'd lost count of my reps.

That never happens.

Except that it has been, several times over the last few weeks, and it's not the only area that cracks have started to form in the strict routine and regimented order I've created for my life.

In the past, those kinds of breaks have felt like painful losses of control, making me feel like I was teetering on the brink of a terrifying abyss, the skin of my body flayed raw, leaving me exposed and in danger of spiraling down into chaos.

And yet, I don't feel any of that right now. Just a mild

annoyance that I'm not sure how many sets I've actually completed.

I lower the bar to the ground and stretch out my neck, then walk over to the edge of the mat and hydrate with four ounces of water. Using the break to examine this odd change.

I have no interest in abandoning the order in my life and no expectation or desire to change entirely, but it's also pleasant in a way I never expected to feel so calm about the unexpected variation in my routine.

I doubt I'll ever stop being haunted by the horrors of my past, but the darkness they bred inside me hasn't spawned the same kind of monster that lived in my mother. I was shaped by her evil, but I wasn't shaped in her image.

The realization is freeing, and when I recap my water bottle and set it down on the shelf, I place it off center, then turn back to the mat to continue my set.

For a moment. The misplacement is too much, and I quickly turn around and align the bottle where it belongs, in the precise center of the shelf. But when I restart my squats, I don't let concerns about the exact number of reps I zoned out on slow me down, I simply pick up from the start of my third set, and the world doesn't spiral out of control. In fact, I shock myself when I finish and enter my bathroom to shower, because my reflection in the mirror is actually smiling.

I quickly correct that, but then strip down and step under the hot spray of water only to be surrounded by the sweet, musky scent of Riley. I fucked her against the glass in here less than twenty-four hours ago, and I'll have to do it again—soon, and regularly—if it's going to keep my shower smelling of her like this.

I soap up and realize I'm not just smiling again, I'm full-on grinning, my cock hard and dripping from the memory. I stroke it, my body constantly insatiable for my wildcat, but then force my hand away because the pleasure isn't something I want to bother with until I can share it with her again.

And I know exactly how I want to do that today. Something I've been planning for a while.

I finish cleaning myself, quickly and efficiently, then dry off and dress before pulling the item I purchased for her out of my desk drawer. I know she'll still be asleep at this hour, and that's fine. She's very, very good at following directions.

I quickly pen a note with instructions, then slip into her room and leave the note and her gift on the pillow next to her. Her face is soft and beautiful when she sleeps, and I'm tempted for a moment to wake her, kiss and defile her, ease the pressure of my arousal in the sweet, welcoming heat of her body.

But that can wait, and it will be all the more enjoyable for the delay.

I go downstairs to start breakfast, my brothers each wandering in shortly thereafter.

"Coffee?" Dante asks us both, heading straight to the machine.

Maddoc grunts his reply, which we all know is and always will be yes to that question, and I give Dante a small nod as I dice peppers for the omelets I'm going to make.

"What's the word from Ruiz?" Dante asks, leaning back against the counter as the coffee brews. "Is he gonna go in on the new supply route with us?"

We slip into a discussion of the partnership we've been working on with the 17th Street Gang as I cook, and just before the omelets are ready to be plated, Riley walks in.

She looks radiant. Always. But there's a particular flush to her cheeks that sends heat shooting through my body.

We exchange a look, and the answering heat in her eyes tells me that she's obeyed my instructions.

I'm tempted to grin, but I school my features through force of habit. The gift she's given me, though—putting herself at my mercy and under my control—has a dark excitement brewing in me that's harder to contain.

I serve up breakfast while the three of them switch from talking about Reaper business to discussing the schools we've been looking into for Chloe. While she was in the safe house with Nathan, she finished up her GED since she missed her high school graduation while West Point held her captive, and now, with the financial resources Riley has, she's determined to follow through on her goal of sending her sister to college.

"That's too far away," she says to Maddoc when he pushes for a school on the east coast that Chloe's expressed an interest in.

"Getting her out of Halston for a while isn't a bad idea, butterfly."

"She doesn't need to go that far! She's not in danger anymore, not now that West Point is gone."

"Come on now, princess," Dante says, tactfully not pointing out that there will always be danger to all of us. "Let the girl live a little. Get out and explore. Ain't that what growing up is about?"

Riley huffs out a breath. "Well, yes, but—"

I slip my hand into my pocket and press the remote, turning on the vibrator I told her to insert into her pussy before coming downstairs.

She stiffens, her voice stuttering breathlessly. "B-Bu-But, um, she..."

Dante raises an eyebrow. "She what? Wants to see a little of the world? We can send people with her, you know. I'm sure Nathan would volunteer. We won't send her off without protection."

"Good," Riley whispers, that gorgeous flush in her cheeks spreading down her throat as she jerks her eyes up to meet mine. "She should... have that."

I grin at her, and her eyes dilate in full.

Then I turn the vibrator off. "I agree."

"You do?" she asks faintly.

"Absolutely."

She hums absently in response, shifting on her seat and picking up her fork, and Dante gives her a quizzical look over her quick acquiescence, then shrugs and goes back to making his case for Chloe spreading her wings.

Neither of my brothers seems to realize just how little Riley is following the conversation anymore, since she continues to manage to contribute little "hmmms" and "uh-huhs" along the way, but her distraction is like a drug that I can't get enough of as I steal her attention, over and over, with the silent remote.

It isn't until after we've finished breakfast and I've cleaned up the kitchen that I realize what the unfamiliar feeling in my gut is.

Toying with Riley this way isn't just arousing, it's also fun.

I'm having *fun*.

"Something wrong, brother?" Dante asks, bouncing the keys to the Escalade in his hand.

I blink, realizing he caught me staring off into space after loading the dishwasher.

I quickly dry my hands and turn to face him. "Not at all."

He gives me a searching look, then shrugs. "Let's head out, then. Madd just got the call from the Realtor."

I nod, and follow him out. With plans progressing so smoothly on the 17th Street Gang partnership, we've decided to buy a new building to provide a legitimate front for the increase in activity. The one we're checking out today is perfectly located between our two territories, and the research I've done into its zoning and construction history indicates it will work for our needs. A visual inspection is the last step.

Maddoc has Riley pinned up against the side of the Escalade when Dante and I get outside, his tongue down her throat and her ass in his hands, and my cock twitches in my pants at the compelling sight. Without thinking, I reach into my pocket again and flip on her vibrator.

She gasps, lurching against him, and he chuckles, stepping back and adjusting his erection. "Don't tempt me, butterfly. The Realtor is waiting."

"Let's go then," she says, pushing her hair back with a shaky smile.

She turns a quick glare on me, and I grin back, increasing the setting by two.

"Fuck," she whispers, smacking the side of the Escalade to brace herself. Her knees look a little wobbly, and her nipples are twin points, clearly visible through the silky material of her thin shirt.

Dante frowns. "You okay, princess?"

"She's perfect," I say. "Would you like me to drive?"

It distracts him the way I intended.

"Hell, no," he says with a wide grin. "I'm taking the wheel."

"Then I'll navigate," I say, slipping into the passenger seat and turning off the vibe.

Maddoc and Riley slip into the backseat, and I tap the building's address into the GPS.

Dante snorts, starting up the vehicle. "That ain't called navigating, brother. That's just data entry."

I keep up the banter with him while keeping an eye on Riley through the rearview mirror. Her arousal is my favorite sight, and the fact that Maddoc is toying with her, too—whispering what I assume are filthy things in her ear while completely oblivious to the control I have over her pleasure right now—just heightens the stakes of the game.

By the time we reach the building, Riley's skin glows with a thin sheen of sweat, the flush on her skin, rapid breathing, and dilation of her pupils all giving away how effective the toy I purchased for her is.

"Excited about doing a walk through on your new building,

yeah?" Dante teases her once we all get out and he catches sight of her aroused state.

"*Our* new building," she says, a strain to her voice that's unmistakable. The glare she gives Dante is pure wildcat, though.

Her inheritance—both from William Sutherland and from Austin McKenna's holdings—may be funding this purchase, but Riley has been insistent that her assets are "our" assets, even though Maddoc has refused to allow her to move them out of her name.

"Ours, princess," Dante murmurs, his eyes heating as they rake over her. "Fuck, I love you."

She flushes even more, and I can't resist. As she sways toward him, I flick the vibrator back on.

She makes an utterly delicious sound, her whole body trembling as one hand shoots out to latch onto Dante's bicep, holding him in a death grip.

"I... love you... too," she says, biting her lip hard. Then she takes a deep breath, visibly gaining control over herself, and lets him go. "Should we go inside?"

Dante raises his eyebrows, then smirks at Maddoc, clearly blaming her state on him. "Sure."

Anything else he might have said is forestalled by the appearance of the Realtor, a mature, high-energy woman with sensible heels and a no-nonsense attitude who quickly steers the conversation toward the building's attributes and features.

She leads us on a tour, and Maddoc's attention shifts to business as he drills her for details along the way. Dante handles most of the physical inspection, knocking on walls and crouching down to check ducts and plumbing fixtures.

I walk next to Riley, my hand in my pocket, finger on the remote.

"You'll notice that the office suites on this floor have all been wired for high-speed internet," the Realtor says, leading us up a set of stairs. "It would be easy to extend that to the manufacturing floor below if that would be useful."

"What do you think, wildcat?" I murmur. "Should we extend it?"

"*Logan.*"

Her whisper is more of a whimper when I activate the vibrator again, and her steps stumble for a moment.

I capture her elbow, steadying her, and Dante shoots us a questioning look.

"Take a look at the setup in here," the Realtor says, leading us into one of the offices.

"I like it," I say, turning off the vibe and drawing inquiring looks from both my brothers.

The Realtor beams at me. "I'm so glad. Do you have any questions?"

"Yes." I turn to Riley, flicking the vibe on again. "Do *you* like it, wildcat?"

She gasps, her cheeks flushing with color again, and reaches out to steady herself on the windowsill. "It's... very nice."

"The view is fantastic, isn't it?" the Realtor says, bustling over to join her there. "It's a commercial district, so scenic isn't really the word, but from this floor, you can see all of eastern Halston."

"Mmhmm," Riley says, her fingers trembling as she raises her hand and presses it, palm flat, against the glass. "It's..." She swallows hard. "Lovely."

Maddoc frowns, then asks the Realtor about something that brings her over to the other side of the room. Riley's got on a tight pair of jeans that frame her ass beautifully, and I can see it clenching and releasing as her breath grows ragged and she leans her forehead against the cool glass, next to her hand.

My cock responds, the memory of how fucking good it feels when I'm buried inside her almost too much to bear.

Dante moves closer to her, leaning down to whisper quietly in her ear. "You okay, princess?"

She nods, still leaning against the glass, and I dial the vibrator up to its highest setting.

Her eyes pop open, looking glazed, and a strangled gasp escapes her as a full-body shudder that's fucking beautiful to see rolls through her body.

My balls pull up tight, aching for release, the control I have over her pleasure right now almost as arousing as the sight of her orgasm.

Dante's eyes go wide too. "You just fucking came, didn't you?" he asks quietly.

She bites her lip hard enough to turn it white, and nods.

I have mercy, thumbing the remote off, and Dante curses quietly under his breath, reaching down to adjust himself as he angles his body between her and the Realtor, sheltering her while she collects herself.

As he does, he catches my eye, and I grin.

His eyebrows shoot up in surprise. "You?"

I slip the edge of the remote out of my pocket so he can see it, and his eyes turn molten with heat as understanding dawns.

"Madd," he calls out, cutting into the conversation Maddoc's having with the Realtor about some of the permits we'll need to be able to mask our activities here.

Maddoc looks over, taking in and analyzing the whole scene with one quick glance, an ability that's helped him rise to the top as our leader and works just as well when he needs to make quick, strategic decisions for other reasons.

Like now.

A wolfish smile flashes across his face, which he quickly schools back to blandness as he turns back to the Realtor. "We're interested," he tells her, his tone commanding and abrupt. "We need a few moments alone to discuss the details, though."

"Of course! There's a coffee stand a couple blocks away. I'll head over there to grab a cup. Can I bring you back something?"

Maddoc turns down the offer and ushers her out, then closes the door to the empty office with a firm click. As he turns back to face us, I flick the remote on again.

"Oh shit," Riley gasps, bracing herself against the window again as we all converge on her.

"What's happening, butterfly?" Maddoc demands in a low purr, stalking toward her. "Why are you trying to distract us from business? You know how important it is that we secure this location. Are you looking to get punished?"

"Fuck, stop. I can't... don't say that," she says with a stuttering laugh, breathless and arousing, as she shakes her head. "Logan's already torturing me enough."

"This is Logan's fault?" Maddoc asks, looking surprised.

"Impressive, yeah?" Dante says with a grin. Then, to me, "Didn't know you had it in you to be so playful, brother. I'm not complaining, though." He rubs his hands together. "This could be fun."

I roll my eyes, but give up trying to mask my grin. It *is* fucking fun to torture Riley like this, and the way her arousal turns me on—turns all of us on—isn't something I'd trade for the world.

The three of us box Riley in, crowding her back against the window. "What exactly did you do to our girl, Logan?" Maddoc asks without taking his eyes off her.

He grabs her jaw, running his thumb back and forth across her lower lip as she pants, staring up at him.

She's still trembling, squeezing her thighs together in a way that probably works the vibe—on the lowest setting right now—right against her g-spot.

"I gave her a gift," I answer Maddoc, pulling the remote out so it's in plain view.

I dial it up to a higher setting, and Riley cries out, her mouth falling open.

Maddoc pushes his thumb between her lips. "Suck."

She whines, her eyes falling to half-mast and her body undulating with her rising pleasure as she complies.

"She seems to like your gift," Maddoc murmurs, his eyes darkening with lust. He slips his thumb out of her mouth, getting another cock-hardening whimper, and steps back. "But why don't you check and make sure, Logan? If she's not wet enough, we might have to work a little harder to help her along."

I move in, backing her against the window. "I can do that."

I rub my hand over her pussy, then undo her jeans and slip my hand inside. The satiny pair of panties she's got on are soaked all the way through, and the feel of her hot, slick folds when I work my fingers underneath the moist material makes me groan, my already erect cock turning to pure diamond.

I push the slick silicone into her a little deeper, the vibrations traveling up my wrist as she writhes against my hand.

"*Logan.*"

Heat bursts through me, sudden and all-consuming. The vibe is enjoyable, but it's not enough anymore. I want to fuck her and watch my brothers fuck her. I want to know she'll let us do anything, anywhere, at any time.

I grip her chin tightly, tilting her head up and sending the bright, colorful waves of her hair cascading over the glass behind her. "Everyone can see you."

She moans, grinding harder against the hand I've still got buried between her legs.

It's not true. The windows on this place are tinted from the outside, so that view the Realtor mentioned only goes one way. But that's not the point.

The hungry look that comes over Riley's face is the point.

The way her body tightens, her breath quickening with excitement, is the point.

The dirty pleasure I know it gives her to be watched, seen, wanted—*that's* the fucking point.

I slide my hand down to her throat, the feel of her delicate pulse fluttering against my palm feeding the insatiable darkness inside me. "You're a dirty girl, and you're about to get fucked like one. Is that what has you so wet?"

"You do," she whispers, her voice broken and the raw, desperate need in it fucking beautiful to hear. "You make me wet. So please fuck me. Right now."

"Is that what you want?"

"Yes."

I press harder against the vibrator she's wearing inside herself for me. "You want to get fucked by all three of us?"

"Please, *yes*," she pants.

"Fucking Christ," Dante says with a groan, palming himself as he watches us. "I need to get inside her already. Unwrap that pussy for us, Logan."

I spin Riley around and pull her jeans and panties down as she braces herself against the window.

"Our realtor ain't wrong," Dante mutters as I slide the vibe out and toss it aside. "This right here is a *gorgeous* fucking view." Then his smile turns wicked. "You see her out there, princess? Is that realtor of ours gonna make it back with the coffee she wanted while my brother's got his cock buried inside you? You want her to catch you acting like our dirty little cum slut, begging all three of us to fill you?"

Riley's breath hitches, the risk turning her on even more.

I can't stand it. I free my cock and drive it into her tight, wet heat, unable to wait any longer.

I bottom out with one thrust, groaning from how fucking good it feels.

"That's it. Fuck her hard, Logan," Maddoc says sharply. "Fuck her until she screams. No one sees Riley come except for us, so get it done before we have company."

He's right, but I still take a moment to just breathe her in, grinding against her perfect ass as I press against her back, pinning her against the glass.

"Logan," she begs, her pussy rippling around my shaft. "God, *please.*"

That feels even better, and when she begs me like that, I *have* to move. Have to fuck her. Have to relieve the pressure that's been building up inside me ever since I delivered her gift this morning.

So I take my brother's advice and flatten my hand between her shoulder blades to hold her in place, then take her apart. "Come on my cock," I demand, my own orgasm rising hot and fast as I pound into her. "Come for me, wildcat. Come while my brothers are watching."

Her body tightens around me as a deep shudder moves through her, and then she's doing it. Coming in a powerful wave that unleashes my release as soon as it hits.

"Fuck," I grit out, the pleasure so intense it's almost blinding. "Fuck, fuck, *fuck.*"

My balls ache with the intensity of it, and when I pull out and see my cum trickle down her thighs, they give one final pulse, sending another burst of pleasure through me as I back away and let Dante line himself up behind our girl.

"Gonna fuck my brother's cum back into you," he says, impaling her. "Can't be wasting that shit, now can we? Gotta keep you nice and full."

"Yes. Fuck, do it," she pants as he starts to drive into her, hard and fast like he's just as pent up as I was. "Give me more. Dirty me up."

"With pleasure," Dante promises, tilting her ass to get a better angle and then fucking her until she screams for him.

When he finally pulls out, Maddoc's eyes are blazing with heat, his cock ready and waiting in his hand.

He moves into place behind her, pulling her shirt above her

breasts and palming them roughly. She's braless again, and my fingers itch to feel those nipples between them. To cause her a little pain.

Maddoc does it for me, pinching them hard enough to make her gasp.

"Press these against the glass while I fuck you," he says, rubbing his erection between her ass cheeks. "Let's give Halston a look at just how hot you look while you take my cock."

He pulls her hair back, bending her spine into a beautiful arch, then slowly eases his cock into her.

"She's coming," Riley gasps, panting with her forehead against the window. "The realtor's... coming back. Fuck me faster."

Maddoc spanks her hard, getting another pretty gasp out of her, and pulls out slowly before plunging in again. "Who's in charge here?"

"She's coming, Maddoc!"

He grins, dark and dirty, and fucks her deep. "Then you'd better come first. Unless you want her to see how fucking perfect you look on my cock."

Riley squeezes her eyes closed, a shuddering moan coming out of her mouth, and when Maddoc finally lets loose, it only takes a few strokes before she's shaking and falling apart for him.

He groans, fisting her hair hard, and fills her up with his load, then quickly pulls out and spins her around, pulling up her pants and smoothing down her shirt.

"Love you," he says, giving her a quick, hard kiss. Then he smirks and smacks her ass while I scoop up the vibrator I tossed aside earlier. "But I'll always love you a little bit more when you're filthy with our cum."

He tucks himself away just as the realtor gives two brisk knocks on the door and walks back in, coffee cup in hand. Her steps falter for just a moment—probably because Riley looks sex drunk and the entire room smells of our combined arousal—but she must scent a commission in the air too, because she just raises an eyebrow and holds out a contract. "Ready to buy yourself a building?"

"We'll take it." Maddoc says, his eyes still on Riley and his voice softening in a way I never heard from him before she came into our life. "It's everything we want."

EPILOGUE

RILEY

"What do you think?" Chloe asks, flipping her hair back.

I grin, loving her so hard it hurts. "I love it."

We've just finished dyeing it a bold magenta, and touching up my own "butterfly" colors too. It's something we could have easily had done in a salon now that I can afford shit like that. It's too fun to do together, though, and I'd never want to give up the kind of memories we make spending time together like this just because I have money now.

Besides, the apartment I rented for Chloe is nicer than most of the salons in Halston, and I feel zero shame about that. My little sister deserves to be spoiled a little after everything she's gone through. Something that Nathan, now that the two of them are officially dating, does a really good job of.

That's not the only reason I like the guy. Besides the fact that Chloe is head over heels for him, I know for sure that his position with the Reapers helped influence her decision to stay here in Halston for college.

I want her close. I can't help it. I don't know if I'll ever stop needing to protect her and make sure she's safe, even now that she's got the entire Reaper organization looking out for her too.

"Are you ready for classes to start?"

She rolls her eyes and throws a pillow at me. "Can you please quit asking me that? The answer is still yes, and there's more to life than higher education, you know."

"Of course there is. I just want you to have everything, okay?"

Her eyes soften. "I know you do, and you've given me that. Maybe it's about time you got everything you want too."

I laugh. "I already have it."

"Really? Does that mean you've made some progress on the convincing-your-men-to-marry-you front?" she asks excitedly. "Because I *really* want to plan your bachelorette party."

"Oh, hell no."

"That's not what Ayla says," she teases me in a sing-song voice that convinces me I never, not in a million years, should have introduced my little sister to that powerhouse of a woman.

Too late now, though.

"But for real, Riley, when are they going to say yes already? I *know* they love you."

I sigh. "I'll wear them down eventually."

Logan and Dante are totally on board, even though they both agree that since I can only legally marry one of them, it makes the most sense that it be Maddoc on the actual marriage certificate. The problem is that he's the one who continues to be a holdout.

Chloe's right. They do love me, all three of them. That's not in question, not even from Maddoc. But marriage is still a prickly issue for him because of our history, and even though I'm determined to get my way someday, I know that every time I bring it up, he has flashbacks about his original plan to marry my sister, and how betrayed I felt.

Not to mention what Austin McKenna did to me.

That's the past, though, and Maddoc, Dante, and Logan are my future. One day, Maddoc's going to accept that and get the fuck over himself, because I *will* get that man's ring on my finger. I want all four of us to be as permanent as it's possible to become in this world.

Chloe teases me a bit more and then drags me into the little room Logan set up a high-end computer system for her in, and shows me some of the new programming stuff she's been working on with him. Some of it goes over my head. Okay, a lot of it. But seeing her happy and knowing she's excited about her own future means everything to me.

I stay later than I mean to, just enjoying her company, but once she starts yawning, I give her a long hug and head back home. The house is dark when I arrive, and for a second, I'm a little thrown. I figured the guys would be home since it's late and none of them mentioned plans to be elsewhere.

Then again, they run what's becoming one of the most powerful criminal gangs in the city. It's not like they operate on a strict nine-to-five schedule.

I park the sleek little sports car they surprised me with a few weeks ago and head inside, and before I can decide whether or not I need to be worried about their absence, I reach the living room and catch my breath.

They're not gone at all. They're here, waiting for me.

"Oh my god," I whisper, my hand flying up to cover my heart as it stutters in my chest.

The whole room is lit by candles. It's like something out of a dream. And the best part is my men, all dressed to the nines, standing in the middle of it.

"What's happening?" I ask, trembling a little as I approach them, my nerves jumping with anticipation.

I'm filled with a giddy kind of excitement that makes my blood feel like it's full of champagne bubbles, but I truly have no idea what's happening until Dante steps forward, taking my hand and going down on one knee.

"Princess," he starts as the hot sting of tears pricks the back of my eyes. "I'm so fucking in love with you. You're the color in my world now. You've been the brightest thing in it ever since the first time I saw you. You're the strongest woman I know, and the sexiest."

That makes me laugh, but I'm crying too, and when his quick, cocky smirk gentles into something soulful and he turns my hand over and places a single kiss on my wrist, I feel every bit of the love he's confessing to me as I let the tears run down my cheeks and drip onto the back of his hand.

"You're the only one my heart is ever gonna have room for," he says, his voice going husky. "You're not just the color in it, you *are* my world, Riley Sutton. Marry me."

"Yes," I whisper, my heart swelling even more at the look my answer puts on his face.

I laugh again, dashing at the tears on my face as he rises to his feet and moves my hand aside to wipe them for me.

"You had to know I'd say yes."

"I hoped. And I believed," he says, looking into my eyes. "But I'll never take your 'yes' for granted, princess, or anything else about you. Until death do us part."

Then he kisses me so sweetly that I can't even be mad for the fact that he just made me cry again, and when he ends it, he puts my hand into Logan's.

Logan, who's already down on one knee.

My hand flies up to cover my mouth, and Logan gives me that secret little smile I fell for the first time I saw it. "I spent most of my life believing I couldn't love, that the darkness inside me had snuffed that part of my soul out, if it had even ever existed at all. I was raised by a monster, and I thought that I was one." He pauses, then pulls my hand up to his cheek, holding it there. "Until you."

"Logan," I whisper, touched more deeply than I'll ever be able to express to him.

Except, maybe I don't have to. He already knows, because he feels it too.

"I love you, Riley Sutton. You came into my darkness and met me there. You saw the monster in me and helped me understand it. You complete me. Now I want to spend the rest of my life completing you. I want to love you and hurt you, protect you and cherish you, until my last breath. Will you marry me, too?"

I can barely get the word out past the lump in my throat, but even if it hurts, especially when it hurts, I will always say yes to this man.

"Yes." I swipe at my cheeks again. "I want to be your wife, Logan."

He gets to his feet with the smooth grace of a striking snake, gathering me up just as fast. "And I want to be your husband," he murmurs before kissing me deeply. "I want to be your everything, along with my brothers, until the day I die."

Brothers. Both of them. Logan just said so, and all three of them are here, so I'm not sure why it shocks me so much when Logan steps back and Maddoc finally comes forward.

He takes both my hands, and I only realize I'm holding my breath when I start to feel dizzy.

Then he drops to one knee.

"Oh my god," I blurt, laughing through a fresh wave of tears. "I was planning on wearing you down!"

He smiles, and I see my forever in his eyes. "You never needed to wear me down. I wanted to marry you from the first time you asked, butterfly. Even before that. I just needed to be sure that you would never doubt why I wanted to."

"I don't," I whisper, squeezing his hands.

"I just had to get out of my own way and trust what we have between us," he says, his voice gravelly. "And I do, because it's more real than anything I've ever felt. Even if I didn't marry you, I would want to spend every day by your side and every night in your bed. I don't ever want to wake up without you again, but I also want to make it official. I love you. We all do. Will you marry all of us, Riley?"

I nod, too choked up to answer any other way. But when he pulls out a ring box—when Dante and Logan go back down on their knees on either side of Maddoc, pulling out ring boxes of their own—I find my words again.

"Yes. Oh god, so much yes. You're everything I've ever wanted. All of you. I want to be your wife. I want... I want all of it."

"And we're gonna give it to you, for the rest of our lives," Dante promises in a voice raw with emotion as they each pull out the rings they bought me—gold, platinum, and titanium— and stack them on my finger.

My heart swells as I twist my hand to admire them, letting the candle light glint off the metal. I'm so full of happiness that I'm not sure how to contain it, so I don't even try.

Instead, I share it with the three men who adore me, who've stood by me, who've fought and killed for me. The men fate thrust into my life, whom I now can't imagine living without.

My future husbands.

BOOKS BY CALLIE ROSE

Boys of Oak Park Prep
Savage Royals
Defiant Princess
Broken Empire

Kings of Linwood Academy
The Help
The Lie
The Risk

Ruthless Games
Sweet Obsession
Sweet Retribution
Sweet Salvation

Ruthless Hearts
Pretty Dark Vows
Pretty Wicked Secrets
Pretty Vengeful Queen

Printed in Great Britain
by Amazon

28532299R00239